SEEING DEAD

EDGAR D JACKSON

Typeset by Raspberry Creative Type in Edinburgh, Scotland
Printed and bound by Clays Ltd in Suffolk, England

'When I think of you, I think of the ocean.'

WHEN CHARLIE WENT

Charlie's disappearance, truthfully, took place over the course of one year. It started on the morning of the fifth of September, 1988. Charlie woke up. He brushed his teeth and hair, as he usually did. He crept downstairs, careful not to wake his mum and dad, as he usually tried. He made his toast, ate his toast. Loaded his bag, shouldered his bag. Then he finally made his way towards the bus stop. The only unusual part was that he didn't make the bus stop.

There was nothing about the street to suggest he wouldn't. The cars were all the usual cars, parked in the usual way – parallel to the kerb. The air was still the same, laced with a late-summer fog and festering with salt from the ocean, which sat on Gealblath's doorstep just one mile outward. Mrs Forsythe was in her garden, her polka-dot skirt folded under her knees as she dug at the flower beds. Charlie waved. Mrs Forsythe waved back. Her gloved hands were caked in soil, and her reddish-grey hair was already beginning to go sticky with sweat.

A few steps further and still nothing was new. The Thorntons had their kitchen window wide open, as they usually did. The voice of Gary Numan was crooning out of a muffled radio perched atop the windowsill. Two doors down from them, Mr Goldman was performing his morning skin routine, crumpled over in his porch chair and rubbing ferociously at his ankles. The pain of his gout always got him up early, so he would sit and spend twenty minutes scrubbing goo into his sore and swollen feet, hissing angrily to himself in a way that made Charlie pick up his pace and stare down at his shoes. On the other side of the road, Mr Striker was making his usual trek down to his expensive seaside cabin. He used to work at the local power plant, but since its closure in 1985, he'd spent most of his time lounging away his life at the beach. Lunchbox in one hand, the morning's post in the other, he wore a slappable smirk that suggested he wanted everyone to know just how very well his early retirement was treating him.

This was the way it had been every day. Everything in the street remained the same. None of the players had changed. None of the scenery. It was like a painting on a wall. And there, where the path began to dip, the bus arrived at the place the bus normally arrived. It would be there for two minutes only, and so Charlie began to jog. He spotted his friend sitting near the rear window and an empty seat beside him.

The fact that there remained an empty seat would soon become a fact that haunted the town he lived in.

CHARLIE COOPER
WHITE MALE, 12 YEARS OLD, 4'7" TALL,
39kg, BLONDE HAIR, BLUE EYES

That was the first police report.

The first witness statement was given by Mrs Forsythe: 'Chirpy kid. Just like every morning. Always walks with a wee strut, that one. Like he's going somewhere. My kids were the same. That age, you're going everywhere.'

Alfie Percival conducted the search. He was a recently appointed detective who was just glad there was something to get him out of the dingy, smoke-filled office for a day. He became slightly less glad when that day turned to two days, then three, then onwards to a week, then two, to the point where his dingy, smoke-filled office started looking like a luxury five-star suite. At first, he liked the respect that came with the job. The looks on the street, the nods, the occasional cigarette packet on the house – unfiltered Raffles, he liked the thick stuff. But after two months, the respect was gone and the looks had turned sour.

'You not found that boy yet?'

'He's not up your arsehole, you know.'

'You take any longer, you'll be finding nothing but skull and bone.'

'What are you lot doing down the station? Measuring cocks?'

Two months more and Charlie's disappearance continued. From absence of body to absence of hope. Alfie quit the job altogether. He left Gealblath in the dust and felt decidedly bitter that the residents seemed to have expected him to pull Charlie out of some magic hat and take a bow. He was no magician, and this was a vanishing act even Houdini would have struggled with. So Alfie vanished to the south of England, to Cornwall, where a whisky on the rocks was waiting to etch away the picture of Charlie from his head.

For Gealblath, that picture remained for months after the case fizzled out. It was plastered along the walls, flickering in the wind on utility poles, stapled to the wood of the 'Welcome to Gealblath' sign. A small boy parked in front of a blurred blue background. Grinning hard. His eyes looking left of camera and a great big

MISSING

hanging under his torso. They couldn't get rid of the memory with a whiskey on the rocks. They had to look at the posters day after day, week after week. Only one was ever taken down and that was just because someone had penned a speech bubble over Charlie's head that read: 'THA-THA-THA-THAT'S ALL FOLKS!'

A respite did finally come in the late winter, however. The clouds were low in the town and the cold wind whipped up the seawater, thinning the posters with salt until the boy was just a faded silhouette. From that point on, the image of Charlie could be forgotten. He became, then, just a muted conversation around a dinner table. He became a few passing lines in a pub at midnight. He became a shake of the head and a 'tsk'. He became a 'shame'. He became a 'poor kid'. He became a 'make sure you're home by dark'. For a small while. Until the conversation changed to some other, more palatable subject.

Then there was nothing.

Charlie's mother, Mrs Cooper, eventually left the town, spurred on by her very public breakdown after finding a poster of her son covered with a poster for a missing cat. But Charlie's father stayed. For some reason – of which the residents of Gealblath were never really sure – the initial phase of the investigation was focused on him. Nothing was ever found to warrant an arrest, but Gealblath was convinced there had to be substance to it. They followed their noses and the smell surrounding him turned sour. Until time passed and there were other things for their noses to crinkle at.

Come late summer, exactly one year after Charlie's walk to the bus stop, it became clear that every inch of the boy had been emptied from the town in which he'd lived. The disappearance was complete. On the street beside his house, all the cars were parked in the same place. Mr Goldman was grumbling to himself and applying his cream. Mrs Forsythe was digging up some worms in her garden. Duran Duran was blaring out of a kitchen window this time. One mile eastward, Mr Striker was sitting outside his cabin to enjoy the rare glares of the sun, watching as some children gathered together to throw stones into the water. He allowed himself a content sigh and the others upon the beach seemed to do the same. Everything was as usual as it had been one year before, and it was clear that Gealblath liked it that way. Normality is important to the human psyche, and a wound left open too long drains blood. If forgetting a lost child paved the way back to a comfortable life, then Gealblath would let a thousand children be forgotten.

And, as it goes, that was how it ended. If the beach was any indication of Gealblath's mindset, then it was utterly and perfectly *usual*. One child was simply gone. But no one noticed that anymore. After all, it was easy to overlook one less stone being thrown into the water.

1

TEN YEARS AFTER

The words were written in red and underlined in black.

MARTY EVANS IS DEAD!

The message was seen by about fifty Gealblath folk, young and old, before finally being witnessed by its intended recipient, Marty Evans. He had to get through a small crowd first. Fifteen school children let Marty through, some with sneers, others with frowns. Sporadic. Like a heart-rate monitor.

'Marty Evans is dead! Marty Evans is dead!' some of them chanted, but Marty didn't listen to them. He was more concerned with Gealblath's new billboard. The words were written on the wall of a wooden castle in the park and some of the spray paint had trickled between each log, so it was messy. It made him feel sick to look at it. His face turned pale and for some reason his eyes started to water. Gealblath Secondary School was located right next to the park, and every child would walk past the castle in the morning to get there. This was no joke. This was a public declaration. And the worst thing was, Marty knew who'd written it.

Despite his being dead, Marty's day played out as usual. He went to class. He put his hand up a couple of times. He answered two questions. One of them was correct. One of them was wrong. Not that he cared. His head wasn't in class, it was still in the park, staring up at those big spindly letters. *DEAD!* He spoke to some kids, hoping by chance they hadn't seen the castle, all to no avail. Of course they had seen the words and naturally they asked him about it. He became a school celebrity, but not the good kind. He hadn't punched the school bully. He hadn't done a grind down the stair rail like Luke McLevin last term. He was dead. Simply that. Dead Marty.

The day went on and the clock continued to tick, speeding its way up to the dreaded chime. Lunch-time. Lunch-time was break time, and break time was dead time. Or so Marty predicted. That was when he would have to come face to face with his apparent demise. He just hoped it was quick and painless. Though he knew he didn't have to worry too much about that. He was the weediest kid in his year. Killing him would be like killing a fish – easy, no resistance. He just hoped he wouldn't flop around on the floor too much before his head was kicked in.

After a few hours of Marty inanely hoping lunch might be cancelled this Monday, the bell finally rang, and the kids bolted in the direction of the lunch hall. The only one walking was Marty. The lunch hall was loud when he arrived. When he walked through the doorway he quickly caught the gaze of a fellow ninth-year, a nice one, one he had talked to in science class that one time. She waved and mouthed, 'Marty

Evans is dead!', pointing at him with a bony finger to assure Marty Evans that he was Marty Evans and that he was dead. Marty took a step backwards and hit into a wall of pudgy flesh and cotton. He turned to see the face of Rory Keeling staring down at him. Eleventh-year. Newly appointed street artist. His face was as ugly as ever, with freckles covering his cheeks and nose in specky mountain ranges, and his under-chin seemed to ripple a bit when he spoke.

'Did you get my message, Weed-kid?' he asked.

Marty nodded, taking a step back into the lunch hall. Lots of the children around him had stopped, eyeing the two of them like they were in a safari park. Marty. The zebra. Scrawny, toothless, and largely ineffective against an enemy. Rory. The enemy. Big, strong, and hungry for blood.

'You're dead,' Rory said, reaffirming the message in case Marty had misunderstood what it meant. But Marty had understood just fine. Dead meant dead, and he was about to be it, unless he said something fast.

'Is this about what happened with the new girl? I didn't do anything, I only...' Marty stopped, realising that nothing he could say could stop a bully as thick-headed as Rory. Resistance was truly futile. It was today. Or tomorrow. Or the next day. His fate was unescapable, and he would have to meet it with as much vigour and punctuality as the park's billboard suggested.

The enemy raised a fist. The spectators held their breath. Marty imagined some of them with binoculars, cameras, and hats with corks hanging from the rim.

Ready for the show, folks? Just watch this.

* * *

One month before Rory's fist landed, a car pulled up to the kerb of the park. It was a jet-black American Lincoln. New looking, windows tinted; the three ninth-years had never seen anything like it before. Marty sat with his two best friends on the climbing frame, his eyes squinting against the harsh light of the morning sun.

'Who's in it, do you think?' pondered Mike.

His large arse was overhanging the pole on both sides. Marty glanced at it fearfully, awaiting the snap that was bound to happen one of these days.

'The first minister?' suggested Teddy. He sat above Marty, wobbling to and fro, his coordination so terrible that he'd tumbled face first into the wood chips at least twenty times in the last two years. Clearly enough to cause some severe brain damage, if his last comment was anything to go by.

'Right,' said Marty. 'The first minister visiting Gealblath Secondary School. What's he doing, brushing up on some algebra?'

'He could be giving us some kind of award or something. First ministers do that sometimes.'

Mike wiped his nose in his ongoing battle against the freshly mown grass. Compared to the rest of Scotland, Gealblath always had hot summers. There was an almost intangible, lingering warmth year-round, even when it felt cold. No one could really explain it. No one really tried to because no one ever complained. Even Mike had accepted the fact that hay fever was just a part of his life. Something he would have to suffer if he wanted to avoid a typical Scottish summer.

'What kind of award would he give this place?' he questioned.

Marty thought about it. 'Award for the best drawing of a penis in a toilet cubicle?'

'Have you seen that too?' Mike laughed and his belly seemed to vibrate a bit. Marty glanced at the pole again. 'Apparently, George Anderson sneaked into school during the holidays. It's pretty good, to be fair!'

Teddy nodded. 'Must be, if the first minister's here.'

'No, Teddy. Just to be clear, it's not the first minister.'

At that moment, the door of the Lincoln opened. All three of them turned to see who would exit. To Teddy's disappointment, it was not Scotland's first minister, but a girl. She looked about thirteen years old, which meant she must have been in their year, and she was new. Her hair was mousy, tangled at the back, and her uniform was kind of worn and baggy. To her chest, she was squeezing a rumpled, grey backpack. She stood and gazed around the park for a few seconds, her eyes resting momentarily on the three boys. Then she turned back to the car, said a few words, pushed the door shut, and headed towards the school. Marty watched the new girl go, oblivious to the hand which was slowly wrapping itself around his right shoe.

'GOTCHA!'

The hand pulled hard, and the next thing Marty knew he was in the dirt, spitting out woodchips and looking up into the green eyes of Rory Keeling.

'You alright there, Weed-kid?'

Teddy and Mike clambered down the poles, fearful that they were about to meet the same fate.

'Unbelievable,' said a boy called Ross Baines, popping up behind Teddy and stuffing a wet finger into his ear. 'You tubes look like you've never seen a girl before. I knew you were paedos.'

'Bugger off!' Teddy squealed and attempted to swat him away.

'Ah, the Teddy Bear's sensitive!' Ross gave him a couple of slaps on the cheek, then began sucking on the previously inserted finger. Of all the bullies in Gealblath Secondary School, Marty found Ross to be the most repellent. He grimaced as he watched him.

'We're not paedos,' Mike stuttered. His voice was high and shaky, as it tended to become when he felt his life was in immediate danger.

'Sure you're not, Chinky.'

Ross halted his sucking act and decided to mimic Mike's accent instead. His Chinese ethnicity had always caused him problems in the school corridors, but no one demeaned him as much as Ross Baines.

'Nah, I don't blame you,' said Rory. 'She's hot as hell. Definitely my type, right, Weed-kid?'

Marty pulled himself to his feet and shrugged. To tell the truth he'd always seen Rory's type as a bit thinner with more of a creamy peanut butter filling, but he wouldn't tell him this. He valued his teeth more than that.

'Sure,' he said instead.

Ross patted Rory on the shoulder. 'Hell yeah, big guy, I'd have a go on her.'

'How d'you mean, have a go on her?' asked Teddy, quite earnestly.

With a bellow, Ross leaped back over and grabbed him by the shoulders, causing Mike to cower once again while Teddy clamped his hands over his ears.

'Let me tell you something, Teddy Bear, when a girl and a boy like each other very much, this...' Ross revealed his index finger to the four of them. 'Goes like this!'

With a flourish, he stripped away Teddy's hands and began penetrating his finger in and out of his left ear.

'HEY! HEY! GET ORRRRFFF!'

'Just gonna have to see what happens,' said Rory, ignoring the 'whoops' and 'wees' of Ross and the yells of his victim. 'You gotta get the new girls early, Weed-kid. C'mon, Ross. Let's leave these tubes to finger themselves.'

On his command, Ross stopped attempting to locate the brain of his victim. 'Remember that little lesson, Teddy Bear. It might come in handy one day, if you get lucky.'

And then they were gone, leaving Marty covered in dirt, Teddy with a decidedly sore ear, and Mike with a slight dampness in his pants.

'Why the hell would two people who like each other stick their fingers in each other's ears?' asked Teddy.

Marty sighed in response, rueful at the poor start to yet another miserable term. Although in all truth, imagining the confusion between Teddy and his future girlfriend was enough to keep his spirits up. For this moment, anyway.

The next two weeks played out much as Marty had expected. School happened. Marty went to it. He hung out with Teddy and Mike. He avoided Rory and Ross. He learned what he wanted to learn, and he ignored everything else. He ate the school lunches, he skived the school sports. Everything was as it had always been. The only new thing was the new girl.

She didn't create much of an impact at first; she sat at the back of classes, doodling furiously in a notebook with her mousy hair covering the majority of her face. She didn't speak. Even when the teacher asked her something, there would simply be a shake of the head, and the teacher would move on. The only subject she seemed to excel in was Art, and that was because she practised so much doodling in all her other lessons. The other girls found her weird. She didn't attend PE, but sometimes they would find her in the changing room alone, complaining that her shoes were too tight and she had blisters growing between her toes. It seemed the only person she liked to talk to was herself. Until she began talking to Marty.

It started in the lunch hall, exactly fourteen days after Marty had spotted her getting out of the American Lincoln. He stood in line, food tray in hand, whistling the *Ghostbusters* theme tune to himself. He was just nearing the end before he noticed that one whistle had become two. The new girl was standing in front of him, her head dipped, evidently deaf to the fact that the original whistler had stopped. Marty leaned forward and tapped her on the shoulder.

'Hello.'

He spoke quietly, but the word was enough to make the new girl jump halfway towards the ceiling. Her tray flew into the air, sending glass and cutlery spiralling over the tenth-years behind her.

'Shit! I've been knifed!' One of them grabbed his scalp. 'I've been knifed! Oh shit, I'm bleeding!'

'You're not bleeding, ya dafty!' said one of his friends.

The scrawny boy fell to his knees. The teachers looked on nonplussed. One took another bite of his sandwich.

'I've been knifed! A knife hit me in the head!'

'What, you mean this spoon?' Another boy bent over and grabbed a small dessert spoon from the floor.

Then the whole lunch hall was laughing. A few sixth-years rushed to surround the felled student and mimicked him with squeaky voices.

'Help! I've been spooned! I've been spooned!'

Marty turned and saw the new girl dart past the gathering mass of school kids, dodging in and out of them before disappearing through the nearest door.

'A spoon attack,' one of the teenagers cheered. 'We haven't had a spoon attack in years, not since the spoon massacre of 1985!'

Another rush of laughter arose around the lunch hall, but Marty ignored it. He turned towards the exit and began running after the fleeing girl.

When he found her, she was sitting in the school corridor, slouched on a bench beside a row of lockers. Her head was in her hands and her fingers were trembling a bit. For a minute, Marty thought about leaving her to it. Judging by the last thirty seconds, he was inclined to agree with the status the new girl had imposed on herself. *Weirdo. Keep away. Hazardous.* But then she opened her eyes, and all options of leaving were robbed.

'Hello,' said Marty, wincing slightly in case his greeting should cause another incident. To his relief, it didn't.

'Hi,' she said back, her voice barely audible.

Marty lowered himself onto the bench. 'I'm sorry, I didn't mean to scare you.'

'You didn't scare me,' she responded. 'It was my fault.'

'No, it was mine. Most people have that reaction when I try talking to them. That was nothing. I caused a pretty big pile-up on the motorway this one time.'

The new girl blinked at him, then stared down at her feet. Marty noticed she was shoeless. Her toes scratched lightly against the school floor, unclipped and slightly dirty.

'Why aren't you wearing shoes?' he questioned.

The new girl hesitated. 'They're too small for me. They hurt. So I took them off.'

A few beats passed between them. *I guess she thinks that's a normal thing to do*, Marty thought to himself.

'What's your name again?' he asked tentatively.

'I'm Amee,' the new girl replied. 'With two E's.'

'That's cool. I'm Marty. With one Y.'

Amee looked up at him. 'Hello, Marty.'

Marty fixed onto her eyes, staring into the irises which were a dark and clean blue. They were unlike any he'd seen before. It was almost like they had a depth, like you could touch them and they would ripple. In a flash, her gaze shot back down to her feet and Marty fidgeted, his heart rate increasing. He was becoming increasingly aware that the new girl was actually quite pretty up close.

'I'm sorry about what happened back there,' he said after a few seconds. 'Do you wanna go and get some food?'

'No thanks,' Amee responded. 'I've got some peanut butter sandwiches in my locker.'

'Oh cool.'

The new girl looked at him seriously. 'I like peanut butter.'

Marty nodded in mutual agreement. 'Same. Peanut butter is good. You wouldn't have thought it, you know, peanuts going into butter and stuff. It sounds kind of disgusting, but it's actually good. I was surprised.'

There was a slight silence. Marty cleared his throat and leant back, feeling a bead of sweat begin to trickle down his temple. He couldn't remember speaking to a girl being this hard before. But then again, he couldn't remember the last time he'd spoken to a girl. *With lines like that, I wonder why.*

'So,' he said, swiftly changing the subject, 'you like *Ghostbusters* too? I've watched it loads. Must be, like, twenty times.'

20

'One hundred and sixteen for me.'

Marty blinked. 'One hundred and sixteen? Jesus, I wouldn't watch any movie that many times, not even my favourite.'

'It's not my favourite.'

Another silence ensued. Amee lifted a finger to untie a knot in her hair, then found another, twirling around the tangles until they frizzed about her shoulders.

'You look like him,' she mused.

'Look like who?' Marty asked.

'Venkman.'

Marty sat up straight, un-creasing his shirt with a tug. Venkman was without doubt the coolest character in *Ghostbusters*, which meant that, in a very loose way, Amee had just described him as cool. It wasn't anything to write home about, but so far this was the best interaction he'd had with a girl since that nurse gave him a lollipop after his measles jab. And to think it had started with a boy being knifed by a spoon.

'You know,' he began, but something stopped him.

A voice called down the school corridor. 'HEY, WEED-KID!'

Marty felt himself slump into a black hole as he spotted Ross and Rory strutting towards him.

'Are they your friends?' asked Amee.

'Absolutely not,' replied Marty.

Rory stopped at their feet, his stature casting a large, fat shadow onto the pair of them. 'Weed-kid and the weird kid. Did you forget our little talk, pal?'

Marty shivered. There was something unnerving about Rory calling him 'pal'. It was like a lion sweet-talking a piece of meat before stuffing it into its mouth. He didn't answer.

'So you're talking to people now?' said Rory as he turned to Amee. 'Trust me, you don't wanna talk to this guy. He's a tube who hangs out with other tubes.' A few seconds passed while Rory awaited her reply, but Amee gave him nothing. 'Listen, the other girls might not like you, but I reckon you're a cool enough bird, once you cut loose a bit.'

Marty had to hold himself back from laughing. He'd thought his attempt at conversation was bad, but if this was the way Rory – who had apparently kissed 'like thirty girls' – went about swaying a female, maybe Marty wasn't so bad after all. Rory kicked at her foot and Marty watched as she finally opened her lips.

'Slimer,' she said simply.

'What did you just say?'

'Leave her alone,' said Marty.

'Look at that,' Ross laughed. 'The weed-kid gets all tough around the new girl. Found some balls, have you?' He reached down and grabbed Marty's crotch. 'Shit, Rory, I can't find them!'

Marty struggled away from him, and Rory laughed.

'You need balls to impress a girl, I'm afraid, Weed-kid.'

'Yeah and apparently you need a brain to talk to one,' replied Marty.

'What is that supposed to mean?'

'I'd say use your head, but we'd be here all day.'

Ross grabbed Marty's shoulders and lifted him to his feet. 'Don't let him talk to you like that, big fella!'

Marty tried to pull away, but Ross's grip was too strong; instead, he could only turn his neck in time to spot Amee racing down the corridor and out of sight. Just the three of them were left in her wake, soon to be two if the retraction of Rory's fist was anything to go by. Marty closed his eyes, questioning how he had gone from his first conversation with a pretty girl to certain death in just a few seconds. But before he could figure it out, another voice came from behind them. It was bored, croaky, and nasal, but most importantly, it was an adult's.

'Having fun?'

The words landed with a graceful thud and Ross darted off immediately. Rory, on the other hand, had clearly had too many puddings to follow him. His face dropped and he turned to the teacher. He wasn't much to behold, Marty thought. He stood just twenty feet from them, his bearded face worn and tired and his hair thin and loose on the scalp, with strands of it splaying out at the back as if he'd just been rubbing his head with a balloon. His clothes were a sad sight too. He was dressed in a frazzled tweed jacket with brown rippled chinos, and his collar was unbuttoned, leaving a tie to flop uselessly on a blue pinstriped shirt. Marty recognised him as Mr Cooper, though he'd never actually been in one of his classes.

'I take it you're Rory,' said Mr Cooper. 'Your reputation precedes you.'

'It's Weed... Marty, sir. He was bullying a girl, the new girl.' Rory put a hand on Marty's shoulder and pushed him towards the teacher, as if he was some kind of peace offering.

The teacher squinted, taking Marty in, examining. 'Bullying? Bit weedy for a bully, isn't he?'

Rory shook his head. 'Sometimes the weediest ones are the worst. They use words, sir.'

Mr Cooper hummed in agreement, and despite his predicament, Marty nearly hummed too. He had to hand it to Rory, that was a pretty profound psychoanalysis of his own kind.

'Thing is, Rory...' Mr Cooper took a few steps towards them, his hands travelling behind his back as if he was about to give a lecture. 'I know you're an arsehole.'

Rory's mouth dropped open, and his two chins suddenly became three. The teacher stared into his dumbstruck face.

'Since I can see your tonsils, I guess you didn't know that?'

'I...' Rory stammered, 'I didn't think teachers could –'

'What? Tell facts? That's actually what we're paid to do.'

Rory gathered himself, straightening his spine and puffing out his chest. It was done in an effort to look tough, Marty guessed. But really it just looked like someone had pumped him up with too much hot air, like you could prick him with a needle and he'd disappear with a 'SHIT!' and a great big pop.

'You can't talk to me like that. You're a teacher. You can get fired.'

'Huh,' the teacher pondered. 'But the only way I know you're an arsehole is because I've been told you're an arsehole. By other teachers. Lots of other teachers.'

Rory's face turned a deep crimson. 'Well, they'll get fired too. I'll tell – I'll tell the headmaster.'

'The same headmaster who called you a wee shite in a staff meeting yesterday?'

Marty laughed, and Rory turned to him, his eyes literally watering with fury.

'You dare to laugh at me? You're dead, Weed-kid.'

'No, he's not,' Mr Cooper responded. 'In fact, if you lay one more finger on him, I'll make sure to get you expelled. You got that?'

Rory glared at him incredulously, every inch of his world falling apart around him. Marty couldn't believe this was happening. It felt too good to be true, like one of those dreams you never want to wake up from.

'You can go now,' the teacher finished, and Rory didn't wait for another invitation. With one more furious glance at Marty, he turned on his heel and chugged defeatedly down the corridor.

'Woah...' Marty muttered.

'To tell the truth,' said Mr Cooper, 'the headmaster didn't call him a wee shite; that was a lie. He called him a fat shite. But I thought that was a bit harsh.' He stuffed his hands in his pockets and cleared his throat. 'Okay. You. With me.'

A few minutes later and the pair of them were in Mr Cooper's office. It wasn't like an ordinary office, Marty thought. When he imagined a teacher's office, he imagined something clean, pristine, kept. That was the word. *Kept*. This teacher's office wasn't *kept*. This teacher's office was un*kept*. The floor had blue carpeting, but it was torn and rough. His desks and bookshelves were chipped and splintered, and a bucket-load of books and stray papers littered both. Some had even found their way to the floor, along with a few ties and jackets. Marty sat in the centre of the office, his legs dangling in the air. Sitting in front of him, behind the un*kept* desk, was the teacher in question. His eyes were glued to some kid's homework. They seemed about as weathered as the room surrounding him. Faded hazel, with a faint greyish tinge staining the bags underneath. He seemed old, but Marty knew he wasn't. Probably early forties. The years had gone by, but it was life that had aged him. The clothes didn't help, Marty supposed. If he had to place him, he'd put him in the 1940s. A professor of maths. A man outside of his time. Perhaps that was why he looked so tired.

'Didn't your mother tell you it's rude to stare?' Mr Cooper's gaze remained fixed on the homework as he spoke.

'You said I shouldn't talk.'

'That's right.'

'So what else is there to do but stare?'

'Not stare.'

'Look, I was just talking to the new girl. Rory was lying. Rory always lies. He's...'

'An arsehole?'

Marty shrugged. 'Yeah.'

'True, but that's not why you're here.' Mr Cooper put down the homework and stretched out his arms with a slight yawn. It seemed to take effort, as if his bones were as crumpled as one of the paper balls that lay discarded on the floor.

'So why am I here?' asked Marty.

'Because you were talking to the new girl. The new girl doesn't talk to anyone.'

'Well, she talked to me.'

'Why?'

'Because I was nice to her, I suppose.'

Mr Cooper pushed himself away from the desk and pointed his chin up towards the ceiling. 'I see,' he sighed.

Marty waited for a few seconds. The office had gone so quiet that he could hear himself picking his nails, a habit he'd had since he was about five years old. His dad used to assure him that if he carried on, there wouldn't be any nails left to pick. But Marty had decided that was stupid.

'So,' he mumbled, after deciding the quiet was too much to bear, 'why am I here?'

The teacher kept his gaze fixed on the ceiling, slowly massaging the bags beneath his eyes as if he was trying to urge some life into them. Some colour, maybe.

'Do you like reading?' he asked.

'Uh, yeah, I guess so.'

'You can read then?'

'Yes,' Marty responded defensively.

'Just checking. You never know with kids at this school.'

'I'm not Rory. I can read. Why?'

'She likes reading too. The new girl. I saw her reading a book by the lockers. Lost amongst kids these days. Now it's all movies and video games. Pretty soon you'll be bringing them into parks. Playing *Space Invaders* in corridors.'

'I'm pretty sure she likes movies too, sir,' said Marty.

'Good illustrator as well,' Mr Cooper continued. 'A little too enthusiastic, it seems. I saw a few confiscated works of hers in the staff-room. They all came from one book, so I assume it's a favourite of hers.'

Marty shrugged vaguely. 'What book was it?'

The teacher made a funny squelching sound with his lips, then drummed his fingers on the table. 'Stick with her. It'd be good for the new girl to have a friend around here.'

'I'm not sure she wants to be friends anymore, not after what happened.'

'Try all the same.'

Marty frowned. 'Why do you care?'

'Because that's what teachers do. They teach. And they care. Now leave, let me get on with my work.'

And just like that, Mr Cooper flicked Marty away, as if he had been nothing more than an annoying fly buzzing about his office.

'FAT SHITE?!'

Teddy pulled on his abnormally large backpack, which was twice the size and twice as heavy as anyone else's. It gave the impression it was crammed full of textbooks and schoolwork, but Marty knew it was just filled to the brim with *Warhammer* models and paint tubs. Teddy and Mike would take them out during break times and colour them studiously, while Marty was left to sit and literally watch the paint dry.

'That's what he said,' Marty replied.

Mike wiped his lip with a wet sleeve. It was pretty much the only thing he could do in the summer. Around this time of year, his nose would warp into a red, weeping ball in the middle of his face. Every now and again it would vibrate with a great big *APOUUUUFFF!*, to which Mike would respond with a gargled 'ooohhh' and pop a tiny white tablet onto the tip of his tongue. Marty had to feel sorry for him. Teddy, on the other hand, found it remarkably funny. One summer he'd even gone to the effort of creating a comic book based on his friend's struggle as a birthday gift. He named it: *Mighty Mike and the Battle of the Pink Flowers*. Mighty Mike was on the cover, one hand strangling a gigantic plant and the other wiping his nose with a tissue. It was creative, Marty had given him that.

The three of them stepped down onto the pavement, their ties loose and their shirts untucked, heading home now that the first miserable day back at school was over. Out of the corner of his eye, Marty found himself watching out for a cool black American Lincoln.

'I wish I'd been there,' Teddy beamed.

'What about Rory though?' Mike's voice was hardly audible amongst the snot and saliva that was clogging up his sinuses. Sure enough, by the time he'd finished the sentence his nose had capitalised on it with a loud *APOUUUUFFF!*

'Ooohhh.'

'What about him?' asked Marty.

'Oh yeah!' Teddy trotted a few steps to keep up with them.

'You mug him off in front of a girl he likes, and then Mr Cooper mugs him off in front of you – he's gonna be pissed.'

'Mr Cooper said if he tries anything on me again, he's gonna be expelled.'

'Holy shizer...' Mike wiped at his lip again, the news of Rory's predicament evidently cheering him.

'Why d'you think Mr Cooper was so easy on you?' asked Teddy.

'There wasn't anything to go hard on; I hadn't done anything apart from nearly getting my head exploded by Rory's fist.'

'That's weird. I've heard stories of how hard he used to be on kids. I guess he changed after everything that happened to him.'

'What happened to him?' questioned Marty.

'You know, like, ten years ago, when his son died. I heard a teacher talking about it once.'

Marty's eyes widened in shock. He forgot to turn the corner, walking into Mike with a bump and an *APOUUUUFFF!*

'Ooohhh.'

'His son died?'

'Yeah.' Teddy nodded. 'Or he went missing at least; they didn't find him. Maybe it made him mellow, maybe that's why he's looking out for you.'

At that moment, an engine rumbled past them, and the three boys turned to see a black American Lincoln shoot down the road. The wheels churned up some rough yellow dust, which swayed and dispersed in the afternoon breeze. Marty kept his eyes on the car, silently contemplating the girl inside; the look of her face, the colour of her eyes.

'I'm not sure it's me he's looking out for,' he said.

Then they continued walking.

2

THE CABINET

The bell woke him up. It began as a distant crackle in the back of his skull, but as he got closer to consciousness it got louder, shaking the foundations of his dream like it had two hands on his shoulders, willing him back to life. He had been with Charlie, walking through seawater at Gealblath Beach. They were following the tide as it went out.

'How far can we walk, Dad?'

'As far as the tide lets us.'

One hand was holding the other; a smaller, softer one.

'What's that?' Charlie's eyes were on the land beyond the sea, sitting in the distance like a paper town; twinkling lights and tiny ash-grey chimneys weeping smoke, a silhouette like in the old movies.

'That's Derling.'

'Will the tide let us go there?'

'Course it will.'

'No way,' Charlie laughed as he stepped towards it, the water kicking up underneath his shoes.

'Yeah way. But only if everything is in its right place. And the moon is with you. Then the tide will let you go anywhere. Derling, Norway...'

'No way!'

They laughed together. Then, once the laughter had subsided, Charlie looked up towards his father and his father looked down at him.

'Dad,' he said.

A faint hum started and the sea began to ripple.

'Yeah Charlie, what's up, kiddo?'

The lips moved, but nothing came out. He could just capture the look on Charlie's face, like he was scared. Like he was holding his hand too tight, or not tight enough. The hum grew louder and Charlie slipped away along with the dream that had surrounded him.

Then life again. David Cooper jolted up in his chair with a grunt, taking a few moments to adjust his eyes to his office. Paper was still strewn across the floor and books still littered corners, stacked unevenly, thick then thin, climbing the walls like a staircase. The walls trembled against the tone of the bell, and David ran a hand through his ever-thinning brown hair, turning his chin up towards the ceiling as he waited for the ringing to stop. That was the fourth time he'd fallen asleep at work now. It was getting bad. And each time he drifted away, Charlie was there waiting for him, his little face looking up at his dad's, distorted by time and drunken memory. The first questions he asked himself were always the same. Had he got it wrong? Were the eyes the right colour? Was his hair the same length? He could check with photographs, David supposed. But all the photographs were locked away in the attic, gathering dust for over ten years now. That had been his choice. Like liquor, tempting yourself with memories could open up a new black hole, far deeper than the one before. So deep it could be impossible to climb out of. They were just pictures anyway. Colour on the page. Like the town of Derling on the distant shore, they were unattainable, and something unattainable was untouchable. What good was a black hole for that? If the face was wrong then the face was wrong.

The clatter of the bell halted, and the sound of scattered footsteps arose in its wake. Voices squeezed through the cracks of the office door and filled the room with a buzz of excitement. The day was over. Time for screams, for cheers, for hushed gossip churned from the depths of the school corridors. *Ryan snogged who?! Matilda did what?! I like him. I like her.* Confessions and adorations admitted, the children on the outside of the dome looking back in like they would never come back. Some strode towards their homes with smiles, others with frowns. Some examined the hours been and spent, others left them on the scrap heap to swelter. Easy enough to do when you were a kid, of course, and bad days could be made better with leftover apple pie and a kiss before bedtime.

David stood and strode to the window, squinting against the sun, which was disappearing into heavy cloud now. It was hateful, in a way, to watch the children move with so much life and vigour, with eyes that could hardly stay open in the light of the afternoon. But then, David knew why that was the case. He knew why he was so tired, and he knew why he couldn't sleep at night. The problem did have a solution. It just so happened that the solution was worse than the problem. Both of which were in the bathroom of David's flat, screwed tight to the wall, locked and secure and doing nothing to harm anyone. The medicine cabinet.

In all three hundred and seventy eight days of knowing her, liking her, maybe even loving her, Gerri Hartman had never asked him about it. She didn't keep medicine. Not for physical deficiencies, not for mental ones, not for anything. Gerri didn't get sick. A throat lozenge a day for a week in the winter, perhaps, if he remembered correctly. And David would remember a thing like that. Others wouldn't, not even Gerri herself, but he would. It was why he liked her, he supposed. In a perverse way. In a way even he did not understand. *Gerri does not get sick. Keep her.* But then, just like that, an infection. Fungal, between the toes, and the damn pills were needed. Pain and a lot of it, first in the feet but then creeping its way up. A headache too, just above the ridge of the nose, throbbing and constant. Tiredness, also. Of course tiredness, it came with infection, but the pain stopped her sleeping. And so, just like that, from nothing to something. Three separate afflictions at once. And Gerri Hartman asked about the medicine cabinet.

'I know what you keep in there,' she had said four nights ago, rubbing her chin up against David's buttoned chest. She was talking about the antidepressants. 'I know what you keep in there, so you don't need to lock the door when you go inside the bathroom. And you don't need to lock the cabinet. It's not something you need to do.'

'Do I lock the cabinet?' David had said back, but of course he knew he did, and he knew exactly where the key was. A small thing, it fit snugly in his pocket. Every pocket at that.

'Yes,' she'd replied, balancing her chin on him. 'You do.'

David remembered how she had looked then. Her eyes hazel and bloodshot. Her face full of pasty smudges where she had dabbed her sponge, then switched to her finger, wiping delicately, then furiously, over one side of the nose to the other. The result was imperfect, but she didn't seem to mind. Or she didn't seem to notice. She had stared at him intently, her breathing fast with the fever and her mind on the pills that lay strewn across the coffee table. She had then asked him a question, one she tended to ask when she thought she knew the answer.

'What are you thinking?'

David was thinking about his arse. The pain, specifically, as he hopped onto his bike and rolled up his tweed sleeves in the heat. It was four p.m, and every child had successfully departed the school grounds, leaving David to retire alone. No conversations, no confrontations, just the way he liked it. It had been ten years since Charlie's case, and eight years since his reappointment at Gealblath Secondary School. But still, that reappointment had caused ripples across the community. The father of a lost child, the father who had been investigated; how could he possibly come back and pretend everything was normal?

'He's a danger to the children.'

'He has anger issues, always did.'

'He beat his wife. I'm sure of it.'

'His son too.'

'I don't want him near my kids, not after what happened.'

'He should be locked up. They were looking at him. They knew it was him.'

'They didn't find anything.'

'I'm sure they tried.'

It had died down. Soon enough the children grew up and their parents stopped caring. They allowed the story of Charlie to fade into the past, but even a healed wound leaves a scar; a spectre of pain that serves an unpleasant, constant memory. David was that pain. He was everything Gealblath had tried so hard to forget. Only he wouldn't leave. He had lived in Gealblath nearly all his life, and he wasn't going to be driven out by some thick-headed detective and his simultaneously brainless investigation.

David twisted the ignition and pulled on his backpack of books, which clung loosely to one shoulder. He kicked his feet off the ground and winced. For fifteen years now, his bike had been violently shoving its way up into his backside. He'd got it when he was twenty-nine. A slick, red Honda Shadow. It was cool then, and his youthful buttocks could take it. But now, at forty-four, he had to pay for it every day. The saving grace was that at the end of the day, he knew exactly where he was riding it to.

The tavern was lit up in deep red, yelling out to a world of dry and balding middle-aged men. GIL'S! Just that. Just GIL'S! A simple name for a simple place. The bar had had a previous life as a makeshift American diner, but the small town in East Scotland wasn't quite ready for the American takeover. It was soon adopted by drunkards wanting a moment's respite from their wives. Funnily enough, not many people wanted to travel out to the middle of nowhere to join them, so it now lay decrepit in the middle of woodland, miles away from anyone or anything. If you stood on the porch and looked closely through the trees, you could spot the lights of the nearest neighbourhood, but they would slowly become blurred the longer the night went on, until the reality of the outside world turned into a soft fuzz, indecipherable and irrelevant. Just as it should be.

David parked the Shadow, turned off the motor, and relieved his butt cheeks from the torture of the hard leather.

For a few moments, he simply stood and breathed, his eyes landing on a pit of water that was nestled beside the pub. David thought of it as a pit because he couldn't bring himself to flatter it. It wasn't an ocean, a loch, a swamp, a creek, or any other natural form of water. It was just a pit. And it stank. It stank of piss, shit, and rotten... something. David didn't want to say fish, because he knew what rotting fish smelt like, and it smelt better than the pit. There didn't seem to be any life in there, anyhow. The red light of GIL'S! that reflected off the dark and murky surface was just about the only thing moving in its proximity, and that was only because the *S* kept flickering on and off.

He walked over to the bank, reached inside his tweed jacket, and removed a torn and crumpled pack of cigarettes. Just one remained un-puffed inside. He put it into his mouth and chucked the box into the darkness, watching as it plunged into the depths of the pit. Light as air. And sinking. David shuddered, casting his mind back to the time he had brought Charlie here, back when he was still alive. He had been playing outside with the kids of some inmates at the bar. David was one of those inmates, craning his neck towards a fifth beer before a scream erupted and two children rushed inside, screaming about how Charlie had tripped and fallen into the water. Like the cigarette packet, he too had plunged right to the bottom. Just a hand was left visible, splayed out and clinging desperately to the world. David pulled him up in time, deciding that he had slipped on the slope and his shoes had got stuck in the mud. A logical explanation. But David was logical back then. His mind didn't wonder. It didn't see anything beneath the surface of things. All this time later, however, and David was wiser now. He knew that the pit was just a no-space. A black hole that sucked in the souls of the living, vowing to never spit them out. He wondered how many others had fallen in there. He wondered how many hands were reaching beneath the black now, out of sight, straightening, just an inch away from breaking the surface...

RIBBET!

David jumped backwards, looking down to spot a frog that had hopped unassumingly onto his shoe. It stared around itself for a moment, its small eyes bubbling, searching for the late-summer flies floating adrift in the wet heat. It found one and flung itself towards it, hind legs splaying before it disappeared into the water and out of sight.

'Huh,' murmured David. Then he flicked the last of the ash from his cigarette, poured a final mouthful of smoke into the evening air, and set off towards the tavern.

It took six beers before he was back on the Shadow. His shoes pushed hard on the pedals and the seat pushed harder against his arse. He propelled himself along a moonlit road, away from the blurry red lights of GIL'S! and onwards to the fuzzier ones on the outskirts of the woodland, a horizon that seemed slightly safer now he'd had a few drinks. Waiting for him there was Gerri and, beyond her, the dreaded medicine cabinet. Usually, it would be the drinking she would fret over, but tonight it would be the cabinet.

I know you're depressed, she would say. *I know what you take. You shouldn't be ashamed of what's in there. Please, David. Please just open it.*

David tried to focus, squinting at the path ahead of him as a van stormed past, its rusted engine coughing into the night. One of these days, that van would hit him. He would end up a motionless body on the embankment, crippled and flattened like roadkill. But he would try to not let that happen, of course. If only for Gerri, the one woman who truly saw him. His ex-wife, Vanessa, had left him soon after Charlie's disappearance, and when she had, David had presumed he would never be able to find anyone again. But then Gerri had come, and she had been warm, gentle, and understanding. She was good. Far better than anyone should be to a man who wasn't quite there anymore. A hollow shell, like the ones found when the tide went out at Gealblath Beach. *Look, Charlie, look at this. Something used to be in there once, Charlie, something lived there.*

David straightened his back. He would open it tonight, he decided. He would give Gerri the cabinet to say thank you. He widened his gaze as he made his way out of the woodland and into the first neighbourhood.

It didn't take much longer before Gerri was sitting in front of him, the aroma of her hairspray blended in with the candles and strawberry tarts that sat atop the kitchen table. She was pretty at this time of night. When the outside went full dark and the inside became a dim orange, her hair became a deeper ginger, her freckles less prominent, her skin smooth, like it was glossed with water. Maybe it was the alcohol. It was usually still burning away at dinner, putting a glow on things, making them palatable.

'What are you thinking?' she asked. She thought she knew what he was thinking, but she never knew.

'Nothing,' replied David.

Gerri placed down her glass. 'I just thought you might be thinking about my father.'

David shuffled in his chair. Gerri's father had ambushed David early that morning, before he left for work. He had given him a key for the boat he kept on Gealblath Beach, but David didn't sail. He didn't even touch the water. It was a test, if ever he had seen one. A peace offering flecked with suspicion. *There you go. You owe me now, laddie, you're in my debt. I'm looking forward to a closer acquaintance with you.* Perhaps he hoped an accident might happen out on the waves. A sunken boat for a liberated daughter. It appeared a good trade, David had to admit. He was no good for anyone.

'David?' said Gerri.

'Yeah, I saw him this morning.'

'And?'

'And he gave me the key to his boat.'

'And that was it? You didn't talk about anything?'

'We talked about the boat.'

Gerri sighed. 'That wasn't the point.'

David began scratching at the wood of the table, watching as his girlfriend frowned, almost sympathetically, like she was trying to reach out to him. *No*, he thought. *No, that wasn't the point.*

'Okay, I'm not thinking about him.'

'Then what are you thinking about?'

'I'm thinking about you.'

Gerri smiled and tucked some of her pretty ginger hair behind an ear. 'What about me?' she replied.

'You're good and you don't need to be.' David talked slowly, careful not to slur his words. He wanted this to be on the right side of drunk talk.

'I know I'm good. And you're good too.'

'I could be better.'

'We all could be better. But we're not, and that's fine.'

David looked to his left, spotting her pills displayed beneath a framed photo of her father. Clotrimazole, ibuprofen, melatonin; the fronts of the packets were facing towards him, as if they were staring, testing. *Open the cabinet.* He turned back to Gerri, who had followed his gaze over towards the medicine. She took a sip of water, then reached over the table and held his thumb.

'We all have demons, David. Some we hide, some we don't. But they're a part of who we are. They come with the package. We don't choose them, they choose us. But do you know what?'

'What?' asked David.

'I chose you. So maybe yours go deeper than most people's, because of what happened, but I chose you. And I'm good. I'll always be good. You don't have to worry about that.'

Another silence passed. David felt Gerri's fingertips on his palms, slowly stroking the skin, her polished nails trailing the cracks like they had carved them on their own. He sighed.

'I know.'

The next thing David knew, he was on the sofa. The television was blaring a re-run of *Now You See It*, with a four-eyed host and his gelled quiff and his belly which overhung a strained bronze belt buckle.

'*If one of our contestants gets this right, then their team will be going home with a huge cash prize of –*'

David pressed the mute button, then ran a hand through his hair, trying his best to ignore the butterflies that were gnawing at his gut. He looked over at Gerri. Her head was lying against the armrest, and her eyes were hidden behind curled lashes. It had taken another couple of pills and a twenty-five minute viewing of an old quiz show to get to this point, but finally Gerri was asleep. Lost to the world. David took a few breaths. Then, as quietly as he could, he fumbled around inside his pocket. His fingers touched something cold and sharp, small and hidden: the key to the medicine cabinet. He squeezed it, then moved over to the coffee table, scooping up the packets of pills. Gerri remained still on the sofa, her breaths low and constant, her mind caught in a dream. He watched her for a bit, taking her in through the low orange light. Then he turned and walked towards the bathroom.

The medicine cabinet was above the sink, pearl white and slightly chipped, David had spent plenty of time contemplating it, standing there every night, too scared to open it up. He had taken in the shape, the shade of the paint, the splinters of the wood, the dark pores, like faces, patterned in the chestnut. But now he didn't have time to stare. Now he had to be brave, and more importantly, he had to be fast. In one smooth motion, David raised the key and put it into the lock, hoping the metal might catch and snap as he twisted, but of course it didn't. The door swung open and the medicine inside was revealed. First were his sleeping pills. Next to them, ibuprofen, Prozac, then his aspirin, his opioids, the cream for his back, the inhalers for his asthma, and beside them, nestled snug in the corner, resting quietly like just another pill, Charlie. Chalk white and grinning, his eye sockets stared like two black holes, looking at his father without seeing him. David reached out and stroked his son's skull, following a crack which went from one end of the head to the other. Jagged. Like a lightning bolt.

'Hi, Charlie,' he whispered, but he didn't mean it. Charlie wasn't there anymore, not truly. He had moved on. He had left his body a long time ago. It was just a shell now. *Look, Charlie, look at this. Something used to be in there once, Charlie, something lived there.* With outstretched fingers, David lifted the skull from the shelf and placed Gerri's medicine in the space it had once filled. Then he closed the door, for the first time in years leaving the cabinet unlocked.

In a few minutes, he would place the skull in his backpack and zip it up tight. Then he would join his girlfriend on the sofa, and she would wake up with him by her side, as if he had never moved, as if they had slipped into the void together and shared the same dreams. She would say, 'Good morning.' And David would smile back at her. She would probably ask him what he was thinking, and for once she would actually know the answer. Because David would be thinking about what she said the night before, about everyone having demons. Everyone did have demons; she was right about that. His would just have to find somewhere else to hide.

3

THE SUBSTITUTE

'Florence.'

A murmur at the back of the classroom. The teacher moved on, as the teacher usually moved on, to Fungus. This always got a laugh or two, but as Marty turned around to watch Peter Fungus squirm in his chair – as he did every morning the universe was reminded of his name – he saw the owner of the first name doodling furiously in a notebook. Her hair was in those tangles and her mouth was in its usual position, clamped firmly shut.

Marty had to wait until break time until he could finally tell his friends. He found them at the climbing frame. Mike was hanging from the top pole, and Teddy was sitting in the wood chips, furiously rubbing two of them up against each other, as if he was trying to cancel them out from the face of the earth.

'Amee Florence,' said Marty enthusiastically. 'With two E's. That's the name of the new girl.'

'Oh yeah?' said Teddy. 'Strange name.'

'Why is it strange?'

'Well,' said Mike, 'it's not normal, is it? Just look at us. Marty Evans, Mike Torford, Teddy...'

'Yeah?' said Teddy.

'What's your second name again?'

Teddy looked up, slowing down the friction momentarily. 'Kowalski,' he replied.

Mike shook his head. 'God, you have to spoil everything, don't you, Teddy?'

'I can't help it if my dad's Polish.'

'My dad's Chinese!'

'Guys, that's not the point.' Marty turned towards the entrance of Gealblath Secondary School, hoping in vain to spot the new girl walking through it. He knew she wouldn't. Marty had never once seen her set foot in the park, not unless she was leaving or arriving. God only knew what she did with her free time, although some of the girls said they'd seen her sitting alone in classrooms, twiddling her thumbs and muttering to no one but herself.

'So what's the point?' asked Mike. 'Her surname's Florence, what's the big deal? You talked to her once and that was a week ago.' He pulled on the pole, attempting to perform a chin-up. His cheeks shone red as his chin failed to venture past his elbows.

'He wants to make it Evans!' cheered Teddy.

'Shut up.'

'You don't deny it. You want her to be Amee Evans!'

'Like Mike said, I've only talked to her once.'

'Oh mate, that's tragic.'

'Well, it's not true, Teddy.'

'It's still tragic.'

Marty sighed. Beyond him, he saw Rory and Ross strolling

across the grass, their eyes fixed on Marty and their fists clenching hard. They didn't come over. Teddy's ear remained unspoiled. He had Mr Cooper to thank for that, Marty supposed.

'Do you want to talk to her again?' asked Mike.

Marty waited for the following *APOOOOUUFFF!* to trail off before he answered.

'If it was up to me, then yeah. She was cool. She called me Venkman.'

Mike nodded in understanding. 'But it's not up to you. It's not like you can just go up and talk to her if she gets scared off easily. She has to talk to you first.'

Teddy hummed in agreement, as if he was all too familiar with this kind of conundrum.

'I mean,' Marty said, leaning his back against the iron poles, 'it can't be as embarrassing as the first time, right?'

Amee Florence found him by the urinals. The voice was small, quiet, but undeniably the new girl's.

'Hello, Marty.'

'JESUS!' Marty stumbled, a stream of piss splashing violently up the wall as he shoved himself into the corner and stuffed his privates back into his trousers. The new girl stood in the doorway.

'That's funny,' she said. 'Normally it's me who acts like that after a hello. You remember what happened the first time you –'

'What are you doing in here?' Marty interrupted.

The new girl's smile disappeared. 'Don't you want to talk to me?'

'No, I do, I definitely do; it's just...' He fixed his eyes on the door behind her, dreading what it would look like if someone

45

were to come in and catch the weed-kid and the weird kid alone together. Especially if that someone was Rory.

'Just what?'

'This is the boys' toilets, Amee. You know, for boys.' He stepped over to the right, covering the urine that was still trickling down the bathroom walls.

'Oh right,' said Amee.

'But that's fine,' Marty added quickly. 'I mean, it's okay. I'm done in here anyhow.'

He pulled hard on his zipper again, even though it was already done up tight, and Amee's smile began to re-emerge between her cheeks. It was small, but Marty noticed that somehow it managed to fill her face. Perhaps because smiling was something she didn't do often. Like the sun appearing in rain, you could really see it.

'Listen,' she said. 'I just wanted to say, I'm sorry about what happened. I'm sorry I ran off, I didn't...'

Marty shook his head. 'Don't worry about it. Nothing happened. Mr Cooper came before they could knock me out.'

'Mr Cooper?' asked Amee.

'Yeah,' Marty replied. 'The teacher.'

'David Cooper?'

'Uh, yeah, I guess.'

Amee stood still for a moment, swaying slightly on the spot. She nodded. 'Okay, that's good.'

'Yeah. Yeah, it is for me anyway. And my face.'

Behind the walls, a bell started ringing and the sound of multiple footsteps erupted in the hallway, coupled with excited screams and end-of-school cheers.

'We better go,' Marty told her, grabbing his bag. 'This isn't a great place to talk when fifty school-kids are busting for a piss.'

'The girls use their bathroom to talk,' said Amee.

'Yeah,' Marty replied. 'There are still better places, I reckon.'

The park was one of them. Every child was now crushing the sun-hard grass in a stampede; some running, others walking, but for two, who were simply observing. Hands in pockets and backs propped against a red-brick wall, Amee and Marty spoke loudly over the revving engines of the cars on the kerb. There was a nice smell in the air. The fresh pollen had been kicked up by every heel, and now it hung in the breeze, swirling back to the two of them every now and then. Marty relaxed into it.

'It's not too, bad is it?' he mused. 'We have the hottest summers compared to anywhere else in the country, apparently. They go on about it every year. I don't get why; I mean it's not like we're in Barbados. We're in bloody Gealblath. But still, I guess it's pretty nice.'

Amee gazed over at him, a blank look plastered on her face. Marty noticed her look and clarified.

'You're new to Gealblath, right? That's why I've never seen you before?'

'I was home-schooled,' she replied bluntly.

'Oh, that makes sense.'

'Why does that make sense?'

Marty stuttered, quickly realising his error. 'Oh, just, you know, factual. Like it doesn't not make sense.'

Amee pursed her lips in contemplation of this, and Marty refrained from punching himself. He always managed to say the wrong thing to this girl; he wished she would give him a full five minutes to prepare each sentence before he said it, preferably with a blackboard and a flow chart for good measure.

47

'Marty,' said Amee then, 'be honest, do you think I'm weird?'

'No,' replied Marty, a little too quickly.

'Tell me the truth, Marty.'

'I mean... maybe a little. But that's okay. Who cares if everyone thinks you're weird?'

'Everyone thinks I'm weird?'

Marty flinched. Flow chart. He needed a damn flow chart.

'Well, not everyone. Some people say you have imaginary friends and stuff, you know. They think that's weird.'

Amee shook her head, turning her gaze towards the park. 'I don't have imaginary friends.'

'No, yeah, I thought you didn't.'

They stood in silence for a while. Marty took a nervous breath and looked down at her shoes. She was wearing some now. These ones must have fitted better.

'I know I seem weird,' said the new girl. 'But I can't help it. I'm just not used to people. At least, not this kind of people.'

'What do you mean, this kind?'

Marty stared at her, but Amee didn't reply. Instead, she simply curled her bottom lip, her eyes narrowing as she looked at the kids around them. Marty cleared his throat, desperate to change the subject.

'So, you like, reading?' he asked, remembering what Mr Cooper had told him.

'Not really. Why?'

'Oh... uh... I saw you reading a book. By the lockers. I guessed you like reading them.'

'*The Hobbit*,' said Amee. 'I like reading *The Hobbit*.'

'Okay.'

Marty wondered why Mr Cooper would care about her

reading that book in particular. Perhaps his son used to enjoy it. Perhaps he read it to him at bedtime. A tinge of sadness hit Marty's chest, but he let it pass.

'Yeah, that's a good book. I mean, I read it just the once. Don't tell me, you've read it a hundred times.'

'No, just twice. I'm reading it again now.'

Marty laughed and Amee joined him. He was just beginning to think this was actually going okay when he spotted Mike and Teddy walking across the grass, their heads swivelling to and fro as they searched for their third friend. Marty ducked slightly. He couldn't even imagine what it would be like if they came over, what with Mike's constant sneezing and Teddy's maniacal enthusiasm for Warhammer; they would blow the whole operation. And Marty was determined to have a conversation with this girl that didn't end with her running away from him.

'What is it?' asked Amee. 'Slimer?'

Mike and Teddy hopped onto the pavement, and Marty breathed a heavy sigh of relief. Amee was still standing beside him. So far, so good.

'So hey,' said Marty, 'if I was a character from *The Hobbit*, who would I be?'

Amee looked at him again, biting her lip in thought. Once again, Marty wished he'd think before he asked things. There weren't many flattering *Hobbit* characters. At least, none as flattering as Venkman. What was he hoping for? Gollum? Amee made a funny sucking sound, her eyes trailing across the road. Then, in one quick movement, she bent over and swept up the bag that had been sitting between her legs.

'I'll answer that. But I've gotta go now.'

Marty pushed himself off the wall, taken aback by the suddenness of Amee's bailing, but then he spotted that familiar black American Lincoln pulling up on the kerb, and he breathed a sigh of relief.

'Do you want to talk again tomorrow?' she asked, looking Marty straight in the eyes.

'Uh, yeah. I mean, yeah, of course.'

Amee smiled that smile again. 'Cool, see you tomorrow then.'

She began making her way towards the Lincoln, and Marty watched her go. She even walked differently to everyone else, he realised. All purposeful and delicate, like she had no shoes. Like she was barefoot on the grass. Marty grinned to himself. Then he picked up his own bag and swung it onto his back.

Mike's puffy cheeks appeared to swell in shock when he told him.

'Wait, so this is actually happening? You're actually going out?'

'No, we're not going out, Mike. She just wants to talk to me again.'

Marty was sitting in the corner of Mike's room, dabbing a brush at one of Mike's Warhammer models that he'd given him to finish.

'That's what going out is though, right?' Mike argued. 'Just arranging to talk to each other.'

'By that logic I've been going out with you and Teddy for about four years.' Marty decided that was quite enough blood on the sword and chucked the figure back over to Mike, who was slumped on a bean bag. 'There you go. Happy four-year anniversary.'

Mike blew him a kiss. 'But seriously though,' he said. 'This is pretty big.'

'It's relatively big. I mean, it's pretty small sized. I mean, it's like...' Marty held out his thumb and fore finger, keeping them about an inch apart. 'In fact, I don't even know why I told you.'

Or rather, he didn't know why he'd sprinted over to Mike's house, knocked on his door, pulled him upstairs, and delivered the information within about fifteen minutes of it actually taking place.

'Are you gonna kiss her?' asked Mike.

'Yeah, and we'll be having sex by next week.'

Mike shook his head in wonderment. 'Wow.'

'Mike, please familiarise yourself with the concept of sarcasm.'

'Just imagine it though, you and Amee, boyfriend and girlfriend. What are you gonna do about us?'

'What are you talking about?'

'Me and Teddy. You can't just leave us. Remember the bro code.'

'What the hell is the bro code?'

'It's the code, Marty. Everyone knows the code.'

'Enlighten me.'

Mike leant forward seriously, like he was about to tell Marty the secret of the universe. 'You don't leave your friends. Not for anyone. Not even a girl.' He leant back, the secret of the universe successfully delivered.

'What makes you so sure I'd leave you?'

'Because you're the cool one of the group,' replied Mike. 'You said it yourself, she called you Venkman.'

'How am I cooler than you?'

'Teddy and me don't belong here like you do. You fit in better than us.'

'They call me the weed-kid. I wouldn't call that fitting in.'

'It's better than some of the names we're called.'

Marty shuffled. He knew what Mike meant, of course. He was right. Even though Marty didn't like it. He saw himself as equal to both of them, so it annoyed him that the rest of Gealblath didn't see it the same way.

'Well, don't worry,' he replied. 'Like I said, it's not a date, it's just a talk.'

'Good. Because there's a punishment for breaking the bro code.'

'What's that?'

'You have to give back the Warhammer set me and Teddy made for you.'

Marty held up his hands. 'Fine.'

He didn't have the heart to tell Mike he'd lost that set two terms back.

The next day in school, Marty sat in the middle of a classroom that was more like a battleground. Paper balls spun through the air, catapulting into walls and Liam Tonson's face. Frazier and Duncan sparred with two plastic chairs whilst Tim McDonnell attempted to force a permanent marker onto his best friend Dylan's inflated cheeks. Above the ruckus there was a clock which read 9.43 a.m.

'Two more minutes and we get to leave!'

'You can leave if you want to get in trouble.'

'Will Collins is a pussy!'

'Shut up, I'm trying to –'

'Can you stop hitting me in the face you –'

'Willy is a pussy! Willy is a pussy!'

'Shut up!'

'Can you put those chairs down, it's starting to –'

'WILLY IS A PUSSY!'

Marty sank into his seat. Ms Robertson was usually late for maths, walking into the classroom with half a McDonald's burger shoved into her mouth and moaning about how terrible the traffic was. But thirteen minutes was pushing it. Perhaps there was a special menu on. He looked across the classroom, ducking slightly to allow a chunk of graph paper to skim over his head and hit Liam Tonson in the face again ('FOR SHIT'S SAKE!'). Sitting quietly in the warzone was Amee, her thumbs twiddling around each other nervously.

Marty thought about going over and talking to her, yet something was stopping him. Perhaps it was the other kids, or perhaps it was his conversation with Mike the day before. He'd laughed it off, but Mike's words had undeniably stuck with him. They clung to his mind and every time he tried to fling them off, they would find him again, hitting him just as successfully as the paper balls were hitting Liam Tonson's face. *It's just a talk, it's not a date. It's just a talk, it's not a date. But she called you Venkman. That means she thinks you're cool. A girl who actually thinks the weed-kid is cool.* Marty shook his head. Then the clock turned to 9.44 a.m. and the door swung open.

The kids all halted. Chairs stopped being swords and became chairs again, one last paper ball was swung at Liam's head, and everyone prepared for another excuse about traffic jams and red lights. But it was not Ms Robertson and a McDonald's burger that entered the room. Instead, it was Mr Cooper. Somehow, he looked more tired than the last time Marty had seen him. His eyes were red, and thin blobs of gloop lined them in weepy puddles. With a zombie-like sigh, he shook his backpack off his shoulder, placed it under the desk, then sat back with a 'humph' into Ms Robertson's chair. Marty noticed black smudges peeking over his collar.

'Okay...' Mr Cooper said, squinting at the class as if they were a million miles away. 'I'm not Ms Robertson. Ms Robertson is ill. Ms Robertson left work for you to do. You'll find it here on the desk. Get on with it, complete it, then sit still until the end of the lesson.' He leant back, his job done and his eyes landing on the cracks in the ceiling paint.

Most of the class was nearly done after just twenty minutes. Papers were finished and handed back to the dozing teacher, and voices were raised in delight as the class could talk freely without the fear of being reprimanded. Marty finished in thirty, but Amee spent most of the lesson biting the spine of her fountain pen and staring at her paper like it had dropped from a different planet. At one point, Marty saw her finally scribbling away, but he soon realised she was just drawing another picture. It wasn't until the end-of-class bell rattled (almost throwing Mr Cooper off his chair) that she finally leant back and screwed the lid back on her pen. Marty sighed in relief, then stood along with her and placed his papers down neatly on Ms Robertson's desk. The rest of the class filed out of the door, but any hopes of joining them were skewered as soon as Mr Cooper raised his arm.

'You stay here. I want to talk.'

Marty pointed at his chest. 'Who, me?'

'No.' Mr Cooper nodded towards the new girl. 'Her.' He waved a hand over to one of the desks. 'Please sit. You can go now, Marty.'

Amee looked over at Marty, trepidation resting clearly in the blues of her eyes. 'Is it okay if he stays?' she asked.

'Don't panic,' Mr Cooper replied. 'You've done nothing wrong. It'll only take a second, Marty.'

Marty waited for a moment, then he slowly retreated to the classroom door, watching helplessly as Amee sat behind

54

one of the desks, and Mr Cooper pulled up a chair that had just forty minutes ago been a sparring sword.

Amee didn't show up to the next lesson. Normally, she would be at the back, her face buried in a textbook, utilising it as a shield to protect her from oncoming stares. But now her seat was filled by George Ripson, who spent most of the lesson engraving something hilarious into the wood of the desk with his pencil. By the look of his grin, it was probably another depiction of male genitalia, a common staple of George's creative work. Geography was much the same. The teacher droned on and on about rocks and erosion, but Marty's brain was still focused on Amee's seat in the corner of the room, empty, screaming out her absence to the rest of the class, none of whom seemed to notice.

It wasn't until the end of the day that Marty's mind was finally set at ease. It started with a tap on the shoulder that made him trip on his shoelaces and cling on to Teddy's arm in fright.

'Hello,' a voice said.

Marty turned to find Amee standing behind him.

'Hey!'

Amee gave him an almost relieved smile, then turned to Teddy and Mike, both of whom stood with hands in their pockets and their postures curiously straighter than they had been before.

'Oh, these are my friends,' Marty explained. 'Teddy and Mike.'

Teddy held out a sweaty hand. 'Hi there.'

Amee took it in hers, unprepared for the hearty shake that he proceeded to perform.

Mike opted to wave. 'Hello.'

'Definitely friends this time?' asked Amee.

Marty gave a nervous laugh. 'Yeah, definitely friends.'

'They won't try to hit you?'

'Well, that depends,' said Mike. 'Are you familiar with the bro code?'

'What's a bro code?'

'Alright, how about I catch you guys up?' Marty stepped in between them, keen to ease Teddy and Mike out of the picture now that the introductions were done with. To his relief, both of them obliged.

'It was nice to meet you,' said Teddy, once again holding out a sweaty hand for her to shake.

'Yeah,' Mike added. 'See you soon.'

And then they were gone, but not without giving Marty a distrustful second glance as they headed outdoors.

'They seem nice,' said Amee, wiping the sweat off her hand and onto her skirt.

'They're okay. I mean, they're a bit –'

'I'm sorry about earlier.'

Marty tripped over his words, taken aback by the force and suddenness of her apology. 'Oh, that's fine, it's not your fault. What did Mr Cooper say?'

'Nothing. I just don't like being left alone with people.'

'What, even me?'

'No.' Amee shook her head. 'Not you, people like him.'

'Oh...'

Marty wasn't sure what to make of that. In the little time he'd spent with Mr Cooper, he thought he'd seemed like a pretty cool teacher. At least, he was the only teacher Marty knew who would call Rory an arsehole to his face, and that had to count for something. Amee sniffed, dragging a strand of loose hair behind her ear awkwardly.

'So, did you decide?' asked Marty.

'Decide what?'

'Which character I am.'

'Oh. No, I don't know who you are.'

For a moment, Marty was a little disappointed. But then, out of nowhere, Amee reached out and took him by the hand.

'But I think you're one of the good guys. And I like you, Marty.'

As if in slow motion, she leant over and gave him a peck on the cheek, the contact momentary but enough to fill Marty's face with a deep red blush, lighting him up like a Christmas tree. She didn't give him any time to spoil the moment after that. Before he could say anything, Amee was striding off towards the door, leaving Marty to sway in shock behind her. A few seconds of nothingness passed. The door swung closed, the school corridor went silent, and Marty Evans touched his cheek. Mike and Teddy would never believe this.

4

DIAGNOSIS

Charlie's skull wreaked havoc behind David's eyes. It had been one week since the medicine cabinet had been opened and Charlie's head had been placed in between maths equations and reports on why Kevin Miles was an arrogant wee shite. He lingered in the bookbag, and he lingered harder in David's head, grinning at him, screaming at every turn and every conversation. *Yes, Laura, it is a shame they're cutting the drama department, but you'll never guess what I have in my bag.* David got sad more and angry too; he'd clenched his fists so hard and so often over the past week he was surprised the knuckles hadn't slipped through the flesh. The skull was messing with his medication, pulling at the threads, placing every inch of him on edge. And Gerri could tell, because Gerri could always tell what David was thinking.

You're acting up, David. I can see it in your face; you're all red. You just need to calm down; it's no big deal. We can even start going to the doctor together, now we're not hiding anything. We'll go out tomorrow – it'll do you good.

Help you sleep better.

But David's sleep was just as bad. Whilst Charlie wasn't alive in reality, he was alive in his dreams. Alive and talking, smiling with teeth, looking with eyes, even breathing. He woke David up now, his impish cries seeming to carry on into the real world. *Let me out the bag! Let me out the bag, you fuck!*

David sat up, kicking the sheet over his legs and squinting against the red shine of the alarm clock. 12.43 a.m. He'd been asleep for half an hour.

'Goddamn it,' he muttered, pulling the pillow behind him to rest against his neck. It was always a struggle to get back to the dark once the veil had been torn, even with the sleeping pills. He had to forget about the real world all over again, but the key to that lock was sleeping soundly beside him. He looked over at Gerri, her bare chest rising and falling in the yellow hue of the streetlight. Her hair was stuck to the sweat on her breasts in a knotted ginger mess. She wouldn't wake up now. She never did once she was deep in her sleep, which was a shame, because she had become a better sleeping pill than the pills themselves when she was in the mood. David lifted his legs over the mattress and placed his feet neatly on the floor. Then he got up and made his way to the medicine cabinet, grabbing a small plastic tub in one hand. They wouldn't work. He knew they wouldn't work.

Oh, take me. Chew / gulp.

Nocturnally.. Chew / gulp / cough.

Forever and ever... Splutter / cough / clench / gulp.

Between your teeth.

The surgery. Ten thirty a.m. David watched through tired eyes as Dr Arnold sauntered across the floor, a clipboard in hand and three thin frowns folding over one another on his forehead. David gulped, squeezing any remnants of saliva into the back of his throat, attempting in vain to wet what was fast becoming the Sahara Desert back there. He'd give anything for a drink; although he wasn't entirely sure if that drink was water or beer. *Beer. Don't kid yourself. You need a damn beer.* Gerri was sitting beside him, her hand on his knee, stroking it gently with a thumb.

'What's the diagnosis, Doc? How long have I got?'

Dr Arnold didn't even look up from his clipboard. 'I couldn't give you the number of people who make that joke to me,' he said. 'It's funny until the bloke who says it has six months.'

David leaned back on his chair. 'Shit. That happened to you?'

The doctor peered over the board and gave a wry, ugly grin. It didn't suit him. His forehead frowned but his mouth smiled; two halves of his face were saying different things. David felt like punching it into one language.

'I'm dreading the day,' he said, perching his arse on a paper cluttered desk which reminded David somewhat of his own. 'But it's not this one.'

The doctor smiled again and David nodded slowly, wishing he would just spit it all out so he could get on with his life.

'So what's the diagnosis?' he repeated.

'Prozac,' the doctor announced, almost triumphantly.

David shifted a little in his seat. 'What about it?'

'You've been on it how long?'

'You tell me.'

Gerri squeezed his knee slightly, sensing the anger in his voice. The doctor made a chuckling sound in the back of his throat.

'If I remember rightly, we put you on it a year ago, give or take. Have you been feeling better?'

'Sure, the roads are lined with daisies now.'

'I mean, the suicidal thoughts are gone?'

'Mostly. Yeah.'

That was partly true. When David first went on the Prozac, he was at rock bottom. It wasn't as if the world had become any brighter since then, but a numbness had taken over. Nothing had to matter anymore.

You're in the dark now. But your bed is made, your sheets are snug, settle in.

Is that memory foam? It feels like I'm sinking. A good sinking though. Pleasant. Drifting.

Enjoy your sleep. And when you wake up, slip another.

I will. Christ, how I will.

That was until he'd had to open the medicine cabinet. Now what was safe and ignored was in the open again, waiting to be found by a pair of eyes other than David's. Waiting to bring down his whole world, or whatever was left of it anyhow. A hot, sick feeling erupted inside David's stomach. This room made him ill. Especially with his bag beside him, nestled right next to his shoe.

'Good to hear,' said Dr Arnold. His gaze sank down to David's fists as he clenched them, rolling the tips of his fingers up his knees and into the palms. 'So tell me what's been happening. In the last week, what's gone wrong?'

'It seemed so sudden,' Gerri chimed in. 'One night he was fine, then the next morning...'

The doctor raised a hand. 'If you don't mind, I would like to hear this from David. I know it's hard, and this sudden change in behaviour can be scary, but these things can happen. I need to hear his side.'

David sighed and immediately regretted it. The breath sounded shuddery, nervous, as if he was on the verge of tears. He fiddled with the buttons of his jacket, making sure he kept the tops of his fingers hidden.

'I...' The words didn't come; they hung in his throat like weeds in the dirt. No matter how hard he pulled, the damn things wouldn't give. 'I...'

* * *

The tavern was dimly lit. Although that went without saying: the tavern was always dimly lit. It was more uninviting than a pig's vagina. And yet the drunkards came. Mosquitos lured by the red light. *Drink / drink / drink / ZAP! / ugh / alive? / another!* Glass down, David shoved his hand into his face and wiped. Gerri nudged him.

'How are you feeling?' she asked. 'How was school today? How's that girl doing?'

'What girl?'

'You know, the one you mentioned a few weeks back.'

David shrugged, though he knew exactly who Gerri was talking about. The new girl, the one who was on her own all of the time. She liked *The Hobbit*. He kept quiet. Gerri sighed, taking a sip of her drink. She hated being here, David could tell, but she did it for him, as if getting him out of the house might solve the problems that had developed over the last week. But Gerri's idea of healing was dubious at best. The two of them simply sat there, problems festering on the stools, muted by the bottle.

David was just beginning to feel his head go when she nudged him again, her eyes rolling to the left. Confused, he turned, simultaneously chugging his beer as he did so. In the corner of the bar, there was a group of bikers. He stared for a moment, wondering what it was he was supposed to be looking at. He breathed a long, drawn-out breath, then gave up. Gerri huffed, pulling her hair to her ear, as if she was trying to show him something. David turned again, and his gaze now fixed on the woman in the middle of the group, the only female there. She was pretty, as far as he could tell. In this light anybody could be pretty, but there was a certain look about her. Quirky but bold, soft but firm. *Fake tits?* He focused harder. *Potentially.* The young woman giggled, turning her face towards the man on her left and gracefully pulling her hair out of her eyes. That was when David saw it. On her right side, just above her brow, lay an ugly black blob of a mark.

'Legs too,' Gerri muttered, pointing down to the woman's calves, where her ripped tights revealed two more blood-dried circles hiding behind the fabric. The three men surrounding her flew into roars of laughter and David frowned, spotting the bruised woman's discomfort from across the room.

'It's messed up,' said Gerri, shaking her head slightly and taking a sip of her rum and Coke. 'Why do these types exist?'

'Bottom of the barrel,' David agreed. 'Anyone in leather is automatically an arsehole, I know it.'

'Not them. Her.'

'Her? But she's the punching bag.'

'And doesn't she know it? Don't tell me she has to stick around. They're not kidnappers; they're her type. She's chosen a type and her type does that.'

David took another swig. *Same can be said for you, Gerri. You've chosen a type and here I am. Getting sad, getting angry, hiding skulls in backpacks.*

'She gets what's coming to her,' Gerri continued. 'I might be a dick for saying it, but she gets what's coming.'

David felt a tug of sadness as the blonde woman pulled her hair back once more. It was slight, subtle, but spoke volumes. *She wants us to see. She wants the world to see. Don't you get that, Gerri? Like scraping a pie from the oven floor with a spatula; once stuck, it takes a bitch and an arm to let go.* David took another deep breath. Watching this made him angry. Watching them laugh, pat each other on the back, gulp down their lagers. She was their dolly, and they'd snipped off the talking string. All of a sudden, David felt his weight go onto the soles of his feet and he staggered slightly.

'What are you doing?' asked Gerri, placing her hand on his old tweed jacket.

David controlled himself, trying to slow his racing heart. 'We're leaving.'

Gerri didn't argue. With an 'Oh yes!' she grabbed her coat from beneath her and took hold of David's hand. They headed across the room, David's eyes staying screwed to the woman. *Don't go,* she seemed to say to him. *Don't go, don't go, see me, fucking see me, open your eyes, goddamnit!* A wolf whistle exploded into the air, squirming its way into David's ears, clicking a switch from standby to go. He let go of Gerri's hand and turned towards the culprit. It was the leather-wearer on the left of the girl, he knew it. Redhead, acne-scarred. He had a triumphant drunk twinkle glistening in his eyes. David approached him.

'The fuck you just do?' he said fiercely. The words weren't as sensical as he had intended, but the whistler seemed to understand them just fine.

'What the fuck did I just do? Just givin' your bird a pat on the arse from here, pal.'

64

His friends laughed. David had ignored everything in that sentence, other than the fact that this was the guy who had whistled.

'Let's go outside.' *That's what people say, isn't it? Go outside?*

'David, leave him! I don't care!' Gerri reached for his arm, but David shook her away, his breaths getting heavier and his eyes narrowing.

'David,' the biker repeated, licking the dry cracks of his bottom lip. 'I know who you are; I recognise you from the village. You're the man whose son went walkies. Or they say he went walkies. The police seemed awful interested in you, if I remember rightly.'

Gerri tugged at his arm again. 'David, please.'

But David didn't move. He remained rooted to the spot.

The biker stood and leaned towards David's ear. 'Where's your boy, my man? Did you tuck him in a bit too tight?'

Without a second thought, David lunged down to the table, swiped up one of the semi-full beer bottles, then brought it down onto the biker's head. A toe-curling cry ignited the innards of GIL'S! and a wave of blood poured from him, landing in a puddle on David's shoes. He stared into the bleeding man's eyes as they looked through him, right over to the wall of the bar and the pit beyond it. The biker let out a shuddered... something. Moan? David decided so. Then he collapsed over the leg of the table and fell to the ground with a thump. Gerri screamed. The blonde woman gasped. The two other bikers stood. And then David got what was coming to him. He closed his eyes, spread his arms, and let it be.

* * *

The doctor made a funny sucking sound with his pursed lips. His eyes had been on the floor for the full time it had taken David to recount the story, but now he pulled them away, looking back into David's soul.

'You were on Prozac at the time you attacked him?'

David tried not to flinch at the word 'attack'. Surely that wasn't entirely fair. He was standing up for his girlfriend; he was protecting her, defending her. Or was he defending the beaten blonde? Or his own dignity? Or had he taken the biker out because he felt like it? Because he wanted blood to pay for what had been going on inside his head?

'Yes, Doctor,' he said.

'And you said you've been feeling angry a lot recently, like you have mood swings, violent waves that rush through you.'

'It's just been this last week,' said Gerri. 'But what happened at the tavern, I've never...' She trailed off, her hand retreating from David's knee. 'That wasn't him doing that. It wasn't him.'

'Has anything happened in the last week that might have brought on this change in behaviour?'

The doctor looked at David, and David was almost sick in his lap.

'There's the cabinet,' said Gerri.

'Cabinet?'

'We have this medicine cabinet. It's been locked, ever since our relationship started, ever since I've known him.' Her hand reached his knee again, scratching at the ripples of his trousers. 'Let's just say, David's feelings and his medication have never been a conversation between us.'

'It can be hard, opening up that side of yourself,' the doctor said.

David nodded. *Harder than you could ever believe, Doc.*

The doctor leapt up onto his feet and paced behind his desk, opening up the drawer and removing a thick stack of prescription papers.

'So here's what I'm gonna do. I'm gonna take you off the Prozac.'

David's heart sank and the room went a little fuzzy for a moment. 'The Prozac? But I thought the pills were supposed to stop feelings of...'

'Of depression. Yes, but you said yourself, you didn't think you were a violent man. And yet these violent urges have arisen, perhaps due to higher levels of stress in the last week. These pills, the Prozac I mean, may be amplifying them. So you'll go on sertraline. The function is the same, but the behavioural changes you've been experiencing should be smoothed out.' He crossed the room, the prescription papers clasped tightly between two fingers.

'And you're sure these will still help like the Prozac?' asked Gerri.

The doctor nodded. 'We can try.'

David sniffed. It was almost laughable, watching these two people try to worm their way inside him, desperately attempting to find out what had gone wrong. It would be easier for both of them if he just opened up the bag and presented the problem like he was the lead in *Hamlet*. Still, if the doctor wanted him on new pills, he'd go on the new pills. He just hoped Gerri didn't get her hopes up. They stood and David gave a small, shaky nod to the white coat.

'Oh and Mr Cooper,' the doctor said before he reached the door. 'If your symptoms persist then come back right away. Rest assured we'll find you something else to help in your recovery.'

David nodded a false promise. He took two steps in one, grabbing the door handle with a sweaty palm as the word churned over in his mind. *Recovery.* Fucking soldiers recovered. And David was sure as hell not that. Not a soldier. Just a sad, angry man in a tweed jacket. Without light, without love, a shell. *Look, Charlie, look at this. Something used to –*

Used to / Used to / Used to / Used to / BRRRIIIIINNNNGGGGGGGGGG.

The sound penetrated David's eardrums with a bastard ferocity. The break bell. Every child in front of him jumped into the sky and swung their backpacks around their shoulders.

'I'm going to the park –'

'You wanna come –'

'Yeah –'

'You got fags –'

'No –'

'Yeah –'

'Mum says we're going to –'

'Can you come –'

'Yeah –'

'Can't come, gotta see –'

'Your girlfriend –'

'Juney's got a girlfriend –'

'I know Juney's got a girlfriend –'

'I do not –'

'June is a dyke –'

'What's a dyke –'

'It means you're gay –'

'Going to the park –'

'Can you come –'
'I said no –'
'Have you kissed her –'
'Shh –'
'Mr Cooper –'
'Mr Cooper's asleep, idiot –'
'Not anymore –'
'Dyke –'
'NO!'

David pointed his chin up to the ceiling, wiping his hand down his face in a long, drawn-out motion. Had he been asleep? Really, actually? That was a new low. Sometimes he would zone out in his lessons, he would leave the classroom and go back to his flat or the medicine cabinet, but he'd never actually slept before. Not with the kids in front of him. Not with his job on the line. Although having said that, his job was already on the line. As long as that biker was in hospital. As long as people were talking and the cops were sniffing about, it wouldn't be long until the headmaster was informed and David would have that conversation, the first under this headmaster but the third in his tenure as a teacher. He was becoming quite the professional at grovelling for his job.

David sat himself up, resting his elbows on the desk. *Dozing off in the middle of a lesson won't help you, idiot.* He sighed, peering out of the window at the rain outside. The water was swaying right to left in the salt-clogged air. Watching it made David feel even drowsier, as if it was one of those watches that hypnotists used. *Right, left, right, left, sleep, now, slip, another.* He shook himself, turning away from the rain, turning instead to the eyes of Charlie's chalk-white skull. *You realise that I'm doing this? You realise*

*it's me who's killing you? I'm gonna weigh you down...
down...down... until you can't find a way out. It'll be like
you're in the pit. Sinking away to join the vermin at the
bottom.* The skull sighed, rolling its eyeless eyes. *You see,
this is what happens when a dad treats a son bad. When
they're dead, a son can treat a dad right.*

David spluttered as the skull was replaced with the face
of the new girl. She stood in front of him, her ice-blue eyes
flashing before his. He swallowed and ran his hand through
his hair. The new girl looked just as alone as she had been
when he saw her on her first day. He wondered if the boy
they called 'Weed-kid' had followed his advice. Marty was
standing beside her, paper in one hand, backpack in the other.
No harm in asking, thought David. *The least you can do is
act like a teacher whilst your job's on the line.* David raised
his arm, determined to get his mind off the skull and into
his life again.

'You stay here. I want to talk.'

'Who, me?' the weed-kid asked.

'No,' David replied. 'Her.' He waved a hand over to the
desk behind the new girl. 'Please sit. You can go now, Marty.'

'Is it okay if he stays?' asked the new girl.

'Don't panic, you've done nothing wrong. It'll only take
a second, Marty.'

The weed-kid hesitated, then nodded and proceeded to
leave the classroom. David took a few moments, wiping his
sore, sleep-deprived eyes before pulling up a chair on the
other side of the table. Amee stared at him. She looked scared.

'It's alright, just relax. I want to know how you're doing.'

'Why?'

'Because I'm a teacher.'

'No, I mean why me?'

'You like *The Hobbit*. I saw you reading it, and I saw your drawings. I liked it too when I was a kid. And I was alone for a while too. Until I made a friend.'

'Okay,' said Amee in a tremulous voice. 'Is that all, sir?'

At that moment, David noticed that Amee's legs were shaking, the soles of her feet tapping up and down on the carpet so hard that he could feel the vibrations shudder through his shoes.

'Just relax,' he repeated. 'You're not in any trouble.'

But the new girl was not relaxing. The blood drained away from her face like someone had pulled a plug. Her lips quivered, her eyes closed, and her breathing deepened, each breath shivering through her nostrils. It was like something was shutting her down one body part at a time.

'Amee,' said David.

He reached over and placed his hand on hers, and at that moment the world around him changed. A high-pitched yell erupted inside the room, so strong that David was surprised he wasn't thrown backwards through the wall behind him. The new girl was suddenly on the floor, scrambling across it.

'GET AWAY! GET AWAY FROM ME!'

For a second, and surely due to his immense shock, David felt like yelling back. But he simply stood and stared. Dumbstruck. Useless. Until his senses kicked back in.

'What did I do? Why are you –'

Amee yelled again, this time even louder. 'PLEASE JUST GO! JUST GO! GO! GO!'

And David didn't need to be asked again. In what felt like one fluid motion, he grabbed his bag from behind the desk, turned, and rushed through the door, slamming it shut behind him and wishing for a thousand bolts to trap the psychotic child inside.

5

THE MISSING STUDENT

'When you tear up an apple, rip the thing in half, what do you see?'

Silence. Marty was sitting in a small waiting room outside of the counsellor's office. Even from where he was sitting, though, he could tell it was an awkward silence. There was a mumble. Incoherent. Then more silence. Then...

'The inside?'

Pause. Even from where Marty was sitting, he could tell it was an awkward pause.

'Yes, and what's inside?'

A squeak of a chair leg, as if someone was getting up, but there were no feet on the floor. His mum's voice spoke up for the first time in five minutes.

'White. Like, it's white on the inside and green on the outside. It's a different colour. I mean, it could be red on the outside too. It depends on the apple. Is that what you're trying to say?'

'No,' the counsellor replied sadly. 'You see pips. If you cut the apple in half, clean in half, then you get pips in both chunks. You could take one half to England, and one half to, oh, I dunno, let's say Japan. After that, you can weld another chunk of apple to each half, but no matter what you did, you would never be able to perfectly replicate the apple that you had before. Why not? You've got the body. It's the same fruit, same colour, same texture, but something will always be missing...'

The counsellor waited. For dramatic effect? Or was it for one of them to answer –

'The pips.'

It was for dramatic effect.

'You'd be missing the pips. The ones on the other side of the world. You would need those very same pips to make the very same apple. Do you understand?'

The seventh silence in half a minute suggested not. Marty shuffled his feet on the dark oak wood, picking at the nail on his forefinger. He let out an audible yawn, loud enough, hopefully, to seep through the cracks in the door and invite his parents to leave. He'd been sitting for over forty minutes now. He heard his dad talk.

'Sorry, but what is this about pips and apples?'

You could almost hear the heart of the counsellor break.

'It's a metaphor. It's supposed to help you visualise the bond you've both created. Your life, your family, your home, your garden. These are the pieces on the inside that if you separate will remain parts of you that cannot be recreated.'

Marty reckoned that was the sixth metaphor he'd heard in the session so far. First was the sea, then a cat with a ball, then a chair and a table, then the sea again – but this time including a beach and a cliff – then coloured crayons, and now this. He wasn't sure what any of them had to do with a failing marriage.

'That's it,' his father said. 'We're out of here.'

Marty was half relieved, half disappointed. This had been their fourth attempt at this, and it was their shortest one so far. They hadn't even reached the hour mark.

'But, sir, I –'

Two chairs squeaked, and this time the sound of shoes on wood followed. The counsellor didn't even have time to tell them 'No refunds!' before Marty's father slammed the door in his face.

The drive home was hell. His mum was yelling this, his dad yelling that. They were saying the same things but speaking in a way that made it seem like they were disagreeing with each other. They did that a lot, Marty had realised. *Let's agree to disagree / Let's disagree to agree.*

'This is the fourth time we've tried this and none of them help. Why don't you –'

'Why are you putting this on me? I'm not the bloody marriage counsellor –'

'Don't swear in front of –'

'Sweet Jesus, if I'd known he was gonna start talking about cats and chairs and apple pips!'

'But it's like you don't try –'

'Bloody apple pips?!'

'You just walked out of there and that was that. All over. Do we actually have to pay for it?'

'I'm not paying for it. He can shove the money up his arse, and throw some apple pips up there for good measure –'

'I told you, don't swear in front of –'

Marty opened the window, hanging his head out slightly so all he could hear was the roar of air. It was bliss, like the war inside had vanished and gone to another reality. He opened his mouth, feeling his cheeks flubber, like they were parachutes trying to slow down his sixty-four miles per hour face. It began to hurt so he pulled his head back inside.

'Constantly, constantly nagging me around him –'

'It's not nagging. I'm just asking you not to use that kind of language. It's not a hard ask; it's not rocket –'

'You're on the bloody moon. I hear him use words a hundred times worse than what I use when he's with his friends –'

'Yeah, and where'd you think he learnt those words? The dictionary?'

'Doesn't matter where you think he learned them. The fact is he's using them, and I don't appreciate how you –'

Marty shoved his head outside once again. The funny thing was, his dad was right. Those words didn't matter. He found it weird how his mum got all uptight about 'damn' and 'shit' and 'bastard' but felt easy about bringing him along to listen in on their marriage counselling sessions. The words he heard in there had the capability to be far more damaging than 'tits'.

Thankfully for her, however, they weren't. The concept of divorce had actually become kind of a pleasing one to Marty. He had never warmed to his dad. He didn't hate him; he just didn't much like him either. It was hard to put into words. They were distant, he supposed. His father had done his job in the honeymoon suite of a villa in Greece, and Marty was the result of that job. Lingering. Present. Selfishly, he felt it wouldn't be the worst thing in the world to have the old man out of the house. He knew it would inevitably make his mum happier, and his dad could finally use all the swear words under the sun without fear of repression. Marty returned his head to the innards of the car as it pulled into their driveway. There was that silence again between his parents now, the one that always came after an argument. It was ugly, upsetting, and it spoke a million words. But boy, was it sweet.

The silence remained for the whole weekend. By Sunday afternoon, it had got so uncomfortable that Marty insisted on Mike and Teddy coming round, despite the fact they spent most of their breath these days interrogating him about Amee.

'So when she kissed you, what was that like?'

'Are you gonna go for the lips next time?'

'I think you should go for the lips. It's the natural progression.'

'What's after lips then, Mike?'

'It's the ears, Teddy. I thought Ross taught you that.'

'Do you think you love her, Marty?'

'He does. He definitely loves her.'

It was vexing, for sure. But anything was better than the dreadful quiet that had befallen the Evans household and, soon enough, Mike and Teddy gave up on their interrogations and proceeded with their new Warhammer set. This included several orcs, one troll, a castle, two warriors, and a dragon; which kept them more than occupied. Marty sat on a beanbag and watched the rain-spattered window as Teddy and Mike came up with stories behind their figures. He was sure they were interesting, as they often tended to be. But Marty zoned them out. His mind was set in reality. That was fantasy enough at the moment. Because Amee Florence had kissed him. Sure, it was only on the cheek, but a girl had decided of her own free will to make physical contact with him. Him. Marty Evans. The weed-kid. That was crazier than a thousand dragons. He didn't even know much about her, that was how fast things had happened. Did she live nearby? Was she in the village? What did her kitchen look like? How many VHS tapes did she have stacked under her television? Were her parents as messed up as his were?

'MARTY!' Teddy shouted suddenly. 'We'll call him Marty, in honour of his recent achievements!'

'No, his name is Valiah the Almighty! You can't call a warrior 'Marty'. Marty's not a warrior name.'

Marty turned to see Teddy holding up a half-painted knight.

'Why can't a warrior be called Marty?' Teddy protested.

'Because Marty's an ordinary person name. Marty, will you tell him?'

Marty gazed back out of the window. 'Yes, Marty is an ordinary person name.'

'Well, why can't an ordinary person be a warrior?'

'Because it sounds stupid. You don't have King Marty the Fourth, do you?'

'But who makes up these rules?'

'It's just common knowledge, Teddy. Now pass me the thick brush.'

Behind the clouds, a rumble of warm thunder hummed in the afternoon sky. Marty sighed, placing his chin into a palm. For the first time, it felt like he'd spent all of the weekend waiting for it to end, just so he could see Amee again. But the closer Monday got, the harder that sick feeling permeated inside his stomach. What was it Mike said? *Go for the lips.* The scary thing was, he was right. That was the natural progression, but the thought alone made Marty feel faint. Did things like that just happen? Was it automatic or preplanned? Why wasn't there a manual for things like this? They managed to make manuals on useless things like how to cut wood or get water out of rocks. Hell, Mike and Teddy were following a manual on how to paint their Warhammer figures. But there were no manuals on things like this, things that actually mattered. Another growl of thunder came through the greyness, and Mike whispered in an overly dramatic tone.

'Oh Jesus...'

'What?' asked Marty.

'A storm is coming.'

'And?'

'Something bad is gonna happen. Something bad always happens when there's a storm. It's called a bad omen. Teddy...'

Teddy looked up, and just at that moment Mike lifted the model dragon and sent it catapulting into his castle.

'*PAACOOORRR!*'

'Bugger off! I'm not done painting yet!'

'You should have listened to me; dragons always come with a storm!'

'What the hell is '*PAACOOORRR*' anyway? It's a dragon, not a crow.'

'You know all about dragon roars, do you, Teddy?'

'Well, I know about crow roars.'

'Oh, crow roars. Yeah, sorry, I forgot you're an expert on those.'

Marty peered up at the clouds as his friends continued to squabble. He sighed. So long as bad omens weren't actually real, Marty would be happy. After all, his next interaction with Amee was just fifteen hours away, and he'd rather no dragons came with this storm.

Fifteen hours later, however, and the dragon *did* come. It just wasn't in the form Marty was expecting. It was podgy, its hair wavy, its forehead full of sweat, and its teeth laid bare in a wide and sickening smile.

'Good news, Weed-kid!'

Rory stood, hands on hips, in front of the school entrance, his giant frame positioned to block Marty, Mike, and Teddy from venturing inside. The rain was coming down hard, and Marty could feel his shirt begin to cling to his bones.

'What?' he said impatiently.

'My father dropped a bit of a bombshell this weekend. He's got a new job down south; I'm moving away, one week from now.'

Marty's jaw dropped in disbelief. Somehow, this actually *was* good news.

'Are you serious?'

'Dead serious, Weed-kid. Funny thing is, it kind of makes this place pretty irrelevant. It's like I can do whatever I want, right?'

'I guess so,' said Marty.

Rory nodded, the smile between his cheeks beginning to make Marty uncomfortable.

'Within reason,' Marty clarified.

'Oh yeah, of course; everything I do is within reason. I just wanna have a bit of fun before I go.' An awkward silence passed between the four of them, broken only when Rory slapped Marty sharply on the arm. 'Well, I'll see you around, pal.'

And then he was gone, gleefully making his way down the school corridor as if he was an inmate whose parole had just been granted. Teddy made a slight gulping sound.

'He's gonna murder you, I reckon.'

'What gave you that impression?' asked Marty.

'Everything about what he just said.'

'Why would he murder me? I've done nothing wrong.'

'Apart from mug him off in front of the new girl,' said Mike.

'Oh and that's deserving of murder, is it, Mike?'

'In Rory's eyes, yeah probably.'

Marty shook his head, but he knew that they were both onto something. Mr Cooper had told Rory if he was to touch Marty again he would be expelled, and so Rory hadn't touched him. But now expulsion meant nothing. It was a fart in the wind. And Rory was Rory. Marty stepped in from the rain, squeezing the water from his shirt miserably.

'Right,' Teddy said with a grin. 'Time to find Amee then?'

Mike laughed, mimicking the act of kissing. Marty punched him on the arm.

'You guys act like I'm so desperate. I'm going to my locker.'

'And then?' pressed Teddy.

'And then see where the day takes me.'

The day in question, however, took Marty nowhere near Amee. It was Amee-less in all respects, and, although the silence of her absence in classrooms was no different to the silence of her presence, to Marty it was deafening. To make matters worse, the dragon came twice more. It grinned at Marty in corridors and stared at him during lunch, which it devoured more quickly than usual, with a far more gluttonous glee.

'Maybe she's ill,' Mike suggested as Marty watched Rory dollop another spoonful of beans into his mouth, his eyes penetrating his soul with a vivid sort of excitement. 'She'll be here tomorrow, I'm sure.'

Marty averted his gaze back to his own untouched plate, flicking over some mash with his fork. 'Maybe.'

But Tuesday was just as Amee-less as Monday, and the same was true of Wednesday, Thursday, and Friday, and before Marty knew it, he was sitting indoors on another Sunday afternoon having not seen her all week. It was Mike's house this time, but the picture was the same. Marty sat on the bed whilst Mike and Teddy lay on the floor with their brushes and Warhammer models.

'It's only been a week,' Mike told him. 'That's not so unusual. Kevin Lee had two weeks off with his urinary infection.'

'She doesn't have a urinary infection, Mike. This is different; she was normal...' Marty thought back to their last encounter. It wasn't normal, of course, but then an encounter with Amee never was. He couldn't judge her by normal standards. 'If I knew where she lived, I could find her, see if she was okay.'

Teddy gave him a suspicious glance. 'That's a bit stalkery, isn't it?'

'It's not stalkery; I'm just concerned. It's been a whole week, Teddy.'

'Stalkers can be concerned.'

'Florence!' Mike almost yelled the name. 'Her surname's Florence; you said it yourself.'

'Yeah. So?'

'So...' Mike leapt up and paced out of the bedroom.

'Does he need the toilet or something?' asked Teddy after a few seconds.

But then Mike returned with a thick book wedged tight underneath his armpit. He threw it over to Marty.

'My mum's telephone directory! Everyone in this town can be found in this book, so you can find her.'

Marty caught it in both hands and gave his friend an impressed smile. 'Alright, Sherlock Holmes.'

Mike performed a triumphant bow, then he picked up a goblin and began mock-smoking it like a pipe.

'No, no, no,' Teddy protested. 'I'm not gonna be part of this. You guys can get a restraining order, but I don't want one.'

'Shut up, Teddy,' Mike responded with a kick to his shin. 'You're an accomplice whether you like it or not. Now pass me the thin brush.'

Marty flicked through the pages with a thumb, scooting over the letters until he landed finally on 'F'.

'Okay, Fairchild, Farrell, Faye, Feck –'

'Hah, Feck!' interrupted Teddy.

'Fergus, Ferguson, Finley, Finn –'

'That's great. What a fecking great guy he must be!'

'Fleetwood...' Marty stopped,

'What's wrong?' asked Mike.

Marty held the book up to him. 'Forsythe.'

Teddy squinted at it. 'Who the feck is Forsythe?'

'It doesn't matter who Forsythe is; the point is there's no Florence. She's not in here. Her family, I mean.'

Mike frowned, rubbing his chin as if he truly was a detective. 'And you're sure she lives in Gealblath?'

'Positive. She said so herself. She said she's always lived here.'

The three of them sat in thought for a bit.

'Maybe you imagined her?' pondered Teddy.

'Or maybe there's a reason she doesn't want me to know where she lives.'

'She doesn't like you?'

'No, Teddy, maybe she doesn't want anyone to know.'

Teddy thought, then shrugged. His attention went back to his Warhammer figure. Marty's attention, on the other hand, remained on the telephone directory. The gap between Fleetwood and Forsythe. The gap where Amee Florence should belong. He sighed. His friends couldn't help him. But there was someone who could, someone who might know more about her. After all, it had been Mr Cooper who told him about Amee's love for *The Hobbit* in the first place, and it was Mr Cooper who had put him in charge of looking out for her.

'So what do we do?' asked Mike.

'Mr Cooper,' said Marty eventually. 'I'll talk to him tomorrow if Amee doesn't show up. He might know more than I do.'

Mike nodded. 'That's if you don't die tomorrow.'

'Huh?'

'Rory's last day, remember?'

Teddy nodded too. 'Oh yeah, he's definitely gonna do something. I've seen it on his face all week.'

Marty gulped, a sudden sick feeling scorching the insides of his stomach. 'Well, whatever Rory's planning, I'm pretty sure I'm not actually gonna die.'

His two friends agreed unconvincingly, and Marty watched as Mike dipped his brush in the paint, revolved it, and splodged one of the warrior's plated chests. He shuffled and repeated, as if to reassure himself,

'I'm not gonna die...'

Monday. Eight a.m.

Marty was only halfway through the park when he spotted a group of kids standing motionless in a horseshoe. Their heads were tilted up towards the large wooden castle, and Marty's heart sank as he saw the words. They were written in red and underlined in black.

MARTY EVANS IS DEAD!

The smell of the paint permeated the air as Marty got closer. He could almost hear the letters being sprayed as he saw them; he could hear the rattle, he could hear the colours mark the wood as they stained his fate in ink. The kids around him started to laugh.

'Marty Evans is dead! Marty Evans is dead!' they began chanting. And the worst part was, they were right.

It was in the lunch hall that Rory threw his first punch. His knuckles collided with Marty's lips, sending one of his front teeth into the back of his throat. He doubled over onto the floor, coughing the tooth up with a thick blob of salivary blood.

'How about that, Weed-kid?!'

The kids surrounding Marty and Rory gasped, some with horror, others with excitement. But Rory ignored them, pushing Marty backwards and stamping hard on his pelvis. Marty gave a small whimper and clasped Rory's shoe before he could lift it up again. This was a bad idea. With Rory unable to retract his shoe, the only way for it to go was down. He pushed it once again into Marty's body, this time square in the gut. A wave of air forced its way out of Marty's lungs with a breathy 'OH!', and he closed his eyes. For the first time he actually prayed that Amee wasn't in school. Not if she was going to see this. His fingers fell away and flew instinctively to cover his face, which was presumably the next target for Rory's shoe.

But the next hit didn't come. Marty peered through his fingers to see Rory topple forward, clutching the back of his head as a knife clattered next to his feet. Mike stood behind him, a look of shock on his face, like the knife had just shot out of his hands of its own accord. But the look wasn't on there for long. Within a couple of seconds, Marty's friend was on the floor along with him, a barrage of fists pummelling his face as if they were tenderising a piece of butcher's meat. Ross Baines squealed in delight, and one of the female audience members screamed, calling out desperately for a teacher to come and intervene. But there was no one. *How could there be no one?!*

'Shit!' Rory bellowed, touching his bleeding head. 'Kill him, Ross! Kill him!'

Ross plunged a knee into Mike's belly and gave his jaw another smack. Marty twisted himself, trying to get to his feet and help his friend. But the pain was too much. With a wince, Marty doubled over and landed face first on the floor again, a high-pitched tone beginning to clog his ear drums and send his head all dizzy.

'How d'ya like this, Chinky?! The best thing is, you threw the knife first! This is self-defence!'

Ross's voice was only just audible over the incessant ringing, and Marty looked up to see another fist land with a crunch upon Mike's nose. He scanned the crowd. No one was helping. No one was stepping forward, because no one would dare touch Ross, or Rory, out of fear for their own safety. So everyone just watched as one boy made another boy bloodier and bloodier, and for a moment, Marty wondered if they actually were going to die. That was his last thought before his eyes closed and he blacked out.

6

DEADY KEVVY

David held the spear in one hand, pulling up his backpack, which was slipping from his shoulders, as usual. He crouched, hiding behind the trunk of a nearby tree, trying his best not to let his presence be heard in the soft silence of the summer forest. He'd seen the rabbit from afar, standing motionless on top of the mossy mound, its greyish-white fur quivering as it drew two breaths every one second. Prey. For the first time in forever. Actual prey. He held the spear tighter, turning it in his hand, relishing the chance for actual, tangible blood to stain the other end. *How sweet would that be!?*

He crouched lower. A bird fluttered out of the leaves above him, making David lose his cool and slip on the loose bark of the tree roots. *Arsehole. It'll be you next.* He yanked himself up to crouching height again, peering from the trunk and breathing a sigh of relief as he spotted the rabbit in the same place, its back still displayed to him. *It should be now.* It had to be now. He wouldn't get a better chance.

David lifted the spear above his shoulder, feeling his hand

tremble slightly. He'd practised this in his back garden. He must have thrown the spear more than one hundred times before it finally reached his intended target of his mother's favourite cushion, right damn *smack!* in the middle. But this wasn't a cushion. This was blood encased in fur. A body. An actual proper body. He lifted the spear higher, remembering his training. *Now. It should be now. Now!* His arm reached back, but before he could release it, the rabbit darted sideways. He lowered his arm. That looked wrong. It wasn't a jump, nor a sidestep. *Can rabbits even sidestep?* It was as if it was pulled on a piece of string, yanked out of harm's way by the hands of God.

He stood, shoving his tin-foil helmet back onto his head as it tilted over his left ear. The rabbit was lying five paces away, but now it had a long, sharp stick protruding from its belly. Kevvy jumped out of the undergrowth, his arms splayed in a victorious 'V' shape.

'I DID IT!'

David gasped. 'It was gonna be me who did it! You bastard, you took my kill!'

'How is it your kill? It's *my* spear in its tummy, that means it's *my* kill, because *I* killed it.'

David huffed. He couldn't fault that reasoning. Still, he was pissed. He was close, *that close*, to being the first nine-year-old in his school who had actually killed something. And Kevin Woods had to beat him to it. Of all the people. Kevvy. Who at this moment was jumping up and down like that time he won first prize in the spelling bee. Kevvy was a loser of course, and so was David, technically, as Kevvy was his best friend. But you're allowed to hate your best friend, and David hated Kevvy right now, as he burst into a song about his victory.

'It's deady! It's deady! It's deady! I killedy!'

'Shut up, prick.'

David had heard his dad use the word 'prick', but he didn't know what it meant. Arsehole, he hoped. He tried to ignore Kevvy, instead choosing to examine the first dead animal he had seen out of a plastic packet. After a while, Kevvy stopped his celebration and joined him, leaning up close to the head of the blood-stained carcass.

'Whoah, Nelly! Look how fast its eyes turned white. That's so cool, isn't it? Weird, but cool!'

David shoved Kevvy out of the way, staring into the whites of the rabbit's eyes. 'Oh shit,' he said bluntly. He knew about this; his dad had told him about it when they were in the car one time. *Why isn't it running, Daddy, why isn't it scared?*

'What's wrong?' asked Kevvy.

'It's blind. I mean, it *was* blind. Shit, I don't think you should kill blind ones; it's unfair. It couldn't see.'

Kevvy stepped back over to the body, his face turning from happiness to remorse. 'Oh,' he muttered.

They stood in silence for a moment, an odd tension in the air, as if they had broken some kind of law.

'What do we do?' asked Kevvy shakily.

David placed his foot on the rabbit and pulled the spear from its belly, taking control of the situation. 'Bury it. Give it a proper burial. Like warriors.'

Kevvy swayed, then began to nod. 'Warriors, we're both warriors, me and you.'

Ever since David's mum had picked it up from the library, *The Hobbit* had been his favourite book. He'd read it all in one night, lapping up every page as excitedly as the last. The only problem was he had no one to share his enthusiasm with. He'd only just moved to Gealblath, and he didn't yet have any friends. That was, until he met Kevvy. David had spotted him reading the book in class, his little eyes scanning the pages like they held the truth of the universe, just as David's had done. He took action immediately, marching over to the reading boy with his hands on his hips.

'Do you want to play with me at break time?'

The reading boy, perhaps a little fearfully, had nodded. And two years later, they were still playing together. Right now, they were not truly in Gealblath. They were in another world, another universe, and they were warriors. Just like the characters in the book. Proper warriors. And like proper warriors, they would respect their victims with proper burials. David leant down and picked up the felled rabbit in both hands, recoiling at the sickly, hot wetness that flooded the creases of his palms. It stank too. A stink that David had never come across before. He would later add it to his list of smells, which included flowers, Mum's cushions, Dad's fags, wet soil after rain, and it would come under the simple word 'death'.

They buried the rabbit under what they called Troll Bridge, placing it neatly beneath a load of fallen sticks and pebbles from the softly running stream. David tried not to grimace as the flies began to land on a puddle of crusted blood, the same blood that had just a few minutes ago flowed like a river before stopping all quick and sudden, like summer into autumn, and green into brown. Instead of looking, he bowed his head, like he knew the warriors would have bowed their heads in his book. Kevvy, on the other hand, said he needed to take a piss behind one of the trees. After about a minute David wondered what was taking so long and went after him. He stopped before he could see because he could hear. Kevvy was crying.

* * *

David awoke crying. He was drenched in sweat, new sweat, sweat after the sex. He looked at the time and swore to himself. 12:03 a.m. Just forty minutes of sleep. For a while he sat there panting, staring out into the semi-darkness as Gerri slept soundly beside him. Then he wiped his face and inspected his finger in the light of his alarm clock. Tears. Proper tears. He'd had nightmares before. Christ, he'd had plenty of those. But this was new; he'd never cried, not in his sleep. David cast his mind back, trying to recall his dream, then he realised that was stupid. No one could cast their mind *back* to a dream, you had to cast it *out*. Right back out to the no-space. That was why it was so hard to remember if you forgot. Besides, he wasn't entirely sure he wanted to remember, especially if he'd been crying. *Charlie. It was obviously Charlie.*

He coughed. Then coughed again. Then one, two, three, culminating in a large phlegmy ball that landed between his thighs. He sat there for a moment, looking at it, his eyes slowly adjusting to the darkness. It didn't take them long these days. After a few moments, he yanked the sheets back, clambered out of the bed, and staggered over to the bathroom to repeat his usual midnight routine of slip / chew / swallow.

David pulled on the light cord and the bulbs clicked to life above the sink, revealing the tubes of pills inside the open cabinet as if it was a holy shrine. He stood for a moment, both hands on the sink and his face bent down towards the plug. Then he looked up, spying his antidepressants and sleeping pills.

How many does it take, he thought.

How many does it take to what? Get better?

David shook his head. *No, how many does it take to sleep?*

Till morning?

No, *how many does it take to sleep so hard that sleep is all you become?* His hand clasped his pills and he opened the lid. *Would it be quick?* he wondered.

Who are you asking?

Kevvy, would it be quick?

Hard to tell.

Will it hurt?

Probably.

Wouldn't the lights go out too fast to feel –

What? Death?

What does death even feel like?

Like a warrmm soup.

What?

Like when you eat soup and it's too hot and OW!

Why are you talking about soup when I'm trying to understand –

Because Mum couldn't cook this morning, so I had to go looking in the cupboards for –

This isn't important, now. I want to know if death hurts –

I had to look in the cupboards and I found soup and I made –

'My own soup. It was too hot though.'

Kevvy jumped down from the bank, his tinfoil helmet only just staying on his head as he splashed into the ankle-deep water. David followed suit, holding his own helmet with one hand just in case it proved to be less successful.

'That doesn't mean you cooked it badly; it just means you didn't wait long enough before eating it.'

They began slushing through the stream side by side, spears in one hand and cardboard shields in the other.

'Yeah, I suppose so,' replied Kevvy, stomping his boots onto the pebbles.

'Don't stomp, you'll scare them!'

'Oh, sorry.' He stopped stomping, then peered down into the water. 'I can't see anything.'

'That's because you kicked all the mud up, prick!'

Prick meant dick; David knew that now.

'Sorry,' Kevvy repeated. He stood still for a moment, waiting for the fog to clear. After a few seconds, he spoke again. 'Do you think we should be here?'

'What?' responded David in confusion.

'Those signs up the bank, you know, saying keep out. Makes me think we should've kept out.'

David rolled his eyes. 'You think the dwarves listened to signs saying to keep out of their homeland? We need to be here. We need to catch fish and eat, otherwise we'll go hungry.'

'But like I said, I had soup –'

'It's the game, eejit!'

'Oh!'

Kevvy shut up and David started walking again, his eyes fixed on the water below them, searching for any sign of edible life. Then, without warning, a hideous low groan erupted out of the clouds, and both David and Kevvy knew they were near a building site so it must have been a digger, but really it was...

'SMAUG!'

David heaved over the sink, wiping the hot, sticky saliva from his mouth with the back of his hand. Kevvy. It was Kevvy. He'd dreamt about Kevvy. Why?

You know why. You cast me out of your mind, didn't you? Until that girl showed up. Lonely, is she? Like you were.

I don't understand.

You forgot about my mum too. I wonder why; you had such a strong hatred once.

Kevvy, this isn't you.

Nothing's me anymore. Nothing's Kevvy. Because of her…

David squeezed his sleeping pills, which were shaking in the tub. *Kevvy,* he thought. *Kevvy, I'm gonna take these pills now…*

She died you know, my mum.

Kevvy, I'm taking the pills.

She died in '89. How about that? She died a whole year after your son got killed, as if you needed another kick in the balls.

Kevvy, I'm gonna take these pills.

OD?

No, I'm just going to take the pills and go to sleep.

Okay. See you in your dreams, fellow warrior. We're both warriors, me and you…

No.

Would you rather dream of Charlie? Would you rather dream of that skull you have hidden away in your bag?

I don't want to dream.

Gah, pathetic. Where's the warrior I once knew?

Shut up.

Do you think I wanted to dream in that car? Do you think I wanted to dream and dream forever?

Don't talk about –

Nighty –

Don't –

Night.

David's eyes opened. Sticky, wet, clamped. But they opened. His heart beat fast as he felt his surroundings. Soft. He'd made it back to bed, and what was more, it was morning: 7:17 a.m. The night was over.

The bathroom door opened, and Gerri stood in its empty frame, a towel wrapped firmly around the top of her head and her bare body dripping with water. She held an empty plastic tube between two fingers.

'You took these last night? Your sleeping pills have run out. I swear you had loads left. You didn't...'

David swallowed and pulled the sheets over his waist. 'They fell down the sink. I dropped them. I was half sleepwalking, I think. I mean, from what I can remember.'

Gerri's shoulders dropped as she relaxed. David didn't know if what he'd just said was true or not, but he hoped it was.

'You woke up last night?'

David nodded.

'Bad dreams? Was it Charlie?'

David shook his head.

'Then who?' Gerri asked.

'My friend, I dreamt about a friend. One I had as a kid.'

He looked up, but Gerri had disappeared into the bathroom, a thick wet puddle marking the place where she had stood. David leant his neck back against the pillow, drawing a long breath as he tried to remember the dream itself. Only fragments were coming through. He remembered looking into a mirror; the bathroom mirror, it must have been. He remembered looking at himself but seeing Kevvy, or a figure he assumed was Kevvy; it spoke with his voice, coming out of the mirror as if it were a television. He shivered, pulling the sheets tighter towards him. Kevvy had been berating him, he was sure. His mind seemed to do that nowadays. First Charlie, now his old friend Kevvy. The faces of the past were judging him, mocking him, throwing him around in their hands like he was playdough.

Gerri returned from the bathroom, a toothbrush shoved into the back of her mouth and her fingers scraping it up and down ferociously. She talked through the foam.

'Why did you dream about that?'

'I dunno,' David replied. But that was another lie. He knew exactly why he'd dreamt of Kevvy.

The conversation had happened in the staffroom the day before. Normally, David would avoid going in there, but yesterday was different. He needed someone to talk to, someone who could help him get his head around the incident that had happened in the classroom. Diana Sadding had spoken to him. A big, fat, purple woman with purple hair, purple clothes, purple nails, and most probably a purple vagina. David hated everything about her. She was jolly like a fat person, she ate all the time like a fat person, and he was fairly sure that wheeze when she laughed ('AGHHAA!') meant heart disease in ten years. She was the only one who would still interact with David now that most other teachers were avoiding him. (Word had evidently got out about the assault at GIL'S!, meaning a meeting with the headmaster was on the cards soon enough.) But she only did so because she loved the sound of her own voice and would jump at any opportunity to hear it. She had spoken between bites of a chocolate biscuit.

'Amee Florence? I have her in my art lessons. She's like all my best students. Talented and strange. Sad, if the rumours are true.'

'What rumours?' David had asked.

'About her mum, the one who shows up in that old black Lincoln. The headmaster deals with her, and he's told me that she's on the buroo. No wonder Amee's a strange case, screaming her head off in classrooms. Poor girl. That's what happens when you have to live in a home like that.'

'A home like what?'

'A home like hers. A junkie's home.'

'Junkie?'

'Mmhm, like...' At that point she had proceeded to demonstrate the meaning of the word by shoving an invisible needle into her huge, trunk-like arm.

'Okay,' David said, stopping her. 'But if the headmaster knows she's a junkie, why's he not doing anything about it?'

'Do what? You can't call the police on every parent you think might be a user, otherwise no one would be safe, especially you! Have you seen yourself lately?'

With a laugh and a wheeze, Diana had whacked David on the shoulder, leaving him with a throbbing arm and an intense desire to make that purple eye of hers truly purple –

'I get sad when you can't sleep.'

The voice was quiet, but it was enough to snap David out of the memory. He turned to see Gerri lying beside him, naked, her chin resting on his shoulder, her hair still tied up in a wet towel. Her eyes were staring, both pupils merging delightfully into dark-brown walls like overflowing pools of milk chocolate. They were pretty, but her breasts were prettier. The cold shower had awakened her nipples and they stood firm and proper like guards on duty.

'It's happening more now,' she said. 'The sleeping. The anger. Is the sertraline working?' Gerri kissed his shoulder. 'Tell me how I can help you.'

'I dunno.'

David didn't want to speak to Gerri, so he leant down and stuffed his mouth with her flesh. She leant back and her breaths got longer and more audible, like he was sucking the life force out of her. She closed her eyes to enjoy his work.

In Gerri's head were images of sex and penis and orgasms and work and her father, who she thought she should call later. In David's head was the skull and Amee and her junkie mother and those piercing screams that would be stuck in there for life, even when they were eventually silenced, there, somewhere at the back, waiting for him in dreams.

7

THE HOSPITAL

When Marty was nine years old, he saw a dead person. Of course, he'd seen dead people in movies, but they were nothing like *real* dead people. They were like us, just with fake blood on them. Mike's nana wasn't like us. When Marty stood up with his friend to support him, no 18-rated horror film could have prepared him for what was waiting inside the open coffin. The skin had changed, for one thing. In life, Mike's nana's skin had been vibrant; her cheeks and ears were rosy, and the tip of her nose never failed to produce a warm red flush. Her name was Ruth but Mike and Marty called her Rudolph, which was often met with the croaked response, 'I ought to hide your behind into haggis!' But the sight of her in the coffin, along with the overbearingly pungent fumes of wood polish, made it seem like the colour had been polished from her face. The life that once resided there had seeped out, like water from a sponge.

Secondly, this was someone Marty knew. Granted, he knew Mike's nana less than Mike himself, but he still knew her. He had still spoken to this person, touched this person, seen this person's mouth and face twitch with movement and essence. But in the coffin, Mike's nana had no essence. Not even an inch. Marty didn't much believe in a soul, but when he stood over Mike's nana's dead body, with that sickly smell of polish shoving its way up his nose, he could see why people would. Dying hadn't just meant the ceasing of movement as it did in movies; dying had visibly emptied her. She was just a shell, and maybe not even that. Death had stopped off at her door with a suitcase and taken everything with it.

It was this memory alone that allowed Marty to know that – 'MIKE TORFORD IS DEAD! MIKE TORFORD IS DEAD! MIKE TORFORD IS DEAD!' – Mike Torford was not dead. He was the first thing Marty saw when he came back around. At first, the object was a jumbled blur. Then a thick bundle of blood-stained clothes. Then, finally, a body. Mike's body. His chubby, bruised head was protruding from one end of a jumper, and his belly was poking through the other. On either side of him his arms were splayed out, both hands gently stroking the rubber of the lunch hall floor as if it was a loved one comforting him. That was the giveaway that the chants 'MIKE TORFORD IS DEAD! MIKE TORFORD IS DEAD! MIKE TORFORD IS DEAD!' were a load of bullshit. Marty shook his head, wincing as a sharp stroke of pain caused a shudder through his body. At the same moment, a singular voice rose above the others.

'He's awake! He survived!'

'What?' Marty mumbled back, blood and saliva flicking through the gap where his tooth should have been.

'MIKE TORFORD IS DEAD! MIKE TORFORD IS DEAD! MIKE TORFORD IS DEAD!'

The chanting continued, and Marty bent over onto his knees to crawl towards his unconscious friend.

'What happened?' he asked one of the girls beside him.

Her voice just about travelled over the jeers, shrieks, and laughter. 'It was Ross and Rory; they wouldn't stop!'

'You've been out for two minutes,' another girl said gleefully.

Marty swallowed, staring at Mike's face. Blood poured from his nose, travelling down onto his lips and dribbling over the first of his three chins. It wasn't just coming from there, though. On his left cheek, a large gash had been ripped into the flesh, and a tear above Mike's eye was causing a flap of skin to hide the edge of his left eyebrow, hanging down the same way a cheese string hangs when you pull it halfway. A gargled noise escaped from Mike's throat and blood sprouted up in a weird bubbly froth.

'HE'S CHOKING! HE ACTUALLY IS GONNA DIE!'

Marty turned to a scrawny eighth-year. 'Will you shut up!'

More laughter ensued from the crowd.

'MARTY LOVES THE FAT BOY! IT'S HIS BOYFRIEND! LOOK, HE'S HOLDING HIS HAND!'

Marty glanced down, realising that he was in fact holding Mike's hand. He let go, a hot red flush staining his face. 'Where the hell are the teachers?!' he yelled.

'People have gone to get them,' another student shouted. 'They were in the headmaster's office; apparently somethings going on up there.'

'Something's going on down here!'

Marty clenched his fists, his eyesight phasing in and out of focus. He looked back down at Mike's face, noticing that both his cheek and eye were beginning to swell up, as if someone was pumping him full of a deep-brown liquid. A ginger boy in front of him seemed to know what he was thinking.

'He had metal. Like one of those metal things on his fingers –'

'It's called a knuckle duster, stupid!'

'Yeah, you see it –'

'Yeah, I saw it, right whack in the face!'

'That's horrible!'

'It had spikes on it –'

'Ross and Rory are so gonna be expelled!'

'Rory can't be expelled, it's his last day –'

'Genius!'

'Prison then!'

'No, prison is for murderers and paedos –'

'Like your dad!'

'Shut the hell up!'

'No one's going to prison, Chris!' Mr Stevens, the history teacher, strode through the crowd. He parted it with a single hand, like he was some kind of wizard from Mike's Warhammer collection. He came against the body and stopped, gazing down at the state of them both. 'Oh,' he said simply.

The next time Marty's eyes opened, he was in bed, but not his own. The mattress was thin, the pillows thinner, and around ten middle-aged to elderly people were sleeping beside him.

'You okay, soldier?' His mum's voice rose above the ringing in his ears, and a hand squeezed his tight, ringed fingers stroking the veins in his wrist.

Marty lifted himself up. 'Mike...'

'Is fine. Go steady. He's okay, just resting.'

Marty breathed a sigh of relief and sat back, his tongue finding the stitches that were holding one of his teeth in place. He poked at them gingerly, felt the pain, then left them alone.

'They found it in some Bolognese,' Marty's mum said with a smile, as if that fact was meant to amuse him. 'Don't worry, they washed it,' she added after she noticed his look.

'I'm not worried about me. When can I see him?'

'When he's awake. Until then, you've got to look after yourself and stay in bed. The doctor said you've got a concussion. You're so brave, honey.'

Marty flicked the sentiment away and felt the back of his scalp, where another pair of stitches was sewn into the skin. They felt wrong, being on his head, like the lunch hall floor had ripped open his world and now there was some string desperately trying to tie it back together. He felt like patchwork, like a busted kid's doll, but he imagined Mike must feel worse. His was just a playtime tear in the fabrics; Mike's was a doll that had been thrown to the family dog. Marty breathed, feeling anger begin to bubble above the pain inside his gut.

'Those cocksuckers.'

'Marty!' His mum stared at him sternly, then realised the appropriateness of his anger. 'I mean, yes, they're nasty wee boys. But they'll be punished. Don't worry, they will be.'

A silence ensued and Marty started to take in the other patients surrounding him. One was an old wrinkled man, his jaw hanging crooked and ajar upon his chest, with a little sliver of saliva wetting the bristle on his chin. Next to him was a woman who couldn't have been older than Marty's mum. She lay with her eyes open, a deep and nasty cut drooping all the way down from her receding hairline to the lobe of her left ear; stitched and patched, just like Marty was. He shivered, turning away and pulling the sheets up to his chin as if to shield himself from their predicament.

'The police found them hiding in the bike shed,' said his mother. 'Apparently, Rory tried to cycle away, but the bike collapsed under him and he broke his nose.'

Despite himself, Marty smiled at that information. It did cheer him up a bit. But not by much. It was Mike he was thinking about. He didn't deserve any of this; he deserved to be at home painting another one of his Warhammer figures, not stitched up in some cold hospital bed. He was just trying to help.

'I'll leave you to get some rest.' Marty's mum gave him a pat on the leg, then bent over to grab a paper cup from the floor. She leant back, swigged the contents, smacked her lips, then stood. 'The nurse says you'll have to stay here at least overnight, but I can stay with you. It just means I'll have to cancel a few dates with the girls. Would you like me to get you anything?'

Marty rested his head back into the pillow. 'No, thanks,' he replied.

His mother smiled at him, gave him a kiss on the forehead, then left Marty alone to stare vaguely into the bright ceiling light. It was ugly, as all white lights were, and almost ominous now that he was staring at it. A precursor, he supposed, to that other white light, the one that hung higher, awaiting most of the patients inside this hospital. But not Marty, he hoped. Not yet at least.

He slept until the next morning. Marty awoke to the sun peeking through the gaps in the curtain around his bed, his head sore and his gums throbbing. Surrounding him were snores from the other patients, but in his dream, they had been an engine. Amee's engine. The cool black American Lincoln. He remembered she had climbed out of it, but as she walked towards Marty, the Lincoln had fired back to life and chased her through the park. Like a huge black cat pouncing fast upon its prey, it swallowed her up into its open hood and she screamed. Marty had tried to run, he had tried to save her, but there were two people in his path. Ross and Rory. Their fists were adorned with knuckle-dusters and their faces wore wide and hideous grins.

'No, please!' Marty had shouted. 'Let me get through, let me save her. I have to save Amee!'

Beyond them, the car had swerved off the grass and hightailed it down the road, disappearing as Ross and Rory backed him up against the castle. When his back hit the wall, Ross had grabbed Marty's chin and turned it towards the words: MARTY EVANS IS DEAD! But the red letters were different this time. What was once thick and crusted paint was instead thin and moving, seeping over the splinters of the wood. Marty had wanted to scream, but there was no voice anymore. All he could do was stand there as Ross pulled his chin back and Rory's knuckles travelled fast towards him.

He awoke upon the first hit. Or he thought he had. Upon sitting up in his bed, Marty had seen a figure by the door, cloaked by the darkness of the room.

'Don't try,' the figure had said, her voice small and familiar.

'Amee? Don't try what?'

'Don't try to save me.' She was gone as soon as he blinked, and darkness had taken him again.

The nurse with the breakfast tray was the first to pull the curtain back, swiftly followed by Marty's mother, who sat beside his bed and proceeded to spoon the contents of the tray into his mouth, as if the concussion had regressed his abilities to those of a two-year-old.

'How did you sleep?' the nurse asked.

'Jesus,' Marty sputtered, ignoring the nurse. 'I got hit in the face, Mum; they didn't cut my arm off.'

His mum didn't bat an eyelid. 'The nurse asked how you slept.'

'Fine,' Marty lied. In all truth the contents of the dream had phased into a numbness now; the emotion was stripped out of it, like walking out of the cinema after a horror movie.

'Mike's awake,' his mum said nonchalantly.

Marty jumped out of the bed. 'And talking?'

'Yes. And you can see him. After you've had your breakfast.'

His mum picked up the spoon and nodded Marty back towards the pillow. For a moment, he wanted to ignore her, but the stern parental look she was giving him would have been enough to make even the bravest of men obey, and so Marty retreated, reluctantly shuffling himself back into the sheets. If a few gulps of milk-soaked oats would get him to his friend, then a few gulps it would have to be, even if it meant yielding to the two-year-old status his mum had thrust upon him.

'Open wide,' she said.

And Marty opened.

When the oats were finished and they finally began for Mike's room, the hospital had fully awoken. Doctors and nurses rushed from one room to the next, reminding Marty of the hustle and bustle he'd experienced when he was here just one year before. It was for a twisted ankle he'd sustained during football practice, and he'd hated the hospital then like he hated it now. It was the way it seemed to take itself with you when you left. The abrasive stench of iodoform, the high-pitched hum from the machines inside the patients' rooms, and that underlying dread that you would be going back there one day; no matter how young and no matter how healthy, the hospital was where you were heading.

They turned a corner and Marty tried to shut off his ears to the *BEEP*s and *BOOP*s of the patients' hearts that seeped from behind each wall. *My heart goes THUMP / My heart goes THUMP / It'll go BEEP one day, trust me.* He shook the words out from his head and kept his gaze on the corridor. His mother walked beside him like she was entirely unaffected, but she had more reason to hate this place than Marty. She'd been in hospitals more times than him, and for matters much worse than a simple twisted ankle. She'd witnessed the deaths of her mother and father in Edinburgh, both of whom had died two years apart, yet by some eerie coincidence passed away in the same room and in the same bed. That story was now told as if it were a sweet coincidence, but Marty considered it horrific. He realised that some things in the world stick your ending to them. Whether it be the car you buy, the passion you choose, or a person you pass. Things *pick* you. And the bed had picked Grandpa. For two whole years it had waited patiently after the death of his wife, anticipating his return, before it was finally granted its wish and Grandpa died peacefully in its arms. Marty couldn't help but shiver at the thought of it all, silently but constantly wondering what in the world had *picked* him.

After a few more minutes, Marty and his mother turned one last corner and came up towards a pale white door. Room B12. Mike's room. Marty's mum turned the knob and pushed the door open, revealing the extent of Mike's condition. He was propped up on one side in the bed, and at first Marty thought he was asleep, but he soon realised it was just the swelling over his one visible eye that had given the illusion. It was funny to look at him, in the worst possible way of course. The left side of his face was puffed up to two times its original size – quite the achievement as far as Mike's face was concerned – and two rows of deep-purple stitches had been sewn into the skin. There was also a stupid-looking cotton bandage hovering over the ridge of his nose, taped loosely and in the shape of a cloud, as if Mike's face had its own climate. He lifted his head as the door closed behind them.

'Hey,' said Marty.

Mike rolled onto his back, pushing his greasy black hair away from his eyes. 'Hi,' he croaked back.

Marty's mum placed a hand on the foot of Mikes bed. 'So glad to see you're doing okay, Mike. Where's your mother? Is she here?'

Mike nodded slowly. 'She's gone to get a tea, I think.'

'Great. How about I leave you two alone for a bit?'

Without waiting for an answer, Marty's mum tapped the rails of the bed, then turned on her heel and left the room. A thick silence followed, leaving nothing but the hum of the machines on the other side of the room to fill the air.

'How do you feel?' asked Marty. 'You look...'

'Shit.'

Marty gave a chuckle. 'Well, I was gonna lie, but yeah, you do look a bit shit.'

'I meant I feel shit.'

The silence came back in a wave. But Mike broke it with a snort.

'It's alright, I know I look shit too.'

'At least the scars are cool,' said Marty. 'I mean, the girls will think you're pretty badass.'

'Yeah, if they hadn't seen me being beaten up like a pussy.'

Marty pulled up a chair and placed it beside the bed. 'Pussy? You threw a knife at Rory's head. If they don't have a mural of you in the lunch hall by the time we get back, I'll be disappointed.'

'A mural of me being pummelled by Ross's knuckle-duster...'

Marty's smile dropped. 'He actually had one?'

Mike nodded, absentmindedly feeling the bulge beside the stitches in his cheek. 'I always said he was a psycho.'

A low vibrating buzz erupted from one of the machines in the corner and Marty stared at it, watching as a blue light flickered, like an eye blinking away a loose strand of hair. A stone sank down into the pit of his stomach.

'That knuckle-duster was meant for me.'

Mike lay his injured head against the plumped-up pillow. 'Ross must have shitty aim.'

'Mike...' Marty looked at him, and Mike shrugged.

'Don't get serious, pal. He put it on me; it's not like I'm dead or anything. I'd do it again too, even if I knew the hospital was where I'd end up.'

'You wouldn't.'

'I would. That's the bro code.'

'I thought the bro code was about girls.'

'This is area two. There's a lot of sections to the code.'

Marty giggled, then pushed himself up and placed his feet on the bed. 'Has Teddy seen you yet?'

Mike looked at Marty's trainers with a frown, then he shook his head.

'He hasn't been to see me either,' said Marty. 'I mean, let's be honest, he's probably not noticed we're gone, has he?'

'Or he just got lost on the way to the hospital,' said Mike.

Marty laughed again, grateful that Ross hadn't knocked any of the humour out of his best friend.

'Speaking of the bro code,' Mike continued. 'Was the new girl there? Yesterday, I mean.'

'I couldn't see her,' replied Marty. 'I hope she wasn't there. Being beaten up isn't really the Venkman look.'

'How are you gonna explain your injuries then?' asked Mike.

Marty thought about it, twiddling his fingers. 'I'll just say I tripped on a rock.'

'What about my injuries?'

'We both tripped on a rock.'

'We tripped on a rock together...'

'It was a big rock.'

'Sounds it.' Mike's gaze returned to Marty's shoes, which were still propped up comfortably on the bed. 'Uh, Marty, you know they don't let you do that. It's germs and stuff.'

'What, they think my feet have rabies or something?'

'Not your feet, but your shoes might.'

Marty stuck a trainer in Mike's face. 'Shoe rabies! Watch out, I'm gonna infect you!'

Mike pushed it away. 'Stop, seriously, they don't allow it. They'll kick you out.'

'Fine, I'll just kick my way back in with my rabies shoe.'

Mike glared at him furiously. So furious, in fact, that Marty felt his feet retreating from the bed and onto Mike's bedside table of their own accord.

'That's better,' said Mike,

'I suppose I should be obeying your every command from now on.'

'That sounds nice.'

'For a week or so.'

Mike pointed at his face. 'What? This only gets me one shitty week?'

'Yes, sir. Only a full-on murder would get you more than that.'

'Great, I'll be sure to remember it.'

Marty nodded happily, then he looked out the window on his left, gazing across the cars in the hospital car park. There were many, sadly, but one in particular caught his eye. In a flash, he jumped onto his feet and moved closer to the glass, peering through it to get a clearer view. But he had seen it right the first time. There, in the car park, between a blue Hyundai and a white Ford, sat the perfectly cool, black American Lincoln.

'Holy shit.'

'What?' Mike pushed himself off the pillows, attempting in vain to look over Marty's shoulder.

'The car.'

'What car?'

'Amee's car. The one I dreamt... the one she has. The one she gets in and out of every day. It's here in the car park.'

Mike hummed, his fingers going to stroke his chin before retreating with a 'Shit!' and an 'Ow!'.

'You don't think she's here, do you?'

Marty turned from the window and paced over towards the door. 'I don't know, but I'm gonna find out right now. I'll go to reception. They'll have her name down.'

'Hold on...' With a wheeze, Mike rolled over on the bed and swung his legs over the edge. 'I'm coming too.'

'You can't come; you're too injured.'

'Oh yeah, sorry, I forgot they paralysed me. Pass me my wheelchair.'

Marty watched nervously as Mike got to his feet. 'You should stay in bed. Your mum will be back soon.'

'She'll be fine, Marty, and I'll be fine. It's only reception, after all. I don't walk with my face. I'm going. And you can't stop me.'

But Mike may as well have been walking with his face. It took them what felt like an age to get through the first corridor, and by that point both of Mike's hands were clinging hard on Marty's shoulders.

'Sto... stop... for... a... mo... ment... please... Jesus.'

'We've walked down a corridor, Mike, not up Mount Everest. You should have stayed in bed.'

'I... know... it's... just... my... Jesus... my stomach... it's... kill... killing... me.'

Marty winced against the weight of him. 'Would you let go? You're starting to hurt my shoulders.'

'I'm... sorry... your... lordship... it's... just... my sto... stomach... feels like... it's gonna... explode... any... second.'

'Let's go back then.'

'No... way.'

'I'll get you a wheelchair.'

'I... don't need... a bloody... wheelchair... stop being... so... melo... dramatic.' With another deep and painful breath, Mike eased off Marty. 'Let's... let's...' He stumbled over his words.

'Go?' Marty suggested helpfully.

And Mike nodded.

When they reached reception, Mike gave a cry of victory and collapsed into a nearby chair, allowing Marty to speed over to the front desk and almost yell at the woman behind it.

'Florence!'

The receptionist jumped, her eyes darting up towards the boy behind a pair of thick white glasses. 'I'm sorry?'

'Amee Florence. Is she here?'

'Who's asking?'

'Me. The guy who just asked it.'

The receptionist looked him up and down, then dropped her gaze towards her computer, scrolling dully with the mouse. Marty tapped the desk impatiently.

'No,' said the receptionist after a few seconds, her voice phlegmy and bored.

'Just Florence then. Anyone called Florence work here? Or a patient?'

'No,' she replied again, this time not even bothering to look.

'But that's impossible. I saw her car outside.'

'Lots of people have the same car, dear.' The woman glared at him, her jaw working slowly on a stick of gum with as much monotony as the tone of her voice. 'Anything else?' she asked.

With an angry huff, Marty retreated from the desk and went back over to his friend. 'Damn it,' he said bitterly.

'Is she here?' asked Mike.

'No,' Marty responded.

'Are you joking? So we walked all that way for nothing?'

Marty fell onto the chair beside Mike, grinding his teeth in frustration. 'That was her car I saw. Amee goes missing for a week and we find her car parked next to the hospital. Doesn't that seem strange to you?'

'Perhaps one of her parents works here.'

'No one called Florence works here.'

'Well, maybe it's someone else's car, then.'

'It was her car. I'm sure of it.' Marty paused for a moment, thinking hard. 'Maybe she is here. Amee, I mean.'

'What?' replied Mike. 'So she's here under a different name?'

Marty stared ahead, absentmindedly picking at a fingernail once again. His father would have given him a whack behind the ear for that if he was here. But he wasn't here. He couldn't even be bothered to visit. So Marty picked.

'Could be. If something happened to her, something her parents don't want anyone to know about, why wouldn't they put her in here under a different name?'

'I think you've been watching too much conspiracy stuff.'

'I just think it's weird.'

'You're gonna think it's weird, then you're gonna go back to school, see Amee there, realise she was off sick, then wonder why you ever thought anything about this was weird in the first place.'

Marty sighed. He hated the role of 'voice of reason' that Mike had carved out for himself since the assault. But still, he could be right.

'Fine. You ready to go back?'

'Yeah, yeah. I'll be faster this time. Just give me two seconds.' Mike took a deep breath, then climbed up onto his feet and took a step forward. 'Owwwwwwwww!' he squealed, and then he fell back into the chair.

Mike was a lot faster on the way back to Room B12. He did the journey in a wheelchair.

That night, Marty found it harder to sleep. The dark came quickly, but his dreams kept him out of it. First there was the car again. This time a driverless vehicle with him and Amee in the back, silently cruising down an empty road with the windscreen obscured by a red and watery substance. The wipers tried to remove it, but the more they swiped, the more the letters appeared to form: <u>MARTY EVANS IS DEAD!</u>

Then there was Mike. He was sitting alone in the hospital bed, his injuries far worse than Marty had observed in reality. His head was hanging by just a few cords of flesh and bone, and his face was entirely mutated to the point of being unrecognisable, warped like it had been recreated by a surgeon who had no point of reference.

And finally, there was Amee. She stood by the end of his bed, watching him intently. Marty had even talked to her.

'Where are you?'

'I'm here,' she said. 'Don't save me.'

A hand reached out to land on Marty's foot; then, somewhere beyond the door, there was a scream. It was distant at first, but then grew into something bigger, like it was travelling down the corridor and heading straight for Marty's room.

Then Marty awoke. On the clock next to him, the numbers 01:27 were illuminated, casting a dim red on the shoebox it was sitting atop. Teddy had brought that shoebox for him when he finally showed up in the afternoon. One for Mike, one for Marty, a box full of Warhammer figures and paint brushes.

'In this one there's a troll, a goblin, two warriors, a wizard and a spaceship, from that new collection they've released. I brought some paint too. Don't mention it. It's just something to pass the time. Relieve the boredom, you know.'

Marty sat up and wiped some goo from his eyes, feeling

his bones shiver and his skin go pimply as he remembered the dream; the blood on the glass, the look of Mike's face, the screaming that had sounded so lifelike, so real, like it really was just beyond the door of his ward. It was something about this hospital. Something about the whites of its walls, the blacks of its nighttimes. In all honesty, he couldn't wait to leave it. The dreams were becoming inevitable and perhaps, once he was gone, there was just a chance that they would stay here without him.

With a shuddered breath, Marty turned over and placed his feet down upon the cold rubber floor. He couldn't go back to sleep now. Not with more of those nightmares waiting for him. He needed a way to forget about them, to shake them off like they were water. He needed a walk, so he tiptoed over to the door and into the corridor.

The corridor itself was long and dimly lit, and Marty tread softly along it. It felt colder at night, he noticed. Like the place was half alive, half dead. The floor still vibrated from a thousand rubber footsteps. The walls still echoed, now with ghost calls, rebounding off the cork boards, thinning, hushing. Before everything became quiet and calm, asleep but awake, before the next sunrise.

Marty was grateful when he finally came across a room with some noise. It came in the form of five nurses, each one sitting with a coffee, quietly gossiping amongst themselves.

'Gruber? Andrew Gruber?'

'That's the one.'

'He still into you?'

'If calling me three times a day and sending me two bouquets of flowers means he's into me, then yeah, I suppose he's still into me.'

'What a weirdo.'

'One bouquet is weird enough; two is just restraining order weird.'

'Can you get a restraining order for flowers?'

Marty moved closer to the open door and lowered himself down onto a seat beside it. It was comforting, listening to the nurses. He could switch off the eeriness of the world around him, forget about those dreams and just delve into their words, like when he was a kid and his mum would tell him a bedtime story before leaving him alone in the dark.

'I think flowers are nice. My boyfriend never gets me flowers.'

'He's not my boyfriend though; that's the point.'

'If anyone got me flowers, I'd be happy. Flowers are flowers.'

'I'd rather something useful, not some plants you put in a vase and slowly watch die for a few weeks.'

'Like what?'

'A television would be nice.'

'I don't think –'

But just as Marty was about to find out what one of them didn't think, they were interrupted. The scream was distant, hardly audible, but most definitely there. It filled Marty's head and set his heart racing. The scream from his nightmares, splitting through the ether to haunt his reality. The nurses stopped.

'Is that something we're concerned about?' one of them asked.

Marty listened closer, trying desperately to hear over the sound of his own heart in his throat. A few moments passed where it seemed the nurses were listening just as intently as

Marty was. Then another nurse spoke.

'No, I don't think so. It's the floor above. Probably Room C19.'

They waited a while longer, then broke into conversation once more, as if the scream had never even happened, as if it was as commonplace as a patient's hearty cough. Marty pinched himself on the wrist, just to check this wasn't another one of his dreams. A sharp pain followed the squeeze, and Marty let go. This wasn't a dream. This was real. The scream was real. It had sounded in the dark as definitely as an owl screeches into the night.

He looked up at the door on the other side of the corridor, the plaque above it illuminated by a dim white light. B37. That couldn't be right. Each floor of the hospital was stacked with twenty rooms. The first two 'A', the next two 'B'. Eighty rooms in total. But the scream had come from *upstairs.* Definitely upstairs. *What did the woman say?* he thought. The floor above. Room C19.

Marty stood up and crossed past the nurses' room as quietly as he could. He kept his eyes on the plaque upon every door. B38, B39. He came to the end of the corridor. B40. The last room in the ward. The last room in the whole hospital. But there, just beside it, was another flight of stairs, with the words 'ENTRANCE BY PERMISSION ONLY' on a sign beside its banister.

Marty swallowed, trying desperately to stop his heart from leaping out of his mouth. *There must be another department. Maybe for sick patients. Really sick patients.* He clenched his fists to stop his hands shaking. *But that scream sounded bad. Why wouldn't they help?* Some laughter arose down the corridor again, and Marty turned, feeling a swell of anger replace the comfort they had given him just moments ago. This was wrong. They had heard it. They had all heard it. He didn't care if it was their department or not; they should want to help – they were nurses. And he was... *the weed-kid?* He shook the thought out of his head. *Venkman. That's what you are. You're Venkman.*

Pulling himself together, Marty began up the stairs, clinging to the banister as if the steps might crumble beneath his feet at any moment. When he got to the top, the first door to meet him was for Room C1. Normal enough. Just like the ones downstairs, in fact. He turned his head and looked down the corridor. It was empty, like the others. But the scream seemed to remain trapped between the walls, echoing over and over again in Marty's ears. A young scream. A terrified scream. A scream that was calling for help.

'Okay,' he whispered. 'Okay, be cool, be calm. Be Venkman.'

Marty tried to shake it out, then he began walking, making sure to keep his eyes on the plaques as he went. C2, C3, C4. He turned a corner. C8, C9, C10. And another. C13, C14, C15. Then one more. C16, C17, C18. And...

Room C19. It was there in front of him, the door as ordinary as any other. Marty took a few steps towards it, his ears pricking up, as if he expected to hear another scream any moment now. But no scream came. Instead, what he heard were voices, muffled and fuzzy as if they were coming out of an old television. He leant in closer, his face pressing up against the hospital door. It only took a few more seconds before he recognised what he was hearing. His jaw hung open in a gasp, and his skin rose in goose bumps once again. He put his hand on the door-knob and twisted.

8

BREATHE

It was an undeniable fact of the universe that since last summer, Kevin Woods had got stronger, and David Cooper had got jealous(er).

'It won't budge. I'm telling you, it's too heavy!'

The felled tree was splayed in front of the mouth of the cave like a hand curling over some goods. A butterfly, a gold coin, a condom found in a parent's wardrobe. *You ready to see? What you got? I'll show you.* Except these fingers were not peeling back. These branches were thick as hell and heavier than a thousand dead dragons, or so it felt like. No matter how hard David tried, they wouldn't budge.

'Get out of the way,' said Kevvy. 'Let me have a go!'

This time last year it would have been David saying that, but 1968 had done something magical to his best friend. It had seeped into his veins and flooded the marrow, bulging them up like water in a sponge. He was taller too, which was also annoying, as it meant David had to have good posture to match Kevvy's height. He stood forward now, rolling his sleeves up his arms and clenching his fists like a ten-year-old Muhammad Ali. David stepped aside and clasped his sheath (cereal packet, scissors, glue, string from the garage). Meanwhile, his best friend grabbed one of the branches, a small bead of sweat trickling down in front of his ear. His spine arched into a 'C' shape as he pulled and a tiny macho groan escaped from his lips. The branch began to groan back and David frowned. *Please don't give, please don't give, please don't give.* The branch splintered with an almighty *SPLLITTT!* and its innards scattered onto the forest floor. *You bastard...*

Kevvy fell backwards with it, but David didn't have time to catch him, and he landed with a thump and an 'Oh!'

David pointed at the cave. 'You're not done yet.'

Kevvy leapt up. 'Rubbish, we can climb through that now!' With his war-beaten fingers, he peeled back some of the green summer leaves and stared into the dark mouth of the woodland cave. 'Woah Nelly...'

David peered over his shoulder, his pride hurt but his curiosity pricked. 'What's Nelly?'

'I can see it...'

'See what?' David held his breath, grabbed the kitchen knife in his sheath, and forgot real life.

'The most precious jewel in this whole kingdom. The Arkenstone.'

In reality, Kevvy's mum was picking them up and taking them to Carlo's Ice Cream Parlour later, then she would drop David off at home.

* * *

The headmaster scribbled words onto one of the papers on his desk, a frown creating an upside-down arch on the bottom of his face, like the opening of one of those tunnels that trains go through. David shuffled in his seat and swallowed deeply. With a long, drawn-out *SWISH!* Mr Aspin underlined a sentence on his blue-lined paper, then paused, examining his work. David made an 'ahem' with his throat. The headmaster sighed, placing down his pen and pulling up his gaze. He was a young man, black, with a handsome face that suggested charm and ignorance.

'Sorry,' he said. 'Busy day.'

David nodded, trying his best to smile at him. 'Every day's a shite.'

Mr Aspin stared, then nodded in unsure agreement. 'So, we need to talk about you, David.'

David tried desperately to calm himself. *Yes, well, that saves us talking about you.* He loosened his knuckles. He couldn't afford to be angry, not in front of this man. Not since his conversation with Diana Sadding. He had to be his normal self; he had to be the man he'd been before Charlie was out of the cabinet.

'Right, okay.'

The headmaster drew a sharp intake of breath, his face contorting in discomfort. That was an odd sign. Potentially a dangerous one. He leaned forward.

'I feel that whilst I hold the position of headmaster at Gealblath Secondary School, I must be able to justify any decision I make to any parent who has entrusted their children to me and this place. And sorry, David, but I just can't justify your employment any longer.'

David slumped his chin onto his chest, processing what he'd just heard. It was a well-devised line, and expertly rehearsed, he knew. He almost respected it. He couldn't justify his position either. Not even to himself, let alone to the parents. All the same, he had been hoping Mr Aspin wouldn't come to the same conclusion. He was in the waters now. He had to fight. *Use the anger, use the impulse, but use it right. Just don't mention her. Honest to God, you're damned if you mention her.* He lifted his head. *Use his first name.*

'George, before you make any decision, you should know that I've had a fall, a bit of a fall, these last few weeks. My depression (*that's right, get in the depression quick and smooth, rub it in his face a bit*) has got worse. It's made me do rash things. But it can get better. I can get better. The doctors, the medication, it can all help –'

The headmaster raised his hand.

Temper flare. Get that anger down. Forget her. Deep breaths. Back of the mind.

'David, it's not about that. I want you to know this school supports you, it supports you completely with your health, and your circumstances. This has nothing to do with that –'

'Then what?' interrupted David. Getting in quick with his responses was important. Fast overtakes and sly undercuts, that was what would keep him alive in this room. For a while anyway. *Just keep that anger down. Breathe.*

'Listen, David, the children must come first, no matter what. Their education, their learning, their respect for their teachers. We cannot have someone who, let's say, cannot control themselves.'

The headmaster stood before David could get in his undercut, striding across the room to slide the window closed at the other end. A last rush of wind whirled inside as he did so, flicking up the pages on the desk, making David shiver under his tweed. He had to stand his ground here. *Break out the big guns.*

'George, I'm not stupid. This has everything to do with my illness and you know it. But I was hired because I'm a damn good teacher (*alright, oversell it*) and none of that's changed. Only my health has changed. This is going to get around, George, don't think it won't. Do you want that? Because that's what they'll all be saying. This school punishes people with depression.'

The headmaster sat, his expression considerably darkened.

Good last line. This is getting good. Collected is good; it could save you. Just remember to breathe.

'David –'

'Look, I'm not trying to threaten anyone. I mean, heck, if you fire me, I probably wouldn't even say anything. I just need you to know, I can get better.'

The headmaster shook his head. 'David, we've supported you throughout all of this. Everything. And we still support you. But we have to think of the kids now. We have to think of what they deserve. They deserve better.'

At that moment, a hydraulic pump thrust down inside David's chest, silently shooting all the blood to his head. His vision went blurry, his body got hot, and his hair stood on end. He repeated one word.

'Deserve.'

Mr Aspin watched him, confused. 'Excuse me?'

David attempted (*too*) to pull (*far gone*) himself back (*already*) to his senses. He cleared the phlegm from his throat and gave his head a shake. *Forget it. Make a comeback. Smart comeback.* But there was no comeback to be had, because the word was still hanging. It rushed through the blood in his veins, tightening the nerves and pulsating the muscles. *Snap out of it! Make a comeback! Stop stalling!* The job had gone now, his silence was steadily ensuring that.

You had him! The job is not gone, you can get it, you can get it back! But then, a stronger voice, stamping out the lines with that hydraulic pump. *Deserve / Deserve / Deserve.* David mimicked it like a silly git mimics a hypnotist.

'Deserve.'

The headmaster straightened, tired of the display. 'David, I think it's best you leave. And maybe get some rest. Please, for your own sake –'

'What they deserve. That's what you said, isn't it? What they deserve.'

David wasn't looking at the headmaster anymore. *Don't mention her. Don't talk about her. It'll be over for you.* But it was over already, David knew. All that was left was a memory and rage. And George Aspin didn't know that he was about to be the victim of both.

* * *

'ICE CREAM!'

Her tits were huge. Big tits. Biggy titty, as David sometimes joked.

'Shut up, your mum has big tits too!'

'Yeah, not as big as yours. It's like she's hiding something in them.'

'Yeah, you idiot, mums have milk in their tits.'

'Wow, she must have fifty pints in there.'

'Shut up!'

'I was wondering why your fridge is full of milk.'

'Gross!'

But David wasn't looking at Kevvy's mum's breasts today, no matter how gigantic they were. Today her face was wrong. What was once a smile had become a weird blankness, like there was really no one there. Also, just below the chin, the white of her skin had turned to red. A nasty red that went both out and in. Out: like a bubble, like you could press down and pop it. In: like beneath the surface, like the redness was burrowing under the flesh and eating away at her like a bug to swat. And it had happened before. David knew, because Kevvy had told him just over a month ago.

'*Weird markings on her face, like scabs, and she goes all weird, like she falls asleep standing up in the kitchen.*'

'*Bullshit.*'

'*It's true! It happened one time at lunch. I had to make my own soup.*'

David grimaced and turned away as Kevvy's mum looked down at him.

'Bonnie day, isn't it?' she said.

Her voice was normal, and David guessed he was thankful for that. He clung hard to his sheath and nodded. Kevvy, on the other hand, didn't seem to care. He jumped into the car, once again crying out into the forest air as if he were informing the birds: 'ICE CREAM!'

The car was a light-blue Morris Mini. It was tight and uncomfortable, with only a small seat for David to nestle in at the back. But it was cool. Far cooler than David's mum's car, which looked more like a juice carton than an actual car. David always cherished his time inside Kevvy's car. He liked the feeling of power it gave him, and how jealous everyone on the outside must have felt to see him in it. He liked imagining himself in Kevvy's mum's position twenty or so years in the future, perhaps with a suit and tie like the kind his dad would wear. But he wasn't cherishing anything today. Today, he was more concerned about how fast the world was rushing by them, and the way the car seemed to swerve from one side of the road to the other. Kevvy, on the other hand, paid it no mind.

'Bubble-gum flavour is the best,' he called back from the front seat. 'But one time Mum took me to Carlo's and we got this weird, kind of a bluey-green one. It's so annoying, I can't remember the name, but if we see it, we've got to get it. It was the best flavour ever, even better than bubble-gum, even though bubble-gum's the best.'

David smiled, or gave something like a smile, then turned back to the road ahead. Another swerve, over the line, back to their lane. David looked at the woman in the rear-view mirror and was horrified to see the nothingness that he had seen earlier. Her eyes were half shut, seeing but not seeing, blue but not blue. A sick feeling arrived in David's belly, and he shuffled on the white leather.

'How long's it going to take?'

That wasn't really a question that needed an answer because David knew exactly how long it took. From the forest, straight on for about twenty miles, then to Canterbury Loch, round the bend, to the right, to the left, to the right again, and then on to Raymurray. It usually took about thirty minutes. They'd been in the car for three. David was scared.

'Not gonna take too long,' said Kevvy. 'Why?'

David sat up, gulping down some saliva which tasted sour. He needed to be reassured. Maybe he was imagining things. Like the orcs, like Smaug, this could all be going on inside his head.

'Mrs Woods,' he said uncertainly. 'What kind of ice cream are you going to get?'

'Mum always gets the boring yellow flavour!' Kevvy chimed in with a grin, compulsively fiddling with the string of the bow he'd made last summer.

David kept his gaze on Kevvy's mum, who hadn't even blinked at the question he'd asked her. 'Mrs Woods?' he repeated.

Nothing. The sick feeling in David's gut sharpened. This was wrong. This was really, really wrong.

'Mum is so boring,' Kevvy proclaimed happily. 'If she had the choice of every flavour in the world, she'd go for the normal flavour. She won't even –'

His words were cut short as Kevvy's mum slumped forward, her head falling on the steering wheel, her elbows drooping down to her thighs, and her pretty dark hair landing in a tangle on her lap. The car veered to the right and down the shallow embankment, and Kevvy gasped, his hand suddenly clutching his mum's upper arm. David's vision felt like it tripled. Everything was so *now! now! now!* and he seemed to look in every direction. His nine-year-old brain took it all in and came to a conclusion: *prepare to die.*

The car rushed into the opening of the woods, going faster, and faster, until the crash. Although the woodland was relatively open, the car landed in a thick mess of trees and brambles. The bonnet crumpled, folding back on itself like a tin of corned beef. Kevvy yelped and was squeezed under the dashboard. His mum's head jerked backward and then forward again and blood started leaking from her nose.

Then there was silence. Apart from breathing. Kevvy's fingers remained dug into his mum's flesh, and David's eyes were still glued to the bent figure.

'What happened? What...?' Kevvy was the first to break the spell of hush. He stuttered over his words, then tried to push himself from the dashboard. He got one leg out and David saw that his shoe was missing. His forehead was cut too, and blood was trickling down into his right earhole.

'Mummy?' he moaned. 'What happened? Mum?' Kevvy shook his mum, but failed to move the body. With tears beginning to fall down his cheeks, he pulled her up from the steering wheel, and he shook her again, harder this time. 'Mum! Mummy, wake up!'

Kevvy's mum's head rocked back and forth. Her neck moved as if it was made of gelatine, like the bone had simply disappeared. With two fingers, Kevvy pushed up her eyelid, but the eye that was revealed was vacant. Kevvy's mum did not recognise her son. It was like knocking on the door of an empty home; she was not there anymore. She'd gone someplace else, disappeared like the bones in her neck.

Kevvy let out a sort of moan and David sprang up from his seat. Immediately, he reached for the door handle, but the already cramped Mini now seemed even more shrunken. The door was a mess of metal and when he pulled on the handle, it didn't give. He pulled again. Nothing. Pushing Kevvy out of the way, he reached over to the other door and repeated the motion. Pull, pull, pull; *no, no, no.*

'It won't open. We can't get out.'

David turned to his friend, but Kevvy was still staring into the blue of his mum's eye, sniffing through a concoction of soft bogey and salty tears.

'My mum...'

David pulled Kevvy's hand from the eye and the lid clamped back shut. 'Kevvy! We need to open the doors; we need to get help!'

Kevvy let out another groan and wiped the river from his cheeks, looking at the hollow shell that was his mum as if it had betrayed him. He looked as if she was there, *right there*, but wouldn't respond to his desperate calls and cries. He was like an animal; he didn't get it.

David pulled again on the door, hoping in vain that he would catch it sleeping and unlock the trap, but the door wasn't kidding. The car was in lockdown. Outside, the forest was carrying on as usual. A red squirrel shimmied down a tree on all fours, stopping only to admire this brand-new animal in its wilderness. A red and black bird returned to its young with a worm in its beak, and a hedgehog hid itself in a bundle of weeds and flowers. There was nothing to suggest their forest had even been dented, while the world of the two boys inside the blue Morris Mini had tilted upside down. David cussed, his eyes glancing down to Kevvy's mum's chest.

'She's breathing,' he noticed out loud. 'Kevvy, she's breathing. She's not dead, she's just sleeping.'

Kevvy pulled up a hand and placed it down on his mum's breast, a flicker of relief passing over his face. 'Her heart's going. Yeah, I can feel it.'

'You see…' David patted Kevvy on the shoulder. 'She's okay.'

Despite everything, including the blatant lie David had just told, Kevvy managed a damaged smile and the flow of tears ceased. 'She might wake up,' he said hopefully.

David nodded. 'Yeah, yeah, she might wake up. She will wake up. We'll just have to wait until then. When she does, she can open the doors and we can get help.'

Kevvy began trying to pull his other leg out, his pants fast and thick. David didn't like the sound of both of them breathing so hard, so he breathed through his nose.

In five minutes, Kevvy would be the first one to say, *I smell smoke.*

* * *

'What they deserve…' David Cooper said the words slowly, flopping them over in his mouth, tasting them, feeling them.

The headmaster huffed impatiently. 'David, I honestly think you should go.'

David looked up, his nostrils flaring and his eyes wet with anger. 'What about what she deserves?'

'She?'

'Amee Amee Florence.'

The headmaster shrugged as if he didn't know who David was talking about. But the fingers which gripped the pen tightened, and the whites of his knuckles revealed themselves.

'I don't follow you…' he said unconvincingly.

'You know her mother. You know she's a drug user. You know Amee is suffering.'

The words came out barely stable; like David, they shook and shuddered, but Mr Aspin flinched at every one.

'I…'

David leant back. *If he denies it, punch his lights out.*

The headmaster shoved his tongue into his bottom lip, contemplating a reply. 'What has this got to do with anything?'

SLAM!

David's fist crashed into the table, causing a cup of pencils to fly onto the carpet and a splinter of wood to shove its way up into his flesh. Just like when the bikers had beaten him up in the bar, there wasn't any pain. Nothing tangible anyway. It was just a mixture of acids, blood, and impulse. Adrenaline cancelled everything out, like morphine coming to boil at the right moment. The headmaster juddered in his seat and raised his hands up in a motion of surrender.

'David – David – I don't know where you've heard – I don't know anything – I just…'

David stood and the headmaster's hands went higher. 'You know she's a junkie. You know that and you have the fucking audacity to talk about what the children deserve.'

'I don't know anything. I was just – I just said – I just mentioned – maybe she is – but I don't have any idea what – if she is.'

The lunch bell echoed behind David's head, but he didn't hear it. He'd heard enough already, enough of everything, enough words. He wanted to punch something now. He had a need to let it all out, and every hit would set them both right. George: because it was right, and it was deserved. David: because like morphine, it would calm the blood and avenge the past. Whose past, he wasn't sure, but no more thinking now.

David jumped into action: he pushed over the desk, grabbed the lapels of the headmaster's jacket, and yanked him onto his feet. Then, with the force of his body and the buzz of those few seconds before *something* happened, he threw the headmaster into the window, sending shards of glass flying down onto the tarmac below.

Mr Aspin roared. 'JEESUUSSS!'

David held the jacket tighter, his teeth clamped rigid, spittle tracing down his lips and onto his collar with every breath. A line of blood slid down Mr Aspin's bald head.

'David – David – David – HELP!' he yelled desperately to a closed door.

David grabbed the headmaster's chin and squeezed, then he moved down to his neck. For the first time, the headmaster fought back. He lunged up at David and punched him in the cheek, then pulled hard on the hand wrapped around his throat. When David failed to budge, Mr Aspin swung again, and this time the force was enough to push David back against the desk. He spat blood, then went all over again. David lunged, hitting his target on the shoulder. It wasn't a hard punch, and it threw David off balance, so the headmaster took his chance. He grabbed David's left armpit, and with an almighty *'GURRGHH!'*, he threw him down onto the carpet.

David landed with a thump, his knee jolting with a sudden sharp pain. Instinctively, he reached down to inspect the damage, and found his fingers wrapping around something thick, jagged, and sharp. *Really? Oh God, really?* He felt the headmaster grab hold of his collar and an arm travelled around his neck like a snake, yanking him into a headlock. David's fingers closed harder on the shard of glass as he spluttered. A warm redness squirmed up through the gaps of his clamped hand and trickled down onto his wrist. He struggled against the headmaster's force.

'Don't,' he gasped, just barely. 'Don't, or –'

The headmaster squeezed tighter, and in one fluid motion David's hand lunged up behind him, travelling fast towards the head of George Aspin.

* * *

David squirmed on the burning leather, panting hard into what felt like nothing. The air had turned against them; it was thick, heavy, choking, and both Kevvy and David were struggling to breathe it in. Forty minutes had passed since Kevvy's mum and her big tits had collapsed onto the steering wheel, and no matter how hard they tried, she wasn't willing to come back. Now she was slumped over on her right side, her tongue lying stray on her shoulder like a dog when it sleeps. She was still breathing, but her breaths had got slower, while the boys' had got faster. Outside the car, the sky was a clean blue. But inside, the air had turned grey. A thin layer of smoke was seeping from somewhere near the bonnet, and with every minute that passed, it seemed to grow thicker. Every attempt to break the windows had failed. Because of the way the car had folded back on itself, David could only turn the cranks two-thirds of a rotation, so they'd resorted to trying to smash the glass. Shoes, hands, even David's knife, but the glass wouldn't even crack. Two vehicles had passed by on the road behind them, but neither driver seemed to spot the smoking Mini, nor realise that there were two young boys slowly suffocating inside. All that was left to do was wait, and hope, and breathe.

The panic had been the first thing. It stripped them down to their nappies, and they'd squealed at the car walls like a baby squeals at the bars of their cot. But soon they figured out that the more they panicked, the harder the air protested.

'Warriors, Kevvy, we have to be calm.'

'I can't!'

'Just think about Thorin; think of what he'd do.'

'But it's so hot!'

'It would have been hot in the dwarven caves too.'

'So this is just like Smaug?'

'Exactly like Smaug. This smoke, it's dragonfire. We just have to keep breathing.'

'I feel sick.'

'Kevvy.'

'It's hard to breathe.'

'Just breathe.'

A short amount of time later and there were no tears anymore. All the moisture inside of them came from the skin, drowning their faces in a deep sweat, making their hair wet and hard like that time David had stolen his dad's hair gel. Kevvy sat panting and choking. His left leg was still trapped under the dashboard, which meant his lungs were the first to greet the smoke. Every now and then, David would hear his tongue slop noisily in his mouth, as if it was attempting to retaliate against it.

'Kevvy,' said David randomly. He wanted to hear his own voice. It was croaky and dry, but still there. He was at least glad for that. Kevvy didn't turn. His body had begun to shake, so David placed a hand on his shoulder.

'Hmm...' came the response.

'You're alright.'

'Hmm.' Kevvy's eyes stared ahead. His hand was clamped fast to his bow.

'Think of *The Hobbit*,' David told him. But even thinking of *The Hobbit* didn't seem to work anymore. At least, not for David. That was more a story than ever now. It wasn't real and it didn't matter. 'You're a warrior, Kevvy. You're a better warrior than me.'

Yet while David truly believed that, Kevvy's newfound muscles weren't exactly helping him now. David turned away, his eyes beginning to squint against the world outside. There was a pain in his head, and it was getting bad. It didn't feel like his head anymore, in a way. A thickness had come over it, like the skull was lined with tiny lead weights. Behind his eyes there was a voice telling him to sleep. It was distant, non-human, but there all the same. He needed sleep. In a way the idea wasn't a bad one. If he slept now, then the world around him would go; he wouldn't have to live in it anymore. And when he woke up, it could all be over. Surely it would all be over. But sleeping now meant he would have to leave Kevvy alone, and that was something

David couldn't do. Not if he wanted to call himself a warrior.

He shook his head, willing himself to stay in the now, but it wasn't too easy. His vision was getting fuzzy, and things that had just before been bright had now become *bright*, like they weren't real, and the sound in his ear drums was becoming muffled, like someone had stuffed them full of cotton wool. It was the void, he could tell. The void was pulling, and David felt like he was sinking down, like it was quicksand that distorted his foundations, distorted his very world.

One, two, three, four, five. Breath. Deep breath. David coughed. The oxygen that he was breathing was only the thinnest of slivers, as if both he and Kevvy had got to the end of the line. *You want some more? That's gonna be another twenty pennies.* He coughed again. His throat was barking, clawing at the edges, demanding clean air like a dog demands water. David wrapped a hand around it, sliding it up and down. *Stroke. Calm down. Breathe.*

He looked over at Kevvy, whose eyes were even wider than before. His panting was heavier too, but the breaths were a weird sort of heavy, like there was really nothing in them. They were futile. A cardboard shield against an orc. A kitchen knife against a dragon.

David leant over again and said, 'Kevvy', but the name came out in a groan. He coughed again and breathed fast. His body was rebelling. *Say nothing. Just breathe.* He felt himself lurch backwards and his back hit the car door. *World going fuzzy. Bright-bright-bright. Don't sleep. Don't sleep now!* The blackness was approaching, things were getting bright and dark at the same time, and David felt like he wanted to be sick in his lap. *No time for sick. No sick, just breathe.* Kevvy started going blurry; his friend was disappearing. It almost felt like it was just David in the car. Just him and his panic now. No one else. But then, out of the darkness, a voice:

'Warriors. We're both warriors. Me and you.'

Kevvy's last words arrived through the cotton. They were a shaky whisper, barely audible, shuddered, stilted, broken. But they undeniably belonged to David's friend. Then the black.

* * *

His eyes were fixed on the carpet. One patch, once blue, now red. Deep red, twenty splashes later, from the palm of his hand, through the air, and into the fabric. David Cooper sat at one end of the room, George Aspin at the other, panting hard, his pupils wide, staring up at the broken window above David's head. Neither of them had spoken for about three minutes.

'I had a friend,' David eventually croaked. 'I had a friend here, a long time ago. He died. His mum, she was on drugs. Heroin. I'm sorry.'

George Aspin averted his gaze from David, touching his left ear lightly. The blood left on his fingers was dark. He stared at it, as if amazed to see the strange liquid that had once inhabited his insides, now on the out, tangible, existing, the workings underneath revealed. *So we don't run on magic, on memory, on the simple idea of living. We're truly flesh and blood, cars on fuel, and* screw *whoever makes us leak.* His gaze turned to David again.

'Fuck you.'

'I dropped the glass. I didn't do it... couldn't... I dropped it.' David's finger wobbled over to the jagged shard on the floor by his feet.

'I bet you did kill your son, you psycho prick. And there's you pretending you're doing this for the kid. You're doing it because it makes you feel good. You're violent, and I'm gonna make sure you go to jail.'

The conviction was there in his voice, but the headmaster didn't get up. He didn't open the door; he didn't leave. He just stayed sitting, pure shock throbbing through his every breath. David shuddered to his feet, and the headmaster cowered, his hands covering his bald and bleeding head.

'Don't!' he yelped. 'I'm gonna call the police, I swear!'

'I know you are,' replied David, walking over the broken glass and towards the door. That was true; he had no reason to doubt Mr Aspin. But before that happened, he had one last thing to do to put things right.

I don't blame you, my fellow warrior. It's what they deserve, not him, not the damn headmaster, arsehole, them.

Sleep now, Kevvy, leave it alone. Please, at the back of my mind, just sleep. It's gonna be over soon.

You know, I don't doubt you. Perhaps you were a better warrior than me after all, but then we're both warriors...

Me and you.

David looked down. 'Where is she?' he asked.

Mr Aspin hesitated. 'Where is who?'

'Amee.'

The headmaster shook his head, still cupping the wound in his ear. 'I don't know.'

'Tell me or I'll hit you again.'

'I swear I don't know. Her... her mother works at the hospital... I'm pretty sure of that. What are you gonna do? David? What the hell are you gonna do?'

But David ignored him. That was all he needed. He put his hand on the door-knob and twisted.

9

AMEE'S ROOM

'Open your eyes.'

And the room met her – the ceiling low and white lit, the paint of the walls cracked and peeling, two film posters covering the worst of it. *Ghostbusters* and *The Land Before Time,* both askew on the nail. By the door on the far side was her television, tiny and old, the plastic on one side coming loose from its glue. Beside that was her bookshelf, a small wooden square that housed a collection of novels and scrapbooks for drawing, and above it, perched beside the door-frame, was the camera. A red light blazed beside the lens. The rest of the room was empty, other than her bed, her bedside table, and the thing in the corner that she didn't like to think about.

'How do you feel?' her mum asked.

'I feel fine.'

'What's fine?'

Amee sighed, looking over to the dinosaur poster. It was a dark image. The dinosaurs smiled as they crossed destitute lands, unaware of the looming green monster with its teeth bared and its eyes a vivid and dangerous yellow. It used to freak her out. In a way, it still did.

'Normal, I suppose.'

'And normal is just fine?'

'In here, yes.'

Her mother laid down her notebook. It was a funny thing. Burgundy leather, thick, with messy stapled pages sticking out of the folds and a black elastic band holding everything in place. She ran a hand through her brown frizzled hair, the moisture of the morning's hair-spray wetting the cracks in her palm. Dark eyes stared into Amee, scanning and surveying her. It was a practice that had become all too familiar by now. Amee knew the score. Her mother held firm to her notebook in every one of their lessons. Each answer was a tick or a cross, every conversation an examination; Amee on one side of the desk, her mother on the other. All that Amee had to do was be good, be cooperative, and wait for it all to finish.

'Did you wake up in the night?'

'No,' Amee lied.

Of course, being cooperative didn't exclude the occasional lie. As long as it was well told. Her mum gazed into her, biting her lip. There was a pause, then she flicked her pen onto the page. Amee didn't even have to look to tell it was a tick.

'And what did you dream about?'

'I didn't dream. I was tired after yesterday, and I don't dream when I'm tired.'

This lie was a bit harder to tell, seeing as she tended to dream the same dream every night, regardless of tiredness.

'You weren't in the water?'

Amee shuffled on her chair. 'No...'

Her mum pulled on the paper and flicked it over, beginning afresh on the page underneath. 'Close your eyes again,' she said, and Amee did so. 'What do you see?'

'Nothing. Just the dark. And the patterns in between.'

'Now open.'

Amee opened her eyes and looked at the room around her once more. She took it all in; the television, the bookshelf, the bed, the walls. Even the thing that she didn't like to think about, the thing that was nestled in the corner, its metal coil curled round itself like a snake sleeping.

'What do you see?'

'My room. And you.'

'And what else?'

Amee pushed herself back against her chair. 'The patterns in between.'

Her mother leaned in, eyes open wide, that familiar curiosity returning to her in one big rush. The lesson had begun. But her mum wasn't the tutor; Amee was.

'Who is it today?' her mother asked.

'I don't know his name,' replied Amee. 'He won't tell me.'

'Ask him now.'

Hesitantly, Amee stared hard into the corner of the room. What she saw was the chipped and crusted cracks where one wall met the other, but knowing the difference between what she saw and what *more* there was to see, Amee allowed herself to look closer.

The boy couldn't have been more than eight years old. His face was busy with freckles and slightly reddened around the nose. Atop his head lay a mop of gingery locks which fell in clumps down to his collar. His clothes looked different to those of most boys his age. His torso was wrapped in a thick scraggly jumper, and his trousers and shoes gave the impression that he went to a more selective school than Gealblath Secondary. He sat and gazed at Amee with a strange curiosity.

'What is your name?' she asked softly.

But the boy just shook his head, his hands gripping his ankles tightly.

Amee continued, 'You don't have to be scared of me; I'm not going to hurt you. What if I tell you my name first?'

The boy sat still for a moment. Then, with a small hum, he lifted his chin in a nod. 'Yes, please,' he said.

'I'm Amee. Amee Florence.'

'I'm Alexander Murphy.'

Amee gave him a comforting smile.

'What is it?' her mum demanded. 'What's happening?'

From the corner of Amee's eye, she saw the boy blur into nothing, his existence replaced by the worn cracks in the white wall. He was still there, though, so long as Amee tried to see him.

'He's called Alexander,' she told her mother.

'And how old is Alexander?'

'He can't be more than nine, I don't think.'

'Ask him.'

Amee turned back to the corner of the room, spotting the boy phase back into her vision and nod his little ginger head. 'He says yes,' she relayed.

Her mum leant forward, pen squeezed hard between her fingers and the nib itching above the notebook. 'And when did Alexander die?'

There was a pause. Amee shivered. She always hated asking this question. Nevertheless, she asked it.

'When did you die, Alexa –'

'Can you help me?'

The small whispery voice cut into her own, and Alexander stared at Amee with a glimmer of hope in his eyes.

'What is it?' her mother enquired.

'I'm lost,' said Alexander, 'and I need help. I can hear... I can hear something. Someone out there, talking to me. Please...'

Amee swallowed, then leaned in closer. 'How long have you been lost?'

'I don't know. It was nearly my birthday.'

'And when were you born?'

The boy closed his eyes, like he had to think about it. 'February, 1975.'

Amee turned back towards her mum. '1984. That's when he died –'

'I feel like I've been lost a really long time,' Alexander interrupted. 'I just want my – I just want to know where everyone is.'

'Where who is?'

'My mum and my dad. They were here with me. They said this was a safe place, that I'd get better here.' The boy pulled his knees hard into his chest, his eyes wide and afraid. 'They told me to wait for them. When they put me to sleep, they told me to wait.'

'Tell me where he's from.' Amee's mother pulled her out of the conversation.

'I don't know,' replied Amee. 'And I'm not going to ask him any more.'

'You'll do as you're told.'

The boy disappeared, and Amee shook her head.

'No.'

There was a pause. With a sigh, her mum leaned back

and pulled her fingers through the wet frizz of her hair once again.

'Do you want him to come? Because I'll send for him, I promise. I'll send for him just as I always do. Unless you do as I ask.'

Amee closed her eyes, her fingers gripping the bottom of her chair. For a moment, she imagined she was somewhere else. School, maybe. With Marty sitting beside her. She heard her mother stand.

'I wish you wouldn't continue to disappoint me,' she said. 'We were having a good lesson.'

When Amee opened her eyes again, her mother had gone. Around her, the room was still the same. The bed in the same place, the television, the bookshelf. Even Alexander was still there, she knew, his tears and sniffles silent to her now that she couldn't see him.

A few moments passed before Amee stood and made her way over to the bed. She sat down on the mattress, shivering as she heard the sound of footsteps begin to approach behind the closed door. With a deep breath, she looked over to the corner of the room, but she made sure she did not see the boy. She didn't want to see him at all anymore. All she saw was the wall and the cracks within it.

'I can't help you,' said Amee quietly. 'No one can help you. And no one ever will.'

The door-knob twisted, the door swung open again, and the tall man stepped forward to fill the frame.

'Little fishy,' he said.

And Amee screamed, feeling the urine stream its way down her leg as she fell backwards onto the sheets.

10

MARTY'S CASTLE

The sun scattered purple and blue stains on the wood beside the window. Marty sat beside it, his hand slipping in and out of the colours, flicking at the motionless flies that had stayed sizzling in the heat for too long. It was hot again today. Walls and corridors dripped with muggy sweat; doctors and nurses paced around with sleeves yanked up to their elbows, foreheads wet and tempers boiled to the brink. Days hated, flies roasted, life decisions questioned, soup and juice shoved in front of Marty's face. Once again, he couldn't wait to leave. And yet he could.

'C19.'

'Amee's room?'

'Yes.'

Teddy was sitting beside Mike's bed, painting one of the Warhammer figures he'd given him. Marty's shoebox was still in his room, unopened, much to Teddy's sadness. Although in all fairness, Marty had other things to think about than toy warriors. He'd just finished telling them about the events of the night before.

'But there's only so many wards in this hospital,' Mike spoke up from the bed. 'They're all in A or B. There is no C.'

'There is. The top floor. Where no one's supposed to go. There are like, I dunno, secret wards or something.'

'Secret wards?' Mike stared at Marty, unconvinced.

'It's true. I wasn't dreaming or anything. Go outside and look at the hospital for yourself; I'll get you a wheelchair.'

Marty went to retrieve the wheelchair from the other side of the room, but before he could, Mike lifted his hand.

'No, no, I get that. It's just... Amee? In a secret ward at the top of this hospital? It sounds a bit far-fetched. It sounds a bit like a –'

'If you say it sounds like a conspiracy theory, I'm gonna kill you.'

Teddy smirked, but Marty wasn't laughing. This wasn't funny to him. This was serious.

'How can you be sure it was Amee if the door was locked?' asked Mike.

'Because I heard the television. I heard *Ghostbusters*.'

'So Amee's the only one who watches that movie? Lots of people watch that movie.'

Teddy nodded in agreement. 'It's a fine movie.'

Marty walked back over to the windowsill, his hands in his pockets and his chin pointed down towards the floor, wallowing in the pool of possibilities that had arisen over the last twelve hours.

'That doesn't explain the scream,' Marty told them. 'That was definitely a girl's scream.'

Mike shrugged. 'Lots of people are girls.'

'And her car is still there.' Marty pointed out at the car park, his eyes squinting against the sun. Neither Mike nor

Teddy could explain that one. 'It was Amee in that room. She's in this hospital; I know she is.'

'So what are you gonna do?' asked Mike. 'It's midday and you're going home in a few hours.'

Marty took a few moments. He'd been weighing up his options ever since he'd walked away from C19. He'd been too nervous to try anything the first time round. He had twisted the door-knob, but it had been locked. And then he had run.

You were the weed-kid last night, he thought to himself. *You ran away. You got scared. But you don't have to be the weed-kid today. Today there will be daylight. There'll be no dark, no cold, no silence. No reason to be afraid. Just go. Be the Marty she thinks you are. Be cool. Be Venkman.*

'I'm gonna go back there,' he said resolutely. 'I'm gonna go find her before it's too late.' Clenching his fists, he marched towards the door. 'Who's coming with me?'

Teddy leaned forward with sudden enthusiasm. 'Oh, can you grab me an Irn-Bru on the way back? I think I saw a vending machine just around the corner.'

With a sigh, Marty opened the door and left the question of Irn-Bru and the possibility of its arrival lingering in the heat of the room behind him.

When he got to Room C19, the door seemed larger than it did the night before, far larger than any other door in the hospital. Marty stood before it, shaking his body into composure as he knocked, first softly, then a bit more strongly, like each knock was filling him with a sort of confidence that he hadn't had before. But then...

'Can I help you?'

The voice came from down the corridor, and Marty turned. A man was stood watching him. He was tall. Very

146

tall. He must have been seven feet at least and his head was nearly brushing the ceiling.

'No,' replied Marty, taken aback by the sheer size of him.

'You're not supposed to be up here. Didn't you read the sign?'

'No, sorry, I didn't know. I was just... I was just going.'

'Just going?' the tall man repeated. 'So why are you knocking on that door?'

'I thought...' Marty swallowed. Even from where he was standing, he felt intimidated by the man's presence. 'Sorry, I thought my friend might be in there.'

'Signs are there to be read, kid. You didn't read it.'

A moment passed, then another, and then, quite alarmingly, the tall man's face contorted into a smile.

'But what kind of young boy reads a sign, anyway? Boot-lickers, that's what we would call those types back in my day. Although, my day was quite a while ago now. Quite a long while.' The tall man shook his head, rustling the tufts of reddish-brown hair that hung parted on either side of his scalp. 'You won't find your friend in there. You'd have better luck asking reception.'

'I've asked them; they said she's not here.'

'Then I guess she's not here, hey, kid?'

'But she is. I mean, I think she is. I think she's in this room. I heard her.'

The tall man walked towards Marty, his hands going behind his back and his features becoming clearer as he stepped into the bright rays of the ceiling lamps. The most prominent feature was his nose. Long, crooked, and squiggling down the centre of his gaunt face. Then came the ears. Low, fleshy, and each one jiggling in the air as he moved. There was a bruise too, Marty noticed. An ugly bruise just on the temple, dark and plum-like, swelling the skin around the edges. Marty wondered whether he got that bumping his head on a doorframe. The tall man stopped in front of him and pointed at the door.

'In here?' he asked.

Marty nodded in response. 'Yeah.'

'What's your friend's name?'

'Amee Florence.'

The tall man gazed down at Marty, folding his red lips on top of each other in contemplation. 'Amee...'

'Yeah, her name's Amee. Are you a doctor?'

'Me? No, I'm not a doctor.'

'A nurse?'

'No, I'm not that.'

At that moment, a woman turned the corner and entered the same hallway, halting suddenly as she spotted Marty and the tall man at the other end. She was panting hard, as if she'd been running, and on top of her head clumps of frizzy hair stood tall and curled in the wetness of the humidity.

'Does he know anything?' she asked. Her voice was soft and shuddering.

'I don't think so,' the tall man replied.

Marty looked between the pair of them, his eyebrows furrowed in confusion.

'Then why are you wasting your time here?' asked the woman.

'My little friend is looking for someone. Amee. Amee Florence.'

The frizzy-haired woman seemed to lurch upright, her eyes piercing into Marty. 'Why?'

'I think he's lost her.'

'I mean why is he looking here?'

'He says he heard her. I was trying to tell him he heard wrong.'

'Then tell him and come with me. I need you.'

With that, she turned on her heel and disappeared, leaving Marty alone with the tall man once again. He wavered for a second, then touched the bruise on his temple. It looked like it hurt, but he didn't even flinch.

'Okay, kid, don't take this as patronising, but we all hear things from time to time.' He reached into his pocket, removed a copper-coloured key, and twisted it in the hole beneath the door-knob. 'Don't be disappointed,' he said, then he pushed open the door onto a pearl-white room.

There was a bed, a couple of posters, a television, a bookshelf, and a weird sort of medical contraption in the corner. But no Amee. No anybody. Marty went to walk forward, but just as he did so, the tall man closed the door in his face.

'Not your room, kid. You see now? Your friend isn't here.'

Marty swallowed, staring into the eyes of the man looming above him. *Even Venkman wouldn't argue with this guy*, he thought fearfully.

'Okay,' he muttered.

The tall man shoved the key firmly back inside his pocket. 'But she'll show up, don't sweat it. Girls like playing elusive. But right now, I suggest you go back to your room. No patients from downstairs are allowed up here. Now you know that, I don't expect to see you again. Here, I'll take you back.'

With a wink, he placed an enormous hand on Marty's shoulder, and the pair of them began walking back towards the stairs, leaving Room C19 far behind them.

'ARSEPIECE!' Marty slumped against the coffee-stained car seat, squeezing Teddy's shoebox, which he'd shoved onto his lap just before they took off.

'Language,' his mum hissed at him.

'It's her room. I heard it. I heard the television in there. I heard *Ghostbusters*, clear as anything!'

'Marty...'

'As clear as I can say ARSEPIECE!'

'Marty!' his mum shouted, taking one hand off the steering wheel to raise a finger at him.

Marty huffed and squeezed his palms into his eyes. He'd known it was a lost cause even before he'd started. If Mike and Teddy hadn't believed him, then there was no chance either of his parents would buy the story. They didn't listen to him about anything, let alone something like this. He kept his mouth shut and glowered for the rest of the drive.

One hour later, a bowl of broccoli landed in front of him with a thump. They were sat at the dinner table, his father scattering vegetables on Marty's plate. The majority of them were coming to rest beside a slice of pink salmon. That other food Marty hated.

'I don't want to eat this,' said Marty.

'Watch your attitude,' his dad said back.

'Why are we doing this? We never eat together.'

Marty's mum was sipping some wine. 'Because it's nice,' she said. 'We're happy you're out of the hospital, all okay. Aren't we, darling?'

She turned towards his dad, who grunted in unconvincing agreement.

Marty shook his head. 'So we're eating salmon and broccoli, two of the foods I hate, in celebration of me?'

'Your father cooked.'

'Okay, that makes sense.'

'Attitude!' his dad barked at him, landing a mountain of broccoli onto his own plate as if to prove some kind of broccoli-related point. 'Anyway, you should be grateful.'

'Grateful for what?'

'Well, your mother had to take two days off work for your little hospital excursion. That costs us, you know.'

'I didn't go to hospital of my own accord, Dad. I wasn't there on holiday; someone put me there. A boy called Rory. Why don't you give him broccoli and salmon if you're that angry?'

His mum set down her glass. 'Marty, your father said atti –'

'Why am I being punished for this?'

'You're not being punished. This is nice. This is dinner.'

'For you, this is nice, Mum. For Dad, this is a punishment.'

His father shoved a dollop of salmon onto his tongue. 'You're overthinking,' he said simply.

Marty's mum leant over to stroke his wrist with a thumb. 'Hmm. You do tend to do that.'

Marty put his fork down, feeling the anger rise up inside him, but he kept it at bay. There were more important things to worry about right now. The question of Amee's room was still churning in his mind. The tall man, the scream, the television. These were all more important than broccoli and salmon.

'Can I be excused?'

'No way,' his dad responded.

'Marty, you've hardly eaten anything.'

'I can't eat. It hurts my tooth, the one Rory punched out. Don't wanna be going back to hospital; it's gonna cost us.'

Marty stared across the table at his father, who glared back, his knife slowly sliding across his fish.

'Well,' his mum said, 'do you want something else? We have leftover leeks and tatties.'

'I'll make myself some soup or something later.' Marty stood and pushed the chair back underneath the table.

His dad spoke through a mouthful of food. 'Marty, you leave this room, you're grounded for two weeks.'

'Fine,' replied Marty, and he slammed the door behind him.

For the next hour, Marty did nothing but sit on his bed and listen. The argument had started as soon as the door swung to a close. His mum had taken an early lead.

'Did you do it on purpose?'

'Do what?'

'The salmon.'

'Well, I don't know what the boy does or doesn't like.'

'Why would you even mention my work?'

'Because taking time off work costs money, in case you hadn't noticed.'

'He didn't put himself in there!'

'Well, that's what happens when you make enemies. It's irresponsible.'

'So that's why you did it then?'

'Did what?'

'The salmon!'

'Why the fuck are we still talking about a fucking fish? Jesus Christ!'

Marty lay against the pillow as they continued, closing his eyes to shut out the light. Amee's eyes appeared in front of him when he did. The irises were made of blue ribbons, some wide, some thin, stretching out from the black and over towards the edge like rivers to a white sea. Was there something in them the last time he'd seen her? Something silent but screaming? She had called him one of the good guys, but what good guy missed a cry for help, however quiet?

Marty moaned and turned in the half-light, staring vaguely at the shoebox, which he had placed neatly on the bedside table beside him. He imagined the warriors in there, their thick and silver armour, their sharp and fiery swords. Ready for anything, anyone, any enemy. Taller than the sun. Greater than a dragon. And then there was the weed-kid. Alone in bed. Beaten by a door and a fillet of fish. Marty sat up and took the shoebox in both hands, jumbling the figures around inside, and lifted on the lid to take a rueful look at the models of strength and resilience which Teddy had given him. The first thing that appeared, however, was neither a warrior nor a dragon, but a sheet of torn grid paper. He stared at it for a couple of seconds, then turned it over. There was writing on the other side.

MEET ME. MARTY EVANS IS DEAD. MIDNIGHT.

Marty gaped, turning the paper over, then back round again, as if to check the words were truly there. He lay against the pillow, taking a minute to sift through the meaning of the message. The thought that this was Teddy went as soon as it came. Teddy would never leave him mysterious and vague messages. He'd had plenty of time to tell Marty something at the hospital, and his brain had no room for ambiguity. The same went for Mike. Barring brain capacity, he didn't even have the ability to leave his ward without wheels. That just left one person.

Marty leapt up from his bed and paced over to the window, his heart beating fast as he gazed into the sky. The stars were just beginning to emerge, dotted against the dark-blue backdrop which was fizzling away into night.

'Amee...' he whispered to himself. Because surely it could only be her. The girl in the hospital, kept in secrecy and hidden from view. How else would she get his attention other than in a way that was just as perplexing as her predicament? At that moment, he remembered the dream. He remembered her standing at the foot of his bed. Or was it a dream? Perhaps she was really there, perhaps that was when she left the note, perhaps...

But surely he would have known. Surely he would have been able to tell the difference between dreams and reality. He checked the clock on his bedside table: 20:56. Just over three hours until midnight. Marty bit his lip in contemplation, wincing slightly at the pain that shot through his reinserted tooth. Beneath his room, a door slammed, and for his own sake, he hoped it would stay shut. If the argument was over, his dad would probably go to the fridge and drown any unsaid words with a bottle, while his mum would sink them all in a steaming hot bath. That was the usual routine anyhow, and usual was what Marty would need. Usual would get him to the front door unseen. If he was going to go, that was. After all, the message could have been left by anyone. Perhaps it was Rory, sending Marty an ominous message to finish the job. Or maybe it was Ross, ready to bust his face in with a Mike-imprinted knuckleduster. Or maybe, just maybe, it *was* Amee. Alone and scared and waiting for Marty Evans, the warrior who wouldn't show because he was too scared.

Marty gulped. He knew there was nothing to contemplate in the end. He was going. He had to; otherwise he'd regret it for the rest of his weed-kid life. All that was left to do now was sit, wait, and watch the clock tick closer to midnight.

When the hour finally came, Marty was already downstairs, creeping as quietly as he could out into the garden. He turned back to peer into the lounge window. His father lay passed out on the sofa, both fists squeezed into balls and his mouth half open, as if he'd fallen asleep still protesting about the salmon. He didn't so much as twitch when Marty clicked the door closed. He had got out of the house successfully. Stage one, tick. Now all he had to do was get to his destination.

Of course, he'd guessed what that destination was as soon as he picked up the note, and it didn't take him long to get there. The castle sat on the edge of the park, lit meekly by a couple of lamp posts on the kerb. A small cloud of sea fog was gnawing into the cracks of the wood. He could see the words MARTY EVANS IS DEAD! had been scrubbed half to hell with buckets of soapy water and bleach. Only the faintest outline remained now: IS DEAD! Insert name here, Marty guessed.

He looked at his watch: 00:05. Five minutes late. There was no room for hesitation now. With a deep breath, he began walking across the grass, pinching himself sensical every time a shadow morphed into Rory, or a prickle of wind was breathed from the lungs of Ross. The dark was trying to trick him, he knew, but Marty wouldn't let it, not now he'd got this far. He broke into a run and stopped directly underneath the IS DEAD! lettering.

He stared about himself. So far the castle was as Amee-less as Room C19, and the park was too. If it really was her who wanted to meet him here, then she was just as late as he was. He leant his back against a splintered pole, attempting to get his breaths back down to a normal rate. The night around him was entirely silent, and as the

155

seconds passed, Marty became one with it, standing as dead and still as the castle billboard suggested.

Then a gust of wind rushed into him, and Marty heard some movement on the grass. Footsteps. Loud ones. Squelching into the wet ground one after the other and heading fast towards the weed-kid. He retreated slightly underneath the castle, his bravery disappearing as he cowered into the darkness.

'Oh shit,' he whispered. 'Oh shit, oh shit, oh shit.'

'You there, Weed-kid?' a voice came in response.

Marty's heart plummeted. The voice was male and low, deep and hoarse, the furthest away from Amee's you could get. He felt faint as he leant down low, holding back a cowardly squeal as the figure peered from behind the wall.

'Weed-kid?' it said again.

Marty gasped. The figure was not Amee, but it wasn't Rory either. Nor Ross. The figure was someone Marty hadn't expected, someone he had never even thought of.

'Get off your arse, Marty,' Mr Cooper said as he took a step towards him. 'You're coming with me.'

11

THE SPY

The cabin door flew open, and Amee fell to the floor, shards and splinters of wood and glass landing in the tangles of her hair.

'Shh. Shh. Shh.' David pulled the door shut behind him and slammed any unbroken bolts into their places. 'Shh. Shh. Shh.'

Amee scrambled into the corner of the room, her breaths hard and fast. David raised a hand in the semi-darkness, his finger placed firmly on his lips. For a few seconds, the only thing to hear was the sea. It was about ten feet from the long line of cabins, the tide slowly but surely rolling its way over to the shore, the curved, mirror-like waves kissing the pebbles over and over again. But then a different sound, coming from beyond the window to their right. The growl of an engine, a splutter of oil, and all of a sudden, a pair of bright-yellow headlights were illuminating the world around them. David ducked to the floor, his buttocks landing painfully on the broken glass.

'Shh! Shh! Shh!'

They were in the first cabin from the road, just beside where the car had stopped. David felt around the floor, feeling over shattered glass until he got to the largest shard he could find. His ears pricked up, and he waited for the click of the car lock. But nothing came. There was just the grumble, and the headlamps, like searchlights, glaring into the cabin, awaiting any kind of movement. David turned towards the new girl.

'Tell me what happened.'

She cowered with her back against the wall, shaking her head so hard that tiny specks of glass flew from her hair. David grabbed her ankle.

'Tell me...'

* * *

David was in the dust, riding his bike behind a pale Ford Anglia. The Shadow was low on fuel, but it wouldn't be long now. Twenty minutes had passed since his fight with George Aspin. Twenty minutes. Twenty minutes to think and to follow. Twenty minutes to remember. Twenty minutes to get mad, to get even, to get *closer*. Twenty minutes to see Kevvy in a car from the past, gulping in the air, his eyes wide and terrified. Twenty minutes to imagine the look of Amee's mother. To imagine her eyes, like Kevvy's mum's, pale and distant. Her son wasn't enough to fill them with colour and joy; the medicine had to do that, the needle, the spoon, dripping hot. Twenty minutes on the skin too. Cracked, broken, scabbed, and dull. Twenty minutes to wonder if the new girl saw the impurities, or whether, like Kevvy, she just saw her mum. Twenty minutes to wonder whether Amee Florence made her own soup.

The hospital was just a mile away; it stood on the end of Gealblath's greener straights. The forest was either side of David, and it wasn't long before he was staring into it, scanning the trees like he might spot a cool blue Mini somewhere in the thicket. He didn't see a Mini, but he did see a boy. He was walking alone. The boy didn't wear a foil helmet; he didn't have a sheath or a sword, a spear or a shield. The boy had grown out of the world he once knew. The boy was walking towards the stream; he was near a bridge that used to be Troll Bridge but was now just a bridge. There were no trolls beneath it. There was no adventure. The boy bent over and started clawing at the wet pebbles, turning them over. The thing the boy was trying to find was not there anymore. But he settled for the skull of a squirrel. He held it between a thumb and forefinger, staring into the empty eyes. The boy frowned at the thing. He wanted the rabbit. He wanted to know what it looked like; he wanted to know how long it took. What did Kevvy's eyes look like now?

David snapped himself to attention, turning back to the road as the green of the trees steadily gave way to man-made structures again. He pulled back on the handle, slowing the bike down to a pedestrian speed as the road began to slope towards a single building. The hospital. This was the place where Kevvy had died. David remembered it well. Kevvy had been in a coma for four months when they decided to turn his off his life-support. The lingering warmth wasn't part of the town's identity back then, so the day Kevvy died, on the ninth of November 1968, was cold. It was wet. It was dark and painful. Now, Gealblath's warmth was a constant joke. It taunted David with memories of that day: the heat, the sweat, the panic, the smoke, the breathing. It reminded him of Kevvy's face, his fear. The way his mother had let him down. It whispered her name on the breeze and it kept her there, forever in his head, branded against his hot heart. Even the hospital looked the same. The darkness was never forgotten. It clung to everything, new and old, like the dark, salty stains which clambered up the hospital's walls, driven from the ocean which lay just over a mile from its doors.

David stopped as he got to the car park. The silence of the world around him unnerved the hairs on the back of his neck, and for a moment, he questioned his resolve. But the thought was gone as soon as it had arrived. His lips quivered, and his fingers shook as he turned the key and sent the Shadow to sleep. He pulled his leg over the leather and began pacing towards the hospital.

* * *

The waves lapped harder on the pebbles, easing the sea fog over the water and onto the beach. It clouded the air now, slipping under the door of the broken cabin and murking the glare of the car's headlamps. The car continued its low rumble and David and Amee waited for the door to open. But it never did. After another minute, the tyres of the vehicle turned, displacing the stones with a sharp crunch as the car swerved away from the cabin and began cruising down the road.

David's grip on the glass loosened, and he watched as Amee stood and clambered away to the other side of the room. He watched her for a few seconds, blinking against the splitting headache that was ringing hard against the walls of his skull.

'They're gone,' he whispered with a shudder. 'They're gone, Amee.' David could make out the trembling of her body as she glanced about the cabin, her eyes attempting to adjust to the darkness. 'You need to tell me now, Amee. You

160

need to tell me everything. I remember driving. I remember getting to the hospital. I was angry, I was going to do something...' David rubbed his hand up and down his throat. There was a pain there too, deep and uncomfortable, like something inside was demanding to be spat out. 'I was going to do something that felt out of my control, like no one could stop me. I was angry. What happened? Tell me what happened after that.'

A moment of silence passed, then Amee pushed a few strands of hair behind her ear with a shaking finger, her gaze finally landing on David.

'An ambush.'

* * *

The receptionist cowered in her chair, visibly disturbed by the state of the tweeded man across the desk.

'Florence. I want you to tell me where she is and do it now, otherwise I'll hold you just as accountable as everyone else. And you don't want that, hen, I can tell you. You don't want that.'

The receptionist pushed her white plastic glasses up her nose. 'There's no...' she faltered, gulping down what appeared to be a thick stick of gum. 'There is no Florence...'

'Look at me,' said David, leaning in close. 'Look into my eyes. Take a good long look. And then tell me I'm not dangerous.'

The receptionist hesitated, pulling her hands away from the computer. 'She's in Room C19, sir. Top floor.'

David removed his fists from her desk, ignoring the stares of waiting patients that were burning the back of his skull. 'Thank you. And don't bother phoning the police; they're on their way.'

He turned on his heel and paced over towards the double doors. *So long as George Aspin is as good as his word and not still snivelling in the corner of his office.* He looked up at the clock; the minute hand was just shy of the hour. Forty minutes had passed since the fight. *I've still got time*, he thought as he pushed the doors open. *Time enough anyway.*

By the time David had climbed the five flights of stairs to reach Room C19, his knuckles were hard enough to knock holes into the wood.

'Open up!' He pounded them against the door, watching as the paint began to peel and split. *Let it splinter, show the anger. Anger is good. Anything else could lead to mercy, and mercy is never justice. Never.* David raised his foot and kicked it into the door. 'If you don't open this door, I'll –'

'You'll what?' said a voice from behind him.

David turned to spot another man at the end of the corridor. He was tall, very tall, and he was leaning calmly with his shoulder against the wall. David stared for a second.

'I'm looking for someone,' he replied.

The tall man nodded, pushing himself off the wall to stride down the corridor. 'Lucky them,' he mused. 'I'm sure they'll be happy to see you.'

David craned his neck up to meet his gaze. He was bigger than him, for sure. But he could have been Al Capone for all David cared. He was getting through this door all the same. He hadn't come this far not to.

'You're going to open this door for me.'

The tall man grinned. He reached into his pocket and removed a copper key. 'Sure thing, chief.'

He placed the key into the hole beneath the handle, and pushed to reveal the room within.

Amee's hair was blowing in the wind which was rushing through the broken window. The waves were getting louder now, each one foaming towards the shore before retreating back like a beaten animal. She watched them for a bit before turning back to David.

'They could come back,' she said.

'But how did they know I was coming?' replied David.

The pain in his neck was getting worse now. It felt as if he'd been strangled from the inside out.

'Because I told them,' said Amee.

'How did you know?'

Amee swallowed. Outside, the clouds peeled back to reveal the half-moon, and Amee's eyes glittered in the silver light.

* * *

Room C19 was unlike any other in the hospital. Windowless, a bed on the far side, a couple of posters on each wall. There was a small television in one corner, a wooden bookshelf in the second, and a contraption that David had never seen before in the third, a metal coil twirled around a grey machine like a snake constricting its prey. The tall man stepped in too, then closed the door behind them.

'Here you go, Amee. You've got a visitor.'

The sheets of the bed rustled, and the head of the new girl emerged, her eyes blinking at David. She was pale, with a hospital gown tied loosely around her neck.

'Mr Cooper?' she said quietly.

'What the...?' muttered David.

'We can explain.' The voice came from behind him, and

David turned to find a black-suited, frizzy-haired woman making her way towards him. She was dragging a plastic chair with one hand. 'But it'd be better if you sat down.'

'What the hell is this?' David questioned.

The woman stared back at him. 'Why don't you sit down?'

'I'm not sitting down. I wanna know what's going on here.'

The suited woman sighed, dragging her fingers through the curls of her hair 'It'd be better if you sat down. You're confused, I can see that. But it's very simple, really. See, our little fishy told us you'd be coming, and our little fishy doesn't lie.'

Across the room, Amee sank lower in the bed. 'I'm sorry, Mr. Cooper,' she whispered.

'What is this?' David continued. 'Why is she here – is she sick? Have you done something to her?'

'She's not sick,' the woman replied. 'She's quite healthy.'

'Then why is she here?'

He stared at the woman in front of him. If she was Amee's mum, she didn't look like a drug addict. The eyes were alive, the skin unblemished. She stood rooted to the floor. She didn't waver; she didn't wobble. She was completely there.

'Why didn't the receptionist downstairs want to tell me you were up here?' asked David.

'Because I told her not to. I own this hospital, Mr Cooper. Everyone inside this place listens to me. The top floor doesn't get visitors. The top floor is off limits to everyone without permission.'

'But... but why...?'

'Look, I could explain the details. I could tell you everything, if I wanted. But I'm of the opinion that you know too much already.'

David gaped at her. What had once been hot, thick rage was now seeping out of him, like someone had put a pin in the balloon and let all the hot air out. The woman could see that too. It was like those eyes could look *inside* him. She could tell she was on top. She could see that she had him. She lifted her other hand.

'But we have a thing for that.'

With a grin, the tall man walked over to the contraption in the corner. He grabbed the metallic tube and unravelled it back across the room. He placed it in the woman's waiting hand.

'What the hell is that?' David breathed.

'This?' the woman replied. 'This is a cure. See, before I came to Gealblath, I worked in a different hospital. An asylum. Back then, practices with patients were primitive. People still didn't understand mental illness; they just wanted them to get better. They wanted everything to be easy. An easy patient is a good patient, after all.' She took a step closer. 'They invented this. Something to instigate a sort of selective amnesia. They thought that if the patients could forget their trauma, then they might be able to recover. Not fully, of course. But enough to become just that. Easy.'

The new girl dipped her head, like she knew what was about to happen.

'It didn't get past the trial stage,' the woman continued. 'People thought it was too cold, too brutal, too uncertain. But not me. I always believed it could be quite effective.'

One more step and the woman began to smile. She was playing with him, David knew. She was toying with him, like a snake with a mouse, ready to unfurl and strike while the heart was still hot and pounding.

'So like I said,' she finished, 'it'd be better if you sat down.'

David yelped, a sharp spike of pain surging through each shoulder as the tall man squeezed him into the chair from behind. A thick set of fingers curled around his head and pulled it back so his eyes were on the ceiling. Then everything happened so quickly. A high-pitched yell erupted from the bed in the corner, and David jolted as the nozzle of the tube was shoved down his throat, sliding so far that it felt as if it was heading straight for his stomach.

'GRRRGHHHH!'

David squirmed, unable to do anything but watch as the woman pushed the tube further, blood and mucus spluttering wildly from his nose and mouth.

'Keep calm,' she said. 'Keep calm. Let it breathe for you.'

David choked again. The protestations of his body were getting weaker and weaker. The world around him started to fade. The tube poured sharp, cold air down into his system, and he spluttered again, tasting the blood merged with the saliva in his mouth. He felt like he was swallowing liquid metal. Then he blinked twice. And the world went full dark.

* * *

David spat a bloody puddle onto the floor, then he wiped it up with a finger and held it before his eyes.

'They call it the coil,' said Amee, her voice still shuddering through every breath. 'It puts you out for two days.'

'What the hell was it?' David swallowed back the pain in his throat, feeling the ghost of the coil that had been shoved inside.

'I don't know how it works. I mean, I don't understand. But it makes you forget.'

David pulled himself up to his knees, trying desperately to keep his breathing under control. His head still roared with pain. His temples were throbbing like they'd been pressed with hot lead.

'But why would they use it on me?'

'Because you were coming to save me.'

'Okay, but who the hell are you, Amee? Why would they do that to me because of you? What makes you so important?'

Amee's blue eyes darkened a bit, just as they had when they were in Room C19. 'You wouldn't believe me if I told you.'

'Well, you're going to tell me.'

A few seconds passed. The new girl clenched the windowsill, her face gaunt and pale in the blackness.

'I can do something other people can't. I don't know how, and I don't know why. I can just do it.'

'What? What is it – are you fucking Spider-Man? What the hell is it?'

'I can see dead people.'

A brief silence passed. David exhaled loudly.

'Holy Christ. And you expect me to believe that?'

'It's the truth. It's the reason they did that to you, and it's the same reason I knew you were coming.'

'And how is that? Because you haven't actually said. How the hell did you know?'

'I was told. By my friend.'

'And who is your friend?'

A loud wave crashed outside as she let go of the windowsill. Amee took a deep breath.

'I'll show you.'

* * *

'Open your eyes.'

The world came to light again. A funny sort of light, like everything was jumbled together, knotted and clumped like a screwed-up ball of string. It only took ten seconds for things to separate though. And Amee came into focus.

'Open your eyes,' she repeated.

With a yank, she pulled the last of the coil from David's mouth and he jumped from the bed, throwing up a load of blood and vomit onto the rubber floor. Amee retreated backwards, grimacing as a few dots of the splatter sprayed her shins.

'We have to be quick,' she said.

David looked up at the room around him, his neck rocking to and fro, as if it was about to snap under the weight of his skull. It was a different room to the one before. No posters. No television. Just a bed and a blank space.

'Whhhuu…'

'Come on, Mr Cooper, we have to be quick. They'll be coming. We have to go and we have to go now.'

She pulled David onto his feet, and he staggered, his eyes spinning wildly.

'I'm gonna…'

'No, don't pass out, don't do that!'

David fell to his knees, both hands pressed against each temple. 'I can't, I can't, oh shit.' He bent over and vomited again. Out of the corner of his eye, he saw Amee sprint over to the doorway and look into the corridor.

'We need to be quick,' she repeated, almost to herself.

'Where am I?'

'In the hospital. Room C20. You've been here since yesterday. But we've got to get out. I've got to save you.' Amee ran back over to him and yanked on his tweed jacket.

'No,' he moaned, pushing her arm away from him. 'Tell me, tell me what happened.'

For the third time, David bent over and retched, but only

a few droplets of blood were making their way out now. He'd spilled all he had.

'There's no time. It won't take them long to find out the keys are missing! Please, we have to go!'

She pulled on his hand again, and David clambered to his feet, both knees wobbling like a newborn animal's.

'Okay, alright. Hold on, I...' One foot fell over the other and David crashed into the wall.

'Oh,' Amee said, a look of hopelessness etched on her face. 'And you need to drive.'

The next thing David knew, he was staggering down a dimly lit corridor, the new girl pulling him along. David heard her whisper under her breath.

'Come on. Just hold him. Be brave now.'

They turned a corner, coming to Room C19. The faint sound of an old television was coming from inside.

'What is that?' David croaked.

'I put it on before I went to get you,' Amee replied. 'So if they got close, they wouldn't think I'd left.'

They stopped for a moment as David caught his breath. The pain in his throat was just starting to ease up a little, but the pain in his head throbbed harder, burning the walls of his skull like a hot fire.

'*Ghostbusters*,' Amee muttered. She turned towards the door and closed her eyes, her breaths long and deep, as if she was resting in the comfort of the tinny voices.

The respite didn't last long however. It only took a few moments before Amee's eyes opened again, and the world around David changed entirely. The scream was piercing. It filled every atom of his being, shooting down the ridge of his spine to shiver his soul.

'What the hell?!' he shouted.

But he saw exactly what was wrong before he had even finished. The tall man was at the end of the corridor behind them, his face a deep red and his eyes flecked with a vivid ferocity.

'No you didn't,' he said through gritted teeth.

Then he began pacing towards them, and Amee grabbed the tweeded man beside her.

'RUN!' she yelled.

And David didn't need to be told twice. The two of them sprinted forward, David trying desperately not to fall flat on his face. *One step after the other! That's all it is! Just one after the other!* He heard the tall man yell over the ringing in his ears.

'Amee, what are you doing?!'

They turned another corner.

'They're close,' Amee panted. 'The stairs, they're close!'

David coughed up another dollop of blood, wiping it away with a sleeve while keeping all of his focus on his footing.

'No stairs,' he panted. 'Where's the lift?'

'It doesn't go up here. No lift. Only stairs. Here! To the right! Now!'

They turned to the right and came up to a stairwell.

'AMEE!' the tall man screamed again.

David turned to find him just a couple of paces away, spittle falling from his chin and one hand curled into a claw, reaching out for the neck of the new girl. Without meaning to, David stumbled backward and hit the opposite wall, his spine sending something hard and round clattering to the floor beside him. The tall man grabbed Amee's neck and pulled her off her feet.

'You little bitch!'

David looked around, looking for something, *anything*,

to fight back with. It didn't take him long to find it. Without a second thought, David reached down for the fire extinguisher, swinging it fast through the air to hit the tall man in the temple. A gargled moan came in response. The tall man crumbled, his gigantic body falling towards the floor so fast that it felt like a barrage of dust and debris would rise in his stead. Instead, there was just a grunt. And then a few seconds of nothingness passed.

Amee and David stood there, breathing heavily and staring at the motionless body.

'We're alright,' panted David.

Amee stumbled onto the first step of the stairwell, her eyes shut and her bones shuddering. 'Don't be stupid,' she said back. 'We're not alright. We won't ever be alright again.'

David knelt down, rubbing against his throbbing head. He was trying desperately to piece together what had just happened, but he couldn't do it. The pain was too strong.

'What happened?' he asked Amee.

'We need to get out of here. As quickly as possible. We need to hide.'

David looked at the stairs. For a moment, his world got fuzzy again, and he felt around his throat. 'What happened to me?'

'Mr Cooper, where are we going to hide?'

David wavered. The stairs realigned. He fought off sleep and picked Amee up from the floor.

* * *

The moon was now a silver stone in the night sky, its glow casting a strange glaze on the beds and cupboards within the cabin. The new girl walked to the centre, tiny crunches of splintered glass echoing her every step. She stopped in front of David.

'I'm going to close my eyes for a second,' she said.

'What are you talking about?' said David.

'It's easier for me if I close my eyes.'

The wind outside continued to blow through the broken window, rattling a pair of handmade wooden hearts hanging from the wall. David peered up towards them, watching as they rapped on the wood, the constant drumming matching the beat of his own heart. He looked back at the new girl. Her eyes were closed to the world now; her body was swaying on the spot. She almost gave the impression that she was calm. But this was betrayed by the violent shaking of her hands that was clearly recognisable in the moonlight. A few more seconds passed. For a moment, David came close to shaking the girl to life again. But just as the thought was contemplated, Amee's eyes opened once more. She gazed over to the left of the cabin, a small but warm smile appearing on her face.

'Hello,' she said.

David pushed himself up onto the balls of his feet and clenched his fists. 'Who the –' he began, but he stopped when he realised there was no one there.

Amee lifted her hand to him. 'It's okay, it's alright; it's just a boy.'

David stared into the dark, the breeze whirling up around him once more. The wooden hearts rattled on the nail.

'Who?' he muttered.

Amee took a breath. 'His name is Charlie. Charlie Cooper. He died ten years ago on the way to the bus stop. And now he's my friend.'

12

THREE PAST MIDNIGHT

It was a small mercy that Mr Cooper had chosen the beach as a place to hide, Amee considered as she dipped her urine-soaked pants into the freezing seawater. She had never been to the beach before, yet it was here that she felt most at home. More at home than she had ever felt at the hospital anyhow. She squeezed her pants, watching as the seawater dripped from the fabric, taking her piss and bits of red and green seaweed with it. It felt good to do this. It felt free. Even more so than Gealblath Secondary School. Her mother had sent her there so she would feel normal, feel like a kid again, probably in the hope that she would become more submissive during their lessons. *How much is she regretting that, I wonder?*

She looked up at the town of Derling far across the water. It was funny to look at it from this distance. There were no people. No life. None to be seen anyhow. There was only a picture. First, the large mountain of green trees, rolling high into the sky. Then, to the right, a hundred red-brick houses stacked on top of each other. To the right of them, you could see neighbourhoods, white and brown dots spotted about the greenery in tiny clusters, like Derling had a skin problem, like you could apply a cream to them and they'd fade out. Amee sighed, leaning back on her hands. The picture was blocky and grey. The surface of things. With nothing behind or beneath. But then, Amee knew there was plenty beneath. Far more than anyone could believe.

'Aren't you cold?' asked Charlie, his blonde hair lying flat and motionless in the sea breeze.

'I don't get cold,' replied Amee. 'Not easily.'

Another wave washed over her hospital gown, and Amee turned her head towards the cabin behind her. It stood small, almost decrepit. Nothing compared to the power plant chimney which towered over the beach half a mile in the distance. The place had been unused for years now. It was just a cluster of cement, with that tower in the middle sprouting up into the sky. Brown from the base and white up top, the chimney stood like an ancient monument of a cigarette, dark and ominous too, with the windows near the chutes making it look like it had eyes.

'I miss the cold,' said Charlie.

Amee turned back to him. 'Is he up yet? Your dad?'

Charlie shrugged. 'What will you tell him if he is?'

'There's nothing more to tell.'

Amee put her pants into the water once again, lapping up the water before squeezing it out drop by drop. That was true. She had told Mr Cooper everything last night. Every lesson, every examination. Descriptions of Charlie, down to the birthmark on his knee, the mole on his right hand, things that she couldn't have known unless she was telling the truth. She'd left him alone to process it. He may not have had any sleep at all.

'And what about Marty?' asked Charlie.

'I put the note in the shoebox, just before I went to Room C20. So long as he opens it, he'll be there. I know he will.'

The sound of wood on stone came from behind, and Amee turned to see Mr Cooper standing half hunched in the doorway of the cabin. With a deep breath, she stood, shoving her salty pants into her pocket.

'Wish me luck,' she said, but Charlie wasn't there anymore. She'd stopped seeing him as soon as she'd heard Mr Cooper. Her legs began to shake as she started up towards the cabin.

The teacher was sitting in the corner when Amee stepped inside, his fingers still pressed against his temple. A few seconds passed before he spoke.

'Is it all the time?'

The words lingered in the salt-clogged air, and Amee felt her legs shake even harder. She clenched the windowsill.

'Is what all the time?' she replied.

'Ghosts. The ghosts. Can you see them all the time?' The teacher cracked an ugly, maniacal smile when Amee didn't answer. 'You can see ghosts. Ghosts in Scotland. Like the stories. You read a lot.'

'This isn't like the stories. This is different. And they're not ghosts.'

'You said you could see dead people.'

'I can, but they're not ghosts. I wouldn't call them ghosts.'

'Then what do you call them? Zombies?'

'I call them people. Like you and me.'

Mr Cooper lowered his hands towards his beard and Amee noticed that he was shivering too. 'Charlie isn't people anymore,' he said. 'Charlie is dead.'

'If you could see him...'

Amee looked at the teacher, only now spotting the hopelessness in his eyes. Charlie had been gone for ten years for him, she realised. Ten years of nothingness. Ink on the card, thoughts in the head. To be told all of this now, by a girl he hardly knew – it was a wonder he hadn't shut her up with a well-placed fist. Perhaps he didn't have the energy anymore.

'And you? You can see him?' asked Mr Cooper.

'Only when I want to. I can see anyone when I want to.'

Mr Cooper stared down at the shoes on his feet. He was sitting like a child listening to a teacher telling the class a story. Amee bit her lip, contemplating her words carefully. *I guess I have to be the teacher then.* She lifted her hand off the windowsill, like a girl re-evaluating her fear of heights up a tall tree. But the violent tremors had her clutching the branch again. *Still scared. But there's a bravery in fear, I know. I'm scared because I'm facing something that frightens me. But I'm facing it all the same.* Amee took another breath.

'It's like the dark,' she began. 'Everything's like the dark for me. When we close our eyes everything is all black, but it's not just that. There's colour as well, patterns in between the darkness. At first, they're hard to see, but the longer you wait and the harder you hold, the brighter and more colourful they get. That's what it feels like. They're always there, the dead people, but I have to really want to look at them. I have to wait, and hold, and then I can see. I saw Charlie not too long ago. I met him at school, and he became my friend.'

Mr Cooper fidgeted, visibly attempting to process all of this information. 'And... and did...'

The teacher stuttered. Amee could tell he'd been waiting to ask this question for a long time. Perhaps all night. She'd been waiting too.

'And did he say what happened? When he went, I mean. When Charlie disappeared. Did he say?' He just about got the words out through the tears that were choking his throat.

Amee took a second, her hand holding the sill so hard that the splinters were beginning to edge against her palm. She winced against their warning shot. *Any more and you'll get hurt. Loosen up, let go. You call this facing your fears? How about you face them with the stabilisers off?* Amee sighed, letting the splinters do their work.

'He doesn't know. He says all he can remember is walking to the bus. Then he saw a shape. But he doesn't know who it was. Man or woman. He can't remember.'

Upon hearing this, the tweeded man shuddered, looking down at his fingers to stare intensely at the wrinkles around the joints. Then Amee took a moment, bit her lip, and let go of the sill.

She leant down and said, 'But he knows you didn't do it, Mr Cooper. He knows that.'

A moment passed. A nice moment, Amee thought. Like it was ten years in the making. Then Mr Cooper broke down in tears and curled into a ball.

* * *

Between midday and four o'clock, the quietest place in all of Gealblath Secondary School was undoubtedly the changing rooms. Amee liked to go there sometimes. When the shrieks got too loud and the looks got too much, she would hide amongst the shorts and shirts, some muddy, some wet, most stinking. She'd eat her peanut butter sandwiches and she'd simply stare. It was nice to be alone for a moment, to soak up the quiet air and pass it through the system, like a sedative.

She'd been at Gealblath School for two weeks, and she was glad that her mum had finally allowed her to go. She liked to get away from the hospital. But sometimes she had to get away from school too. So the occasional respite, no matter how brief, was just nice.

Today, she sat amongst Lily Tigerson's things, her buttocks going a bit numb against the wooden bench and her fingers rubbing at her toes. Her shoes were too tight and they were beginning to send irritating pulsing pains into the bones of her feet. She breathed, revelling in the calmness. If only it could have lasted a little longer. Only two more minutes of serenity passed before Amee heard a rush of footsteps from behind the door. They were followed swiftly by three high-pitched giggles and a scream of, 'HE KISSED ME! HE ACTUALLY KISSED ME!'

The door swung open and the three teenage girls charged in.

'Give us the details! Give us all the details!'

'Was he good? I've always thought he'd be really good!'

'Daisy's had wet dreams about it.'

'Shut up, Evelyn, I haven't! I've had dreams, but they've all been dry.'

'You wake up with a monsoon between your legs and don't you deny it.'

'Shut the hell up; this is about Tessa. Tell us everything!'

'Yeah, we need to know everything!'

The girl in the middle held up her hands. Her name was Tessa Thompson and she was Amee's least favourite person in school.

'I'll tell you everything, but...'

Tessa stopped, staring towards the corner of the room. Amee tried to conceal her face behind Lily Tigerson's kit, but it didn't work. Tessa's eyes widened with delight.

'Look who it is,' she said excitedly. 'The new kid!'

'What the hell is she doing here?' said Evelyn. 'She doesn't do any sport.'

'Maybe she's found a quiet place to stroke herself.' Tessa walked forward, a sly grin spreading fast across her face. 'Well, new kid? Were you stroking yourself?'

Amee didn't respond.

'You don't talk much, do you?' Daisy piped up, twiddling her ginger locks.

'She doesn't like talking,' said Tessa. 'She just likes sitting and being weird. That's your thing, isn't it? Being weird. I bet she thinks the boys like it. Trust me, new girl, it won't work. If you want to know how to get boys, ask me. I just kissed Peter Dunchan.'

Amee had the feeling Tessa would make sure the whole of Gealblath School was aware of this fact by the end of the day.

'Well?' said Evelyn. 'Aren't you gonna say anything?'

'Peter Dunchan,' Tessa repeated, as if Amee hadn't heard the name properly.

'She probably doesn't know what kissing is,' laughed Daisy. 'Not real kissing. She's probably only kissed her mother.'

'Yuck!' Evelyn squealed.

'Do you even know who Peter Dunchan is?' Tessa moved closer, putting her face right up to Amee's.

Amee stared back. As a matter of fact, she did know who Peter Dunchan was. She'd never talked to him, but she'd exchanged a few words with his dead grandfather. He used to work at the school as a gardener. He tended to stay close to Peter now, incessantly watching him with a crinkled gaze and a disapproving raised eyebrow. Amee smirked slightly, imagining Peter's grandfather having to watch Peter and Tessa smack their lips together. Her least favourite person in school started to frown.

'What are you laughing about? Something funny, new girl?' With her thumb and forefinger, Tessa gave Amee a flick on the chin. 'What's so funny about me and Peter Dunchan?' She flicked her again, and Amee finally looked up into Tessa's eyes.

'You,' she said quietly.

'What?' Tessa stopped flicking.

'You're the funny part. No one saw that coming. Maybe not even Peter. You sure he remembered his glasses today?'

There was silence. Tessa's friends dropped their jaws halfway to the floor.

'No way...' Evelyn whispered.

Tessa leant in closer, her lips curling back to reveal her gritted teeth. 'You think that's funny?' she spat.

For a second, it looked like she was about to hit Amee, but then Daisy grabbed her by the shoulder.

'Leave her, Tessa. She's not worth it.'

Tessa paused. Then, after a few deep breaths, she glanced down and spotted Amee's bare feet.

'Well, new girl, I've got something funnier.'

In a flash, Tessa bent over, swiped the shoes off the floor, and held them aloft in the air. Amee jumped up from the bench, attempting in vain to snatch them back.

Tessa jeered, 'The new girl wants her shoes back? Daisy, cover her eyes, let's have a game of hide and seek.'

Laughing a little like a hyena, Daisy grabbed Amee by the shoulders and wrapped a hand around her face. Her vision went black.

'Where shall we put them, Evelyn?'

Amee heard Tess and Evelyn race around the changing room, searching frantically for the least convenient place for her footwear. They found it after a few seconds, somewhere up high, most probably, given that Evelyn shouted 'Great throw!' in her most blatant display of kiss-arsery yet. With a 'WOOP!' Daisy let go of her, and Amee watched the three girls come together and high five.

'Come on, girls,' said Tessa. 'We'll talk about Peter somewhere else. Give the new girl some peace and quiet.'

Tessa gave Amee one last flick for luck, then led her two giggling girlfriends towards the door of the changing rooms. When the door closed, Amee closed her eyes, waiting until she could see the colours begin to form in the dark. When she opened them, she wasn't alone anymore.

The boy was beside the pegs, hidden slightly by a swimming suit, in the same way that Amee had been, and he was smiling. That was the way it tended to be whenever Amee saw someone new. It was like they knew she could see them, or they could sense it anyhow. They didn't tend to ask questions or act surprised. She simply saw them and they simply saw her back.

'Where did they put them?' she asked immediately.

The boy pointed near the showers, where rows of lockers were propped up one after the other, all of them at least three times the size of Amee. Her shoes were nestled on top, completely out of reach.

'Great.' Amee sighed bitterly and sat back down on one of the benches, elbows on knees and her chin balanced in the curve of her palms.

The boy's features began to come into a firmer focus. He was around her age, blonde-haired, blue-eyed, white-skinned.

He wore the Gealblath School uniform, with brightly polished shoes on his feet.

'If I could get those for you, then I would,' he said after a few seconds.

'It's alright,' replied Amee. 'I don't care. They're too small for me, anyway.'

'Doesn't give them the right to throw them up there. Just so you know, I would get them. If I could. My name's Charlie, by the way –'

'I think I should leave this place,' Amee interrupted. 'I think this was a mistake.'

'You think what was a mistake?'

'This. All of this. I don't think I'm ever going to fit in.'

'Fit in with who?'

'The other kids in this school. I'm not used to this. I don't think they'll ever like me.'

Charlie furrowed his eyebrows. He gave the impression he was leaning on the wall behind him, but Amee knew he wasn't. Not really.

'They will. There will always be someone who likes you. You've just got to find them. It took me a whole year to find my friends.'

'When did you go here?'

'Oh. I'm not sure. It's... I'm not sure.'

The blue-eyed boy swayed, and Amee nodded in understanding. She'd done enough lessons in the hospital to understand why he'd struggled with the question. Queries of time were always hard for dead people to compute, especially if they'd been in their purgatory for so long. It wasn't the same as living. Things just happened around them and they were there for it. They didn't live it in the same way that living people did. They didn't *experience* things.

'That's okay,' she said.

Charlie smiled again. 'It took me ages,' he said. 'You'll find a friend, though, someone who might help you get your shoes back.'

Amee smiled too. She decided that she liked Charlie. But then again, she liked a lot of dead people. It was the living she had a problem with.

'So, what do you...' Amee stopped as soon as she saw Charlie jolt slightly in front of her. He peered up at the ceiling as if he was scared it would cave in. 'What is it?' she asked.

Charlie gazed around the room. 'I thought I heard something.'

'What did you hear?'

She asked the question, but Amee was pretty sure she already knew the answer. She'd spoken to lots of dead people. And lots of them thought they heard something. Before Charlie could say anything, the lunch bell began to clatter behind the walls. Amee turned, a heavy stone sinking inside her chest as she realised she would have to rejoin her living classmates with no shoes on. She turned back to the dead boy.

'I'll talk to you again. Wish me luck.'

But his features were already beginning to fade, and by the time she blinked, he was gone completely.

* * *

Amee sat in silence. There were no waves now. The tide had made its way out towards Derling to reveal the grey sands under the water. There were no stars either. The clouds hung low in the sky as if they were threatening something. Maybe rain, perhaps a storm, but definitely something. Four candles lit the cabin. Three strong, one barely flickering. They made the shadows move and put them all in the wrong place. Amee sighed, pricking up her ears to hear the road behind the beach, waiting patiently for the hum of an engine. They were overdue now. Surely overdue. Gealblath Secondary School was no more than a ten-minute drive away and yet the time was thirty minutes past midnight. That was late. Curiously late. Worryingly late.

She squeezed at the nail of her thumb until it hurt, trying to make her body understand the stress in her head. Amee's mother was out there now, she knew. Somewhere in the night. Both her and the tall man. But she tried not to think about it. She'd got away from the hospital, and she would never have to see her mother or the tall man again. Although, of course, Amee knew that wasn't true. Something deep inside her said that she would see them again. Before the end of all this, she would see them, and she would have to live with that.

A rumble sounded from the road outside and Amee sat forward, her heart picking up its pace.

'That's him,' a voice said, and she turned to find Charlie Cooper standing on the other side of the room. His pale features were easily visible despite the darkness. She hadn't meant to see or hear him. In that way, he was different to the other dead people she saw. But then, maybe Amee always kept herself open to Charlie. Even when she didn't mean to.

'Is Marty there too?' she asked.

Charlie nodded. 'Why is he here again?' he asked as the engine of the bike cut out. 'You know it's risky, you know it's not –'

'Because I want him here. Because I have to say goodbye.'

A slight knock, and then the door opened, the tweeded

man entering with a bag on his shoulder, swiftly followed by Marty Evans.

'Holy shit, Amee!'

Marty stared at her with a smile, and Amee couldn't help but return it. It was strange, but seeing him for the first time in just over a week caused a flutter inside her. It was like she hadn't seen him in a whole year, like she had really missed him.

'I knew you were in the hospital. I knew –'

'I knew you were there too.'

Mr Cooper placed the bag down and sat, wiping fiercely at his beard.

'What took you so long?' asked Amee.

She already felt more confident with Mr Cooper now that Marty was there. It was like he was a source of strength, a friend to rely on in all this.

'I had to go into the school,' the teacher replied. 'I had to get something.'

'What's going on?' asked Marty. 'What is all this? Because Mr Cooper –'

'I'm sorry,' she interrupted. 'Did he tell you?'

'I told him,' Mr Cooper intervened. 'But he didn't believe me.'

'It's true, Marty. He's telling the truth.'

'But that's – but it can't be true.' Marty gaped at both of them, as if he was trying to work out whether all of this was one big trick.

'I'm sorry,' Amee said again, and then there was silence for a while. Charlie remained in the corner, his eyes darting between them all.

'You can see dead people,' said Marty. It wasn't a question, so Amee didn't nod. She just stared at him, fighting a strange impulse to kiss him on the cheek. 'And what...' Marty hesitated. 'What are they like?'

'What do you mean?'

'Are they still like us? Or, like, you know, like *Ghostbusters* or something?'

'No. Not like *Ghostbusters*. They're like you and me.'

'See-through?'

'No. Like you and me.'

Marty swallowed. 'So, so that's what happens. When we die...'

Mr Cooper had been sitting motionless, but at this point he jolted up, staring at Amee as he waited for her answer.

'No,' replied Amee solemnly. 'No, this isn't what happens. It's not meant to be like this.'

'What do you mean?'

'It's meant to be something else. Something warm. That's what they say. They say they can feel a kind of warmth, like it's behind a door that's shut. They're stuck. Stuck between this life and the next one, in a sort of mid-space.'

A car passed behind the cabin, and the three of them froze, peering through the window, waiting for the engine to fade into nothingness.

'It's like the road,' Amee continued. 'The people I can see, the dead people, they're not supposed to be here. They've told me. But something is stopping them from moving on. They're on one side of the road, but they can't cross over to the other.'

'What do they mean, warmth?' asked Mr Cooper. 'What's on the other side?'

'I don't know. They won't know either until they cross. They just say it's somewhere warm.'

'And why can't they cross over?'

'They don't know that either.'

'Do they know anything?'

Amee bit her lip, squeezing at her thumb again. 'One thing. A sound. One they can all hear.'

All of a sudden, Charlie became more vivid, and Amee glanced at him, seeing the fear in his face.

'What kind of sound?' asked Marty.

'This is why I'm here,' replied Amee. 'This is why I escaped the hospital, my mother, everything. Something's talking to the dead people, like a voice they can all hear. I think...' She looked down at Mr Cooper, then up at Charlie, the son that he couldn't see. 'I think it could help them.'

The breeze picked up outside and the air moved around them, rattling the wooden hearts against the wall again. Amee stood in the chill before taking a step forward.

* * *

The girl was not pretty, Amee had to admit. Her nose was hooked, poking out from the centre of her face in a 'D' shape, and she had a cleft lip. One cheek was rosy, the other not so, and her hair was a boring shade of dark brown, with grey streaks already beginning to stream through it. She couldn't have been more than twenty-one years old. Amee sat in her usual position, her mother in front of her, with that thick burgundy notebook in her right hand and a fountain pen in her left. The ink dripped from the nib, dotting black holes into the page below.

'Can you say it again for me, Olivia?' asked Amee.

The girl scratched her temple, then moved to the top of the scalp. She itched roughly, irritably, like she might have nits. The session had been going on for an hour, and Amee was getting impatient. A few more seconds passed, then Olivia bit at her split lip before obliging.

'*When I think of you, I think of the ocean. If you're scared that the green monster is coming, come find me. I'm in the house on the cliff waiting for you.*' She talked slowly, like she was reading off a distant autocue. '*Find me and we can cross together. Into a better place. Into a warmer place. But you must find me.*' She finished, looking back at Amee as if in hope of some kind of reward. Instead, Amee recited the words back to her mother, who followed each one with the tip of her pen.

'Okay,' she said, running a hand through her curls. 'Okay, let's move on.'

'*When I think of you,*' said Amee, '*I think of the ocean.* That's usually how it ends, but she didn't finish with that. Why did she finish differently?'

'She didn't. Sometimes they hear bits, but it's always the same. There's no more to it; we'll move on.'

'But this is important,' Amee interrupted. 'It's getting louder. That's what they're saying: it's always getting louder. We shouldn't just move on, Mum.'

Her mother rubbed her thumb and forefinger together, spreading smudges of black ink between the cracks of her skin. 'Ask her when she died,' she said.

Amee sighed, shuffling irritably in her seat. She went to turn, but her mother grabbed her hand before she could.

'Don't sigh at me, little fishy. Unless you want me to call him. He's been so looking forward to seeing his girl, you know. It's been a whole week.'

A moment passed, small and quiet. Then Amee nodded. With a deep breath, she turned to look at the ugly girl once more, trying not to grimace at her lip as she did so. Olivia spoke first.

'Can you help –'

'Can you tell me when you died?' said Amee before the girl could finish. 'I know it's hard, but we need to know. Tell us when you died, and then we'll be done.'

* *|*

Small patters of rain began to speckle the windows that weren't broken. Mr Cooper stood up from his chair, frowning at Amee Florence.

'What's that supposed to mean?' he rasped.

'I don't know,' replied Amee. 'I don't even know if it makes sense.'

'I'll tell you. It doesn't.'

He walked over to the window, staring out at the tide. The clouds still hung low in the sky. The night was blacker than black.

'But it could be their only hope.'

'How can that help them?' asked Marty, and Amee turned to him, tucking her mousy hair behind one ear.

'The voice talks about crossing over. If we could find the source…'

'In the house on the cliff?' he asked.

Amee nodded. Outside, the rain started hitting harder, rattling the tin of the cabin roof like thunder inside a cloud.

'And what's the green monster?' Marty continued. 'What does that mean?'

Amee looked over at Charlie. He remained in the corner of the room, the only one who wasn't dimmed in the shadows. 'We don't know,' she said. 'But whatever it is, it could be coming. That's why we need to find the house as quickly as possible.'

Marty cleared his throat. 'Have any of them seen it? The dead people, I mean?'

'No,' replied Amee.

'Maybe that's why they're here. Maybe whatever this green monster is, it trapped them. Maybe it wants to keep them here to... I dunno... feed off them or something?'

Mr Cooper scowled at him. 'Jesus Christ, Marty, she said this wasn't *Ghostbusters*. If you're gonna come up with stuff like that, go home and watch movies, don't say it here. Grow up.'

Marty's red face was just about visible in the candlelight. He was clearly embarrassed, but in Amee's opinion, what he had said was not an outrageous possibility. Some of the dead people had claimed to see something strange out of the corner of their eyes. They'd heard the stamping of feet, the grinding of teeth. One of the dead had even insisted he was being chased. Chased by something large, something hungry, and something green. Amee shivered at the thought of it. Nightmares, her mother had told her. People could be very suggestive. Her mum believed that if they were told there was a green monster, then they would see a green monster. It didn't make it real. But still, Amee shivered.

'So tell me,' said Mr Cooper, 'you're going to find a house on a cliff?'

'If it can help them cross, yes.'

'And you know where to look for this place?'

'No.' Amee shuffled her feet. She knew how stupid that was, but it was true. *I have to tell the truth, no matter how crazy it might sound.*

'So that's it. Nowhere to start and no idea where you'll

end up. That's what you've got going?'

'If it can save them, if we can find it and bring them to the source of that voice, then I've got to try. Maybe that's…' She faltered. 'Maybe that's why I can see them. Perhaps I was always meant to help.'

Mr Cooper smirked, a hint of anger glistening in his eyes. 'That's a nice story.'

'I don't know,' continued Amee. 'But I need to do it. My mum would never even let me try. All she cares about is seeing them, learning about them. She never cared about the voice because she never cared about letting them go. That's why I've got to do this on my own.'

'But not completely on your own,' said Marty. 'If you're going somewhere, going to this place, I'll come too. That's why you brought me here, isn't it?'

Amee smiled sadly. 'No.'

'No?'

'I didn't bring you here to help me. I brought you here so I could say goodbye.'

Amee couldn't help herself. Without thinking, she leapt forward and caught Marty in a hug, squeezing his shoulders together and nestling her chin into his neck.

'Thank you, Marty,' she said, her voice slightly muffled against his collar.

'Thank you for what?'

'For being my friend.'

At first, Marty let her hug him, but then he pushed her away. 'No way. I'm coming. I want to help. Whatever this is, I want to help you.'

Amee shook her head. 'You can't come. There are people who'll be following me. You don't know what they're like. You don't know what they can do.'

'That's exactly why I should come. You can't do it on your own.'

'Marty, this isn't a film. This isn't *Ghostbusters*; it's not *The Hobbit*.'

'Why are you saying that? I know that. I don't want to be a hero, I just want to...' He stopped, swallowing back whatever he was going to say next. 'I just want to help you.'

Amee cupped his cheek. 'You can't help me.'

At this point, the tweeded teacher leant back on the chair, the old and splintered wood creaking. 'And what about me, then?' he asked.

Amee turned to him, considering her words carefully. 'He's your son. He's there in the mid-space. I know him. If you want to help...'

Mr Cooper put his hands on his knees and then, quite slowly, he reached down and opened the bag beside him. What he pulled out was hard to recognise at first. It was round and white, with two gaping holes carved into the front and a long lightning-esque crack tracing its way along the middle. Amee squinted at it, trying to take it in.

'Do you know what this is?' asked Mr Cooper. 'This is Charlie. My Charlie. I found him a year ago now. Alone and cold. This is what was left of him. The real him.'

'A skull?!' exclaimed Marty.

Amee turned to see the dead boy staring back at her.

'I'm sorry,' he whispered. 'I didn't know how to tell you.'

'My son...' Mr Cooper stroked the skull, then traced the crack with his finger, finishing as he reached the row of teeth.

'But how do you know it's him?' asked Marty.

'I know my son. I know his face.' Mr Cooper stroked the

skull again. 'What other kid has gone missing in Gealblath?'

'Where did you find that?' Amee cut in, and Mr Cooper glared at her.

'It doesn't matter where I found it. The fact is, this is my son.' He held the skull tightly, then bent over and placed it back into the bag. 'This. This is my son...'

A moment passed. Then, in a flash, Mr Cooper jumped up from his chair, grabbed Amee by the shirt and flung her up against the wall so hard that the whole cabin shook. A sharp shot of pain streaked through her spine and Amee screamed, clamping her eyes shut. All she could hear was Marty's shouting.

'What are you doing?! What the hell are you doing?!'

She peeked and saw the teacher's face up close to hers, a bubble of spit tracing down into his beard. Behind him, Charlie disappeared into nothing.

'MY SON!'

'I'm not –' Amee choked out, but she couldn't finish.

Marty grabbed Mr Cooper, trying desperately to pull his arms away from her.

'My son is dead, but whoever did this, whoever killed him, they're still alive!'

'He doesn't know,' she pleaded. 'He doesn't know who –'

'But we can find them! As long as you can see Charlie, we can find them! We can find who killed him!'

Amee shook her head, both hands clasping Mr Cooper's. 'I want to help Charlie! I want to help all of them! He wants it too!'

Marty began hitting Mr Cooper in the stomach. 'Stop it! Just let her go! Stop it!'

A few seconds passed. Mr Cooper lowered Amee down until her feet were on the floor. But her legs were weak. With a groan, she fell all the way, crumbling onto her knees and wrapping her arms around her chest. Marty rushed to hold her, but Amee wished he wouldn't. The wetness of her urine went all the way down her thighs, and she knew it would start to smell soon.

'We can find them,' Mr Cooper repeated. He was quieter now, but there was a wildness still in his gaze.

'But he doesn't know who killed him,' cried Amee. 'I told you, there's just a –'

'A shape. A shape that he can't put a face to, I know. But we can put a face to it. We can do that if we have Charlie. So long as he's still here, so long as you can see my son, we can end this. What other father gets that chance?'

The rain started punching the cabin so hard it felt like the ceiling might collapse.

'It's not a chance,' pleaded Amee. 'It's not a chance. You've got to let me go!'

'You're not going to the house on the cliff, not if it sends him away.'

'You don't understand.'

'I understand that if you find that place, then Charlie could be gone for good. I want to find out what happened to him before he goes. I want to find the bastard who took him from me, and I want to kill him.'

'If you do this, then they could be stuck forever. Or something worse.'

'I don't care about the dead, Amee. I care about the living, and people getting what they deserve.'

'You'd condemn them. If you don't let me do this, you'd condemn them.'

'They've been condemned already. Clean yourself up and get yourself together. We'll go when the rain stops.' Mr

194

Cooper paced back to the chair and sat down, removing a packet of cigarettes from his jacket.

'Go where?' said Amee.

'There's a man I want to find. A man who needs to hear Charlie's testimony. You just make sure you can see him, and make him remember. Remember everything that happened on that day.'

With a shaky breath, Amee propped herself back up against the wall. Marty held her tighter despite the wetness, whispering into her ear.

'You're alright. It's alright.'

But Amee wasn't listening. She was staring across at Mr Cooper, at his face, quivering in the candlelight.

'I think you're a bad person,' she said then.

The tweeded man shrugged, lighting the cigarette between his teeth, letting the smoke seep out from the corners of his mouth.

'Then you shouldn't have saved me.'

Outside, the rain began to calm.

'When I think of you, I think of the ocean. I think of its blue waves, its mountains, made of coral, spiralling down the vistas until everything's black, and cold, and different, and new all over again.'

13

THE BILLIONAIRE DETECTIVE

He was sixteen when he joined the mile-high club. It was a Boeing 707. A streamlined seventy seater, almost as perfect a vessel as the girl in the red shorts.

She was sixties. So sixties. Proper sixties. Her red hair was in a semi-beehive, and her legs dangled smoothly off the seat like they were made of marble. A real girl, like she had hopped straight out of the silver screen. And she liked him. He knew it. It was his looks, he assumed. He looked older than he was. His skin was pimple free, and small patches of stubble were already beginning to poke out of his chin. His hair was thickly gelled, his jaw was smoothly chiselled, and his clothes were so slick and fancy they may as well have been tailored for James fucking Dean. A real sixties man, he supposed.

And so the two collided. She talked to him first, and it was immediately evident that she thought he was someone other than who he really was. A businessman perhaps, with a jacket lined with pound notes. Why else would he be on a 707, flying first class to OR Tambo Airport in South Africa? He had the look of a businessman about him, and that was being modest. Alfie Percival was a good looking sixties guy. If not *the* James Dean, then sure as hell the next James Dean.

Then again, his accent didn't half give him away. Alfie had been born in a modest, working-class town in Scotland, but his father had come into money. They quickly travelled down south, where Alfie was enrolled in the most expensive school his parents could find, meaning his working roots were shed for something far quainter, more trimmed and proper. But he didn't suppose that mattered. The girl liked him, and she thought he was rich. Him. Not his father. So long as she kept thinking that (without finding out he was going to South Africa as a latecomer to his school's Duke of Edinburgh Award trip) then Alfie was sure he would be the first person in the world to lose his virginity at thirty-five thousand feet.

'How old do you think I am?' she had asked him at one point, swivelling in her seat and placing her red-painted nails on her waist.

Alfie had swallowed and put on a half-smile. 'You couldn't place an age on that,' he'd said, but really he assumed she must have been twenty-nine, verging dangerously close to the thirties.

'You're too sweet,' she had said back, rubbing a hand on her thigh.

It was around twenty minutes after the exchange that Alfie found himself in the aeroplane toilet. It was his first time, so he was worried he would be bad at it, but actually, he found the whole thing decidedly easy. The space seemed to help in a way. It was so small that no moves were expected, nothing imaginative, nothing eye-catching. They got in, she undid his buckle and trousers, she bent over, he found the right hole, and then they were away. Two minutes and thirty seconds, if he had to count it. She was quiet during the whole thing, but he supposed that was more to do with the fact there were seventy people directly behind the door.

When he was done, he relieved himself in the toilet. She kissed him three times on the mouth, and then they were back in their seats, preparing to land in Johannesburg. He didn't speak to her; she didn't speak to him. But Alfie didn't care. That flight was the best seven hours of his life. Not just because of the sex, but because it had taught him something. He didn't have to be a catch to get into a girl's red shorts; he just had to act like one. Wear the right clothes, smile the right smile, put the right amount of gel in his hair, borrow his father's suit, and man, he had it made. So long as he remembered that, Alfie knew his life was going to be a sweet one.

* * *

Thirty-five years after that flight and Alfie Percival was sweating underneath the Cornish sun. He was sitting on a sun-lounger, itching the skin under his swimming trunks whilst his mouth moved up and down on a chalky piece of mint. In one hand was a gin and tonic filled with cucumber and melted ice. He'd been nursing it for a whole hour.

'For Christ's sake.' The woman in front of him lifted her arse off the cushion and pushed her lounger out of the shade before sitting back down and cursing under her breath. 'It's every ten seconds now, I swear, every ten seconds.'

Alfie nodded, placing the rim of his glass against his mouth but making sure he didn't let any of the liquid pass his lips. *Yeah*, he thought. *The sun moves, honey. You want something still, go lie under a lightbulb.* Although, to look at the woman, Alfie wasn't sure that she hadn't done so already. Her flesh was a deep shade of brown, almost charred looking, like you could pull bits off in crispy chunks. And except for the eyes, she wasn't pretty. But then, Alfie could make do with the eyes. *You're not that good-looking either,* he thought to himself. He looked down at his belly, which was overlapping the strings of his shorts. In all truth, he had let himself go over the past few years. But the girls didn't seem to mind. They saw beyond all that. *Bigger pants, bigger pockets.*

'You were saying?' the woman said, lying back down and turning her head towards Alfie.

She was an American. A rich girl on holiday from her husband in Florida. A beautiful mid-point, too. She was rich, but only rich enough for a three-month sabbatical. Not quite the highest of flyers, but not very close to the dirt either. She'd glided straight into Alfie's arms.

'Nothing,' replied Alfie, wiping some of the sweat from his forehead.

'So what type are you anyhow?'

'How d'you mean type?'

'You're clearly a millionaire.'

Alfie had to stop himself from laughing up a lung. 'Hmm,' he mumbled instead.

'Don't deny it. I've been around Europe long enough to know that if anyone owns a Sunseeker, they're cruising. That's why you hang around here. Don't think I haven't seen you trying to reel in a few women over the last few days. Luxury hotel in St Ives; fresh water, fresher pussy, am I right?'

Alfie had to laugh this time, although he made it sound like he was laughing *with* her rather than *at* her. In all truth, he had been hanging around this hotel for the last few days and for the precise reason that this woman was suggesting. But it was hardly a millionaire's digs, and her pussy wasn't going to be the freshest of fresh either.

'You saying I'm old?'

'I'm saying you're a millionaire. And you're old.'

'You got me.' He grinned.

'How much? Don't tell me, you've lost count. The same, all of you. All of you are the same.'

'Not quite the same.'

'Tell me then,' she said as she sat up, peering at the sweaty man over her rose-tinted sunglasses. 'Tell me how you're different to any of the other millionaires I see, waltzing their big cocks about the place like they're Casanova.'

'Some of us are billionaires,' said Alfie. He slurped the rest of his gin and tonic as the woman gave a raspy laugh. 'And some of us have little cocks,' he finished.

'So you're a billionaire.'

Alfie raised both arms. *You said it, honey.*

'You're outrageous.'

As outrageous as you want me to be.

She laughed again. 'Alfie. Alfie, Alfie, Alfie.'

He laughed with her, then stood up from the lounger, shoving his feet back into his sandals. 'Another drink?' he asked, pointing at the empty glass beside her head.

'If you're buying.'

'Of course.'

She put the glass in his beefy hand, and Alfie strolled over to the pool-side bar, chuckling giddily to himself. *Billionaire. I'll be, that's a new one.* He wasn't going to get a lot of brain power out of this woman for sure, but she'd be good fun all the same. Even if she wasn't the freshest catch of the day.

The Idle Salt Hotel, which sat just five miles from Bamaluz Beach, north Cornwall, was a perfect place to pick up women. It had been for a while now. Gullible and sun swept, they littered the place with bikinis and dark freckles, attaching themselves to anyone they thought might have a substantial amount of cash. Alfie had even sorted out the problem of rooms. It was all very well hanging around the outdoor pool of a luxury hotel, picking up women of an afternoon, but it wasn't going to end well if Alfie brought them home to his weed-filled caravan park. That was why he passed the harbour every second Saturday. Most of the time, it was filled with ordinary yachts and fishing boats, but on occasion it had been known to house a particularly fancy-looking number. And every time it did, Alfie knew he could pounce. After all, how good was a room when you could have a boat?

Alfie walked down onto the pier now, arm in arm with the deeply tanned woman, who might very well be called Zara. His eyes were scanning the moored yachts, quickly but casually searching for the Sunseeker he had spotted just a few days before. This was the perfect time to take advantage, when the sun had gone down and the true owners of the boat had made their way into town for the evening. Taking momentary ownership of a boat like this wasn't actually that hard to do. The rich pricks practically left their back door open.

'Beautiful, aren't they? Just beautiful.'

Zara held his arm tight, and Alfie gave her a quick

squeeze on the arse. *Let's keep this tasteful, honey. We're gonna shag on one of these things, not eat a candlelit dinner.* He spotted the Sunseeker three moorings to the left. It was relatively fitting for a billionaire, he supposed. He could pull it off if he said he was feeling thrifty at the time of the purchase. Zara spotted it too and gasped.

'Now that's a billionaire's boat!'

Yeah, definitely brain-dead, thought Alfie.

The two of them came up alongside it, looking up at the boat as if it was a mansion of the waves. Thankfully for Alfie, it seemed empty.

'How do we get in?' asked Zara as he looked around for a ladder.

I'm trying to work that out myself, darling...

'Here,' replied Alfie, spotting the silver ladder near the bow. He let her go up first, making sure to give her arse a quick slap for good measure, ever the British gentleman that he was.

'It's so huge,' she cried as she got to the deck, and Alfie winced, clasping the cold rungs of the ladder.

If you don't keep it down, you'll be saying the same thing about the local jail.

After a few seconds, he had reached the top too. His ears pricked up slightly at the high-pitched voices echoing from a yacht on the walled side of the harbour. *So long as we act like we own the place, we should be fine.* Zara stared about the deck, giggling as Alfie tried the handle of the nearest door. *Locked. Okay. If this one is locked, then they're all locked.* Zara grabbed hold of his arm, her mischievous smile gleaming an unnatural white despite the darkness of the hour.

'Let's go in. I want to see the whole place.'

Alfie felt around in his pockets. 'Goddamn it.'

'What's wrong?'

'Forgot the key. Must have left it in my suite at the hotel.'

Zara bit her lip, visibly disappointed with this information. The sound of champagne popping came from the deck of the yacht nearby.

'So what do we do?' she asked.

Alfie huffed, staring up towards the night sky. 'Well, it's pretty dark.'

'How d'you mean?'

He waited a beat, then leaned down and slid his tongue into her mouth. He set up shop there for a little while before letting go, looking at her and gauging her reaction. To his relief, she kissed him again, and then he started taking her clothes off.

Alfie put the hose in the hole and squeezed. He'd always hated the smell of petrol, so it was a wonder he worked at the station. On the other hand, free petrol always smelt a little sweeter. He wriggled the nozzle in his old and busted Ford, keeping one eye on the shop as the morning midges hovered about his neck. Of course, it wasn't supposed to be free. But what idiot wouldn't give his car a quick spurt if he was left in charge behind the counter? It was easy enough to do. Just as easy as it was to convince blazing brunettes to fiddle about with his own hose. Although in all honesty, half of the catches he made these days weren't exactly blazing, at least not by the standards of his younger self.

He shook his head. *You were James Dean once. You had the pick of the apple tree. The ripest, the reddest, the leading ladies of all the world's pussy. Now you have to settle.* Alfie hated that word. Settle. Zara had been just that, a girl to settle on. She wasn't the best of them. She wasn't the best of anything; she just had the right accessories. Perhaps he'd got relaxed about the whole thing. Or maybe he just wasn't a catch anymore, now that those razor-sharp cheek bones of his youth had dissolved into a soft wall of pillowy pudge.

Alfie placed the hose back on the rack. *You should have died young. You should have been taken out quickly on some sun-soaked road like the real James Dean. At least then you wouldn't be out here pedalling husks on the weekends.* Settle. He chortled miserably, heading back inside. All of this was the punishment of survival, Alfie knew it. The punishment of age. Or, he supposed, it could be that other kind of punishment. The kind that Zara had reminded him of the night before.

He remembered them lying on the deck together, cigarettes hanging from their mouths and their clothes only half put on in the dark light of the midnight hour.

'What do you do?' Zara had asked.

'I was a detective,' Alfie had replied truthfully, seeing as there was no need to lie anymore.

'A detective? How can a detective make all that money?' It took Zara a few seconds to come to her conclusion. 'Ah! Inherited. That makes sense. Although why would a billionaire take a job solving murders?'

Why does anyone? Alfie remembered thinking. *Because they're naïve. Because they have no idea how badly a dead boy's face can haunt them, can follow them into their sleep or stare at them in the mirror.* Not even a million whiskies on the rocks could fade that boy, and Lord knows, Alfie had tried.

'You're not much of a talker are you?' Zara had said then. 'You're more of a listener. I reckon you were a good detective in that way. But man, oh man. A billionaire who chose to be a detective. And now look at you, living the way you do. I don't think many detectives get that kind of reward, huh?'

Later that morning, Alfie had dropped Zara off back at the Idle Salt Hotel and promised to see her again. Same place, same time. The sad thing was, the poor girl seemed to believe him. Most of them didn't. Or at least, most of them had a feeling by that point. But not Zara. She'd smiled at him, given his cheek a sloppy kiss and his cock a quick squeeze, then she'd waved goodbye and said, 'See ya poolside, baby!'

Alfie walked up to the counter and coughed away some phlegm that had been lodged at the back of his throat. *Sorry, Zara, this baby has a nine-to-five, pumping petrol into old bashed up Hondas. Ah, it's a billionaire's life for me.*

He imagined her there now, a gin and tonic in one hand, keeping the sun lounger beside her free. Would she cry when he didn't show up? Was Alfie enough to cry over? *Of course you're not; you're an old man who lied to her, fucked her, and gave her arse a few slaps. You're nothing to cry over, just something to regret. Something that might make her feel a bit ill in the pit of her stomach when she thinks about you. You're not who you were once, remember?*

A carton of milk landed on the counter in front of him, and Alfie looked up to see an aged, grey-haired man swaying by the desk. *That man is my mirror. That face is my face. When did that happen?* Alfie scanned the milk and then shoved it into a bag. *It happened when you let that boy down. Isn't that what Zara said? This is your reward.* She was right, he supposed. This whole thing was a reward, not a punishment. How else would you reward what happened during that case, if not with time, with reflection, with dark days and darker nights?

The old man turned and tottered out of the shop, allowing a little girl to stand in his place. She placed a pair of flowery flip-flops beside Alfie's hands.

'How much?'

Alfie turned them around to show her the tag on the soles. 'Can't you read?'

'Oh, sorry,' she said with a fake smile. Then she reached into her pockets and took out a five-pound note. 'I'm just tired today, I guess.'

Alfie shook his head, shoving the note roughly into the till. *You don't know tiredness, kid. Spend a night in my head, then try to read the price tag.*

A couple of hours later and Alfie was finally able to clock out. His shifts seemed to take longer as he got older, like every second was a lead weight getting heavier and heavier, but mercifully, they did eventually end. He was sitting in his car now, scanning the road for oncoming traffic. No vehicle caught his eye, but there was something that did. It was a person watching him. He was middle-aged and smartly dressed, a cigarette dangling limply from his lips as he leaned against a wall on the other side of the street. There was something unusual about him, Alfie thought. Something that he couldn't quite put a finger on. Alfie leaned over the steering wheel to get a closer look, but just as he did so, the smart man turned on his heel and walked away. A horn sounded from behind him, and Alfie glanced in the rear-view mirror to see a scrawny teenager giving him the finger.

'Get a move on, dickhead!' he shouted.

'Eat cocks,' Alfie muttered back. Then he propelled his car forward.

The caravan park lay just ten miles from the Idle Salt Hotel, but the two worlds couldn't have been further apart. Where there was a luxurious sapphire pool by the hotel, there was a stinking grey quagmire by the park. Tiny black flies buzzed about the weeds, and fat rats gnawed their homes into the mounds, biting the ankles of whoever passed too close. The park lay in the underbelly of St Ives, in a place called Penderleith. Miles away from any town; miles away from the life he'd once known. But Alfie made do with it. The place had been occupied by travellers and their static caravans for several years, and to their credit, they had accepted his quiet arrival with zero questions asked. He had become a ghost on the fringes of their world, unnoticed but for the times he arrived and left. A place for him to disappear. And that was just what he needed. A place to exist without existing.

Alfie parked up, chucking a cigarette into his mouth as he stared out across the park. *Here we are, my billionaire's retreat. I'll never see you again, Zara, and you should be counting your lucky stars every night.* He lit the cigarette, stepping out of the car and slamming the door behind him.

'Yer keep shutting it like that, one day yer'll be picking glass outta yer shoe.'

Alfie turned to spot a lanky man slumped on a deck chair beside his caravan, a creaky hand wrapped around a tin of lager. 'You telling me you've never had a bad day, Mack?'

'Plenny er those, plenny er bad nights too. And all my hinges aren't even squeaking.' Mack leaned back smugly, crunching up the empty can before cracking open a full one.

Alfie strolled past him, puffing a dollop of smoke into the air above his head. *A man with silent hinges is a man who hasn't opened many doors. I've opened lots in my time, pal, and you'd best believe I've left them all broken.*

His was the caravan at the end. Almost fifty feet from anyone else's, just enough distance to be able to call it peaceful and secluded. Alfie opened the door and crashed onto the sofa, flicking on the tiny plastic television that was balanced skilfully upon a stack of magazines.

'And many of these animals make their nests inside the –' FLICK.

'This is what you call standing your ground, so when the first one –' FLICK.

'Over for dinner, that's exactly what you said last time.'
'Last time was with YOUR mother! –' FLICK.

Alfie dropped the remote, settling for a show that featured two old men with rifles strapped to their backs walking through a damp forest. He relaxed to its buzz, pushing hard on closed eyes, waiting for the patterns to form in the dark. After a few seconds, he let go and watched the hunters make their way down a slope.

'This is where you have to be really quite careful –'

He coughed, eyelids beginning to droop slightly in the vague orange fuzz of the hanging light. It wouldn't take him too long to reach the realm of sleep. He wasn't one of those guys who needed a pill or a tin of beer to turn himself off. All he needed was a sofa, a television, and a load of memories that were better off in the dark. He squinted at the dimming picture, seeing a deer trot into the frame, its eyes a deep hazel and its fur smooth and pretty. One of the moustache-wearing men drew his gun and knelt down beside a bush, attempting in vain to fade into the background of the forest. He lifted the rifle, but Alfie never found out if he got the kill. Within a couple of seconds, he had closed his eyes again, his body sinking into the warm fabric of the sofa while his mind flicked through images from the last few days. It culminated with Zara's naked body on the boat. Alfie said her name for some reason, and then he fell asleep.

'HOT DOG!'

Something pounded the door three times, and Alfie was ripped out of his slumber. He spluttered up some saliva, his eyes coming to focus on the television in front of him, where an animated hot dog was surfing an ocean wave.

'WATCH IT GO!'

The door crashed again, and Alfie leapt off the sofa. He clambered to the cabinet beside the fridge, pulling out his old PPK pistol from his days on the force.

'POLICE! FUCKING POLICE!' he yelled, pointing the barrel of the gun at the door.

For a moment, Alfie questioned whether it could be Zara behind there, come to exact some kind of vengeance upon him. He couldn't think of who else it could be. He never had visitors.

'Who's there?!' he called out again.

'HOT DOGGY DOG!'

Alfie cursed, rushing over to the television and pulling the cable from the wall. It turned off with a *ziiiip*.

'Who the fuck is there?' he repeated.

'Can you help me?' said a voice from behind the door. It was young, small, and most definitely a girl's.

Alfie kept the gun raised. 'Who is it?'

'I need help. I'm lost. Can you help me, please?' She knocked on the door again, but this time the knocks were decidedly quieter.

Alfie hesitated, his finger quivering slightly on the trigger of the pistol. The girl had a slight and soft Scottish accent, and it reminded him of home in the worst way possible.

'What do you mean, lost?'

'Please help me,' she begged him. 'I don't know where my mum and dad are. Please. It's late. Can you help?'

Alfie lowered the gun. *It's a child. It's a damned child. Get a grip, old man.*

'Okay. Okay, hold on. I'm unlocking the door.' He shoved the gun between his belt and arse, walked over towards the door, and pulled the bolts out of place.

The girl stood on the second step, staring up at Alfie, her fingers twiddling nervously. Alfie recognised her almost immediately, and it didn't take him long to work out why. The flowery flip-flops were attached to each of her feet, the price tag still poking out of the left sole and the cheap rubber already starting to fray near the tips. The girl from the petrol station. Mousy hair and ice-blue eyes, staring up at Alfie on his doorstep. She climbed another stair.

'Thank you so much.'

Alfie felt wildly about his waist. 'Don't come closer.'

'What's wrong?'

'Who are you with? Don't tell me you got all this way by yourself. Who are you with?'

Alfie's fingers wrapped around the pistol and he pulled it out, causing the girl to gasp and fall backwards down the stairs.

'I don't know what you're talking about,' she said fearfully.

'Like hell you don't. Don't tell me you're alone!'

'She's not alone.'

The voice came from the shadows, and Alfie turned to see a smart-looking man emerging out of the darkness, the same person he'd seen when he'd clocked out of work. The strange thing about him that Alfie had been unable to grasp just a few hours ago was now obvious. He was tall. Very tall. It had been hard to tell with the distance and the otherwise empty street that he had been standing in, but the man was almost unnaturally tall. Nearly seven feet if Alfie had to put a number on it. And now he was on his doorstep.

'What the hell are –'

'Jesus, look at you,' the tall man interrupted. 'Living in this dump, pointing guns at little girls. I suppose this is what that case made of you, huh?'

A woman came up alongside him, a burgundy notebook squeezed under one arm. 'Why don't you put the gun down?' she said. 'You're scaring the child.'

All three of them had Scottish accents. It was like they were ghosts from a previous life, come to haunt Alfie's door.

'Who the fuck...?' Alfie stuttered in shock. 'I'll put it down as soon as you tell me what this is!'

He turned the barrel towards the woman, and the tall man took a few steps closer, seemingly unfazed by the gun as he reached into his pocket to remove a pack of cigarettes. In his left hand was an antique-looking lighter. Bronze and scuffed, with a small ruby embedded near the spark wheel.

'We're just here to talk,' he said with a smile. 'It's been a long nine years since that boy disappeared, detective. And we've got a lot to talk about.'

14

BILLY AND LUCY

The hotel was located on Trevelling Road just beside the trading estate, which boasted a bunch of warehouse stores and takeouts. It was dingy, but Mr Cooper never stayed anywhere that wasn't cheap. Nor did he stay anywhere they could get noticed, and he'd decided no one was going to notice them here. Still, the hotel room had a bed, it had clean sheets, and it had a small cabinet shower room, and that was a lot better than some of the other places the three of them had stayed over the last month.

Marty climbed the stairs and knocked on the door of room number seven. One, two. One, two. One, two, three, four. For a moment, only silence followed, but then the door was unlocked and David Cooper was standing in front of him.

'Anyone see you, Weed-kid?'

'Some saw. Don't think anyone recognised me though.'

The former maths teacher nodded. In all truth, he was right to be concerned. Other than his usually black hair being dyed blonde, Marty looked almost exactly the same as he had when he left home. Mr Cooper, on the other hand, was another sight entirely. The tweed jacket and chinos were gone, replaced by a thick brown leather coat and blue jeans. His thin brown hair was entirely shaved off, and his beard was so long it could be curled into his armpit hair. Not a particularly pleasant sight, but Marty supposed that was the point. People would rather avert their gaze and keep their distance than approach him for a closer look.

Mr Cooper stood aside and let Marty into the room. Amee was sitting on the bed, her hands gripping the sheets. A wide smile spread across her face as she saw him.

'You're back.'

'Yeah,' replied Marty. 'I only went for a short walk around the estate. Were you alright on your own?'

She had a look in her eyes that suggested she hadn't been, but she nodded bravely. In truth, Marty knew that she was never alright when she was left alone with Mr Cooper. She still hadn't told him what that tall man did to her in the hospital, but it had clearly had a lasting effect. She struggled with being alone with any adult male, but she always powered through. She was always brave. By this point, it was hard to tell there was anything wrong at all.

Marty sat down on the windowsill, pulling the curtains back to look at the Cornish street below. He gazed down for a moment, then turned back to Amee. She looked different too compared to a month ago. Her long mousy hair was now dyed black and cut right up above her shoulders, and all the clothes she wore were boys' clothes. There were no cops on the lookout for her, of course. She wasn't on any Gealblath register, and her mum wasn't going to draw attention to herself by reporting Amee missing. But still, there was always the possibility that the three of them would find a cool black American Lincoln parked outside. Marty remembered what she had said that night in the cabin.

'They'll be looking for us. They'll always be looking for us.'

Mr Cooper had told them that they would have to change. He meant himself and Amee, because he hadn't accounted for the fact that Marty wasn't going to let them leave without him.

'I'm coming with you. If you're taking Amee. I'm not leaving her.'

'No chance,' the teacher had replied.

'You can't leave me. If you do, then I'll tell the police. I'll tell everyone.'

'Marty, if you come with us, then you'll send them after me. The town, the police. They're gonna think I took you.'

'Then you can't go. You're gonna have to listen to Amee. Help her let the dead people cross over.'

The words had come out of Marty's mouth with fiery intent, and there was nothing Mr Cooper could do. It was a stalemate. And Marty had the upper hand.

'You think a weed-kid like you can stop me? No, she's not doing that. We're going to Cornwall whether you like it or not. I'm going to get my justice. By any means necessary.'

When they left the cabin at one thirty a.m., Marty could hardly believe it. The teacher had chosen to turn a whole town against himself in order to find retribution. Not even guilt, sin, or punishment could cloud his desire to catch Charlie's killer. And one month later, that desire still hadn't faded. They sat in the Margle Hotel with Mr Cooper's intent burning stronger than ever. But then, Marty's intent was strong too, and it was becoming a distinct possibility that neither of them would ever fold. Both of them were damned, but at least Marty knew he was doing this for the right reason.

Amee pulled her legs up onto the bed now. 'You look pale,' she said, her head tilting slightly.

'You can talk,' replied Marty.

A fuzz of static filled the room, and Marty turned to see Mr Cooper perched beside a radio. His bony knuckles twisting the knob until he found the station he was looking for. Marty shut out the sound, as he had done ever since he'd heard his mother plead for him to come home.

'Please just come home, Marty. I need you. I love you, we all love you, and we just want you to come home.'

He shuddered as he recalled her voice. Her tears. That emotional tremble that he'd never heard before. *I need you.* He wished that he could have just reached into the radio and told her where he was. But he couldn't. She wouldn't understand. He needed to do this. But still, that didn't make him feel better. He was still upset. He was still sorry.

'Is he with you?' asked Marty, trying to clear his head.

Amee looked up. 'Hmm?'

'Charlie, is he with you?'

A moment passed. Then she shook her head.

'He was with you.'

Marty shivered and he checked over his shoulder, as if he'd be able to spot the dead boy behind one of them. Charlie had been with them the whole time according to Amee. He'd followed their every movement, listened to every word, hovered near every breath. Even when they slept, he was there. Sometimes Marty woke up to find Mr Cooper sitting in the blackness, his eyes wide open, staring beside a sleeping Amee like he was trying to see his son. It must have been hard for him to be so close again. But for Marty, the whole thing was just unnerving. Especially when Amee would break into a fractured conversation every now and then, her eyes looking intently into nothing. The scenes were so bizarre that sometimes Marty struggled to believe them. But then he remembered what Mr Cooper had told him back in Gealblath, and he shook himself out of his doubt. Amee needed someone who believed her. Amee needed someone. And Marty had to be just that.

The radio went silent, and Mr Cooper stepped over towards the bed.

'Pack your things, Weed-kid. We're leaving this place in an hour.'

'Do you know where we're going?'

'Our man likes hanging around hotels here. Barman said they'd traced his details after he claimed he owned the place to a guest. I said it wouldn't take long for someone to recognise the name.'

Marty huffed, pushing himself up onto his feet and stretching out a knot in his back. *Wouldn't take long.* They'd been lingering around north Cornwall for a whole week now, and south Cornwall for three weeks before that. Asking around a county for somebody while trying to lie low had proved to be more than a bit difficult.

'Where is he?'

'Caravan park near the Idle Salt hotel. Apparently, there's a couple of parks around there; we'll go to the closest.'

'Caravan park? I thought you said the guy was a detective.'

Mr Cooper didn't answer. Instead, he sat on the bed nearest the wall, stroking his beard. He had a queer smile on one side of his face, like he had found comfort in something. Marty looked at Amee.

'Are you ready to go?' he asked.

Amee nodded. 'The longer we wait, so do the dead.' She grabbed her bag and swung it over one shoulder. 'I'm ready.'

It was four o'clock by the time they got to the first caravan park. By then the sun was already beginning to dip. Marty threw his bag down, rubbing his ankles and biting his lip against the pain. He stared up towards a row of twenty caravans that sat just left of the road. After a five-hour walk, they were finally on the outskirts of the town, and Marty could feel it.

'Shit, shit, shit.' He pulled his fingers away, wincing at the blood that stained the lines in his skin.

Mr Cooper stuffed away the map, scanning the field of caravans. 'Shoes leaking again, Weed-kid?'

'I swear it's like cheese graters.'

Marty slipped off a shoe and winced as the warm air sucked at his wounds. Amee knelt beside him as if she was about to give him medical attention. Instead, she just looked at the blood sympathetically.

'Are you okay?' she asked.

Marty ignored her. 'I need new shoes, Mr Cooper.'

'Well, maybe we can find some here,' Mr Cooper replied.

Marty gazed up at the caravan site and grimaced. 'If the air smells like this, I don't wanna know what their shoes smell like.'

'Is the pain really bad?' asked Amee, putting a hand on his shoulder.

'Yeah,' whispered Marty.

'You'll be alright.'

'That's easy for you to say; your shoes aren't fighting back.'

Amee tucked her sweaty black hair behind one of her ears. 'Here,' she said, as she pulled off her own trainers. 'You can take mine if you like; maybe they'll fit you better.'

She presented them to him, and Marty noticed the blood stain on the fabric. He looked down and saw the same blood on the white of her socks.

'Oh,' he murmured. 'No, thanks.'

At that moment, a forced and throaty laugh erupted from the gate, and Marty turned to see Mr Cooper standing in front of a slightly insane-looking elderly man. He had a bald head, but his beard was longer than Mr Cooper's, tied into three bristly knots. Mr Cooper stood with his hands placed firmly behind his back, just as they had been when Marty had first seen him, back when he had called Rory an 'arsehole' in the school corridor. The man with three beards gestured towards the caravans, then shook his head. Amee put her shoes back on her feet.

'He's not here,' she said.

Mr Cooper began treading back towards them. 'Not here,' he confirmed. 'This is a holiday camp.'

'Holiday camp?' said Marty. 'Why the hell have you brought us to a holiday camp?'

'I didn't know that, did I? Still, don't fret. It means we know where he is now.'

'That's great,' said Marty. 'I mean, we walked five hours to the wrong caravan park, but hey, let's look at the positives.'

'That's the attitude, Weed-kid. Now get up. If we move fast, we can get there by nightfall.'

'Nightfall? It's already getting dark.'

'Better move quickly then.'

Amee glared at Mr Cooper. 'He's hurt,' she said firmly.

Marty felt his cheeks go red in embarrassment. *So are you,* he thought. *But I haven't heard you complain.*

'I don't care,' replied Mr Cooper. 'We've got somewhere to be, and I'm not gonna let a weed-kid stop me because he's got a cut on his heel.'

Amee turned away and stormed across the road, leaving Mr Cooper alone with Marty at his feet.

'Get up, Weed-kid.' Mr Cooper grabbed his collar and pulled, but despite Marty's nickname, he couldn't pick him up from the grass.

'I'm not walking anymore,' said Marty, lying down on the ground and rolling away from the teacher like a toddler in a tantrum.

'For shit's sake, Weed-kid!'

Mr Cooper clasped the back of his shirt, but before he could do any more, a voice echoed from across the road.

'I hear you gents are looking for a place to stay!'

Marty looked up, spotting the elderly man at the gate, and Amee standing beside him, a smug smile resting on her face.

'We're fine,' Mr Cooper called back, but the elderly man shook his head.

'The nearest town is miles from here. It's gonna rain hard tonight, and this one's just told me how tired you all are. Wouldn't feel right to let you go on. Stay the night. We're friendly, all of us.'

Marty looked at Amee, who gave him a wink. Then, with a sigh of defeat, Mr Cooper tilted his head towards the sky.

'Fine,' he said.

Not long later, the three of them were sitting in the heart of the caravan park. A fire in front of them was crackling loudly inside a rusty firepit, glazing the world with a soft, quivering orange and filling their nostrils with the scent of wood, plaster, and rubbish. It was set up between two caravans, sheltered by a parasol and surrounded by three chewed-up deckchairs. The deckchairs were set upon a large crimson rug bridging one door of a caravan to another. Just where the fabric met the grass there was a thick bulge that shuffled every few seconds, but Marty tried not to look at it. He remembered something his dad had told him once, about how there was always a rat at least five feet away from you. He didn't think that was true, but in the heart of this caravan park, it very well could have been.

The man with three beards was reclined on the other side of the firepit. His white vest was smudged with smoke of days past, and spaghetti too, Marty was fairly sure. He watched as he knocked back a tin of Tribute, then smacked his lips with the rough part of his sleeve.

'Rain is gonna be big tonight,' he said roughly.

Marty looked up. Above them, the rain was beginning to fall in a rhythm. The bustle of people who had been wandering around the park had moved indoors.

Mr Cooper scoffed. 'You don't know rain. Try living where I grew up.'

The man with three beards stared at Mr Cooper. 'I didn't catch where you grew up.'

Mr Cooper lowered his tin. 'I was born in Glasgow,' he lied.

'How's it like?'

'Like here, just without the stink of shit.'

Marty froze, glancing over to their host. He eyed Mr Cooper with a half-raised eyebrow, then burst into raucous laughter.

'You aren't the first to say that,' he beamed at the three of them, as if he was proud of the fact. 'Par for the course if you're out in the countryside. Trust me, you stay out here long enough, it's the cities that start to stink. Not here.'

A piece of rubbish spat from the firepit and the elderly man stamped his boot onto it. A silence ensued. Amee was sitting on the rug beside Marty, her knees up to her chin and her eyes staring intently into the flames. Marty was going to warn her about the rats, but he decided not to in the end. She would probably be fine with them anyway.

'So who's this Alfie you lot are looking for?' the man with three beards asked.

'Just a friend,' replied Mr Cooper.

'Uh-huh. And why're you heading on foot? Don't you own a car?'

'Too expensive these days. Besides, a little walking never hurt anyone.'

That was half true, Marty supposed. Mr Cooper had taken money out of his account in Gealblath to sustain them, but only enough to live on. Cash for buses, for food, for cheap accommodation and second-hand clothes. But not enough for a car, not nearly enough. Marty rubbed the cuts on his feet again.

'These your kids?' asked the three-bearded man.

Mr Cooper nodded. 'Yeah,' he replied.

'Good thing the missus is asleep; she would be doting on you right now. Always wanted kids. What's your name, son?'

The three-bearded man peered over towards Marty, his fingers squeezing his beer tin until it was moulded to his palm print.

'Billy,' Marty lied.

'We've got a Billy. Here with his mum three homes back. He's a little shit.'

Mr Cooper chugged the last of his beer. 'Must be a Billy thing.'

'And what about you, girlie?'

'She's Lucy,' Mr Cooper answered for her, squeezing his own can and wiping one side of his mouth with a sleeve.

'Lucy. Hey, I like that name. I'm Andy.' The man called Andy held out his hand for Amee to shake. She did so. Andy smiled. 'Well, you've got two beautiful kids. And they've got a great daddy. Even if he's got you walking. Dads always know best.'

'You got that right.' Mr Cooper chucked his empty tin into the fire and lifted his chin towards the stars.

'You want another one of those?' asked Andy.

Mr Cooper shook his head. 'We've got to be getting some sleep if that's alright with you. Long day tomorrow.'

'No worries. I won't lie, it's going to be awfully tight in the sleeper. Might be room on the sofa but –'

'On no account. We'll be alright out here.'

Marty jolted. 'What?'

'We've got shelter.' Mr Cooper glared at him. 'It's warm out.'

'Bollocks is it warm out.'

'Watch your mouth, Billy.'

A rush of wind blew into them, making one third of Andy's beard swirl into the open air as he scratched his head.

'Well,' he mumbled, 'do you want some blankets at least?'

'Yes,' Marty cut in before Mr Cooper could reply.

Andy nodded, then turned and headed into his caravan.

'Why the hell are we staying out here?' Marty hissed as the door closed.

'Because he's a man we don't know,' Mr Cooper responded, 'and this is a place we don't know. You wanna get locked in a stranger's caravan tonight, you be my guest.'

'You know, there's a chance not everyone's a bad guy.'

Mr Cooper smirked. 'Time for another lesson, Weed-kid. There are two types of people in this world. The bad guys and the good liars.'

'Yeah, forgive me if I don't take it from you.'

The door opened and Andy chucked over two blankets. 'You're gonna have to share; or else I'll be the one shivering all night.'

'We appreciate it,' Mr Cooper said as he caught the bundle.

The three-bearded man peered through the rain with faint concern. 'Alright, well, you lot sleep tight.' He took one last bewildered look, then closed the door.

Mr Cooper passed one of the blankets to Marty, who let it roll from his fingers, grimacing at the thick tufts of dog hair which were clinging to the wool. Or at least, the hair he *hoped* was dog hair.

'You two can go under that one,' said Mr Cooper. 'I'd try to get to sleep fast; we'll be getting up before the sun.' He stood from his chair, then set himself down against the other caravan, pulling the blanket over his lap.

'You're not a teacher anymore,' said Marty.

'I'm the best teacher you'll get, Marty. After all, dads know best.'

It was starting to pour harder now, each drop thundering against the parasol, dripping over the edges to create a damp circle around the three of them. Marty turned to Amee and held out the blanket

'You going to sleep?' he asked.

'No. But you can.'

Marty turned away and lay down on the rug. 'Fine.'

The fire was still crackling in the pit as he pulled his blanket over himself, but his body shivered in the wind, so he pulled harder, making it cover everything but his eyes. In the window of the caravan, he could see the faded face of the three-bearded man staring at them. An orange light was hanging from behind him, casting a shadow over his body and smudging the kind wrinkles which Marty had seen before. There was an unsettling vagueness about him. He kept staring for so long that Marty considered saying something. But he closed his eyes before he could, and sleep took him as quickly as a speeding bullet.

He dreamt of Mike and Teddy. They were in his room, Warhammer figures scattered across newspaper. Rain poured hard onto the sill beneath the open window. Mike was dabbing a paintbrush against a small castle.

'Dragons always come with a storm,' he said, his face still bloodied and bruised from Ross's knuckleduster.

'When do you think Marty's coming back?' asked Teddy, his own focus drawn to a figurine which looked a bit like Mr Cooper.

Mike placed down his brush. 'I'm going to let this dry,' he said.

The words MARTY EVANS IS DEAD! were written on it.

'I'm not dead,' Marty exclaimed.

But his two friends took no notice of him. It was as if he was entirely invisible. No matter how hard he shouted, their eyes remained on the figures.

'Mike, listen to me; I'm not dead!' Marty roared at his friend, shaking him by the shoulders. 'I'M NOT DEAD!'

'Okay, okay, you're not dead.'

Marty opened his eyes, spotting Mr Cooper hunched over a round white ball. The shadows of the fire were flecked across his face.

'You seem pretty anxious about whether you're dead or not, Weed-kid,' Mr Cooper smirked. 'Don't worry, I can see you too.'

Marty grunted, wiping moisture from his forehead which may well have been rain but was probably sweat. He looked at Amee, who was stretched out by the firepit, covered by the bottom half of the blanket. He sat up and blinked at Mr Cooper.

'Bad dream,' he said.

'About Amee?'

'No. About my friends.'

'Hmm.'

Marty rubbed his eyes and looked at Mr Cooper more closely, noticing that he was in fact hunched over the skull of his dead son.

'Charlie,' he muttered.

Mr Cooper often took his son's skull out at night. He stroked it like there was still hair on the head. He pinched it like the cheeks might still twitch and giggle. Sometimes he whispered things, like the ears were still listening. In a strange sort of way, Marty guessed they were.

'Why do you...' Marty started, but paused. He had wanted to ask him something for a while now, only he'd never had the courage. He shook himself and forced the words out. 'Why do you still have him, Mr Cooper?'

'I told you,' said Mr Cooper. 'I found him.'

'Yes. But why do you still have him?'

'Because if the main suspect turns up at the police station with the skull of the victim years later, it doesn't look too good for the suspect.'

'So you kept him all this time.'

The wind picked up around them, whirling the thinnest flames inside the fire and spitting them out into the cool open air. Marty glanced up towards the window where Andy had been watching them. He was relieved to see that he was gone.

'I'd lost him for nearly ten years,' said Mr Cooper, 'and then he found me again. After all that time, he found me. Yeah, I kept him. It was senseless, I get that. But it felt like my duty.'

'But why don't you acknowledge him then? You're doing all this because you believe Amee, but you don't talk about him. Ever. And when she mentions him, I can see you don't like it.'

Mr Cooper kept his gaze on the skull, but his thumb stopped stroking. 'This is my son. This is what was made of him. This.'

'But there's more. After all of this, after we're just bones. There's more. Amee's proved that. In a way he's still alive –'

'No, Marty.'

'But he still exists.'

Mr Cooper pulled his gaze from the skull. 'No.'

There was another silence. Marty fidgeted on the rug, noticing a second lump twitching beneath the fabric about five feet from him. He stared at it for a while before another thought hit him.

'He's still here. You just don't want him to be.'

Mr Cooper's eyes flashed. 'What the hell was that, Weed-kid?'

'You're afraid to talk to him. Why?'

'How about you shut your mouth and go to sleep.'

'You're not a teacher. Not anymore. You can't tell me

227

what to do.' Marty kept his voice quiet. He didn't want to be hostile; he didn't want to anger Mr Cooper. In fact, for the first time since he'd known him, he actually wanted to help him. 'You should talk to him.'

'You should shut the hell up.' Mr Cooper reached for his bag and slid the skull inside.

'If you just ask Amee, you could talk to him through her. You just need to ask.'

'Go to sleep, Weed-kid.' Mr Cooper lay down on his back.

Marty leaned in closer, speaking softly, like his mum used to do when she would try to comfort him. 'Ask her, Mr Cooper. Just ask her.'

The rain began to slow, the tapping on the parasol getting lighter and lighter.

'I've been talking to him since I found him,' said Mr Cooper after a few seconds.

Then he turned onto his side, leaving Marty with nothing but the back of his head for company. Marty sighed, pulling the blanket up towards his chin and gripping it hard as he lay back down.

'You've never actually told us where you found him,' he said through gritted teeth. 'That's another thing you don't want to talk about. But have it your way.' He closed his eyes, hearing the rain return in a rush of wind.

It took a whole minute before Mr Cooper's voice whispered back.

'I found him by the ocean.'

15

SEEING DEAD

Ten thirty a.m. and David Cooper needed a drink. Not a big one; he wasn't an alky or anything. He just needed something to dilute the nerves and numb things a bit. Warmth. That was what it was. For the last week or so, David had felt really cold, like he was close to freezing, and the drink had become the warmest thing in the world. Like a radiator in a cold room, he needed filling, and so he stopped the bike and ran to the nearest petrol station.

The whisky was fourteen pounds, thirty pence. David had thirty pounds on him, so he bought two bottles. He took a gulp, then another, then three, and with wincing eyes he hissed, 'Ahh...' The sharpness of the liquor stained his throat, and his gasp was like the soft gasp of burning wood. He took another, then screwed on the bottle cap, walked back outside, and placed the whisky inside his bag. It would be enough, he decided. Enough for the day to come. He got back on the Shadow and started her up.

The church was a small one, ugly looking, almost

dilapidated. The white wood was stained black and brown, and one corner was propped up with a few bricks due to a nearby sinkhole. Around fifteen people stood outside of it. All of them were dressed in black, some with sunglasses, others with gloves, scarves, and coats. It was the twenty-first of October 1994. The air was sharp and bitter, and everyone huddled beside the door of the church like moths by a warm lamp. Vanessa was the only one who stood beside the hearse. It had been six years since David had last seen her, and she frowned as he pulled up.

'You're here,' she said bluntly.

'Yeah,' replied David. He killed the ignition. Faces inside the hearse glared at him.

'We've been here for ten minutes,' Vanessa growled. 'I told you on the phone, half past ten. I told you twice.'

'Yeah.'

'I didn't think you were coming.'

'Well, I'm here.'

'Yeah, you're here. You'll stand in front of them.' Vanessa nodded towards the congregation. 'But you won't carry it.'

The doors of the hearse opened, and three middle-aged men stepped out and walked towards the boot. He recognised them all from their wedding. Vanessa's side of the family. Her father, her brother, and her best friend. They reached down and pulled out a small, narrow wooden box. Inside it was Charlie's life as they had known it. His favourite toys, his pyjamas, the photos of his birthdays, the teeth that had once hidden beneath pillows. The very essence of him, about to be buried in the dirt.

'No, I won't carry it,' said David.

They held the box between them and began to walk slowly towards the church entrance. Vanessa walked behind them, and David followed suit.

'So why are you here?' she asked.

'Because they want me to be,' he replied, staring up at the people waiting for them by the door.

Vanessa laughed coldly. 'It's about you. Okay. Yeah, that makes sense. It's about you.'

David pulled on his cufflinks. 'You wanted to do this. If I didn't come to this circus, then it'd refuel the fire.'

'Did you just call our son's funeral a circus?'

'It's not a funeral. We're not burying him; we're burying a box. That's what you've come here to do.'

'I've come here for closure, David.'

'If burying a box was closure, why didn't you just bury one back in Perth? Or wherever it is you're living now.'

Vanessa shook her head. 'You just called our son's funeral a circus. Don't talk to me.'

'It's not a –'

'Don't talk to me.'

She moved ahead of him, placing one hand on the finely polished box as they began heading past the congregation.

The service lasted twenty minutes, no longer. David sat at the back, listening to the priest as he recited Genesis 1:14, then Psalms, then something else that involved loving your neighbour. None of David's neighbours even looked at him. By the end of the service, he knew every inch of the backs of their heads. Upon the last prayer, the priest slapped his book closed, Vanessa's side of the family picked up the box once again, and the congregation walked towards the graveyard.

The plot was waiting for them, a shallow hole dug neatly in the corner of the yard, with a polished stone embedded just in front of it.

Here Lies the Memory of Charlie James Cooper.
May They Warm the Earth with His Smile.
1975 – 1988.

The group stood solemnly for a moment, then they lowered the box inside, the same way one would lower a coffin. Vanessa cried. The others watched with vague shadows under their eyes. David remained at the back, slowly puffing on a thin cigarette that he had rolled earlier the same morning.

When the crowd finally dispersed, just Vanessa was left standing above the grave.

'David.'

The name carried on the autumnal air, and David dropped his cigarette and stamped it beneath his foot. When he came alongside her, his son's box was already beginning to sink into the wet mud. The memory of things were being eaten by the earth.

'You came,' Vanessa said softly. 'And I don't care what you say about them, you came because you wanted to. I believe that.' She raised a hand and wiped something from his face. 'And it's nice to see you again. I hope you're doing well. I'm doing okay now.'

David didn't say anything.

'There's a gathering in the town hall,' said Vanessa.

David nodded. 'I know.'

'I don't want you to come.'

'Okay.'

Another pause. Vanessa took one last look at the ground and then turned and walked away, leaving David alone in front of the hole and the box, his thin hair blowing in the October wind. He took another cigarette out of his pocket, lit it up, and sucked in a stream of smoke. He rested against one of the nearby gravestones. He hadn't planned on going to the town hall, but all the same, Vanessa's words stung. That woman had loved him once.

'Once...' he whispered to himself.

A lot of things were different once. David had learned to forget that. To bury it in the dirt like Charlie's box. He sighed and squeezed his arms around his body. Another gust of wind bit into him. Cold. But warm. Somehow still warm, just as it always was in Gealblath, even though it wasn't. He watched something small and black swoop down from the church roof, and a raven landed skilfully on one of the gravestones. It ruffled its feathers and dipped its beak in David's general direction.

CRAWCHH! it shouted at him.

David flicked his cigarette towards it, then turned away, already thinking about the whisky waiting for him in his bag. But before he could get very far, a voice came from behind him.

'Hey!'

David's heart jumped and he swivelled, seeing the raven feasting upon the cigarette, its little head shooting up to stare at its supplier before dipping back for another taste.

'Who said that?' he asked, half expecting the raven to reply, *ME!*

But thankfully, the true source of the voice was a man in a woollen coat, who stepped out from behind an oak tree in the corner of the yard.

'David,' he said.

The raven took flight with the cigarette stuck firmly in its beak.

'Alfie Percival,' David realised.

'I'm surprised you're here,' said Alfie as he approached him.

233

'Feeling's mutual.'

David watched as Alfie slid a packet of cigarettes out from his coat pocket and rattled the sticks inside. 'Got some? Or did you give your last one to the bird?' He picked one out and slipped it between his teeth.

'I'm okay,' said David.

The former detective lit the cigarette and blew a stream of smoke into the morning air. He was different to when David had last seen him, fatter and greyer underneath the eyes. Time and reflection had affected all of them since Charlie's disappearance, but they'd certainly done a job on Alfie.

'I don't like graveyards,' he murmured. 'My mother used to tell me they were haunted.'

'What are you doing here? I heard you were living in England now.'

The detective paused momentarily. 'I am. But when I heard about this, I had to come. Thought it my duty. Same as you, I guess. Though maybe those are different duties.'

'I didn't see you in the congregation.'

'After everything that happened, I didn't think that was a good idea. Do you?'

David shook his head, trying hard to get his pulse down to a normal level. 'No, I do not,' he replied. 'I should punch your teeth out here and now for what you did.'

'What I did?'

'Yes. What you did. You were so hell-bent on me, you let the real culprit get away. You're the reason my son was never found, you're the reason...' David stopped because his voice was starting to shake.

'You're right,' said Alfie. 'I was hell-bent on you. I still have been, these last six years, to tell the truth.' The detective breathed in another cloud of smoke. 'So how about it, David? How about putting an old man out of his misery?'

'Is that what you came here for? A confession? You think a day like this would get the better of me, the way you never could?'

Despite his anger, David almost had to laugh. Alfie Percival was just as hopeless as he had been on the case. But he was glad to know he was still messed up by all of this. He wondered how many dark nights Alfie had spent with the drink, slowly and torturously contemplating if David really had done it. He hoped there were a lot of them. He hoped he didn't sleep at all.

'That's not why I came.' Alfie pulled on the lapels of his coat, buttoning it up around his chest. 'Like I said, it's my duty.'

He spoke the words like they meant something, but to David, they meant little to nothing.

'How does news about this get to England anyway?' asked David.

'I'm living in Cornwall, David, not a different planet.' Alfie turned his head towards Charlie's plot on the edge of the yard. The tree above it was already starting to dispatch brown, oaky leaves into its open mouth. 'I mean, I tried to leave this all behind when I went to Cornwall. I tried to cut it all off, be a new man. I thought I could. I thought time would, you know, put distance on things. Like it would all fade into the past, and I could be on the other side of it. But there's no distance because it won't let go. It's like there's a tether between me and what happened that can't be torn. It's like I can't disconnect.'

He swayed as he talked, and for some reason David found himself nodding. Because he knew what Alfie meant. He knew the feeling one hundred times over. All the same, he still hated him.

'That's what happens when nothing's solved,' said David. 'When it's all left open. I mean, that's what all this is, right?' He raised his arms towards the graveyard. 'This attempt at some kind of closure. It's like a plaster.'

The detective dropped his cigarette to the ground. 'When nothing's solved,' he repeated. 'And you're the man telling me this.'

'Yes. Innocent.'

'If that's still your story.'

Alfie began walking past David, his boots leaving soggy imprints on the wet, autumnal ground.

'You want to be disconnected?' David called after him. 'How about you release everything? The leads, the suspects that you had, everything to do with the case. Make it public knowledge. Then maybe someone can finish what you failed to.'

The detective stopped and looked back at him. 'Someone like you? You want people to point the finger the other way, I guess?'

'There'll never be closure if it's all kept in the dark.'

Alfie shook his head and pulled his coat tight around his body. 'This cold is getting to me,' he grumbled. He went to leave again but hesitated. 'You know, she said this is where the ghosts sleep, my mother. The rest of the time they're out in the world, creaking floorboards and opening wardrobes.'

'I can't get you to believe it wasn't me.' David glared at him. 'You. The man who believes in ghost stories.'

Alfie stared at David with a sad smile. 'We're the only ghost stories I believe in,' he said. Then he turned away and began trudging towards the road.

* * *

The morning sun appeared behind the far caravan, causing a warm glaze to light the strands of Amee's black hair.

'Anything new?' asked David.

His voice was slightly raw. He had no idea how much sleep he'd got last night, but it couldn't have been much. He could feel it in his throat, in his head, in the way he breathed. Maybe thirty minutes. Maybe not even that.

'No,' replied Amee after a few seconds. She was sat on the rug, her blanket still curled around her shoulders. 'There's just the shape.'

'Man or woman?'

'He doesn't know. Just the shape.'

David sighed, leaning back until his deck-chair winced. The 'shape' was all they had got out of Charlie. It was the only thing he remembered from before he died. There was the walk, then the bus, then the shape, and that was it. But still, a shape meant something. And that was more than nothing. All they had to do was try to help him put a face to it, mould the shape into something Charlie could remember. And to do that, they would need the detective.

'Okay,' said David.

'What about you?' asked Amee.

David stared at her, taken aback. 'How d'you mean?'

'Anything new with you? Did your sleep make you think about what you're doing? Did your dreams bite back?'

David frowned, his bottom lip curling towards his teeth. He didn't take the bait. Instead, he stood and gave the sleeping weed-kid a firm nudge with his shoe. 'Get up, Weed-kid,' he growled. 'We're leaving.'

Marty awoke with a splutter. 'Ugh…'

He glanced about himself with his eyes half open. The caravan park was still deserted; the firepit was eking smoke with no warmth. The ground beneath them was still wet with the night's rain.

'What time is it?' he murmured.

'Doesn't matter.' David swung his backpack around one shoulder. 'Get up. I want to leave before anyone asks more questions.'

Five hours into their walk and the sun was glaring down at them. They were treading another long, worn tarmac road, David in front, with Marty and Amee just about managing to keep up behind him. The weed-kid held his shoes in one hand.

'Damn it,' said David, staring down at the thin sheet of a map that he'd taken from the motel.

'What's wrong?' asked Marty.

David stopped, wiping the sweat on his neck. 'This map has got to be wrong. It's this way.' He dithered, then he continued walking.

'Are you sure?'

'We can hope. How's your feet there, Weed-kid?'

'Better now they're not being grated to death.'

'You'll have to put those back on pretty soon; this tarmac will start to cut your feet up. And if we are going the wrong way, we'll have to head back and take a raincheck.'

Marty shook his head. 'I wouldn't put them back on if we were walking on glass.'

Despite the confusing map, the lack of sleep, and the heavy ache in the centre of his skull, David found himself smirking at that. He was actually in high spirits today. Perhaps it was because they were closer. Closer to Alfie, closer to answers, closer to deliverance. It made him happy in a way nothing else had in a long time.

Another twenty or so minutes passed before one of them spoke again.

'What was that thing again, Amee?' asked Marty. His voice was low and hushed, but David heard it.

'What thing?' replied Amee.

'That thing you said the dead were hearing.'

'You want to hear all of it?'

'Yeah, all of it.'

She proceeded to recite the words from beginning to end. Then there was a pause, and the two of them started slowing down. David slowed down with them.

'What's the ocean thing?' questioned Marty, almost in a whisper.

'How d'you mean?'

'*When I think of you, I think of the ocean.* That's what the voice keeps saying. What does that mean?'

David pricked his ears up, recalling the conversation he'd had with Marty the night before. He'd told him about Charlie. About where he had found him, washed up on the pebbles of the tide, seaweed clinging to his skull and his eye sockets filled with coral and sand.

'I don't know,' said Amee. 'We don't know what any of it means, not really. My mum didn't linger on it.'

'Why not?' Marty replied.

'She wanted me to see dead people. That's all she wanted me to do. That's why we were in the hospital. The dead always stay where they die. The hospital had a lot, and I saw them all.'

David stopped, turning around to look down at the two kids. 'So you've seen Kevvy,' he said.

There was another pause. David had wanted to ask her about Kevvy as soon as he'd believed her, but he hadn't done it. There were more important things to think about.

'Kevvy?' she asked.

'Young boy. Skinny. Blonde hair. His name was Kevvy. Kevvy Woods.'

Amee thought, then shook her head. 'I don't remember a Kevvy.'

'But you said they stay where they died. Why wouldn't you see him in that hospital?'

Amee glared at him. 'Don't pretend you care about the dead now.'

A wave of cool air washed down the road, sticking David's clothes to his body. He glared back at her.

'But Charlie doesn't stay where he died,' said Marty. 'He follows you, doesn't he? He moves.'

'Charlie's different to the others,' replied Amee, almost defensively. 'I don't know why. He just is.'

David shook his head. There were times when he forgot just how young Amee was. She claimed she knew the dead people. She claimed she knew how to save them, but the truth was, she knew as little as anyone else. She could only see. But seeing didn't mean understanding. Seeing was just that, staring through a glass door at a world other than her own. A door without a handle, and a world beyond comprehension.

Amee went to say more, but as she did so, a horn sounded from afar. The three of them turned to see a truck hightailing its way towards them.

'Quick,' said David, pushing Marty and Amee to the side of the road. 'If it stops, don't speak. I speak. No tricks this time, Amee.'

The truck started to slow and the wheels spurned off hot steam. It halted on the verge, and through the gap in the window, David saw a lanky man with strangely muscular arms squinting down at them.

'Yer lost?' he asked over the rumble of the engine.

'Not lost,' replied David. 'Just walking.'

'Walkin' where?'

'Where we need to go. No business of yours.'

The man glared down towards the two kids. 'Unusual seeing a man and two little'uns out in the middle of nowhere. He yer dad?'

'Like I said,' said David before Amee or Marty could reply. 'We're just walking.'

'Just walkin' don't answer my concerns. In fact...' The man squeezed the wheel, leaning his elbow outside of the window. '... just walkin' gets me even more nervous.'

'What are you, the patron saint of this road?'

'My name's Mack Goody. Lived around here for longer than the three of yer have lived anywhere. So yeah. Pretty much. They look scared to me. They look tired. Something about this isn't right.' The man opened the door and stepped down onto the tarmac. 'You there, girl.' He pointed at Amee. 'He yer dad? Answer me straight. I can tell if yer lying.'

Amee didn't give him anything. She was looking at something else, something just behind Mack's shoulder.

'Alright, that's enough.' David grabbed Mack by his crumpled jacket. 'How about you get back in your vehicle and mind your own business?'

'Yer not the boss of me.' Mack pushed his arm away. 'If yer want, I can get the rest of the boys down here. How d'yer like that?'

David frowned. He looked between the truck and then Mack. 'Boys? Are you a traveller or something?'

'What's it to you, beardy? If these kids don't tell me where yer going, then what does that tell me? It tells me that –'

'We're going to a caravan park.' Amee's small but curt voice cut him off. She wasn't looking over Mack's shoulder anymore, but staring at him right in the eye. 'The one near the Idle Salt Hotel. He's got a friend there, my dad. But we're a bit lost. Do you know how to get us there?'

Mack eyed David suspiciously. 'Yer got a friend in camp?' he asked.

David shuffled. 'Yeah, a friend,' he replied.

'And he *is* your dad?' Mack looked back towards the two kids, who nodded in response. 'Strange. That's where I'm heading. I live there myself.'

'So can we go with you?' asked Marty hopefully.

Mack sniffed, still glaring at David. 'If that *is* where yer going, sure. Suppose then I'll know yer word is yer word. And if it isn't, yer heading to the wrong place to lie, boy.'

David glared back at him, unblinking, watching as Mack curled a lip and spat onto the ground.

'You can jump on the trailer,' he said, then he turned and climbed back into the driver's seat.

David clasped Amee's shoulder. 'What the hell was that?' he hissed. 'You didn't hear what I told you?'

Marty pushed him away from her. 'Hey, you said it yourself, we were lost. He doesn't know our names, and he's going where we're going. That's a good thing.'

'Yer gonna have to hurry up though,' Mack shouted. 'Yer on my time, remember?'

David huffed. Getting to Alfie was what mattered, he

supposed, no matter how it happened. Getting to Alfie was *all* that mattered. He muttered, 'fine'. And then the three of them climbed onboard.

For the majority of the journey, David stared a hole into the map, occasionally lifting his head to check they were heading in the right direction.

'Close now,' he muttered every so often. 'We have to be.'

Marty was sitting beside him, his long blonde hair blowing wildly in the wind. After a while, he spoke up. 'Why are you staring at that thing?'

'Just making sure,' replied David. 'Get ready to jump the minute he takes us somewhere else.'

'Jesus. What's so suspicious about a guy giving us some help?'

'If you don't find that man suspicious, I can't help you, Weed-kid. The caravan park was miles from where we were, and he just happens to be heading there when Amee mentions it. Plus, he's a gypsy. Being trustworthy isn't exactly his forte. You think he just bought this truck?'

'Being a gypsy makes him untrustworthy, does it?'

'No one's trustworthy, I thought I told you that. There's no reason that this man should –'

'No.' Amee's voice was only just audible over the roar of the wind.

'What?' said David.

'He doesn't have to help,' she clarified. 'But he will. He thinks it's his duty.'

'How do you know?'

'Charlie.'

A familiar sinking feeling shivered hard inside David's gut. Hearing that name still unnerved him, especially now it was said in the present tense.

Marty sat up. 'But how did he know?' he asked.

'He didn't. I wanted to see Charlie, so I opened my eyes, but I saw someone else instead.'

'A dead person?' asked Marty.

Amee nodded. 'Yes. A boy in the truck.'

'It doesn't matter,' said David bluntly. 'What matters is where we're going. Alfie isn't going to be very cooperative. He won't believe anything I tell him, but he'll believe you, Amee. So tell him everything you told me. Everything and more. If you do that, he'll help us.'

'Help *you*,' said Amee.

David resisted the anger which was stinging his chest. 'The house on the cliff,' he said. 'How do you go about finding that, by the way? You dream about helping them. I get it. But you have no idea how to even begin. How long until you realise that? How long until *your* dreams bite back?'

Amee said nothing in return. She peered down the road, perhaps to look for Charlie, David didn't know, and he didn't care. She and Marty could hate him all they wanted. They could argue, moan, and cry, but it wouldn't change anything. They were close to the caravan park now, close to the old detective, whom David hadn't seen since Charlie's box had been buried in the dirt. They were close enough to touch the morning David's son was taken, and that was what was important. He rested his back on the wall of the trailer and returned his gaze back to the map.

When the engine finally rumbled to a halt, the sky had turned dark. Night was hours away, but grumbling rain clouds had spread a thicket of blackness above the treeline, smudging the blue sky like an ink spill. Mack slammed the door of his truck, then walked around to David, Marty, and Amee. Their eyes were glued to the park, swallowing in the ugliness of the place, their noses crinkling against the smell of burnt rubber and damp laundry.

So this is where he ended up, thought David. *A caravan park amidst a sea of shit and soil.* He climbed down from the trailer and stretched out the painful knot in his back. *Could've been a lot worse*, he considered. *It should've been a lot worse.*

'Who is it yer looking for anyway?' said Mack as he stuffed the car keys in his pocket.

'Percival,' replied David. He figured he may as well tell him now that he knew the man was good to his word. 'Alfie Percival. We were told he'd be here.'

'Jesus,' Mack spat. 'Who told yer? 1997? I knew that man; he used to park his car up near here. But I've not seen him for around twelve months now.'

A ball of bile fell into the pit of David's stomach. 'Twelve months?'

'Oh, you've gotta be kidding me,' the weed-kid moaned.

'Sorry about that. Would've thought yer'd know, he bein' yer friend and all.'

'A whole year?' questioned David. 'Did he say where he was going?'

'Nope. At some point, he just stopped showin' up.'

'What,' Marty intervened, 'you didn't check up to see if he was okay?'

Mack scowled at him. 'This isn't no neighbourhood, son. He wasn't one of us in the first place. He was an outsider. Probably figured he'd found somewhere better. Kidding himself more like. I reckon he's ended up in an alleyway shiverin' in the rain, like a lost rat. He always thought he was better than us people. I could see it on his face. He never talked to anyone and he never wanted to know. Why would I look out for him?'

'You said his home is still here,' said David. 'Which one is it?'

Mack stumbled onto the grass and pointed towards a caravan at the end of the stretch, static like the rest of them, alone and desolate by a dense forest. 'He kept himself up there, away from everyone else. Like I said, yer guy thought he was better. He wanted to be alone.'

'I don't doubt it. We'll go there.'

David attempted to convey a sense that all was not lost, but he knew it wasn't looking good. They may even have to go back to square one.

'What yer goin' there for?' asked Mack.

'Yeah,' Marty concurred. 'What's the point?'

'Because we're here and we can look. There could be something inside which might explain where he went. Thanks for the help, Mack, but we're good by ourselves for now.'

Mack scratched his temple. 'Well, alright. Just so yer know, I'd get out before the sun goes. Yer lucky yer've got me; not everyone here's gonna be so accommodating. Yer get any trouble, I'm in the nearest.' He pointed towards the caravan by the grass. Beside it was a low wooden rocking chair in front of a bucket of empty beer cans. 'Not for you, mind, for the kids.'

'Fine,' mumbled David. 'But I don't think we'll –'

'Thank you for your help, Mack,' Amee interrupted, giving Mack a kind and sympathetic smile.

Mack wavered, then nodded, slowly turning away from her before trudging towards his home. Amee turned towards David and Marty.

'It was his son,' she said simply. 'The boy in the truck. That's why he's looking out for me and you, Marty.'

And with that, Amee began walking towards Alfie's caravan.

The park itself was like a maze when the three of them were in the midst of it. The majority of dwellers were inside, but the ones who weren't glared at the three of them. One moment, Alfie's caravan would be in sight, the next it would be lost in a wall of plastic, rubbish, and suspicious gazes. It took five minutes, three dead ends, six dark stares, and four wrong turns before they were finally away from the dwellers and standing in the doorway of the detective's home.

'Jesus,' mumbled David.

He tried the handle, but there was no luck.

'Are you okay?' whispered Marty from behind him, and David turned to find Amee staring at the caravan, a queer and nervous look plastered across her face.

'I don't know,' she replied, taking in her surroundings. 'Something about this place feels strange.'

David jumped down onto the grass and peered in through the foggy windows. 'Blinds are closed. Can't see in.' He scratched his beard and looked back towards the park. 'Marty, keep a lookout. I'll kick the door down.'

'What?'

Without hesitation, David landed his foot square in the middle of the door, knocking it back as if it was barely even being held by the hinges.

'Jesus!' Marty jumped as the door fell onto the carpet, pumping out dust like white chalk into the cooling breeze.

David took a moment, then he stepped inside. The caravan smelled foul. It was deserted, for sure, but not empty. Alfie's things were still littered around the place. Random items of clothing were strewn about the floor; the sink on the far side was filled with plates and cutlery, flies and other bugs clambering over them. Next to the wardrobe, there was a television propped up on some magazines. In front of that, there was a sofa with a bundle of fabric resting against the armrest. It was only when David took a step closer that he realised there was something inside that bundle.

The skeleton was slouched to the right, the skull nestled into the neck and the arms rested down onto the knees of the jeans, as if it was watching television. Beside the legs, a host of maggots squirmed in and out of a lopsided shoe, like they believed there was some flesh somewhere deep inside. Around the collar, a spider had set up shop with a giant cobweb, and around twenty plumped blue-bottle flies were caught above the tip of the arched spine. Dead. Just like the body they were clinging to.

'Holy shit,' whispered David, spotting a hole in the temple of the skull and the gun that lay on the cushion. 'Alfie, what the hell did you do?'

'Oh my God,' came a voice from behind him, and David turned to find Marty and Amee walking inside.

'No! Don't come in!'

But it was too late. The two children stared with wide eyes at the skeleton, Marty cocking his head a little like a scared but curious dog.

'Is that...' he began.

'Alfie,' David finished quietly.

'He's dead.'

'Yes.'

A few moments passed. David waited. He allowed Marty and Amee to take in the sight, soak up the emotions, work them out, put them into some kind of order. He hoped they could. But there was every chance they wouldn't be able to. Things like this shouldn't be seen by the young. Seeing dead was for the old, the learned, the already experienced. Experience was a wall, after all, and innocence was just the foundation. A foundation already damaged would lead to a shoddy wall. Or perhaps no wall at all. David really hoped they could cope.

'Are you okay?'

The voice was low, but it wasn't David who'd asked the question. Amee was looking over at Marty, her deep-blue eyes now decidedly calm in the dim light of the caravan.

'Yeah, of course.' Marty attempted a weird, affirming smile at her.

'Are you both okay?' asked David. The two kids nodded. 'Good. Because I need you to be.'

'What do you mean?' asked Marty. 'Shouldn't we call the police or something?'

David shook his head. 'Think smart, Marty. The last thing I want to do is tell the police where we are.'

His eyes landed on Amee, who peered up at her former teacher with a look that suggested she already knew what was coming. They had come all this way, across grass, roads, and borders. They had come so far, and David wasn't going to let death stand in his way now.

'He's dead. But that doesn't mean we can't still talk to him. Can you do it? Is he still here?'

A silence fell across the room. Only the wings of flies, the shuffle of maggots, and the deafening presence of the body on the sofa remained. Then Amee took a shaky breath.

'I can see.'

16

THE GIFT

The dead man was in two places. One, dead, on the sofa. His body rotted to the bone, his veins drained, his eye sockets emptied, his creases and corners cobwebbed. But two, in the corner, Alfie Percival. Alive but not really. Not alive as anyone knew it. Not alive as anyone *should*. Amee opened her eyes and saw him.

'Hello.'

The man was by the sink. He was watching all three of them with a look of confusion that Amee often saw in the dead. It was a look that you would expect to see on someone in his predicament. In the room, but not in the room. With people, but not really. The look you would see if you were to glance in a mirror in the midst of a dream.

Mr Cooper stared at Amee with wild desperation. 'He's here?' he asked.

Amee nodded. The blinds of the caravan were closed, so it was dark, but Amee still tried not to look at the skeleton on the sofa. She didn't like seeing Alfie there twice. The dead had always been so real to her. They had always felt as alive as anyone else. But seeing the body on the sofa, seeing the fabric still clinging to the bones like it still kept them warm, and then seeing Alfie in the corner of the caravan... the dead had never felt so dead. *Charlie's in the bag too, remember.* That was true, she supposed. She didn't find that scary, but then she never truly made that connection with Charlie. There was no body, no clothes, no inkling of a past. It was like the thing in the bag wasn't really him at all. It was just a stone, a strange piece of rock that had lost all suggestion of life.

'Alfie,' she muttered. 'Are you able to help us?'

The dead man cocked his head and spoke in a gravelly tone, like there was still phlegm stuck in his throat. 'You can see me?' he asked.

'I can see you,' replied Amee. 'Don't worry. Everything's alright.'

'I don't understand.'

'You don't have to understand. It's okay, you don't have to.' Amee walked forward, careful not to step on any of the maggots that were roaming near Alfie's feet. 'How long have you been here?'

'I don't... I don't know. It feels like I've been here a long time. I feel... I can feel something warm. But I can't get to it. I can't move. I...' He stopped. 'David Cooper. Is that David Cooper?'

Amee glanced at Mr Cooper.

'Tell him what we need,' the teacher said. 'We can't be here too long.'

Amee frowned. His eagerness reminded her of her mum. That firmness, that look, that inhuman focus on getting answers. It was like they weren't even people anymore. But Amee knew they were. And she was the one who spoke to the dead.

'Alfie, can you tell me what happened here?' she asked.

Alfie shook his head. 'What do you mean?'

Amee gestured towards the gun on the sofa. She never tended to ask directly. Sometimes people in the mid-space were so confused they didn't even realise they were dead to begin with.

'This,' she clarified. 'How did this happen?'

At that moment, a pang of something strange flowed inside her. It was the feeling she'd had outside the caravan. Something like a wave of emotion; the one that rushes through the body when you remember something happy or something sad. Only with Amee, it culminated in nothing. It was an emotion she didn't recognise, a memory she couldn't quite place. She tried to shake it out.

'People,' said Alfie simply.

Amee hesitated. 'What do you mean, people?'

'There were people here.'

The stretching of old plastic sounded in the background as Marty sat down on a table. His legs were clearly shaking, but he tried to hide it by squeezing his knees and placing his feet firmly on the floor.

'They asked me,' Alfie continued. 'They wanted to know about the boy. The case. I didn't solve the case.'

'I'm not talking about people,' said Amee. 'I'm not talking about that. I just want to know what made you do this.'

'We know what made him do this,' said Mr Cooper.

Amee ignored him and pointed at the body. 'Why did you do this, Alfie?'

'This? This wasn't me. This was someone else. The people.'

'What do you mean, people?'

'It was the people. People came here. They knocked on my door, and they shot me with a gun.' Alfie pressed a

252

finger up on his temple. 'Right here.'

'Someone killed you?'

'What?' Marty and Mr Cooper said together.

'Someone. Yes. The people.'

Alfie turned his back for a second. He moved over to the sink and tried to touch the insects hovering around the dishes.

'Why did someone kill you?' asked Amee.

A bump suddenly sounded from behind her, and Amee turned to see Marty clinging hard to the string of the plastic blind behind him, his face shining white in the darkness of the caravan.

'Can I open the blinds?' he asked. 'Get some light in?'

'No,' said Mr Cooper harshly. 'What's he saying, Amee?'

The dead man stared at Mr Cooper. Amee knew about the hatred that had existed between them. Mr Cooper never failed to show it in the way he talked. But now that they were finally reunited, none of that seemed to show. There was nothing for Mr Cooper to see, and Alfie stared with a vacancy not dissimilar to his skeleton on the sofa. But then, that was the case for all in the mid-space. They should have been completely disconnected from this life, but they were being held against their will, looking at things from a hundred feet up, waiting for someone to cut the line and let them go.

'They wanted something from me,' murmured Alfie. 'They wanted to know things, things that had happened a long time ago.'

'They wanted to know about Charlie,' said Amee.

'They took my gun, and they told me to tell them everything I knew.'

'Who were they?' questioned Amee.

'There were three.'

'Can I get some light in?' Marty stood up from the table, a look of desperation on his face. 'Please. I don't feel good. Can I open the blinds?'

'Shut up, Weed-kid,' Mr Cooper hissed at him. 'If you can't deal with it, go outside. Amee?'

Amee peered from her friend to her former teacher, spotting the sweat which was now threading into his beard.

'They wanted everything,' said Alfie. 'Everything on the boy, the suspects, the leads...'

'But that's why we're here,' Amee revealed. 'That's what we want to know.'

'I had nothing. Nothing to tell. Nothing to give. So they shot me.'

There was a short silence. Amee tilted on her feet slightly, looking over at the dead man with a sense of dread.

'What's happening?' whispered Mr Cooper.

Amee turned back to him. 'People came here for the same reason we did. They wanted to know about Charlie. They wanted to know everything he had on him.'

'And what does he have? Suspects, leads, what?'

'Nothing.'

'What do you mean, nothing?'

'He had nothing to give them.'

'That's bullshit.'

'David always wanted to know,' said Alfie. 'Everyone wanted to know. But the truth is, there was always nothing. The boy didn't go missing. He disappeared. Disappeared into thin air. There was nothing to hold on to. I thought it had to be David. His alibi was the only one that didn't add up. I said there was nothing else. There was no one else it could have been. I was so sure. But they didn't believe me.'

Amee watched as Mr Cooper lowered himself into a chair,

pressing his hands together, twitching with violent tremors.

'He can't have nothing,' Mr Cooper muttered. 'That's bullshit...'

'It's not,' whispered Amee. 'Mr Cooper, he died because he had nothing. He's not lying.'

For a while, there was silence. The dead man stayed by the sink. Mr Cooper sat still, scratching his fingers, digging into the skin as if spilling blood would help alleviate the despair streaming through him.

'But why would people do that?' Amee turned to the dead man. 'Why would people kill you for that?'

Another bump sounded from behind her, and Amee turned again to see Marty pulling on the blinds. A soft rush of light entered the caravan, and Alfie's eyes widened, his expression changing from emptiness to bleak horror. He gaped at Amee.

'You...'

Amee took a step back. 'Me?'

'You're the girl at my door. You've been here before. You were here with them, weren't you?'

Amee didn't answer. She swallowed back a sick feeling which was beginning to swell inside her gut.

'You were here when they killed me. You look different. But it's you.'

'No,' said Amee firmly. 'I've never been here before.'

'You were with them. I know your eyes.'

'What's he saying?' asked Marty.

'I don't know,' replied Amee. 'I don't know what he means.'

But Amee did know. She felt it again, that pang of remembrance, that undeniable feeling that she knew this room. She knew the sofa, she knew the television, she knew Alfie himself. She'd walked on this carpet before. *But that's impossible,* she thought. *How could I not remember?*

'You were here,' said Alfie. 'I remember the last eyes I saw and I'm looking into them now. They're the same.' The dead man started to shake as he talked. A shot of anger had been pumped into him, reinvigorating the blood like it was flowing once more.

'No,' said Amee, backing away.

'It was you,' he cried. 'I know it was. It was you!'

At that moment, Alfie pushed himself forward, moving towards her with his arms outstretched. He lunged as if he meant to throttle her on the spot.

'YOU!'

'NO!'

Amee fell backwards and clamped her eyes shut, squeezing both palms into her face and pulling her knees up to her chest. The voice faded into nothing and the room was plunged into a harsh silence. Marty came up beside her, his face pale and confused.

'Amee, are you okay? What happened?'

She looked up. The dead man was gone now. Only his body remained, slouched over on the sofa, as if he hadn't just charged at Amee with a roar of fire and fury. But he had. And he was still there, Amee knew. Alfie was there now. Still in the room. Still full of fire. His hands could have been around her neck at that very moment. She gasped and pulled herself up.

'I want to go!'

She looked at Mr Cooper. He was still sitting on the chair, staring at the body.

'Okay, we're going,' said Marty. 'We're going. Aren't we?'

They waited, but Mr Cooper didn't respond. He was staring at the skeleton, gazing into the black and empty eyes that had given him nothing in life and given him less in death.

'We're going,' Marty said again, and without waiting for the teacher, he pulled Amee onto her feet and led her through the doorway.

* * *

'Do you know what I said to you the first time I found out what you were capable of? Do you remember?'

Mrs Nightly stroked Amee's cheek, spiralling the small droplets of tears into warm wet circles. She'd been crying for two days now. Her face was red, hidden behind a tangle of mousy hair. Her nurse, Mrs Nightly, smiled at her.

'You've forgotten, haven't you? When they sent me to you, they said you were damaged. They said you were ill, confused. They said that one time you tore the curtains down in your room and burned them in the garden, because your imaginary friend didn't like them being closed when you weren't there.'

Mrs Nightly held the side of Amee's face gently, and Amee shivered. She had always liked Mrs Nightly. She was a good nurse. Kind, warm, and comforting. But now she could hardly even look at her. Mrs Nightly leaned forward, two long strands of pretty blonde hair falling from her shoulders as she did so.

'They called you a burden. But you're not a burden; you're none of those things. Do you remember what I said you were?' Her smile dropped, and she scrubbed away the wetness on Amee's cheeks with her thumb, cleaning her up like a lioness cleans her cub. 'I said that you were a gift. A special gift. More special than anyone could believe. Everyone else pales in comparison to you. Even me. No one else matters. You shouldn't cry over anything else, you mustn't.'

'But I don't understand,' cried Amee. 'Why did he have to die?'

Mrs Nightly leaned backwards and her chair creaked beneath her. 'You're not listening to me, are you, Amee? All we care about is you. Your gift, what you can do, what you can achieve. One man's death is not important, not when it gets us closer to finishing our work.' Mrs Nightly waited a moment, watching Amee as she continued to sob. 'It won't be like this forever. One day, all our lessons will be over. You'll see then; you'll see how right I was, how special you really are. Until then, whatever we do, we do it because we must.'

Amee shook her head, her whole body beginning to tremble uncontrollably. 'But I don't want to do this anymore. Not now.'

There was a pause. Mrs Nightly stood and paced over to the nightstand beside the bed to retrieve her messily bound notebook.

'We've talked now, Amee. There isn't any more to it. Let's start the lesson. Can you close your eyes?'

'No.'

'Close your eyes for me, Amee.'

'I don't want to do what you say anymore. I want to...'

Amee stopped, wincing as she looked about the room. She felt like the place was closing in on her, like the walls were getting smaller, tighter, falling around her body like a trap. A feeling of horrible dread rose inside her belly.

'I don't want to be here anymore. I want to go. I don't want to do what you say.'

'Amee...'

'I can't.' Amee felt herself breathing faster, panic billowing through her veins, tightening her muscles, constricting her head, her thoughts, her very being. 'I can't be here anymore!'

'But you're –'

'I don't care what I am! I can't help you anymore! I want to leave!' Amee jumped from her chair and ran over to the door. 'I want my mum! I want my mum! Please, oh God, I want my mum!'

She kicked the wood over and over again until it felt like her toes were bleeding beneath her socks. Then a pair of arms wrapped around her from behind, and Amee whimpered as she was pulled to the floor.

'Shh! Shh! Shh!' Mrs Nightly held her head and pressed her lips right up close to her ear. 'Okay! It's okay!' She kissed her cheek, and Amee bawled out loud, the room blurring in the midst of her tears.

'It's not okay! I want my mum!'

The door opened and the tall man stepped through. His dark eyes glared down at them both. 'What's the little fishy crying about now?' he said.

'I want my mum! I want my mum! Please help me, I want my mum!'

'She wants her mother,' Mrs Nightly told him. 'She wants her mother and she'll get her.'

The tall man nodded, staring down at the girl as she squeezed her knees tight into her chest.

'It's okay,' whispered Mrs Nightly. 'You'll get her, Amee. I'll bring her here. Just you watch me. I'll do it. You'll get your mother.'

Mrs Nightly kissed her a few more times and then there was silence, broken only by the ever-flowing waterfall which was landing in damp patters on Amee's lap, before disappearing entirely into the fabric.

* * *

Amee stared at the stars through the trees. She liked looking at the sky without a clock, with no indication of how early it was or how late. No indication of whether the stars were filling or fading, starting to glow or beginning to dim. Was the sky going blacker? Or was dawn about to turn the page? Perhaps neither. Perhaps the night would go on forever. Like maybe there was no order to things. Maybe the morning didn't have to come, if it didn't want to. Amee liked that, the feeling that maybe the world didn't follow the clock, the feeling that maybe the world followed its own instinct.

A rustle of leaves sounded from behind her. Amee turned to see Marty walking forward, carrying a clog of branches in both arms. She was perched on a log. Shivering. Remembering. *Tell him. You should tell him. You should tell someone.* She knew she should, but the truth was, Amee didn't want to tell anyone. How could she expect anyone else to understand when she couldn't even understand it herself? She had been there. At some point, at some time, she had been at the caravan. She was sure of it. She had seen Alfie Percival before. His body intact, his veins filled with blood instead of maggots, his aged and damaged eyes looking into her own. She remembered she had talked to him. Her. The tall man. And the woman. That woman.

Amee touched her temple gently. Mrs Nightly. Her nurse. Where had she gone? Disappeared into a warped and fuzzy memory. She remembered the blonde hair, and the suit, a black suit. Amee pushed harder on her temple. The memory was clouded, coming through in bits, the emotions strong but the pictures faded. She squinted her eyes and tried to remember, but the whole thing was like a distant dream, a door in her mind that was locked shut. She let go of her temple and tried to stop herself trembling. *Calm down,* she thought to herself. *Be strong. It's a locked door, but opening any door is possible; you just have to work out how.*

'I'm not getting any more.' Marty dropped the branches, letting them tumble and snap beside his feet. 'Especially if I'm not getting any help.' He glanced over at their former teacher.

Mr Cooper was sitting with his back against an old oak, his chin clamped to his knees and his gaze as empty as Alfie's. He'd been hardly any help since they'd left the park. They'd walked for four miles, and all he'd given them in that time was a slight grunt when Marty suggested they should get some rest in the forest overnight.

'Lighter.' Marty walked over to Mr Cooper and pointed at his bag. 'Mr Cooper, we need a lighter.'

The teacher didn't respond. He scratched the back of his head, ignoring Marty's voice as if it had been just another squawk of one of the nearby owls.

'For shite's sake.' Marty marched over to the bag and sifted through the contents. When he returned to the branches, he bent down low and shoved dead leaves into the midst of the bundle. 'Freezing. It's actually freezing.'

'Sorry, I should have helped.' Amee tore herself away from her thoughts, reaching down to push some of the forest floor into the bundle herself.

'It's fine,' Marty replied.

'No, I should have. I'm sorry.'

'Don't be.'

Marty pulled out the lighter and pressed it up against the wood with a quick flick. To Amee's relief, it caught straight away. Marty sat down beside her, both his elbows resting against his knees as he blew into the rising flames.

There was a brief silence. Amee shuffled uncomfortably. She'd been expecting questions for two hours now, but none had come. No one wanted to talk about what had happened in the caravan. The shock was still streaming through them, the confusion, the fear. It was like they had to let it linger for a while. Get some sleep. And then they would be in the right place to discuss it. That was what Amee had thought. But with Marty, it was like he didn't even want to look at her. Like he was angry. She'd sensed that much the day before, after he'd come back from his walk. In fact, she'd sensed it for a while now.

'Are you okay?' she asked.

Marty nodded, picking up a stick and prodding the fire with the pointy end. 'I'm fine.'

'You're not fine.'

Marty tilted his head, peering above Amee's shoulder in the way he usually did when he was scared Charlie might be listening. But Charlie wasn't there right now. After what had happened in the caravan, Amee didn't want to open her eyes to the dead, not even for her friend.

'How do you know I'm not fine?' asked Marty.

'I can see more than just the dead people, you know.'

Marty leaned back and dropped the stick into the fire. 'It should be me asking that.'

'What do you mean?' asked Amee.

'I was pretty useless back there. I've been pretty useless for all of this.'

Amee stared at her friend, watching as his face glowed and flickered in shadows. She wondered whether it was the smoke making his eyes wet, or something else.

'I don't know what you mean,' she said.

Marty stretched his fingers out to the flames, glaring at the ash as it danced into the air. 'When I first decided to come with you, I thought I could... I dunno. I thought

262

I could be something more.'

'You don't want to be here anymore,' said Amee suddenly.

'No, that's not it. I just…' Marty sat up and took a deep breath. 'The truth is, Amee, you're stronger than I thought you were. When I decided to come with you, I did it because I thought you might need protecting. I thought you might need me.'

'But I do need you.'

'No, Amee, you don't. Ever since you left Gealblath, you've been strong, way stronger than I ever thought you could be. When I started all this, I thought I could be more than who I am. Like I could actually be someone better than the weed-kid, like I could be brave. But I'm not. Back in that caravan, when you were there talking to Alfie, with his body on the sofa, I felt like I was gonna be sick. I was useless and scared. More scared than I've ever been. It's stupid.'

'But Marty, I do need you. You don't understand. Without you…' Amee peered over at Mr Cooper and felt a shiver go through her spine. 'I couldn't do this if I was alone with him. You stop me being afraid. Remember the first time we met? Gealblath Secondary School was terrifying to me. I'd never been to school before. All those people, all those teachers, Rory…'

'Yeah, but Amee, that's just school. It's stupid.'

'It wasn't stupid for me. I was scared. There was one morning, these girls threw my shoes up onto a locker, and I felt so alone that I was gonna leave. It was the same day I met you, and you made me stay. You made me better.' She stumbled over her words, trying desperately to find the best way to say it. 'That's what you do, Marty. You make me better. You keep me calm amongst all this, just by being my friend.'

Marty kept his eyes down on the flames, picking incessantly

at his nail. 'Just being here doesn't make me strong though. Just being here doesn't make me brave.'

'Of course it does. Marty, I *had* to leave Gealblath. If I hadn't, then the dead would never even have had a chance of getting to the other side. Don't you see? I had to be strong for them. If I'm the only one who can save them, then I have to become brave, even though I'm not. It's like it's not even my choice. But with you... no one made you do this. There wasn't some higher calling. You chose to come with me of your own accord. That's brave. That's braver than anything I could ever do.'

Marty visibly took in what she said, mulling over her words. 'Yeah?' he said after a few seconds.

Amee reached over and placed her hand on his. 'You remember what I said to you the first time we saw each other? I said you were Venkman. And you are. You're the best person I know. Seriously, the best.'

Marty sighed, a familiar smile spreading across his face. Amee hadn't realised how much she'd missed that smile.

'But you still haven't decided what *Hobbit* character I am.'

'No, I haven't,' laughed Amee. 'But you're the good guy. That's all you need to be.'

Marty nodded. 'That's nice. But after a few weeks without a shower, I think I'm definitely verging on Gollum.'

The pair of them giggled, and Amee swayed on the log, bending down to smell her armpit. 'Then we're both Gollum. Mr and Mrs Gollum.'

'Sounds bonnie to me.'

Amee smiled. She realised that her hand was still clasping Marty's. She looked down, and he did too.

'You know, I...' Marty began to move his hand away,

but Amee clasped it harder, staring at Marty as he shivered in the light of the fire.

He looked handsome in the embers. Prettier than he'd ever looked before. An impulse caught her then, the same kind of impulse that she'd had in the school corridor that one time. Without even thinking about it, Amee leaned forward and pressed her lips against his. There was a moment when it felt like he might be about to pull away, but then he grabbed hold of her shoulders and began to kiss her back. Amee stayed rigid on the log, moving her lips up and down in an attempt to imitate the way kissing was done in the movies. She dreaded to think what it looked like from the outside, but from the inside, it felt okay. *Don't think. Don't think about it. Just do it.* She left her brain behind and fell into him, her eyes flickering open for just a moment to take everything in. This was the closest she'd ever been to Marty's face, she realised. The closest she'd been to his skin, his eyelashes, his eyebrows, the strand of hair which had fallen from behind his right ear. It felt nice to be this close. It felt right. She closed her eyes again, trying hard not to smile. A couple more seconds passed, and Amee finally let go, inching backwards and staring at Marty to gauge his reaction.

'Was that okay?' she asked, her voice shaking a little.

Marty smiled. 'Yeah.' His voice was shaking too. He squeezed her hand.

'Yeah,' she said back.

And for that moment, Amee was happier than she'd ever been in her life. For that moment, she forgot everything. She forgot her mum, that nurse, the tall man, the dead body, and the way it had raged at her. She forgot everything that wasn't that moment or that night. She wished it never had to end. She wished they could stay on that log forever. She wished the fire would never die and their skin would always be warm beside it. She wished Marty would hold her hand for that night and for the rest of time. And perhaps the morning wouldn't come.

17

THE SCOTTISH SNAIL

When Marty awoke, the sky had gone funny. Four streams of red clouds striped the surface like bleeding gashes, staining the rest of the space with a light shade of pink. Just where the horizon began to dip, there was a quiet speckle of stars still hovering over the tree line. He lay against the log and watched them for a while, his breath swirling into the air in its own cloud, every so often fading the stars from view. He twisted, spotting Amee lying asleep beside him, and his heart *kerplunked*. It had been racing all night, and now it was racing again. Just the sight of her sleeping there, puffs of white air slipping delicately from her lips. Her messy black hair and her small, curled-up fingers... Suddenly everything that had happened the day before, the terrible things he had seen, the terrifying dread that he had felt, it had all become meaningless. Because last night, Amee Florence had kissed him.

'How was it?'

'I'm not gonna give you the details, Mike.'

'It's your duty to give us the details. We need them. You know, as research. Preparation.'

'Preparation for what?'

'Our maths test next week. What the hell do you think?'

'So everything that happens with me and Amee, I have to relay back to you and Teddy for your own research?'

'Yes, that's the rules of the bro code. We thought you knew.'

'What section is that, then?'

'It's in there.'

Marty sat up on the forest floor, craning his neck from left to right until he heard a click. Of course, kissing Amee had been amazing, but it seemed to have opened up a void that had been resting deep down inside him. It made him miss his friends. He imagined how excited Mike and Teddy would have been. He imagined Teddy's jaw dropping in shock. He imagined Mike's eyes widening in horror. The bro code would have undoubtedly been called into question, and Teddy's confused ramblings on female interaction would have indisputably taken place. But Marty would never truly know. Because his friends were miles away, in another country, with no idea of where he was or what he was doing. For all they knew, he could be dead. He sighed sadly. It wasn't like he could talk to Amee about it. And he certainly couldn't talk to Mr Cooper.

Marty looked over to the oak tree, expecting to see the teacher slumped over in his sleep. But the teacher was gone. Nothing but his bag remained in the midst of the oak's shadow. Marty clambered to his feet.

'Mr Cooper?' he called out.

Amee fidgeted, her eyes still clamped shut against the world. Marty frowned. They had left Mr Cooper to his own thoughts all night. But now he was gone, with nothing but a few cigarette butts left in his wake. *But he can't have gone far*, Marty thought. *All his stuff is still here.*

He stared into the undergrowth, attempting to look past the thick tangle of twisted branches. *Maybe he's gone for a walk. To clear his head, perhaps.* Somehow Marty doubted that. But nevertheless, he began walking further into the forest.

It didn't take long before his mind fell back to the fireside again as he walked. He thought about what Amee had said, about his being brave enough to come with her in the first place. She was right, he supposed. He was wrong to feel so cowardly and useless, and he was stupid to feel jealous of her. But he still had to prove it. Being told he was brave was one thing, but it meant nothing if he couldn't show it. He just needed the chance. And when the chance came, he had to pull through, not cower in the corner like he'd done in Alfie's caravan. This whole thing could still be his story. All he had to do was rise to the pages.

Marty trod over a clump of brambles and shook himself back to the task at hand. He called out into the forest.

'Mr Cooper?'

There was no response. Perhaps he'd left them, Marty pondered. Perhaps he had left them both now that his plan had come to nothing. Perhaps. Or perhaps something else had happened. Marty felt his heart start to beat faster. Perhaps something worse had happened, he thought. Perhaps something unthinkable.

'Mr Cooper?' he called again.

Marty broke into a jog. Rushing water sounded from beyond the trees, and he turned, cursing a little as a string of branches whipped into his face. He tore them down and began sprinting. After a few seconds, the mesh of branches began to thin and the trees around him grew sparse. He slowed down as he ventured into an open space. Surrounding him was grass, with four rocky streams tangled around it as messily as the woodland behind him. The air was still and peaceful. The streams were like veins, almost pulsing, like Marty had stumbled upon the heart of the forest.

Mr Cooper was sitting and staring into the smallest stream. His legs were crossed and his arms were folded. The skull of Charlie Cooper was perched neatly atop a stone in front of him. He had never taken it out in the day before. Marty had only ever seen it in the nighttime, a small white thing in the darkness.

'Marty,' the teacher said, acknowledging his arrival.

'I didn't know where you were,' Marty panted.

The teacher didn't respond. Marty took a few steps forward and sat down on the rock beside the skull.

'Are you alright, sir?' he asked.

'I thought I'd bury him,' said Mr Cooper, ignoring the question. 'When all this was over, I thought I'd bury him.'

Marty didn't quite know how to respond to that, seeing as Mr Cooper had never really wanted to talk about Charlie before. But Marty had always wanted to know more about the skull, so he decided to encourage him.

'Why didn't you before?' he asked tentatively.

'He came to me,' replied Mr Cooper. 'On the beach. He was just sitting there, like he was just another shell in the ocean. He came to me, but I couldn't do it. I couldn't put him in the ground, say the words, walk away.'

Mr Cooper shook his head, then leaned over and picked up the skull, holding it firmly in both hands. Forest water dripped from the crack in the head, falling into the teacher's lap with a quiet *tap, tap, tap*.

'Rest in peace,' Mr Cooper mumbled scornfully. 'There's no peace without justice. There's no rest when those responsible still walk on the ground you're buried beneath. How could I do that? Keeping him close was the only thing I could do.' He placed the skull back on the wet stone, his eyes finally looking up at Marty.

'So what now?' Marty asked.

The teacher slouched. The essence of his resolve had gone; Marty could see that now. That drive, that compulsion, that will. All of it had been stripped away back in the caravan, gnawed to the bone like the dead man himself.

'There's nothing we can do.'

'But the detective –'

'Had nothing. No leads, no suspects, nothing. All he had was me. No wonder he was so hell-bent.'

'But the detective was killed,' Marty argued. 'Some people came to his caravan asking about the case. They killed him. That's what Amee said. Whoever they were, maybe they had something to do with it. Maybe they wanted to make sure there were no loose ends or something.'

'And how do you find them?' said Mr Cooper. 'Where do you begin?'

Marty hesitated. He couldn't think of an answer to that, and it surprised him that he had even tried. Ever since the cabin, all he'd wanted to do was get as far away from Mr Cooper as possible. To take Amee's hand and run as fast as he could. After all, it was Mr Cooper who had taken Amee against her will. It was him who had led them into another country to find justice and revenge. But now Marty had seen the people they were dealing with. He had seen what they had done to Charlie, to the detective, and in a strange way, he couldn't help it. That small burning feeling had struck him too.

'If you give up now,' said Marty, 'they'll be out there forever. They'll get away with it.'

Mr Cooper looked up, evidently just as surprised as Marty. 'I used to come to a place like this,' he said then. 'Me and a friend of mine. We used to come and pretend the world was something different. His mum would come and pick us up, and most of the time she would be sober. But she loved two things, the addiction and Kevvy. And one day she loved the addiction just that little bit more.'

A gust of wind rustled the trees around them, and Marty shivered underneath his shirt.

The teacher continued, 'When he died, they put Kevvy in a box and put that box in the ground. Everyone was saying words about the kind of kid he was. But all of them were wrong. None of those words described my friend. They were all about someone else. A memory I was meant to recognise. They put a stone over him with his name on it, then someone came up to me and told me not to blame her.'

Marty watched as tears began falling down the teacher's cheeks.

'They sent her away,' he said shakily. 'She did time, but not a lot of it. And then she lived the rest of her life. Everyone lived the rest of their lives. Everyone moved on, and no one blamed her. But none of them saw my friend the moment he was about to die. No one saw the look on his face, or heard the sound of his voice. Only I did. All I felt after he went was anger. I gave myself up to it, let it take over, become a part of who I am. But justice isn't a word the world understands. I should have realised then that the world doesn't give you justice, and any attempt to get it only deepens the anger more. It spreads the roots, makes them sink, until that's all there is.'

He looked Marty dead in the eye.

'Don't give in to it, Marty. Don't even let it start. Because when it starts, it grows, and when you get to the other side and the world is no different, there'll be nothing else left of you.'

The last of the autumn leaves fell to the water, darkening and then sinking, moulding themselves around the wet stones. Marty watched as the teacher dropped his gaze, wiping away his tears.

'So what now?' he asked again.

'Now...' Mr Cooper paused. 'Now you should get back to Amee. You don't want her to be alone when she wakes.'

The voice had turned monotonous again, and Marty could tell Mr Cooper wanted him to leave, so he pulled himself up from the forest floor.

'What about you?' he asked nervously.

'I'll be with you in a second, Marty. Don't worry about me. Just give me a bit more time.'

Marty swayed on the spot, then turned slowly and began walking back towards the trees. He looked back only briefly to see Mr Cooper still staring at the skull, his thumb rubbing circles into the temples and his breath blowing small clouds into the face, warming his son's cheeks like they might just go red once more.

When Marty got back to Amee, she was still asleep, her head now buried under a mess of greasy black hair. Marty looked at her for a moment, smiled, then perched on the nearby log. He reached down to remove a half-eaten cereal bar from his backpack, and just as he did so, Amee shuffled and pulled back the black strands of hair from her eyes.

'Sorry,' said Marty through a clump of sticky granola. 'I didn't mean to wake you.'

'I'm fine,' replied Amee, blinking the world back into consciousness.

'Want some?' Marty held out the cereal bar.

'What is it?'

'I dunno – fruit and nut, I think.'

'Do you have any more peanut butter ones?'

'No. No, you ate all of them.'

'Oh.'

Amee dipped her head disappointedly, then she sat up and gazed around the forest. Marty swallowed the rest of the cereal bar in a hurry. *She hasn't said anything,* he thought to himself anxiously. *Maybe she's forgotten. Maybe it was all a dream to her.*

But then Amee looked up at him and smiled. 'You okay?' she asked.

'Yeah, I'm okay. Are you okay?'

'I'm grand.'

There was a brief silence. Then both of them started to laugh. They did so for thirty seconds before the sound of twigs breaking cut them off and Mr Cooper appeared from the undergrowth.

'What are you two so happy about?' he grumbled.

'Mr Cooper...' Marty began, but he stopped as soon as he noticed the teacher's hands. The skull wasn't with him. It was gone. Mr Cooper's hands were bare, naked, and clinging onto each other as if they could sense the emptiness between them.

'We're leaving,' he said simply. Then he trod over towards his bag and swung it around his shoulder. 'We're leaving now.'

Twenty minutes later, they were back on the road. Marty

was still shoeless. He'd put them on to start with, but it hadn't taken long before he was wincing in agony, and he had ripped them off and flung them as far as he could. Only four vehicles passed by as they walked, and every time they did, Mr Cooper had them on the verge, their faces away from the windows and their eyes down on the ground. No one stopped. To everyone else, they were just ghosts on the road. Three more dead leaves blowing wherever the wind would take them. They weren't so wrong about that, Marty supposed.

After another ten minutes, Amee finally whispered to him, 'What's happening?'

Mr Cooper was ahead by a few paces, his head bowed and his hands held tight in his pockets.

'I think it's over,' replied Marty.

'What do you mean, it's over?'

'I mean the detective's dead, and he doesn't know who did it. I think Mr Cooper's giving up.'

Marty winced as the soles of his feet began to leave traces of blood in the wet cracks of the tarmac. He glanced at Amee and was taken aback slightly by the look on her face.

'Oh,' she replied simply.

'What's wrong?'

'Nothing. Why?'

'I thought you'd be relieved. After all, this means we can start looking, doesn't it? The house on the cliff, the place we need to get to. That's a good thing, right?'

Amee didn't say anything to that. She had a look in her eye, the same look that Marty had seen there many times before. She wanted to tell him something. She wanted to say something important, but she couldn't do it.

'What is it?' he asked softly.

But Amee shook her head. 'Nothing.'

The rest of the journey was passed in silence. The closest town was only around three miles away, but the journey felt more like three hundred miles. By the time they got there, Marty was miserable. Any remnant of last night's euphoria had eked out of him as steadily as the blood on his feet.

The town was weird looking. It was cramped and narrow, grey and decrepit. The houses all looked the same, and the roads were cracked in the heat. Chunks of black tarmac stuck up a few inches from the ground, like the road was supposed to be cobbled. There wasn't a sea breeze. The only thing remotely Cornish about the place was an overabundance of pasty shops. Marty felt his tummy rumble at the smell, but it stopped rumbling when the scent was replaced by the taste of sour beer and cigarette smoke from an inn in the middle of the street. Mr Cooper stopped in front of it. The inn was small, wooden, and slanted. It looked a bit like the gritty taverns Marty had seen in old Western movies. The sign on the front looked like it had been sponged to an inch of its life.

THE SCOTTISH SNAIL

'This seems fitting,' said Mr Cooper.

'It seems shit,' said Marty.

'What are you talking about? It's a home from home. Perfect.'

Marty tilted his head to the small banner underneath the sign. *Welcome to Benny's Sleepy Eatery*. 'This says eatery,' he pointed out.

'Says sleepy too,' replied Mr Cooper. 'Unless we find the

diners sleeping on tables, this should be fine.' He bowed his head and pulled open the door.

Nobody was sleeping inside. While the place wasn't exactly full, the few diners who were there were making such a ruckus it would be easy to think The Scottish Snail was the hottest place in town. Most of them were in the corner, glasses of beer in their hands and lines of froth fuzzing their lips. Their voices were so loud that they almost drowned out the music that was being played at the far end. Marty looked up to the platform. Two cellists were stroking their strings in staccato, and an elderly man was coughing up his lungs into a long silver flute.

Mr Cooper noticed Marty's look and shrugged. 'Like I said. Home from home.' He pointed towards one of the booths by a dusty window. 'There's a table over there.'

'What about you?' asked Marty, but the teacher was already marching over to the bar.

A strange-looking man was eyeing his approach. He had a small hump beneath his neck, causing him to hang forward as if the floor was tilted askew. Two big badges were stitched to his lapels. 'MY NAME IS BENNY SNAILER', one said. 'ASK ME ANYTHING', said the other.

Marty smirked. Snailer. Perhaps 'Weed-kid' wasn't such a bad nickname after all. He followed Amee to the booth, wincing slightly as he stepped inside. He inspected the damage to his feet. They were both bleeding, and one of his heels was badly bruised, but Amee didn't offer her shoes this time. In fact, she didn't take any notice of him. She was watching Mr Cooper.

'What's he doing?' she questioned.

The teacher remained at the bar, the humpbacked man in front of him. He gestured to the ceiling, then opened a book, taking a ballpoint pen from the pocket above his badge.

'I don't know,' replied Marty.

The teacher scribbled something down in the book, then turned and came back to them. 'You've got a room here,' he said as he reclined in the booth. 'Last one available.'

'Us?' asked Amee.

'You. I'll stay here for a few hours, see you're settled in, then I'll leave.'

The cellists shuddered their strings to a finale, and the flautist stood, the veins in his temples beginning to bulge as he tried to keep up with them.

'What do you mean, you'll leave?' asked Marty.

'I mean what I told you, Weed-kid. We're done. That's it.'

'But what about me? What about Amee?'

'You can stay here. Pick up the phone, call home, tell them what you want. The police will come and get you. You'll be fine. I'll be gone.'

Marty sat up. 'We can't find whoever did that to Alfie Percival, but –'

'Marty.'

Mr Cooper raised a hand, his face stern enough to make Marty realise he'd said that a little too loudly. Marty quickly surveyed the bar. Content that no one had heard him, he spoke a bit more quietly.

'But what about Charlie?'

Mr Cooper's face twitched slightly at the mention of the name. 'Like I said, you can do what you want. Go find whatever it is you're looking for or go home. It's up to you.'

'But you can help –'

'No.'

'You can –'

'No.'

The flautist breathed his last note, and the other inn-mates began to cheer and clap.

Marty looked over at Amee. 'Come on, Amee, tell him.'

But Amee was still expressionless. She was staring at the teacher as if it didn't matter to her either way. But it mattered to Marty. He didn't know why, but it did.

'You'd be leaving her,' he said to Mr Cooper. 'What if her mum finds her again? What if she takes her back to that hospital?'

'She won't go back. There are plenty of people who can make sure she never goes back to that hospital again. Like I said, you two can take it from here. It's up to you.'

'Coward.' Marty couldn't stop the word from leaving his mouth. The anger had been starved too much. The line had been crossed. His emotions were at breaking point. But it didn't even faze the teacher.

'Good eyes, Marty,' said Mr Cooper sadly.

Then there was a silence. Marty pushed his back up against the leather with a huff, his gaze sliding away from the teacher to land back on the bar. Benny Snailer was still there, but now he was staring at the three of them, his brows furrowed slightly.

'Mr Cooper,' Marty nodded towards the man, and Mr Cooper followed his line of sight.

He slowly took hold of his bag. 'Come on. The room's upstairs.'

When they entered the room in question, a thick smell of damp wood was lingering in wait for them. It oozed out of the cracks in the floorboards like poisonous fumes, wetting their eyes and creasing their noses. Green mould coloured the walls and bed posts, like a kid had got loose with a crayon, and in the corner, a clump of the windowsill had been eaten away to splinters, with the skeletal remains of dead cockroaches providing the smoking gun below it.

'This really is shit,' said Marty bluntly.

'Beats the woods,' replied Mr Cooper.

He began pacing around, inspecting the place as if he didn't trust the screws that held it together. A strange creak of wood sounded from outside the door, but Marty ignored it. He imagined the whole place was just a few creaks from caving in completely.

'Single bed,' he groaned.

Mr Cooper turned away from a tilted painting of a British garden snail. 'Floor space.'

'So I'm on the floor again.' Marty dropped his bag and let out a sigh. He'd been looking forward to the comfort of a mattress, even if that mattress was damper than any floor he'd been sleeping on for the last month.

Mr Cooper clapped him on the shoulder. 'Very gentlemanly of you, Weed-kid.'

Amee moved over to the window, gazing out at the drab street below, her fingers tapping slightly on the wood. 'So you're leaving us?' she muttered.

A creak of a floorboard sounded from outside the door again.

'Yes,' came Mr Cooper's reply.

'You're leaving Charlie.'

'Charlie left a long time ago.'

'No.' Amee clenched her hands into fists, turning to face the teacher.

'What do you mean, no?' he questioned.

'He never left,' answered Amee. 'If you could talk to him, if you could see, you would –'

'I'd what? My son is dead, Amee. You seeing him doesn't help that. It doesn't help him, it doesn't help Alfie Percival, it doesn't help any of them.' Mr Cooper squeezed on the strap of his bag, his nails digging into the loose strings of old fabric. 'I came here to find the detective. Nothing else.'

'This isn't about Alfie now. This is about Charlie.'

Marty watched in shock. Amee had never spoken to Mr Cooper like this before.

'You're scared,' she said resolutely. 'You're scared, and you don't have to be.'

At that moment, another creak of wood sounded from behind the door. An entire floorboard loosened with a sharp *iirrrrkkkk*, and this time, Mr Cooper noticed it too. He raised a finger to his lips, then trod quietly over towards the entrance and wrapped a hand around the door-knob. He pulled the door open and grabbed whoever was standing behind it.

'OH J-J-JESUS!'

Mr Cooper pulled the intruder into their room and kicked the door closed. It was Benny Snailer, the humpbacked man with the badges.

'What the hell are you eavesdropping for?' the teacher growled at him.

'I'm sorry, I'm n-not eavesdropping, sir. It's just, uh, ow!' The man's shoes slid across the wood, his hands clinging to Mr Cooper. 'I heard you talking. I didn't mean to.'

'You didn't mean to sneak up and listen?'

'Downstairs!' he yelped, his voice high-pitched and squeaky with panic. 'I heard you talking downstairs! I heard a n-name! Hard to miss a n-name like that when you've heard it before! You were talking about Alfie, Alfie P-Percival.'

Mr Cooper hesitated. He loosened his grip, letting the humpbacked man slip away and stumble back into the corner. 'You know about him?' the teacher asked.

'No.' The humpbacked man patted himself down. 'No, not me. But there was s-someone who did. He came from out of town not t-too long ago. Stayed here for a few nights. See, I'm not just f-front of house. I'm the owner. Benny Snailer, sir.' He pointed at his left badge desperately, 'MY NAME IS BENNY SNAILER'.

'The owner?' said Mr Cooper.

'Yes, yes.'

'Why do you care about Alfie, then?'

'I don't care. I don't know the man; no one around here does. But the man who stayed here, he cared. He asked s-something of me. He wouldn't say why, he just asked it. Maybe it was the b-badge.' Benny pointed at the other badge, 'ASK ME ANYTHING'.

Mr Cooper began to unclench his fists. 'Asked what?'

'I've got a reputation around this place, you see. The p-people know the p-pub. This town's so small, you can find everyone in here most days. Streets are empty, then The Snail's plenty. That's what my m-mother used to say. And the p-place has been here a long time, too. Nearly a hundred years. One of the oldest p-pubs in Cornwall to be owned by one f-family. My d-daddy had it, and his d-daddy before him. My son would have had it too if –'

Mr Cooper raised his hand. 'Why are you telling us this?'

'Because the man knew it. He knew that if you want to know what this town is saying, then you come to The Snail. He came here and asked me about Alfie Percival. He t-told me, he said, anyone comes round here with that name on their lips, he wants to know about it. He w-wants to know badly.'

Marty furrowed his eyebrows. 'Why?' he asked.

'He w-wouldn't say why.' Benny looked down at him. 'Just asked me to do it. I'm the man for it, you see. It's why this place has b-been here as long as it has. Good deeds.' He scratched slightly at his hump, and then there were a few moments of silence.

Beneath the floorboards, another band started up. An electric guitar was strummed, and a woman began singing groggily into a microphone. Mr Cooper pulled at his backpack, glancing between Marty and Amee before landing back on The Snail's owner once more.

'What's his name?' he asked.

And Benny Snailer gave a strange smile. 'Let me show you.'

18

A HELPING HAND

The room was small, the ceiling was low, and the desk was so close to the ground that Mr Cooper nearly hit his shins into it when they walked in. Benny Snailer was fumbling amongst the clutter of his drawers. His whole body was bent over, and his long nose was stuffed into files like he was a blind mole digging around in the dirt.

'In here,' he whispered to himself. 'In here s-somewhere. Sure it is.'

David sighed impatiently. He looked over at Amee, who was looking up at the walls. They were covered with kids' drawings. In the middle was a neatly polished portrait. Benny Snailer was there in the centre, his hair thickly gelled and his face white and shining. A middle-aged woman was next to him, squeezed snugly under his right armpit. To the left of them was a boy, well dressed and finely groomed, with a small wooden truck in his hands and a smile beaming brightly between two pointy ears.

Benny pulled his head out of the drawer and spotted

Amee's interest. 'Oh, that's me and the family,' he said with excitement.

'Yeah,' replied Amee.

'Took a while to get a p-professional.' He began rifling again. 'They c-cost so much these days, j-just to p-press a button.'

'You're the one paying them,' said David.

'Oh, yes sir,' said Benny. 'I am. I wanted a good picture before my son left us. I had all these colouring-ins that we'd done together. But I wanted a p-proper picture. He was sick as anything by that point.'

'Who was?' asked Marty from the back of the room.

'My boy. Kidney disease. He left us about a month after that.'

Benny waved a hand towards the frame, and David looked back up at it, staring at the smiling boy in question. He didn't look like he was about to die. He didn't even look sick. He looked happy. But then, anyone would look happy at that age, when death was one of those abstract concepts at the end of a long rope. David swallowed, then turned away, watching Benny.

'We thought we'd bury him in Scotland. That's where my ancestors lived b-before they came down here. Hence the n-name. That's where they're all buried too. I guess you're from up north, too? I can hear it in your accent.'

David faltered, suddenly self-conscious. 'Uh, yeah, up in Glasgow –'

'Yes, here it is!' Benny closed the drawer and placed a scrap of white paper in David's hand, completely uninterested in his fake backstory.

'Roman Guild,' mumbled David as he examined it.

'That's right. Nice man, t-truly. Here...' Benny stood aside and pointed at the phone. 'Feel free. And if you ever need a f-favour from me, all you have to do is ask. I'll do it; that's why The Snail is still standing in this town. Good deeds.' With a shaky nod, Benny put his hand on David's shoulder. 'I'm sorry, I'll give you some q-quiet. My wife says I can t-talk for England.'

He squeezed past David, flashing Marty and Amee a kind smile as he went out into the hall and closed the office door. Then there was silence for a few moments. David stroked his beard, his thumb slowly tracing around the page.

'Alfie,' he said faintly.

'You're going to call?' asked Marty. 'I thought you'd given up.'

'Maybe he knows something.'

'Or maybe he was just looking for Alfie. You know, like we were.'

David shook his head. 'Benny said he came from out of town. He was here for a few nights, three miles out from the caravan site. No, he knew where Alfie was.' David began dialling. He held the phone right up close to his ear, and it rang for what felt like forever before there was a click and a rustle on the other end.

'Hello?' A male voice answered.

'Roman?' asked David.

'Who is this?'

'My name's Ryan. I'm in The Scottish Snail.'

'The Scottish Snail...' The man on the other end of the line dragged the last syllable, lingering on the name like it was a long and distant memory.

'I understand you know Alfie Percival,' said David.

Roman let out a long and muffled sigh. 'Oh,' he said simply.

'What do you know about him?'

'Benny gave you my number?'

'That's right,' confirmed David.

Roman sighed again. 'He's a friend of mine. Old pals on the force. Years and years back now. You're police, right? I mean, I've got that right – I'm talking to police?'

'What makes you say that?'

A shuffling sound came through the small speaker, like the man on the other end might be sitting down.

'I came down not too long ago. Passed it off as a reunion, but it was more like a check-up. I was worried about him. See, after he moved down south, the airwaves kind of went silent. And when I got there...' Roman paused. 'I don't know. The way he was living in that park. Nobody should be living like that, not alone anyway. You're police, aren't you?'

'You wanted to know if his name came up,' said David, ignoring him. 'Here in The Scottish Snail. Why?'

'Like I said, Alfie was alone, cut off. Took me ages to even find him. I stayed in The Snail when I visited. I dunno, what with his airwaves being silent, I just thought I could trust on Benny to keep me updated.'

'Updated how?'

'Let's just say, if Alfie Percival's name was on the lips of anyone in the town, I'd know why. He was a lost man. Suicidal, I was sure of it.'

There was a moment of silence. David heard the band move into a crescendo downstairs. The female stopped singing and she was met swiftly by a cacophony of cheers and wolf whistles.

'He's dead, isn't he?' said Roman.

Another pause. David sighed, that ball of anger and emptiness beginning to knot in his stomach once again. *A friend*, he thought ruefully. *This guy was a friend. A worried friend who wanted to know whether Alife had ended his life.* The hope started to spiral away.

'You're just a friend?' asked David dejectedly.

'Yeah,' replied Roman. 'Yeah, I'm his friend.'

'You don't have anything that could help us?'

'Help you?'

'Listen, if –'

'What d'you mean, help you?'

David wavered. Roman's voice had changed suddenly. It was sharper, stronger, his lips pressed right up against the plastic.

'You don't know anyone who meant him harm?'

'You think someone else was involved?' asked Roman.

'Someone,' said David. 'Maybe some people.'

'Well...'

David leaned forward. To his surprise, Roman actually seemed to be thinking about it.

'I can help,' he said finally.

David nearly dropped the telephone. 'How?'

'I can come down. I'll come down.'

'No, no, you can just tell us. How can you help? What do you know?' His heart began pounding like a hammer drill inside his ribcage, drumming at the bone like it was attempting a prison break.

'I can't tell you on the phone. I'd like to drive down. I can help. Trust me. Stay where you are. I'll be there by morning.'

There was a click, then the line was cut off, leaving nothing but the dead tone.

'What did he say?' asked Marty after a few seconds.

'He knows something,' replied David.

He scratched his beard, his mind racing, rifling through everything he had just heard. The guy knew something. David could tell just from the way he had talked, the way he had breathed. The guy could help. And he was coming to The Snail. Hope was spreading inside David like wildfire. It felt like a hand had reached into the blackness and grabbed him by the lapels, pulling him out of a hole and into the light. But then, the light could have been anything. It could have been the guidance he needed, or it could have been something else, something brighter, closer, hot enough to burn him when touched. The man was Alfie's friend, of course. And any friend of Alfie's was bound to recognise who David was. But that was a chance he'd have to take. It was the last one left anyhow.

'What does he know?' asked Amee.

'You got the last room,' said David as he turned towards her.

'What?'

'I need...' David stopped, his eyes creasing a little as he stared at the portrait on the wall. Benny Snailer beamed down at them, that warm and welcoming smile spread between his cheeks.

'Mr Cooper,' said Marty impatiently, 'what do you need?'

'I need a good deed,' said David. Then he laid the phone back in its holder.

The humpbacked man's face lit up as soon as David's request left his mouth. Benny was back behind the bar, his hand wrapped around a black pump.

'Another room, is it? That was a quick f-favour. You t-talk to Roman?'

He yanked down on the pump, using all his body weight. Benny Snailer was only a small man, five foot six from head

289

to toe and not much muscle in between. It took every ounce to get a few squirts of beer into the empty glass. David glanced around the bar. None of the eyes were on him. Most were over towards the platform. A dark-haired woman was still singing there, with an elderly, bearded guitarist accompanying her.

'Yeah,' replied David. 'I talked to him. Can you get me another bed?'

'Sure I can, sure I can. Seeing as you were so g-gentlemanly with me, it's the least I can d-do. Deborah, how about you f-finish this off?' The owner beckoned to the woman beside him, then stood aside and wiped himself down.

Deborah was bigger than her boss. Beefier and scary looking, with a body that was almost entirely made out of bosoms. She filled the glass with one pull.

'Upstairs,' said Benny as he lifted the hinged countertop. 'Upstairs all the way.'

By 'all the way', Benny meant three flights. One past the bar, another past the rented rooms, and one more into the living quarters of the owner himself. It took them about five minutes to get there. Benny Snailer was so slow that David began to wonder whether the hump beneath his shirt was actually a snail's shell.

'Sorry about the p-pace,' he stuttered. 'I walk slower these days.' Benny began fiddling with a bunch of keys. He shoved one into the nearest door and opened. 'You'll have to excuse the m-moth balls.'

The four of them stepped inside. The wood beneath David creaked, his shoes leaving imprints in the dust like footprints in the snow. He took it all in. The room was virtually empty, but for a bed and a cupboard. It had been uninhabited for a while now, he was sure, but it was liveable for a night or two.

'This is great,' he said.

'Well, it's not m-much to look at, but it should do just fine. Gave the same place to Roman back when he was here; he had no c-complaints. I won't make it a habit though. Only for the needy. Just hard to do anything with it, you know.'

'A few whips of a duster would help,' said Marty.

'Manners, Billy.' David flashed him a look.

'Anyway,' said Benny, 'I'll leave you to it. Hope you're happy. My p-pleasure.'

The humpbacked man tottered from the room, making sure to keep a small distance between himself and David just in case he decided to rough him up again. A cloud of dust swayed into the air when the door closed.

'What are you doing?' asked Marty. 'Why is Benny giving us this room?'

'Because I asked for it,' replied David. 'Good deeds keep The Scottish Snail standing. You know that by now, Weed-kid.'

'No, I mean why do we need this room at all?'

'Because I'm staying.'

'What? After all that?'

'Roman knows something. He said he could help, and I've got to stay if I want to find out how.'

'He's coming here?'

'Yes, he's coming, and I'm going to be here when he does.'

'But you said –'

'I know what I said, Marty, I know.' David straightened his back; his voice was beginning to shake a little. He took a deep breath to try to calm himself. 'I'd given up. I thought it was over. I believed it was. Hell, I still believe that; I believe every word of it. But that's the thing. That's just the thing. Any light is worth following when you're in the dark. And

I'm in the dark now, Marty, I'm all the way in it. I've got to try. I've got to.'

David didn't know why, but it felt like he was pleading with the two of them, willing them to understand. He'd never done that before. He'd never felt the need to. But he did now. Marty glanced over at Amee to gauge her reaction. She was by the cupboard, biting her lip as clumps of white dust began to settle on her dyed black hair. She nodded.

'Okay...' Her voice was cracked and quiet, hanging in the air with the dust.

'So I'll stay,' said David, trying desperately to get his emotions back in check. 'Until tomorrow. And I'll hope that he can help, whoever he is.'

Below them, the voices from the inn began to get louder, undoubtedly spurred on by the fast-flowing drinks now that the nighttime was approaching.

'So what do we do until then?' asked Marty. He sat down on the bed and pulled his bloody feet onto the mattress.

David looked down at them. 'You can ask Benny for another good deed, if you want.'

The weed-kid threw his hands up in victory. 'Thank fuck for that,' he said.

And despite himself, David gave a slight smile.

Later that evening, David joined the ruckus. His drink sat on a cracked wooden table, the froth slowly sinking its way back into the amber liquid. For some reason, he wasn't actually drinking it. Something was stopping him. Perhaps it was association. When David used to drink, he did it because it clouded things, put a dampener on them, made them misty enough to be palatable. But now he didn't want the mist. Now he wanted the opposite. Thanks to Roman

Guild, his mind was straight again, his path was clear, and he didn't want to blur it up.

He pushed the glass aside a few inches and looked up towards the ceiling. Marty and Amee were upstairs in the bedroom. They were talking things over probably, trying to understand. David didn't blame them. He found it hard to understand himself. One moment all was lost, and the next there was hope again. Like the tide at Gealblath Beach, the search for those responsible played tricks on him. One moment there was nothing but dark, murky water; the next it was gone, peeled back to reveal all these new unturned stones. The kids used to play a game when that happened. They called it crabbing. The first one to find ten crabs was the winner. They couldn't think, they couldn't stop to work it out, all they could do was act fast and turn over as many of those stones as they could before the water came back. That was what David was doing now. He was crabbing. Because the people behind Alfie's murder were under one of those stones, he was sure. And Roman could be their best chance to find them. He believed that, and he hoped Marty and Amee would too.

David leaned forward and wrapped his hand around the glass, then he hesitated and let go again. *No drink. Not now. Remember, you don't need it.* He sat back and peered up towards the stage. The live set was over now. The elderly, bearded man was perched on his stool. He was clinging to the thighs of the dark-haired woman who had replaced his guitar, the same one who had been singing earlier in the day. David looked at her eyes momentarily, wondering whether she was happy or sad. She turned and saw him, and David averted his gaze, but the woman had caught him looking. Before he knew it, she had leapt off the bearded man's lap and sat down in front of him.

'Like what you see, huh?' she said raspily.

The woman was older than she looked from a distance. The creases beneath her eyes were evident, along with the lack of colour in her face and the slight grey tinges amidst the dye in her hair. She must have been nearing forty.

'I was just looking,' said David.

'Looking at me.'

'It's a small pub; it's hard not to look at people in it.'

The woman smiled, and David noticed yellow smudges wedged between the lines of her teeth. 'People look. People look all the time. But you looked at me, at my eyes.'

David shuffled uncomfortably. The woman was clearly high on something. Her pupils were wide, her nose was blocked, and her voice was shuddering. Coke, maybe. Or something heavier. Whatever it was, David didn't want anything to do with it. He made to get out of the booth.

'Thought you might be calling me over,' the woman said, almost disappointed.

David stopped, his arse half on the seat, half off it. 'You sing nicely. I heard your set. But I'm not interested. I'm sorry.'

The woman pointed at his beer. 'You're not drinking that?'

She stared at him expectantly, and David shook his head. In a flash, she lifted the glass and swallowed nearly all of it down in a few gulps. She smacked it back onto the table and wiped an amber moustache from her lip.

'Thirsty?' David found himself asking.

The woman didn't answer. Instead she looked him up and down, her eyes trying to focus through the blur. 'What's your name?' she asked.

'Ryan.'

'I'm Maisy. What's your deal, Ryan?'

'What deal?'

'You like my set, but you don't like me?'

David glanced at the man on the platform, and Maisy laughed.

'He doesn't mind,' she said. 'He knows he's dispensable. For a night anyway.'

'I'm not worried about him.'

'Then what? You're married?'

'I was.'

Maisy took another gulp of beer. 'You got a woman?'

David sat back into the booth, arching his back. 'No.'

'You must really hate me.'

'No. I've just had bad experiences with women in inns.'

'So it's time for a good one.'

'No.'

'You get caught before? Get into trouble?'

'Didn't get caught, that's why I got into trouble.'

Maisy huffed and reclined against the leather. She looked okay in the cool blue light of the bar, David thought then. Perhaps on any other night he might have taken her up on the offer. He certainly would have done so a couple of months back. But he wasn't the same person now, and the last thing he wanted to do was get distracted. Besides, Amee and Marty were upstairs, and they probably wouldn't take too kindly to an arrival like this one.

'So why'd you look at me then?' enquired Maisy.

'Same reason I just said.'

'No, I mean why did you look at my eyes?'

David was taken aback slightly by that question. He *had* looked into her eyes. But there hadn't been a reason for it. Or at least, there had been as much reason as there ever was. 'Why does anyone look someone in the eyes?' he said.

'Because they're the best indication of what's going on behind closed doors. Of the soul. We're the same, I think. Your soul's as lost as mine. That's why people like you and me connect.'

'You saying I don't have a soul?'

'Everyone has a soul; some people just lose it along the road.'

David nodded slowly. 'It's a long road.'

'And not all of it's lit.' At that, Maisy slipped a packet of cigarettes from her shorts and fumbled about inside with her deep-blue fingernails.

'No, it's not,' David agreed.

She stuffed one of them into her mouth, sparked it up, then tipped the packet in David's direction. He declined it.

'I'm doing fine,' he said. 'I thought I was lost for a moment there, but I'm fine now.'

Maisy blew out a thin trail of smoke with a smirk. 'I've thought that too,' she said. 'I've thought that lots of times. But I always end up back at square one. You will too. Like I said, we're the same.'

There was a brief silence. Maisy reached out and touched David's hand. Her fingers were cold and kind of rough, like they'd been sanded down by all the years spent on the hilt of a microphone.

'Spend the night with me,' said Maisy.

David looked her in the eyes. 'I don't think a night in an inn will solve either of our problems.'

'I'm not looking for a solution; I'm just looking for a good fuck.'

'Maybe that's why you've never found your solution.'

Maisy removed her hand, then took another long drag. 'Okay, Mr Philosopher. Explain why you look as lost as me.

Because I'm sitting in front of you and I can see it. I can see it in your eyes as clear as this table.'

David shook his head, pulling on the cuffs of his leather jacket. 'Maybe it's because you're drunk. Maybe it's because you're high out of your mind on whatever it is you've been taking.'

'Or maybe it's because you're not looking at yourself, just the world around you.' Maisy squinted at him, her face tilting in the blur of smoke, distorted by the haze of blue light. 'You do that, you'll see how lost your soul is. Then you'll be as wise as I am.' She grinned, showing off her yellow teeth, and a greyish-pink tongue to go with them.

David let the words linger for a moment. They swirled slowly in the air like the smoke from her cigarette, rising and falling above the table, and the longer they stayed there, the less David seemed to like them.

'I told you already,' he said, deciding that this conversation had run its course. 'I've found the light to my road.'

'Maybe it's the wrong road,' replied Maisy.

'Maybe I don't care what a drugged-up whore thinks.'

'Maybe you need someone to tell you how to think –'

'I don't.' David slid out of the booth. 'But thanks for the offer.'

He gave the table two taps with his knuckles, then he began making his way over to the door.

'Which one?' Maisy called after him.

But David didn't answer.

By the time he had got back to the room, Marty was there waiting for him. He was sitting on the windowsill, a sheet and a pillow on the floor beside the radiator. David closed the door.

'Where's Amee?' he asked.

'Upstairs in the other room. She wanted to be alone.' Marty kept his eyes on the window, staring down sombrely at the darkening street.

David moved over to his bag and began rustling through the contents. He faltered for a moment when he remembered Charlie's skull wasn't there.

'What are you looking for?' asked Marty.

David didn't answer. 'How are the shoes?' he asked instead.

Marty looked down at his new, slightly tattered trainers, which were about two sizes too big. 'They'll do.'

'Nice of Benny to give you them.'

'I suppose.'

Something upstairs went bump, and David looked up towards the peeling plaster. 'We should get some sleep,' he said then. 'It's been a long few days, and we need the rest. You can take the bed.'

'What?'

'The bed. You can take it. I'm good with the floor.'

Marty hesitated. He stood up from the windowsill and walked over to the bed, a suspicious crease under his eyes. 'Why are you being nice?'

David unzipped his jacket. 'I'm always nice.'

'No,' replied Marty curtly. 'Did something happen down there?'

'Just take the bed, Weed-kid. No more talking; I'm tired of it.'

Despite looking as if he wanted to talk back, Marty shook his head, pulled off his trainers, and sat down on the mattress.

David turned off the lights and lay down in the dark. A dim glow from the streetlamps illuminated the room around them, casting strange shadows along the mouldy walls. David tried to shut out to the murmurings from the pub beneath them. Maisy would still be there, he knew. She would be there prowling, drinking, asking someone else to share a bed with her for the night. He wondered if she'd find anyone. Then he stopped, shaking the image of her out of his head. *Forget her. Forget everything she said. You need to be focused for tomorrow. For Charlie, you need to be focused.* He turned onto his side, yanking up the sheets until they covered everything but his eyes.

A small voice came from the bed. 'Why did you leave Charlie there? In the forest, I mean.'

David felt his heart shudder slightly. He cast his mind back to those streams, the rocks, the water trickling down every crevice. He wanted to say he had left the skull there because he had given up, but that wasn't true. He had left it there because it was nice. It was quiet, gentle, and calm. A place to rest. Without punishing whoever killed him, that was all David could give Charlie now.

The springs in the mattress creaked, and even though David couldn't see, he could tell Marty was still sitting upright.

'Go to sleep, Marty,' he said.

And Marty didn't speak after that. The room went silent, and the gaps between David's blinks started to close, each one lasting longer, deeper, until he dissolved into a fuller and blacker darkness.

In his dream, David was on the road. At first it was just him. He was alone, a long stretch of tarmac in front of him, with streetlamps above it flickering on and off. He was walking, but the longer he walked, the longer the road seemed to be. It soon became clear that the road was all there was. But then a female voice arose from behind.

'You look lost.'

He turned to see Maisy leaning up against one of the streetlamps, that familiar smirk illuminated by the light of the bulb.

David tilted his head. 'You said that before.'

'And I'll say it again.' The woman walked forward. With two hands, she clasped her top and pulled it over her shoulders. Her torso shone in the dark. Her breasts were small but pert, and her skin was awash with tiny brown freckles. 'Are you sure you don't want to spend the night with me?' she asked.

David swallowed. 'I told you, I'm not interested.'

Maisy took another step forward, her face coming up close to his, her cool blue eyes gazing into him with a strange ferocity.

'Liar,' she said bluntly.

'I'm not –'

'Liar.'

'I've got to go.'

'Go...' Maisy nodded behind David's shoulder, and he turned, staring out across the road. 'You know, those lights don't last forever.'

David began to tremble. 'So why are you here?'

'Some of us don't have any other roads but the dark ones.' Maisy touched his hand, then pulled it up and placed it on her left breast, rubbing it softly until her nipple went hard and pimply. 'Spend the night with me.'

David shook his head. 'No.'

'Spend the night with me.'

'No!'

In a flash, he pulled his hand away and started retreating. The world around him faded into blackness. Maisy walked after him, her footsteps clearly audible on the tarmac. *IRRK, IRRK, IRRK*. She followed David into the darkness, the road creaking underneath her, squeaking, bending, wincing, until...

David awoke. His body was almost entirely out of the sheets and his clothes were hot and damp with sweat. *IRRK, IRRK, IRRK*. David tensed his neck as he heard Maisy's shoes continuing to make the road creak. *No. Not Maisy. Not her. She's not here. That was just a dream. Just a dream. It wasn't real. None of it was*. But the sound continued. *IRRK, IRRK, IRRK*. As clear as it had been in the dream. It wasn't Maisy though, and it wasn't the road either. David looked up. It was the wooden floorboards upstairs, creaking in the dead of the night. The spare room was directly above this one.

'Amee,' he whispered to himself. 'It's just Amee.'

David took a deep breath. He tilted his head towards the clock in the corner. 12:15 a.m. He'd been asleep for only two hours. With a sigh, he leant back again and tried to slow his racing heart. The bar below had gone quiet now, but a low growl sounded from outside, and he watched as an approaching car's headlamps caused the shadows in the room to twist and change. The car stopped, and David listened to it for a while. After a few minutes, he said Maisy's name, just once, and let it linger on the tongue like a sizzling mint. He thought about her face, her eyes, her breasts and the size of them. He thought about her words and her hand reaching out to place his own upon her body. Then he closed his eyes, shut his mouth, and fell back into a dreamless sleep. He didn't hear it, but the rumble of the car's engine switched off with him. It ended with a splutter and left nothing but silence inside the inn.

19

ROMAN GUILD

'*When I think of you, I think of the ocean. If you're scared that the green monster is coming, come find me. I'm in the house on the cliff waiting for you. Find me and we can cross together, into a better place, into a warmer place. But you must find me. When I think of you, I think of the ocean.*'

The waves lapped in further on Gealblath Beach, colouring the edges of Amee's feet, bubbling, fizzing, then retreating back. Amee's hair blew erratically in the sea wind. Her bones shivered and her teeth rattled, but she didn't mind. She liked being out in the open. The sea was like an old friend. She knew the waves on top, the pebbles underneath, the ripple of the water and the lick of its touch on her bare skin. She recognised it when she saw it and she smiled when the waves came up to meet her.

'Amee...'

The voice came from behind, and Amee turned to see Mrs Nightly standing beside one of the cabins. She was wearing her black suit today. A pair of thin dark shades was perched neatly atop the ridge of her nose. That familiar burgundy notebook was held in one hand. Her pretty blonde hair blew just as wildly as Amee's.

'Yes, Mrs Nightly?' said Amee.

'How many now?'

'Just one.'

Mrs Nightly went to write something, then she stopped. 'One?'

'One.'

Amee looked back into the ocean, where the boy was still standing amongst the waves. He was young and handsome, dark skinned with a messy afro. A normal boy, if it hadn't been for the world around him. The water gave it away. There were no ripples, no breaking of the waves. He was entirely unfazed by it, just as the water was entirely unfazed by him. Two immovable objects acting as if the other didn't exist: one, the ever-changing source of life; the other, a lingering remnant of death. They were never going to complement each other, she supposed. They were never going to work.

'Why is it one?' Mrs Nightly walked down the beach towards her. 'Why isn't it more? Why isn't it much more?'

'I don't know,' responded Amee truthfully.

In all seriousness, she had thought the same thing. Amee didn't tend to see many dead people, and the ones she did see seemed to have died recently. There was never anyone from the distant past. No clansmen in kilts, no old people wearing cravats. It was strange, she supposed. But Amee didn't ponder it. She had other things to think about.

'All you should see is dead people,' said Mrs Nightly. 'There should be countless of them. Why do you only see one?'

303

Another wave crashed down upon her feet and Amee shrugged. Her nurse still spoke about them wrongly. She spoke as if they were numbers on a flow chart. Unreal, meaningless, just something to be worked out and understood. If only she could see them like Amee could see them. Then maybe she would understand. They were so much more than that. They were real. They were human.

Mrs Nightly tapped the pen against her notebook. 'It means the others have crossed. They've got to the other side. So why not them? What's stopping them? What's changed?'

'I don't know, Mrs Nightly.'

'Ask him again.'

'Do I have to? What's the point?'

'You don't need to know the point. You just need to do it.'

A few moments passed, and Amee turned back towards the young-looking boy. 'Can you tell us when you died? If you can remember, can you tell us?'

The boy was staring up at the beach, his brown eyes flicking from one end to the other with a glint of fear. He looked as if he was searching for his mother in a big crowd, but the beach was empty. It was just the three of them now. The summers had passed, and this boy would never have to look for his mum in a big crowd again.

'Please,' Amee urged him. 'It would really help us.'

'I remember it was summer,' said the boy. '1981. My mum said it was supposed to be the hottest one yet...' He stopped, his lips starting to tremble. 'I'm scared,' he muttered.

'I know you are,' Amee said to the boy. 'I know you're scared. I understand that. But you –'

'I'm scared of the green monster.'

Amee felt her legs tensing beneath her tights. 'Don't be

304

scared of the green monster. You don't have to worry about that. You need to –'

'Help me.'

The boy seemed close to tears now. He spoke to Amee as if she was an adult, as if she had some way of protecting him. In many ways, he even looked hopeful. But any hope of salvation was in vain, because Amee knew this wouldn't last. Pretty soon she'd be leaving. She'd be getting in that car and driving back to the hospital, back to her room, and she would never see the boy again. He'd just be a memory that she would try to block out. An image that was best forgotten. That was the horror of all this, Amee thought. For the dead, talking to the living was like holding onto a rope, a connection between life and death that meant they weren't alone or forgotten. But the rope wasn't real enough to save them. It didn't even hold. All Amee had to do was blink and the boy would be gone. And she would. Any second now, she would, because what else could she do?

'What's he saying?'

Mrs Nightly took a step forward, her high heels crunching into the stones. A salty breeze surged around them. It flicked the pages of the notebook and flapped the lapels of Mrs Nightly's black jacket. Amee would be able to taste that salt tonight, she knew. It would be on her lips, on her hands, in her clothes, and in her hair. The seaside would leave an imprint on her, just as she had left a footprint here. But both would be washed away eventually. They had that luxury.

'Can you help me?' the boy pleaded.

Amee hesitated. 'I...'

'I don't know what the green monster is, but it's coming. It's coming to get me. It's coming to eat me. I want to leave here. I want to go to the place that feels warm. Please help me.'

Mrs Nightly's hand curled around Amee's shoulder. 'When did he die?' she asked.

'He died in 1981,' replied Amee. 'In the summer.'

'How?'

'I don't know. He's too scared. I don't think he'll answer.'

Behind the dark shades, Mrs Nightly stared at her silently. She wanted her to ask; Amee could tell. She wanted to know the answer. But Amee couldn't ask. The boy was scared, confused, and close to tears. She couldn't bring herself to ask that question.

'He won't answer,' she affirmed, and Mrs Nightly sighed.

'I think you need to be stronger. I think you need to be much stronger.'

The boy began to dissolve in Amee's peripheral vision.

'I don't want to force them,' she said quietly.

'And that's your weakness. If you don't make them cooperate, then we'll never get answers. Your weakness will always be hindering our lessons.'

Amee felt her heartbeat pick up in her chest, the skin beneath her clothes beginning to rise in goose pimples. It was like she could sense what was coming.

'And you know what happens when you hinder our lessons,' said Mrs Nightly.

'No. I'm not. I asked, but he wasn't –'

'You're not listening to me, Amee. You have to be stronger. If I can't get that through to you, then perhaps there's someone else who can.'

'No,' replied Amee. 'Not him. You don't mean him.'

'If you can't learn, then what other choice do I have? You have to start, Amee. You have to start being better.'

Mrs Nightly looked at her expectantly, and Amee took a

deep breath. She looked back over to the water. The boy was there again, staring back at her with that hope she had seen earlier.

'I need you to tell me...' Amee paused, struggling to get the words out. The boy's eyes were small, lost, and lonely. 'I need you to...'

Mrs Nightly shook her head and the boy faded away again. 'Little fishy,' she tutted in a whisper. 'Little fishy.'

Amee knew what was coming now. She knew what her punishment would be. The nurse took her hand and began walking her up the beach towards the waiting black Lincoln. When they reached the top, Amee turned and looked at the ocean one last time.

* * *

Amee watched the water spiral down the sink. It was quarter past midnight and she had been in the bathroom for over an hour, staring into the scum-stained mirror that hung askew just above the sink. It reflected her pale face, the room behind her, and the shadows which covered everything from the bath to the shower. It reflected her world and every inch of its matter. But it didn't reflect what she saw. Not everything she saw. The pattern in the corner of her eye shifted a little before speaking.

'Why are you still here?' asked Charlie Cooper. 'Don't you think you need sleep?'

Amee wiped her face, allowing the cold sting of the water to bite her skin. 'I don't want to sleep,' she replied.

'Why not?'

'Because there's someone coming. Someone who says he can help, who says he knows something.'

'I know,' said Charlie. 'But that's good, isn't it? If he knows who killed the detective, then that's a good thing.'

Amee dipped her head down towards the sink. 'Yeah...' She nodded slowly. 'Yeah, I know, yeah.'

'So why don't you wanna sleep?'

Amee looked up at the dead boy. He was staring at her sadly, solemnly, but suspiciously at the same time.

'There's something else, isn't there?' he said. 'This isn't about Roman; there's something else going on.'

'I don't know what you mean.'

'There's something you're not saying. Something you're keeping to yourself. I've seen it on your face for a while now. I think Marty has too.'

Amee felt her hands start to tremble, and she used one of them to push a strand of black, greasy hair behind her ear. *You have to tell him*, she thought then. *You have to tell him now, or else it will eat you up inside and leave nothing behind.*

'I can't sleep,' she muttered. 'And when I do, I have nightmares, the same ones I have when I'm awake. Nightmares that feel more like memories, like I'm remembering things that have been blocked out for a long time. There's another one now. I'm at the beach with my nurse.'

'Your nurse?' Charlie interrupted.

'I had a nurse a long time ago, one that I've forgotten. It's hard to remember. All the images are blurry, and they're not quite together. But we were at the beach. I thought I'd never been to the beach before, but I have. Of course I have. I'd just forgotten. It's like there was a trigger. A trigger that made all of these memories come back.'

'What was the trigger?'

'I was at the caravan. The detective's home. That's when

308

all this started, when all these memories started coming back. I'd been there before. I'd been there with the others. My nurse and...' She stared hard at Charlie, her upper lip beginning to quiver a bit. 'I was there when he died, Charlie. I'm sure I was. I was there.'

'You know who killed him?'

'I don't know. Maybe...' She looked down at her feet, stopping herself from saying more. She didn't know who had killed the detective; that was true. All she knew was that she was there, and her nurse was there, and...

'The tall man?' asked Charlie.

Amee shivered. 'Yes. Maybe.'

'So then the woman, this nurse, she's your mum?'

'I'm not sure. I don't think so. She was called Mrs Nightly. And she looked different, I'm sure. Different hair. Only...'

'Only what?'

'The notebook. My mum, she has a notebook, but Mrs Nightly had one too.'

'Maybe it was given to her,' said Charlie.

'I don't know,' said Amee. 'Like I said, they're just memories. I can't see them. Not properly.'

'Why haven't you told my dad? Why haven't you told Marty? They're here because they want to find out how the man died. They're here to know the truth.'

'How could I do that? I wouldn't even know where to begin. I was there when the detective died, Charlie. I was involved.'

Charlie tilted his head, evidently pondering everything Amee had just said. He didn't understand it; that was obvious. He didn't understand any of this. But Amee didn't expect him to. He could never understand if she couldn't.

'So what are you going to do?' asked Charlie.

'I don't know,' Amee replied. 'It's like my mind's in two places. Here, now, and back there.'

'I mean, what are you going to do about Roman? If this guy knows something, then he might know about you. You need to tell my dad and Marty before he tells them.'

'I know what I need to do,' said Amee. 'Why do you think I can't sleep?'

'I'm just saying that you need to do it now –'

'I'm the one living this. Not you. I don't need your advice.'

Charlie hesitated for a second. His body had long since faded to bone, but those words had clearly cut through him. He stared back at Amee with a frown, and his mouth quivered as if he wanted to respond, but before he could, Amee blinked and Charlie faded away. He left nothing but the empty white bathroom in his wake.

When Amee got back to the spare room, she was already feeling guilty. A surge of regret swelled in her chest, and the more she kept it in, the more sour it tasted. Charlie didn't deserve to be treated like that. He had only ever tried to help, to sympathise and to understand. He didn't deserve to be pushed aside.

With a sigh, Amee sat back on the mattress and rested her head against the pillow. The room was dark orange, illuminated dimly by the streetlamps outside. Beneath the floorboards, the sounds of merriment had ceased. Voices that had just before been booming were now low whispers. On the other side of the window, car lights bent the shadows, making the place look different until the engines spluttered and the room returned to normal again. Amee sat there alone. The memories were overwhelming her, she could tell. They were locking her inside of herself, isolating her from her friends. But Charlie and Marty were the only friends she had. The last thing she should be doing was rejecting them. She needed friends now more than ever. Alive and dead.

Amee closed her eyes and held the dark for a few seconds. 'Charlie...' she whispered. Her eyes opened, and she prepared herself to see him, but the person staring back at her wasn't Charlie.

The boy stood in the glow of the streetlamps. His smile was not dissimilar to the one he had cracked in the picture, but this time there wasn't a wooden truck squeezed in one hand, and his parents weren't beaming beside him, either. He was on his own. In more ways than one. Benny Snailer's dead son raised a hand in greeting.

'Hello,' he said politely.

Amee pulled herself up, watching as the boy grinned more widely, both ends of his smile almost touching his small, pointed ears. 'Hello,' she responded.

'Are you new here?'

'Yes. I arrived this morning.'

The boy took a step closer, but the dust didn't move with him. The room was entirely undisturbed by his presence. 'I saw you in my room,' he said excitedly. 'I wanted to talk, but you didn't see me.'

For a moment, Amee thought about blinking him back into nothingness, but the happiness in the boy's eyes made her reconsider. A sense of happiness. Relief. That was the biggest burden of her ability, she supposed. For the dead, she was a lighthouse. They were lost at sea, but through the clouds, there was a light, a single light that brought them hope. But it couldn't guide their boats back to shore. They could look, and hope, and believe, but the tide would always turn, and the light would blink before morning.

'I'm seeing you now,' she said then, relenting to the weight of her burden.

'Yes, and I'm seeing you.' The boy put his hands behind his back, as if that was the way he had been taught to stand while speaking to a lady. 'So, what's your name?' he asked.

'My name's Amee. With two E's.'

'I'm Jack.' He held out a hand like he meant for her to shake it, but then he realised his mistake and put it back behind him.

Amee sniffed. Jack Snailer seemed far more mature than a typical child. He was eloquent, expressive, and friendly. A perfect heir to The Scottish Snail by all accounts. Apart from the small problem of his being dead.

'Do you want to do something, Amee?' asked Jack, looking at her hopefully.

'What do you mean, do something?'

'I don't know. It's quite lonely up here on my own. I miss playing. Do you want to play?'

Amee shook her head. 'I can't play with you, Jack.'

The dead boy looked at her sadly, but his disappointment was short-lived. 'What about colouring?' he asked suddenly. 'Do you like colouring?'

'I do some drawing. Why?'

'My dad used to colour with me all the time. We didn't do much talking in the beginning, you see. When he talked to me he was all tuh-tuh-tuhs and buh-buh-buhs, but he could colour in alright. That's how we spent our time together. We were halfway through this book. Maybe you could help me finish it?' Jack turned and beckoned her over towards the cupboard in the corner of the room. 'It won't take long. It's just in there, if you'd open it.'

Amee stood up and opened the cupboard, grimacing

slightly at the foul hit of old moth balls. Jack's clothes were hanging on the rail in front of her. Smart-looking trousers and shirts, church ties and black laces hanging to the right, a blue and red cap hanging to the left, and just below, a row of polished size elevens tipped up smartly onto the toes. It was a picture of life, like it had never gone away. But then, Amee understood that just fine. The death of a loved one could never be easily swept out of the house. Sometimes insignificant things remained. Clothes they wore, cups they had drunk out of, crosswords they never finished. Remnants of a life could only ever become more meaningful in death. Because it held their bodies, because it held their attention. One morning's newspaper could be thrown away, the next morning's could be kept forever. Because it was real, touchable, and bound by so much more than just the material to begin with. Mr Cooper would know that too, Amee was sure. Mr Cooper would know that better than anyone.

'Can't you see it?' Jack teased. 'Look up top.'

Amee allowed the dead boy to form properly in the corner of her eye so she could see where he was pointing. It was to a shelf above the clothes rail, a thick yellow book poking out over the edge. She reached up and grabbed it, turning it around in her hands to read the title: *THE HOBBIT: COLOURING AND ACTIVITY BOOK.*

A familiar sinking feeling started to bubble in her gut.

'That's it,' Jack enthused. 'We couldn't finish it though. Do you think you could do it for me? Now that you're here, do you think you could help?'

'I... I don't...'

Jack's smile wobbled slightly. 'What's wrong?' he asked.

'I had a book like this,' replied Amee. 'I mean, I think I did.'

'What do you mean, you think you did?'

Amee turned the page to a vast open landscape with rolling hills and two huge eagles soaring towards a blue ocean. The smell was strong and the crayon was thick, so thick that she could feel the ugly green clumps that had formed on the paper. She ran her fingertip over them, then a rush of something cold entered her head, and she closed her eyes, allowing another memory to sweep her up and place her down some place new.

* * *

'Green. Too much green if you ask me.'

Mrs Nightly sat in front of her, a faint look of tiredness and boredom spread across her face as she stared down at the page. It was four o'clock now. The lesson was long finished, and Amee could spend her time doing whatever it was she wanted to do. She sat on her bed, drawing in her colouring book while *The Land Before Time* played on the television at the end of the room.

'Maybe for you. For me, it's the right amount. And I'm the artist.' Amee licked the pencil, then rubbed it up and down in a blur. 'Do you think Picasso listened to people when they said too much abstract?'

Mrs Nightly shrugged. 'Hardly Picasso. Don't you think you're a little old to play with colouring books now?'

'I'm not colouring. I'm drawing.'

The nurse tilted her head, watching Amee start to draw the shape of a house. 'Why do you draw in colouring books?' she asked.

'Because sometimes I like to fill in my own blanks.'

'What do you mean?'

'I like drawing my life into the pictures. Putting my world

into their world. Making it more interesting. See...'

Amee lifted the book and flicked through the pages with a thumb, demonstrating the work she had done so far. She ended on the page she was working on now. There was the house, and the sun, setting into a red horizon. Mrs Nightly admired it, then her smile quivered slightly. Her finger began tapping on the fabric above her knee.

'Amee, I'd like to ask you something.'

Amee lowered the colouring book back onto her lap. 'What?'

'Yesterday, on the beach, you know why I got upset, don't you?'

'Because I didn't do what you asked?'

'But do you know why that upsets me? Do you know why you were wrong to do it?'

Amee didn't want to answer that question, so she kept quiet. Mrs Nightly leaned in, her cold, long fingers stroking Amee's hand.

'Would you like to know?' she asked.

And then she wrapped her fingers around Amee's hand and stood up from the bed.

Two minutes later, Amee was being walked down the hospital corridor. The corridor in question was empty, with nothing but the sound of their own footsteps and the hushed patter of rain on glass. The nurse walked ahead of her, leading her around one corner and then another, until they came face to face with Room C10.

'Here we are,' said Mrs Nightly, letting go of Amee's hand to place a key into the lock.

'What are we doing?' asked Amee.

Mrs Nightly pushed the door open. The room on the other side was pretty vacant for the most part. The walls were long, painted in a lime-green colour, and there were two beds in each corner.

'Sit on the bed, Amee. I'll be back in a moment.'

Amee did as she was told. Mrs Nightly smiled at her reassuringly, then she left the room and closed the door. When the door opened again, it was the tall man that walked through it.

'No!' Amee leapt from the bed. 'Not you! Not again!'

'Calm down, little fishy.' Mrs Nightly followed him inside and pushed the door shut. 'I'm here. You're alright when I'm here, aren't you?'

The tall man turned and pulled a strange grey apparatus into the room, rolling it slowly into the centre.

'I need him to be here,' said Mrs Nightly firmly. 'And I need you to be alright. Can you do that, little fishy? Can you be alright?'

Amee took a few breaths, trying to slow her racing heart. She could be alright. She knew she could be alright, so long as Mrs Nightly stayed, so long as she was always with her. She couldn't be here on her own. Not with him. 'Please stay with me,' she told her.

The tall man chuckled, glaring at Amee with spine-tingling glee. 'You hurt my feelings, little fishy.'

Mrs Nightly turned towards him. 'Be quiet. Just play it.'

Amee's breaths quietened down and she watched as the apparatus began to hum to life. A strange white light flickered at the top. 'What is that?' she asked.

'A projector,' replied Mrs Nightly.

The tall man bent down and began attaching something that looked like black tape to its side. The wall in front of them shone into life.

Amee frowned. 'Is this a film?'

'Yes,' replied Mrs Nightly. 'But not the ones you're used to. I'd like you to watch it. Can you do that for me?'

'I don't –'

'Just watch.'

Mrs Nightly walked over towards the door and turned the lights off at the wall. The tall man followed her. After a few moments, the green of the wall turned to white, then to red, and then there were all sorts of colours blurring together to form somebody's living room. It looked old, almost tattered, but homely. In the centre, there was a brick fireplace with a steel grate. Beside that, there was a small sofa, with a white, coffee-stained blanket hanging over the arm. To the left, there was a six-foot Christmas tree, with a load of neatly wrapped presents stacked in wait underneath.

By the time Amee had taken it all in, the camera had swerved to focus on a pot-bellied, elderly man. He was sitting with his legs up on a long olive sofa, pulling on the ribbon of a present. He went to say something, but Amee couldn't hear what it was. After a while, the man gave up on the ribbon and pulled at the paper instead, ripping it all off until he was met by a cardboard package. *LONSTA 4500 FRUIT JUICER: JUICE YOUR FRUIT TO FRUIT YOUR JUICE!* The man laughed and said something, then the camera panned to the left, where a young girl was fidgeting about in the mountain of gifts. Her hair was blonde, not unlike Mrs Nightly's.

Amee turned towards her nurse. 'What is this –'

'Just watch.' Mrs Nightly flicked away the question, her own gaze holding firm on the wall, as if she was hypnotised.

Amee turned back. The camera was approaching the girl now. She lowered herself down onto the carpet, her blue nightie crumpling under her knees. With a cheer, she wrapped her fingers around a present and began opening it, strips of pink and blue paper swishing behind her head as the gift was steadily revealed. Then chaos broke loose. The girl exploded into a ball of delight, leaping up from the floor and shooting about the living room. The camera struggled to keep up with her as she flew into the elderly man's arms and wrapped him in a warm and joyful hug. He hugged her back, his mouth curving into a great big, inaudible laugh.

The girl pulled away again and ran to the other side of the living room to sit. She yanked the present out from the remains of the wrapping paper and turned it to the lens. Amee squinted to read the box. *BIG BARBIE TOWNHOUSE – 4 ½ FEET HIGH – 4 FLOORS OF FUN – FANCY FURNITURE FOR 7 BIG ROOMS – ELEVATOR STOPS ON ALL FLOORS.*

'Who is she?' Amee found herself asking.

'Her name's Grace,' Mrs Nightly revealed finally. 'She's the reason we're here. She's the reason we're doing all this.'

'What do you mean?'

Mrs Nightly took a step forward, her gaze now set on Amee. 'What you need to know, Amee, is that everything we do here has a purpose. Every lesson. Every question. Every answer. Anything and everything I ask of you, it's all because of her.' Mrs Nightly pointed at the living room on the wall. The girl was sliding the Barbie house out of its packet, her eyes wide and her smile stretched. 'She needs us. She needs you. And every time you let me down, or misbehave, you're letting her down too. You're forsaking her, and I don't think you want to do that. Do you, Amee? Do you want to do that?'

Amee turned and watched as the girl began placing miniature bathtubs and furniture into the rooms of her new doll house. Her small body bounced up and down in excitement.

'No,' replied Amee. 'No, I don't want to do that. But –'

'Then don't. When I ask you to do something you don't like, if I want you to do something that you don't feel you're capable of, all you need to do is remember her. Remember her face. What happened yesterday on the beach, that can't ever happen again. Do you understand?'

'Yes. Yes, I understand.'

Mrs Nightly nodded, and the film behind her began crackling to a close, the frames quickening faster and faster until the living room dissolved into black and white splodges.

'Good,' she said simply. Then she turned towards the tall man. 'Make sure, if you would. Make sure she understands.'

That familiar heavy ball sank deep into Amee's stomach, and for a moment she went dizzy. 'What do you mean?' she asked tremulously. 'You don't mean it. Please, Mrs Nightly, you can't mean it.'

But before she could protest further, Mrs Nightly bent down and pulled her into a hug. 'I love you, little fishy. I love you a lot. But…' She tilted her head and whispered into her ear, 'I love her more.'

With that, the nurse made for the door, leaving Amee to shiver and tremble without comfort, her nails already starting to dig deep into the cracks of her palms.

'Mrs Nightly, you can't!' she screamed. 'You can't! I understand! I swear I understand! You can't leave me with him again! You promised!'

'Remember her face, little fishy,' said Mrs Nightly as she reached the door. 'Remember her face.'

'Please!' Amee cried.

Urine seeped through her tights and created a small yellow puddle on either side of her shoes, and the tall man shook his head, tutting as Mrs Nightly left the room.

'Little fishy, little fishy...' He grinned, his long, ugly nose twitching slightly at the smell, and his pupils seeming to sharpen in the projector's dim, incessant glow. 'Why do you make a mess?'

Amee pulled her eyes shut, trying desperately to close herself off from the world around her. Her next scream formed itself into one word. A single word that she didn't even mean to form.

'MOTHER!'

* * *

The dust fell from the spine of the colouring book as Amee stroked it, flittering briefly, almost prettily, through the long orange glow which was cast in shards through the window. *How did I forget that girl?* she thought to herself, clenching the book tightly. She could recall the memory even more vividly than the others. She could see the girl's happiness, her eyes, brimming with life. She could remember her hugging the old man and she could remember the way he laughed so soundlessly. She could remember everything, and the fact she was only *now* remembering made her want to be sick in her lap.

Jack Snailer noticed something was wrong. 'What's the matter?' he asked.

Amee shook her head. Everything, she wanted to say. Everything was wrong. Nothing was right. Nothing was in the correct place. Her head was now abuzz with doors she could open and walls that were crumbling down. But she didn't know how many there were, she didn't know what was hiding behind them, and she didn't know why they'd been erected in the first place. She wanted to scream, but she couldn't do it. All she could do was stand there and simply stare at the colouring book.

'You don't have to if you don't want to,' said Jack awkwardly. 'It would just be nice to have some more help.'

Amee took a breath. Her grip on the book loosened and one of the pages flicked over, going from a blur of messy scribbles to something more pristine, with colours perfectly within the lines.

'Oh, my friend did this page,' said Jack. 'I wish the whole book looked like this. I was never that good at colouring. Neither was my dad. '

Amee wavered slightly. 'Friend...'

'Yes. My friend. Roman. The last one who came to this room.'

At that moment, the growl of an engine vibrated the air outside, and the shadows in the room swerved once again, changing Jack's form from clear to blurred.

'Roman Guild?'

The dead boy nodded. 'That was his name. He did some colouring too. He wasn't here long, but he got a few pages finished. Why? Do you know him? Is he coming back? That would be great if he was. Maybe he could finish it for me, if I ask nicely.'

Amee froze, squinting over at Jack as if she might have misheard. 'What do you mean, ask nicely?'

'Well, I asked nicely the last time. We spoke about a lot of things, and I asked him about the colouring book. There's no reason why he wouldn't do it again, is there?'

'He spoke to you...'

'Yes,' replied Jack. 'You two are the only ones to have spoken to me since I left my dad. It's really very nice of you.'

He smiled, but Amee didn't smile back. Her grip failed completely and the colouring book fell to the floor, causing a pile of dust to rise into the sharp orange air.

'You're lying,' she said, her body suddenly shaking.

'No. Why? Is everything okay?'

Jack took a step forward but he was already beginning to disappear now. He merged with the dust, fading back into darkness and leaving Amee with nothing but the sound of her own beating heart for company. She stood there for a few seconds. Then she ran over towards the door and opened it onto the landing.

Both feet crashed hard against the floorboards as she made her way down the staircase and towards Mr Cooper's room.

'Mr Cooper?' she called out, knocking three times on his door. But there was no answer. Amee knocked again, then pushed, and was surprised to find the door unlocked. 'Mr Cooper, there's a boy! The boy from the picture –'

She stopped as she saw her teacher. Mr Cooper was lying on the bed, just under the framed picture of the large garden snail, with both of his hands placed delicately upon his belly. Marty was beside him, in the exact same position, with his mouth hanging slightly open and a dribble of drool making a puddle on the sheets beneath his chin.

Amee squinted as she stared at him. 'Marty...' she breathed, but Marty didn't answer. He was entirely motionless, just like Mr Cooper.

At that moment, a bump sounded from the corner of the room, and Amee turned to see a figure stepping towards her. He was lean, with a sickly smile curving across one side of his face and an almost hawkish gaze. A hawk that had finally spotted the fish through the rippling water. The look of relief, the look of concentration, the look before the kill. Roman Guild wiped the tip of a long, dripping needle with a small handkerchief.

'Little fishy, little fishy...'

Amee's vision blurred and she felt herself sink into darkness, every essence of her wanting to scream out and tear away from her reality. The tall man pointed at his face mockingly.

'Remember me?'

20

THE DEEPEST FALL

'ONE! TWO! THREE! FOUR! FIVE! HEADS UP, SHOULDERS BACK –'

'COCKS OUT!'

Marty swallowed against the feeling of dread which was beginning to tickle at his insides. There was a whole Sunday morning's breakfast in there. His mum's egg and soldiers, a side of malt wheaties, orange juice, plus a monster bag of Wotsits he'd had later on in the day. His stomach growled dangerously against the swell of the day's matter. But Marty kept it in. He had to keep it in. Any food coughed out now would take with it any remnants of his dignity. And that was something he could ill afford to lose. He had little of it to start with, he was pretty sure.

'Let's have a dick contest! The boy with the smallest dick has to jump in first!'

'That's not how this works! We have to keep this orderly! We have to be organised!'

Rory Keeling slapped Ross Baines around the back of the

head, then grinned at the five boys in front of them. They were standing in a line, and each had his shirt off, apart from Marty.

He didn't know either Rory or Ross too well. They were in the year above, and he hadn't ever actually talked to them. He'd only been at Gealblath Secondary School for a month, but it wasn't hard to know who they were up against. These two were the crème de la crème, the Nazi Germany of school bullies, and they weren't to be crossed under any circumstances, unless you wanted to risk death.

'We start on the end! Gibby! You can go first!' Rory pointed down the row of boys, his plump finger coming to a halt at the end of the line.

The smallest of the five of them, Gilbert Darrow, was waiting for him there. Marty winced in pity. He had it on good authority that Gibby was a newcomer to Gealblath. He'd heard that his father, who was a banker, had retired from Edinburgh and snapped up one of the Mason properties that would have cost an arm and a leg in the city. It was one of those red-brick houses with a gate, a drive that swooped in a semicircle, a fountain at the front, and a hot tub round the back that had cool multi-coloured lighting. By all accounts, it seemed that most people of Marty's age range saw Gilbert Darrow as the luckiest kid in town; by which they meant the richest. But he wasn't very lucky anymore. He was at the end of the line.

'COME ON, ARSEHEAD!' Ross pointed his sharpened stick. 'JUMP TO YOUR CERTAIN DEATH!'

Gibby gasped, then looked over the edge. Marty sighed and looked along with him. The drop was at least fifty feet, if he had to guess. It fell all the way down to the still surface of the swimming hole, where the dark-blue ripples and wild green plant life made the water look almost inviting. If it weren't for the fact that hitting water after this kind of drop would almost certainly mean your arsehole coming out of your mouth. Marty swallowed. Gibby really would be an arsehead then. If he made the jump, that was.

'We don't wanna wait all day, Gibby!' yelled Rory.

Marty glanced to the right, where Mike and Teddy were quaking beside him. Mike's bare tits jiggled, and Teddy's thin black hair was splayed out in loose strands. They looked at him with the same question on their minds: Why? Why had they chosen today to make the hike to Gealblath's power plant? But the truth was, Marty knew exactly why.

It had started three years ago, when the teenagers of Gealblath first discovered the place. Having been abandoned for more than nine years, the power plant became the ultimate playground, with huge empty warehouses to run through, rusty construction poles to climb up, and, of course, the swimming hole, which was in fact just a large rain-filled crater. For Marty, Mike, and Teddy, who had been too young to come here on their own, the prospect of spending the summer at the power plant without an adult to tell them what to do was almost too good to believe. They lived for the day they would be old enough to do it.

But then the summer of 1994 came, and the power plant's rat problem went through the roof. Millions of them, according to the eleventh-years, some as big as cats, with teeth like trimmers that could chew through a whole block of hard cement in just under fifty seconds. Well, Marty wasn't sure about all that. But he was sure about the rats. His dad had told him so. They'd been there since forever, apparently, small enough but plentiful, and in 1994, they only got worse. They chewed through the warehouses, churned up the land, and came pretty close to making the whole place uninvestable.

That was bad news for Jonathon Taper, the property developer who had bought the place just one year before. He sure as heck wouldn't own anything uninvestable, so he invested in some rat poison. Nearly nine thousand small, sweet-looking cubes of strychnine, which were spread across the ten acres of land that he owned. It sent plenty of rats to hell, that was for sure. Problem was, it also sent Jimmy McKenzie to a hospital bed for three months when he mistook one of them for a discarded piece of his favourite sweet. A pick 'n' mix for mice, he must have assumed. The poor bastard couldn't have had much juice up there in his skull. But thankfully for him, his lack of juice got the parents five thousand pounds in a nifty settlement, and the next thing Jonathon knew, five more children had had the same bright idea. Or rather, the parents had. Marty's dad couldn't help but crack up at that.

Since then, the power plant had been closed off. Gealblath's ultimate playground had become a pleasant memory for those who were fortunate enough to have played in it. Three years to the day, however, another group of Gealblath students found their way back inside, and it didn't take long for word to get around. They were back in business. The only issue was, that word had got around to more people than just Marty, Mike, and Teddy. It got around to Rory and Ross too.

'OKAY, GIBBY! I'M GONNA COUNT DOWN FROM TEN!'

Marty shivered against a rush of late summer air and pulled on his shirt. He hadn't taken it off like the others yet. He hadn't come to terms with the fact he was going in. With a deep gulp, he peered over the edge of the crater and into the dirty water below.

'You sure you're able to do that, Rossy?' Rory laughed at his friend, and Ross slapped him on the thigh with his stick. 'OW! YOU ARSEHOLE! OW!'

Rory hopped up and down in pain. For a moment, Marty had a vague hope that they might start a civil war with each other, allowing the five of them to sneak off. But the hope was short lived, because a few seconds later, Rory was laughing it off and patting his friend on the shoulder.

'Jesus, that stick smarts!'

'I know!' replied Ross proudly. 'That's why I chose it.' He pointed the spear over at Gibby again. 'ALRIGHT, RICH KID! HERE WE GO!'

Gibby swayed on the spot, three small droplets of sweat trickling down from his temples. It wasn't the sun doing that, Marty knew. It was fear. Pure, unfiltered, unadulterated fear. A bird crowed behind him, and Marty looked up towards the huge cigarette-esque chimney about fifty feet away from them. He could see two sea eagles circling around it. They soared up high, entirely unafraid of the drop. Marty looked back towards the swimming hole and felt his breakfast curl into a ball in his stomach.

Then Ross yelled out like a maniac, 'TIME TO PROVE YOUR WORTH!'

The sea eagles shrieked and Marty closed his eyes, waiting for the first number.

'TEN...'

* * *

Marty opened his eyes and winced against a fierce pain in his wrists. He moaned groggily, blinking hard in a vain attempt to comprehend his surroundings. It was pitch black.

So black that for a moment, Marty thought he could be blind. But after a while, his vision adjusted to see a small line of soft yellow light shining from a slit above him.

'Hmm?' he mumbled, and he attempted to sit up, wincing again as his head thumped into a ceiling. *What the hell is that?* he thought as his heart began to clatter in his chest. *Where the hell am I? What the hell is this?*

The questions buzzed quickly through his mind, and he tried to turn his body. A shot of fiery heat met him in response. His wrists were stuck behind his back, he realised, tied together with some sort of hard plastic. *Okay, okay, shit, what's happening?*

Marty pulled hard, but as he did so, the plastic seemed to tighten, and after a few seconds, he felt a warm trickle of something wet slip towards his thumb. *Stop! Stop that! Fucking stop!* his head screamed at him, and he resisted the human instinct to pull again, to tear the restraints and break free. He calmed himself and halted movement entirely.

Blood. That's blood. I can feel it. That's blood. I'm bleeding. I've been tied up in the dark, and now I'm bleeding.

A sudden jolt against his spine sent him up in the air a few inches, and he landed with a thud, his eyes widening in fear as he realised where he was. It was a car. The boot of a car. It had to be. Beneath the carpet, there was a low humming. A cough of exhaust sounded as the vehicle picked up speed, cruising fast down what seemed to be a straight and endless road.

Okay, so you're in a car. You're tied up in a car, that's where you are, that's what's happening. So how do you get out? Come on, stop the snivelling, Weed-kid. You've got to find a way out, so find a way out.

For some strange reason, it was Rory's voice that Marty was hearing now, taking over from the comforting tones of his own. Rory Keeling from school. The bully who'd made Marty's life a living hell for the last two years. He tried to shake it out.

Come on, Weed-kid. You can't just curl up in a ball and cry. I know that's what you want to do, you pathetic arsehole. That's what you've always wanted to do. Ever since you decided to come on this ridiculous mission. But you can't do that right now, you hear me? You've got to do something.

Despite his efforts to stop hearing Rory's voice, Marty started listening to it. With another moan, he tried to turn the other way, but as he did so, he hit something soft and pudgy with the strong smell of campfire oozing out of it. He recognised the stench immediately.

'Mr Cooper,' he gasped.

The teacher didn't respond. He lay motionless. It was so dark that it was impossible to tell whether he was even facing Marty or looking the other way. A lump of bile rose up into Marty's throat, and he spat it out, letting what seemed to be half saliva, half vomit trickle down his chin and stain the neck of his t-shirt.

Okay, said Rory, *so you're being sick. That's fine, that's cool, I mean, that's what any normal person would do in this situation, right?*

'Please,' Marty muttered randomly. Then he rolled back onto his hands, trying to understand what had happened to get him into this predicament. They had been in The Scottish Snail, he knew that much. They were talking to Benny, the owner, and then... No, they had talked to Benny. They had talked to him already and then they were waiting. Waiting for Roman. They were waiting and...

Marty remembered now. He had come. Roman Guild had come, and he had recognised him. It was the same man from before, the one who had been at the hospital, the one who had talked to him just before he tried to get into Room C19. It was him. He had come and... Amee.

Marty shot up onto his arse again, but his head hit the same obstacle, rebounding off the roof of the boot with an almighty thump and a 'Shit!'.

'Amee?' he whispered. 'Amee?' He blinked into the blackness once again, but there was nothing. It was just him and Mr Cooper in there. 'Amee?!' he tried again. 'Amee, are you there?!'

Shut your bloody guts up, Weed-kid! You don't want the driver to know you're awake, do you?

Marty clamped his jaw shut, but it was too late. The vehicle appeared to slow, gravel churning up beneath the wheels as it came to a stop. Then there was silence. For a moment.

Marty waited. The pain in his wrists reached breaking point as he felt his whole body seize up, every hair and every goose pimple rising in anticipation of the next sound. *CLICK!* The car door opened, then closed, and Marty listened as the gravel was dispersed by something other than rubber. *One, two, one, two, one, two.* The footsteps parted the stones, moving quickly towards the boot, towards him.

Oh shit! You realise what you've done? You weedy little git, you realise what's happened? He's heard you. Whoever's out there has heard you and now he's coming this way. He's coming and...

No. No, he wasn't coming. Marty twisted as the man walked past the car.

Oh, you lucky arsehole. You always were a lucky little prick. Ever since I first laid eyes on you, I knew it. So where is he going? Let's think about this. Let's be rational here. Come on, take your heart out of your mouth; it's making it hard to think with all that kerthumping! You're tied up in the boot of this man's car. You're tied up and you're on a long road by the sounds of things... Oh wait, no, I've got it. There's no need to think. He's probably off to a field where he'll dig a hole in the ground to bury you in. Gosh, Weed-kid. I think this actually might be it for you.

Another car door opened, followed swiftly by a pair of hard soles landing with a crunch on the gravel. Then there were voices. Two of them, one male, the other female. Marty tried to listen to them, but they were quiet, muffled, and he only heard bits.

'Long journey... black... snail...' the male one said.

'Good... it's... good... did anyone... where?' the female one replied.

'In the back.'

The two of them seemed to walk forward, approaching the boot of the car so fast that Marty was close to vomiting down his shirt again.

Shit, shit, shit. They're coming. They're actually coming. Here we go!

A door was opened, but it wasn't the boot.

'Here,' the male voice said, far clearer now.

'How long will she be out for?'

'Not too much longer.'

'Is she okay?'

'She's fine. She'd been making friends with the same people I had. Jack Snailer, the owner's dead son.'

Marty felt his heart shudder. *Him too?* he thought. *That's impossible. Amee's the only one who can see dead people. Just her. No one else.*

332

There was a heave, the sound of a seat belt retracting, the scrape of leather, and then more gravel being dispersed.

'I'll take her back to the hospital,' the female said. 'If you're alright to deal with the others?'

'It'll be my pleasure.'

'I don't want any stalling; I don't want any games. We've had enough of that now. Just get the job done.'

'And what about Amee?' said the male voice. 'What are you going to do about her?'

'I've been lenient enough. God knows I did everything I could to make her comfortable, to make her accept me. What else can I do? Our little fishy will always want to leave its bowl.'

'If it were me, I'd snip the fins.'

'Perhaps it's time I started listening to you, Roman.'

The voices trailed off again, and Marty turned onto his front, biting into his bottom lip as the pain began to swell around his wrists.

Shit, said Rory. *That's painful. I mean, that's properly painful. That's so painful I think you're starting to see stars. Wait. Are those stars? Do people actually see stars? I thought that was only in the movies. Oh shit, you aren't about to pass out on me, are you, Weed-kid?*

Marty winced as the door of the other car shut and its engine sparked to life.

Earth to Weed-kid. You're not allowed to pass out. I don't care how much of a wuss you are. I don't care that your arms are on fire. You can't pass out now!

Wheels churned hard against the tarmac as another car swerved back onto the road, the growl of its engine gradually fading as it drove off into the distance. Then there were footsteps again. The shoes on the gravel got louder and

Marty reclined his head all the way back. Something banged hard on the top of the boot.

Don't do this, Weed-kid! He's opening the boot. He's opening the boot and he's gonna have a shovel or something. He's gonna bash you over the head, and he's gonna bury you! You need to be awake, you need to fight back, you need to run, you need to not pass the fuck out!

Marty felt his eyes close and the carpet beneath him suddenly became comfortable, soothing, as if he could simply sink into it and let the fabric wrap him up into a nice warm cocoon.

Okay, so your eyes are closed. This is actually happening. Fucking hell, Weed-kid! I knew I could count on you to be a soft pussy!

The locks of the boot clicked out of place and Marty gave a quiet groan.

Okay, no more time to mess around. Here's what we're going to do. Action stations! I'm gonna count back from ten, and when I do, I want you to open those eyes and snap out of it, alright? You on the same page as me, Weed-kid? We've only got one shot at this, so you better give it your all. I'm counting on you. Okay, here we go. Ten, nine, eight, seven, six...

The voice faded away, the boot opened, and Marty's body fell into a soft and dreamless sleep.

* * *

'FIVE! FOUR! THREE! TWO! ONE!'

Gilbert Darrow leapt up into the air and fell towards the water below him. The boys held their breath, their muscles tensed and their buttocks clenched as he flailed around in the wind, both arms swinging in crazy circles and his legs kicking into nothing as he got closer and closer and closer. Then there was a scream. Not a big one, just a little one, like a whimper, pathetic and disquieting. And...

SPLASH!

'WOAH!' screamed Ross. 'THAT LOSER JUST GOT FUCKING DUNKED! DID YOU SEE THAT? DID YOU SEE THAT, RORY? THAT WATER FUCKING OWNED HIM!'

'Course I saw it. What do you think I was doing, tying my shoelace?'

The two kids hopped giddily on the crater's edge, and Marty stared down, watching the ripples spread across the swimming hole. Gibby's friend, Kit Miller, did the same.

'Is he out yet?' he asked. His being a Cub, this one was nerdy looking, with smart grey shorts, knee-high socks, and a thick compass for a watch on one wrist. He looked as ready for the wilderness as anyone in Gealblath, but he hadn't reckoned on beasts like Ross and Rory. Not even his trusty pocketknife could help him now.

'He's fucking dead!' squealed Ross with delight.

But Gibby wasn't dead. Two seconds later, the rich kid's head was rocking up and down on the surface, his long black hair clinging to his scalp in strands like seaweed on a bobbing buoy. The four of them breathed a sigh of relief.

'You okay, Gibby?!' Kit called down to him.

'Uuuuuuuuuuuhhhhhhhhhhhh...' came Gibby's reply.

'He's fine,' decided Rory. 'You're next!'

'I actually think he's hurt!'

'Uhhhhhhhhhh...'

Ross raised the pointy end of his stick towards Kit, jabbing it through the air threateningly. 'You wanna help him, why don't you go join him?'

Gibby's friend took a shaky breath, glancing hopefully from Teddy, to Mike, to Marty, as if he actually thought any one of them might be able to save him. But they couldn't save him. They couldn't do anything. They were all in the same predicament. They were all going to have to comply, even if it meant falling fifty feet to their death.

Ross repeated his stabbing motion. 'C'mon, pussy! It's an easy choice. Either you get wet, or you go back to your mummy one eyeball short!'

With a slight gasp, Kit touched his left eyelid, rubbing the skin meekly as if he was only now realising how much he'd miss the eye. 'Fine,' he replied fearfully. 'Fine.'

'You want us to count you in too, do you?' Rory stamped his foot, kicking some more yellow sand into the air.

Marty looked below again, watching Gibby thrash wildly about in the water. Kit took another step closer, his hands hovering on either side of him like he was on an imaginary tightrope.

'What if I hit him?' he asked the two adjudicators.

Rory grinned maniacally. 'Then you're gonna have to pay for my new pants because I'll be pissing myself laughing.'

Kit touched his eye again, putting the tip of his foot cautiously on the last remaining jagged piece of rock. He took another breath, and so did everyone else.

'Please,' he muttered. And then he was in the air, his body flailing about in the breeze as he hurtled towards the swimming hole. His mouth was clamped shut, so unlike Gibby, he didn't scream. Instead, there was just a pause, lingering and unnerving, until his body hit the water.

KAAAAASLIIIIIIP!

The sound echoed over and over, dispersing some birds from their nearby nests and dislodging some more of those soldiers from the depths of Marty's stomach. He looked over the edge and saw another huge ripple edging away from the impact point. The blue of the water turned stark white and foamy.

'AHOOOOO!' Ross jumped up and down, his stick swishing to and fro in the air. 'BULLSEYE! OH, THAT'S A SWEET SOUND! YOU OKAY DOWN THERE, KITTY BABY?'

Kit's head pierced the water and he made a similar groaning sound to Gibby. Then Marty began to sweat, because his turn was coming soon. It could be a few seconds from now, it could be a few minutes, but it was going to happen.

'Two down, three to go! YOU!' Rory pointed at Marty. 'Why isn't your shirt off? Think you're not going in, huh?'

Marty looked down at his shirt and tensed, his fingers stroking the fabric slightly. He was afraid they might say that. He reached down and pulled the shirt over his head, allowing his bare torso to be kissed by the summer wind.

'Holy shit!' yelled Ross. 'He's weedier than my stick!'

Rory laughed. 'What's your name?'

'Weed-kid,' Ross answered for him. 'That's his name! It's Weed-kid!'

The two of them cracked up again, and Marty looked back over towards Teddy and Mike, both of whom were watching the water, their eyes wide and their lungs panting. He wondered once again how the hell they had got into this predicament, and why the hell they had to see it through. They had done nothing wrong. They didn't deserve any of this. They were just in the wrong place at the wrong time, and they were being punished for it.

Ross stopped laughing. 'Okay, you're next. What's your name?' he gestured over towards Marty's friend.

'T-T-Teddy,' he stuttered back.

'Alright, Teddy Bear, in you go!'

Marty looked at Teddy, beginning to feel anger bubble up alongside the mush of soldiers and Wotsits. Perhaps they didn't have to see it through, he realised suddenly. Perhaps they didn't have to be on the losing side. But then, this was Ross and Rory. The school bullies. The school psychos. Going against them was like going against a lorry travelling at a hundred miles per hour. It could surely only end in one big *splat!*

But all the same, the urge remained. It outweighed the fear, rewiring the brain to make it foolish. Marty took a few breaths. If he was going to do anything, it had to be now. He knew that. It would have to be now, and it would have to be fast.

'You don't want me to come over there, Teddy,' Rory bellowed. 'I can kick you off the edge if you can't do it yourself!'

Marty's legs began to shake, and he searched himself for courage. He hadn't needed it before; he hadn't needed it ever. But he needed it now. The problem was, he didn't even know if it was a part of him. Courage was only recognisable once it was tested. There could be something behind the veil, just waiting to come out when the curtain was pulled, or there could be nothing. Just an empty stage. Hollow. Dark.

'THAT'S IT, TEDDY, YOU'VE HAD YOUR CHANCE!' Rory began walking over towards Teddy, and Marty took a deep breath.

Guess it's time to find out, he thought. And then he prepared to pull the curtain. *Where is your courage now?*

* * *

The stars were the first things to greet him. They darted about the sky like autumn flies, spinning high above Marty's head until he blinked once, then twice, and stilled them.

'Blerrrrghh...' He smacked his lips together, grimacing at the smell of vomit that permeated the cracks. 'Blergh.'

A breath, a deep breath, and then a memory. *Oh shit!* Marty pulled on his wrists, but they remained stuck behind his spine, quite numb now, as if all the blood had been squeezed out of them. He lifted his head to see Mr Cooper lying about ten feet away in front of him. They weren't in the car anymore, that much was for certain. Instead, it appeared that they were on the grass in the middle of a large and empty valley, disrupted only by some woodland about a quarter of a mile to the right.

Marty felt his heart pick up again as Rory's voice echoed through his head once more.

How was your sleep, Weed-kid? Comfortable? Relaxing? I hope it was, because you're back in the fire now.

His nose wrinkled at the smell of smoke, and he rolled on the ground, squinting at a small campfire which Roman Guild was kneeling beside. His tall stature was silhouetted against the two glaring headlamps of the cool black American Lincoln. They lit up the scene from behind him, the engine still emitting a cold and metallic hum.

'Look at that,' Roman said with a smile. 'The kid's awake. I thought you'd never come back. Here...' He trod over towards Marty and propped him against a nearby log. 'That's better, right?'

Marty didn't answer. He simply sat and stared as Roman walked back over towards the fire. After a few seconds, he opened his mouth. 'You're the one,' he croaked. 'The one on the phone, the one who knew about the detective.'

'And you're the one from the hospital,' said Roman. 'The one who was curious about his lost friend. She is your friend, isn't she?' Roman looked at him, but Marty didn't answer. 'That's nice. That's awfully nice. You know, before all this, I was Amee's only friend. She and I used to spend quite a bit of time together.'

Roman slipped a hand into his pocket and took out a cigarette and a lighter. The lighter looked strange, like it was an antique. Decorative metal pieces wrapped around it like a snake, and the spark wheel was like a large cog that had been stitched onto the end. He flicked it on, and Marty felt like he could feel the flame from here. It was big and roaring, like it could set an entire log on fire. Instead, it burned the cigarette in Roman's mouth.

'Where is she?' Marty felt the muscles in his arms begin to twitch violently as he talked.

'She's gone home,' replied Roman. 'Where she belongs.'

With great pain, Marty pulled his wrists higher, a sting of heat pulsing around his collarbone as he did so. He winced, and Roman saw it. A sickly smile twisted the symmetry of his face.

'I'm sorry, Marty, but the restraints are necessary. I've seen how far you dogs can run when you're let off the leash. And you're more clever than most; you don't leave any tracks.' He peered down towards Mr Cooper. 'His doing, I suppose.'

'How do you know my name?' Marty whispered. The words struggled to escape the dry tunnel of his throat. It was like a slide with no friction, and they barely came out.

'Hard to miss a story like yours in Gealblath. Marty Evans. Disappeared into thin air, like Charlie Cooper before him. You're a nasty little one, aren't you? Your family must be hurt.'

'I had to come. I had to be with Amee.'

Roman laughed and blew out a harsh cloud of smoke. 'I'm sure she appreciated your protection.' He prodded the fire, blinking against the sparks which were rising spontaneously into the air, twirling like moving stars around the tall man's face.

Marty bit his bile-encrusted lip. 'What are you gonna do to me?'

Despite his efforts, he couldn't help the tears lodging alongside the words in his throat.

Oh, well done, Weed-kid. Beg him. You beg him good. That's what will get you out of this.

Roman ignored Marty's question. 'Seriously, Marty, I thank you for it. Being there for Amee. Imagining her alone with him...' He nodded down to Mr Cooper. 'I can hardly think of it.'

The teacher was still motionless on the ground, his left cheek pressed hard into the grass and his legs lying slightly crooked. He was on his front, so it was hard to see if he was breathing, especially in the darkness of the valley.

'Did you kill him?' asked Marty. The question was blunt, and for a moment, Marty couldn't believe he was asking it. It wasn't a question he'd thought he'd ever have to ask. It came straight out of a film, a story. Not real life, not his. But the question was in the air now, and Roman Guild soaked it up.

'I'm not sure,' he responded.

Roman stood and walked over towards the body. Without warning, he landed his shoe directly into Mr Cooper's groin.

The body groaned on the grass.

'Not dead,' said Roman. 'Just sleeping.'

The teacher opened his eyes. 'Wha...? Where...?'

'What's that?' the tall man teased him.

'Where am I?' Mr Cooper turned his head, his eyes wide and afraid as he took in his surroundings and tried to sort them into an order that made sense. He looked up at Roman. 'You... What have you done?'

'Last time I saw you, you knocked me out with a fire extinguisher. My methods of tranquilisation are a little more uniform.'

Mr Cooper's head lolled back, his neck tilting so far that Marty thought he might slip back into sleep. But then his eyes were open once more and he was focusing on Roman as he returned to the fire.

'Roman Guild...'

'Yes,' the tall man replied.

Mr Cooper wheezed. 'Where are we? What is this?'

Roman looked set to answer, but before he could, the teacher appeared to find his strength. He jolted up, his lungs panting and his legs flailing. He tried to lift his neck, but whatever was left of the tranquiliser didn't allow it. His bones were weak. Useless.

Roman lifted his hand. 'No,' he said, almost like a parent. 'Over. Over now. It's done, David.'

Mr Cooper stopped struggling and Roman flicked on his lighter, letting the fire blaze bright before his eyes.

'We can have this conversation alive or dead. It's your choice.'

Mr Cooper peered through the flame. 'What the hell are you talking about?'

'He can see dead people,' said Marty suddenly.

Roman frowned. 'How did you know that?'

'I heard you. In the car. You were talking about Benny Snailer's dead son. You can, can't you? You're like Amee. You can see them.' Marty stopped, the voice in his head urging him not to go further.

What the hell are you doing? Seriously, this man's tied you up in the middle of nowhere and you want to engage in a conversation? Are you as stupid as you look, Marty?! Besides...

Besides what? The thought hit him like a ton of bricks. He could see dead people. Roman, the tall man, the one Amee knew better than she knew Marty himself. Surely she would have known too. Surely she knew who was coming. But if she did, why hadn't she told them?

'Yes,' said Roman. 'I can talk to dead people. But I try not to make a habit of it. Dead people are a bore. The living tend to be a lot more fun.'

'You can see dead people?' said Mr Cooper.

Roman ignored him. 'It was good of you to call by the way. It's been a long month and we were starting to lose hope. We thought we'd never find you.'

'But I don't understand,' Mr Cooper moaned.

'You think you're the only one with questions for Alfie Percival? That man has a lot to answer for, and more to answer to.'

'What reason could you have to talk to him?'

'Me? Oh, no reason at all, but I don't work for myself. I work for somebody else.'

There was a pause. Mr Cooper took a deep breath. The words seemed to teeter on the edge of his tongue. 'Did you kill my son?'

Roman smiled. 'No.'

'Do you know who killed my son?'

'No.'

'You're lying.'

'No.'

The fire spat a small ember at the tall man's feet, and he cocked his head, his thick brown hair blowing about in the nighttime breeze.

'Are you disappointed?' he asked, but Mr Cooper didn't answer.

He heaved in pain, closing his eyes as he stuck his nose into the grass. Marty could feel it too. His own arms were spasming even more vigorously now, throbbing like a jackhammer against concrete. He had no idea how long they'd been curled up in that car.

Roman shrugged. 'You want to know who killed your son. That's why you went looking for Alfie. It seems our paths are similar, if not identical. We want to know what happened that day too. That's why we talked to the detective, just about a year ago.'

'And you killed Alfie?' asked Marty, before he could help himself.

Roman turned, his eyes ablaze, a cool mixture of orange and green, with smoke blurring the lines in the middle.

Why did you ask him that? hissed Rory. *Why did you have to ask him anything? What the hell did I tell you? Just keep your weedy arse quiet, and pray you stay alive. That's what you're supposed to be doing.*

'A mistake,' said Roman, 'by all accounts. But a pleasant one, by mine. His death wasn't planned, and neither were the consequences. Thankfully, I made a friend in Cornwall. I knew I could count on him, old Benny Snailer.'

'Count on him to do what?'

What did I just say, Weed-kid?

344

'You tell me,' replied Roman. 'You're the ones who called.'

'You wanted us to call you?'

This isn't fucking funny now!

'I knew that if Alfie's name came up in The Scottish Snail, then word would have got around about his death. The phone call was for me to gauge how much I was needed, if I was needed at all. How much of a trace had I left? Were people saying suicide, or were people saying more? It was messy, I'll give you that. These things are when you don't plan them, when they happen on a whim. What happens afterwards is just a plaster over a bleeding wound. But it's funny how things work out because look where it led me. If I'd never killed the detective, I would never have found you. That's destiny.'

'But I don't understand,' said Marty. 'Why would you want to know about Alfie? What could you do?'

'Oh nothing, nothing at all. Don't you remember? I'm just a friend. I'm just a concerned party who always knew the poor detective was gonna pull the gun on himself. Such a shame he did it. He didn't deserve a bullet through that skull. I hope he did it right and saved himself any pain.' He dipped his head in a sort of weird performance. Then he raised it again.

'Unless that isn't what happened. Unless, maybe, the caller knew something else. What was it you told me, David?' He looked over towards Mr Cooper. 'You were looking for some people? Well, there I knew I could help out'

With that, the tall man stood up straight and marched towards the rumbling Lincoln. He leaned through the open door and pulled something from within. Marty heard a clink of steel. Roman was holding a strange machine in both hands, something Marty had never seen before. But

Mr Cooper had. That much was clear almost immediately.

'No! No, no, you can't! You won't!'

'Shh, shh, shh.' Roman began removing what appeared to be a long, metallic tube from the machine. 'No more talking now. It's okay. It's alright. There'll be pain, but don't worry. You won't remember it.'

He walked towards them, and Marty felt his heart clattering in his chest.

Well? Well?! Where is your courage now?

* * *

'PUSH THE FUCKER TO HIS DEATH!'

Rory walked towards Teddy, his chubby cheeks red with anticipation. Ross raised his stick in a stabbing motion, but this time Marty was ready. He grabbed the pointy end in one hand and pulled as hard as he could, swiping the stick from Ross's grasp before jumping towards him and holding him in a head lock. Rory heard the scuffle and turned, watching with wide eyes as Marty jabbed the stick up against Ross's abdomen.

'WHAT THE –'

'Don't move! If you move, this stick will spill his guts!'

There was a moment. Both bullies stood still. Rory gaped at Marty with a bewildered look on his face, and Marty's two friends weren't that much different. Another hoarse moan came from the swimming hole fifty feet below them.

'We're not going in there,' yelled Marty. 'You're gonna let us go!'

Mike squealed. 'Marty! What are you doing?'

'We're not going in!'

Rory let out a long and dangerous sigh. 'A troublemaker.

Look at this, Ross, we have a troublemaker.'

Despite being locked in Marty's grasp, Ross giggled. Marty poked the stick in further, hoping an extra inch or two of pain might cut him off.

'I'm serious! We're not going in! You're gonna let us go!'

Rory took a step towards him. 'Or what?'

'I've already told you! I'll spill his guts!'

'Oh, you'll spill his guts?! You hear that, Ross? Weed-kid's gonna spill your guts!'

'Fucking hell!' Ross almost spat with laughter. 'The weed-kid's gonna do me, Rory! He's gonna do me right here and now. Jesus Christ! Tell my mumma I love her! The weed-kid's gonna do me!'

Marty jabbed further, but the more he pushed the stick, the harder Ross laughed.

'OH, DO ME, WEED-KID! SPILL MY GUTS, GO ON! I CAN'T WAIT TO SEE MY INTESTINES ON THE FLOOR! OH, WEED-KID, YOU'RE A FUCKING HERO!'

Teddy and Mike watched in terror as Rory took another step.

'Go on then,' he said confidently. 'You heard him. Spill his guts.'

Marty felt his heart beating in his mouth. One of the nearby eagles called into the wind. The sound spiralled around the chimney over and over again like a cyclone.

'I'm warning you. Don't take a step closer...'

'Are you not listening to me, Weed-kid? I want you to spill his guts. I want to see them on the floor.'

Marty hopped from one foot to the next. Regret for his decision was streaming through him, but he couldn't have predicted this reaction. He couldn't have predicted any of this. They were unfazed. They were entirely unfazed. Ross, if anything, seemed to be having even more fun than he was before.

'WOOHOO! C'MON, WEED-KID, STICK ME! STICK ME! STICK ME! STICK ME!'

Rory was only a couple of feet away now, his eyes glimmering and his tongue curled onto his lip in concentration. Marty felt the bile begin to bubble in his stomach.

'Go on then, Weed-kid,' said Rory. 'Prove your worth.'

Marty held the stick tighter. *Go on*, he thought. *Go on. Go on. Do it, just do it! You have to do something if you want to get out of here!*

'Well?' said Rory.

A moment passed, and then Marty's fingers peeled back, the stick fell, and he bowed his head and threw up onto his shoes.

'UGH!'

Ross squirmed from his grip, just about managing to swerve out of the way of Marty's regurgitated Sunday breakfast. Rory bounced in excitement.

'I knew it!'

Another load came out and Marty spat, his head beginning to sway and the sand starting to blur. Every grain swirled beneath his feet like a hurricane ready to spin him into the air and send him over the edge. But he didn't need a hurricane to do that, because Rory was already behind him. He clamped Marty in a head lock.

'Oh, Weed-kid, you're gonna pay for that!'

Ross retrieved his stick and stuck it into Marty's belly, pushing so hard that the tip was stained with red.

'Don't hurt him!' screamed Teddy.

'It'll be you next!' Ross roared back.

Rory began whispering in Marty's ear. 'You think you

can take us on? You think you can be the hero?'

He drove his knee into the back of Marty's leg, and Marty winced in pain, his belly churning up some more breakfast to stain the sand on the crater's edge.

'You know what you are?' said Rory. 'You're a weed-kid. That's what you are.'

'YOU FUCKING SKINNY PUSSY!'

Ross drove the stick into him again, and this time Marty yelled out, but not because of the pain. The stick had barely broken the skin. He yelled out because he had lost. He yelled out because he had tried to find his courage, but it wasn't there. He yelled out because they were right.

'That's what you have to remember,' said Rory with a grin. 'You're a weed-kid. That's what we're gonna call you from now on. That's what everyone is gonna call you. You're a weed-kid, and there's nothing you can do about it.'

'DUNK HIM, RORY!' whooped Ross.

And Rory obliged. With a large swing, he twisted his body, then kicked his shoe into Marty's spine, sending him flying off the edge of the crater with no mercy. All Marty could do was close his eyes and pray he wouldn't hit the rocks.

* * *

Do you remember the water? Do you remember the way it wrapped itself round you and sent you cold? Do you remember how you felt? Well, Weed-kid? Do you remember?

Roman Guild continued to uncurl the tube, his brow furrowed in concentration and a slight sweat trickling through his hair. The fire was high now. The flames kissed the wind loudly. The wood blackened, shifted, peeling off into ash and then into nothing. Perhaps the stars? Did the ashes go high enough? Marty's eyes followed them into the darkness. He watched them rise, like they were falling in reverse, spiralling down into a big pit of black water.

Do you remember the water? Rory's voice returned.

Marty closed his eyes. *Why do I have to remember?*

That summer day played out in front of him. The way he had stood on that crater's edge, the shriek of the sea eagles spiralling around the power plant's chimney, the sound of those boys groaning in the swimming hole. He saw himself falling. But he didn't want to remember that. Not now. He didn't want to. *Please*, he thought. But was it him thinking it, or was it his teacher calling out? Mr Cooper was still squirming on the wet grass, his screams echoing across the valley.

'Please!' he yelled. 'Please! Please! You can't do this!'

He begged the tall man, but the tall man only smiled, his eyes focused on the strange machine as it began to wheeze and breathe of its own accord. Marty knew what it was now. He'd heard Amee and Mr Cooper talk about the coil. About how they had tried to use it on Mr Cooper back in the hospital.

The deep end is here again, Weed-kid. It's Roman, and he's calling to you. Do you remember the water? Do you remember how it felt?

'Roman!' shouted Mr Cooper. 'Talk to me! You don't have to do this! You can't do this!'

I remember what it felt like, Marty told Rory. *I remember it all the time. That was the day I found out who I was. That was the day I couldn't find my courage.*

'ROMAN!'

So find it now, if you can. Find it. Pull on the restraints; break free.

'ROMAN STOP!'

I thought you said I wasn't a hero. I thought you said I was just a weed-kid. I thought you said I'd always be a weed-kid.

'YOU CAN'T DO THIS! I'M TELLING YOU, YOU CAN'T DO THIS!'

We all get second chances, Marty. You don't have to be the weed-kid anymore, not if you don't choose to be. That's why you came. That's why you wanted to protect Amee. To prove your worth. To show you're something more than what you are. Marty, listen to what I'm saying. Fight back.

Roman started turning one of the gears on the machine. Marty didn't know what was about to happen, but from Mr Cooper's reaction, he knew it was bad. He knew they only had seconds. He pushed himself up against the log.

What if I'm too afraid to fight back? Because I am afraid, Rory. I'm really afraid.

Another spit from the fire, the ash rising up, up, up, into the stars.

Don't be afraid. Just do it.

Marty heard the teacher scream again. *How do I do it?* he asked himself.

Pull, came the reply. *Pull hard. Pull harder than you've ever pulled in your life!*

Marty clamped his teeth and started pulling on the plastic behind his back. Tears began to fall down his cheeks as he anticipated the pain which was sure to come. But it didn't come. To his surprise, the pain was less than it had been in the car. There was no blood; there was no jab of pain in the wrist bones. It was almost as if they weren't the same restraints.

Looser. Are they looser? How can they be looser? He kept pulling, his heart beginning to thump harder as he watched the tall man pick up the strange-looking coil again.

They're not, they can't be; it's the adrenaline. Just keep going.

'Roman! Don't do this!' yelled Mr Cooper at the top of his lungs.

Roman walked over to him. 'We've done this before, David. You don't have to panic.'

He knelt down beside the teacher and stroked the top of his scalp. Then he grabbed his jaw and began shoving the coil down Mr Cooper's throat. The teacher gagged and spluttered as Roman drove it further and further, cutting off his air supply with the thick metal tube.

Jesus Christ! C'mon, Marty! Pull! Pull hard! Otherwise that's gonna happen to you!

Despite everything, Marty began to feel his left hand easing out of the plastic, his thumb now pushed right up into his palm.

Come on! You're doing it! I don't know how, but you're doing it! Keep pulling! Keep going! Come on! One last pull now, c'mon, do it, go!

Marty winced, yanking down towards his arse until his left hand slipped free from the restraints.

I'm out. I'm actually out! I did it! I did it, Rory! I did it!

Marty swayed on the spot, his vision going a little blurry for a moment. The tall man was kneeling over the teacher now, the coil in one hand and the machine beside him whirring.

Calm down! Calm yourself down! Get your bearings!

Marty let himself take a few breaths. His heart was now beating so fast that it felt like he was going to go into cardiac arrest right there and then. He tried to calm down, but he couldn't calm down. He was out. He was out of the restraints. Somehow he had done it, and now Mr Cooper needed him. Roman could be killing him. Marty needed to act, and he needed to act fast.

Okay. Go. Just go. GO!

Marty sprang onto his feet and rushed to the fire. He reached down and grabbed the nearest blazing log. The pain was almost immediate, but he ignored it. His hands was already numb enough. Without wasting another second, he swivelled backwards and stumbled towards the two struggling bodies, raising the log above his head and preparing to bring it down as hard as he could onto the head of Roman Guild.

You'll have one shot at this. Just one. So this has to work. This just has to work. Do it. DO IT NOW!

For some reason, it felt like everything was happening in slow motion. The wind rushed into his face, the fire coughed into the air, the log came down towards Roman, and Marty braced himself for impact. Then a hand came up to meet it. A big hand. It wrapped itself around the hot wood as if it was nothing, and Marty's heart stopped in its tracks.

'Oh, Marty,' said Roman, the smile still present on his face as he turned. 'I was hoping you'd do that.' He tugged the log from his grasp and threw it behind his shoulder. 'I was really hoping I could have some fun.'

Marty struggled to form the words. 'H... how...?' he breathed.

'You think I'm the only one with eyes here?' said Roman.

Marty didn't know how or why, but the next thing he knew, he was on the ground. Roman was standing over him, his fists clenched and his gaze fierce.

How did that happen, Rory? whispered Marty inside his head. *Are there dead people here, do you think? Are there dead people?* Rory's voice didn't reply, and Marty felt Roman's boot digging into his gut. *Did he loosen the restraints for me, perhaps? When I was sleeping? Did he want me to fight back?* The boot squeezed down hard, and Marty felt one of his ribs crack. *I don't understand. I don't understand what's happening. It feels like I'm falling again. Is this my story?*

Marty felt something hit his cheek, and it could very well have been Roman's fist, because it felt big, and round, and hard, and Roman laughed after it happened. *In the movies, the hero always rises up again. After they fall, they always fight back. I thought that was supposed to happen. Why didn't that happen?* Another sting of pain shot through Marty's nose, and he heard a crunch. *Rory, why won't you talk to me?*

The stars began moving again, some darting this way, some the other. Some spiralled into a small circle, almost like a cyclone, like they were preparing to whirl Marty up into their arms like a mother with her child. Roman's boot landed on Marty's head, and then he realised what was happening. He was being beaten up. Roman was a bully from school. He was Rory. He was Ross. He was beating Marty up on the lunch hall floor, and he was enjoying it. *What if he never stops?* Marty felt an excruciating pain in his neck. *Rory, what if I'm going to die?* The stars began growing dimmer, fading, cooling, like they were going out one by one. *Don't tell me the stars go out, Rory. Don't tell me they leave.* Roman's fist came down onto Marty's temple, and then everything fell into darkness.

Do you remember the water? Do you remember how it felt? Do you remember the way it swirled around you and swallowed you down, until there was nothing left?

Shit, I'm sorry, Weed-kid. I thought this time it could be different. I thought you might really do it, like the way it happens in the movies. The good guy always takes a fall, but he always rises back up again. He always beats the villain in the end. But I guess this isn't a movie, huh? This is life. This is real. And this is the way it's ending. You're in the water again now; you're all the way in it.

Do you remember how it felt the last time? I can tell you, if you'd like. Last time everything went black. You wondered if you had died, but you hadn't died. You were alive, just broken a bit, just beaten. But you didn't know that. Not in that moment, not in that split second of blackness. You thought that death had come to you and there was nothing left. You felt frightened, you felt sad, you felt cold. You felt like there was no warmth left in the world at all. Just for a moment.

Thing is, Weed-kid, this time you might not reach the surface. In fact, I kind of doubt that you will. I think this is it for you, so think about someone. Think about someone who makes you happy, someone who brings a light to the darkness. Think about Amee, if you can. Think about her face, her smile. Think about that time you watched her walking like she was barefoot on the grass. Take her with you into the deep end. Make her the last thing in your head and feel warmer for it.

I think you deserve some warmth down there, after all, Weed-kid. I think we all deserve some warmth at the end.

21

QUIET IN THE VALLEY

'How far can we walk, Dad?'

'As far as the tide lets us.'

The water retreated from David's toes, trickling delicately from rock to rock, fizzing, frothing, diminishing steadily, like it might lead them all the way to Derling, or someplace else entirely. Charlie squeezed his hand tighter.

'How far is Derling?'

'One mile, maybe two; it's closer than it looks. One time the water let me go all the way there and back again.'

Charlie laughed, then sniffed in the breeze. The bite of the wind was giving him a bit of a fever. His forehead was turning red and his upper lip was moist with snot. 'Not possible,' he said.

'Of course it's possible.'

David squinted at the faraway shore, watching as some clouds fell from the sky, hiding the vista of a distant forest in a mess of grey. When he looked back at his son, Charlie was staring at him. His blue eyes were wider now, almost suspicious.

'Why did you stop dreaming about me?'

David stopped walking. Or had they stopped walking a long time ago? He didn't know. Or couldn't tell. 'What do you mean?' he asked.

'You haven't dreamed in a long time. Not about me, not about this. You used to. You used to dream about me a lot. And the ocean.'

David swayed a little, the sand creasing quietly under his shoes. 'I don't dream lately,' he replied.

'That's not true.'

Another wave of wind hit them, and Charlie wrinkled his nose, a strand of blonde hair catching in the corner of his eye.

'Okay,' said David. 'Well, I'm dreaming now.'

'No. No, you're not.'

'What do you mean? I'm dreaming about you, kiddo. I'm dreaming.'

'You're not dreaming. This isn't a dream, Dad. You have to understand that, this isn't a dream.'

David turned back to Derling. The clouds were now covering the entirety of the landscape. He was staring into a wall of nothing. 'I don't understand,' he muttered.

'You're not dreaming, Dad. You're not dreaming. You have to wake up. You have to wake up or those clouds will keep going. They will cover everything you know.'

David squinted his eyes again, and now he could just about make out Marty and Amee standing in the water. The clouds were engulfing them too, distorting their features, erasing them until they were nothing but shapes in smoke. David started to panic.

'Fuck. What the fuck? What's happening?'

His head started to hurt, and his throat began to twitch, like it was attempting to push something out. A fur ball, a lump of sick, or something else, something thicker, longer, like a snake curled up inside a tunnel. He coughed, but the thing remained. He coughed again. One, two, three. But nothing happened. Nothing but more panic.

'Oh, what the fuck?!'

'Wake up, Dad.' Charlie squeezed his hand so hard it felt like he was crushing the bone. Then, with a heave, he pushed him. 'Wake up. Now!'

And David felt himself falling backwards towards the sand.

He awoke on grass and spluttered into the cold evening air. Tears were streaming down each cheek, blood was trickling along the cracks of his fingers, and a long, cold tube was halfway down his throat, pumping what felt like sharp air down into his system.

'Blerrghh...' he moaned.

Then he pricked up his ears. The only things to hear were the hooting of owls in the nearby woodland, the metallic rumble of machinery, and the sound of flesh on flesh and breathing along with it. David felt his heart beating in his chest, and he lifted his head. He spotted the blurry outline of the tall man just a few feet ahead, standing over a lump on the ground beneath him.

'Blerrghh...'

He coughed again, this time whistling a few droplets of blood into the sky. With a shudder, he tried to take a deep breath, but the tube inside his mouth stopped him from doing so. That was when David started to panic. The speed of his heart tripled in his chest, and he struggled on the ground, trying desperately to jerk the tube from out of his throat. The sound of flesh on flesh continued, this time accompanied by a loud and toe-curling howl.

'OH, I'VE MISSED THIS!' The voice was hoarse, high,

and familiar. It was Roman. Roman Guild.

David's eyes widened as he began to remember. Roman had found them in the inn; he had taken them out to a wide, empty valley; he had shoved the coil down David's throat, just as he had done back in the hospital one month before. And now David was at his mercy.

He stopped struggling and tried to think, the breath from his lungs only just managing to escape through his flaring nostrils.

He remembered the hospital. He remembered how Amee had pulled the coil from his throat, how he had thrown up onto the pristine rubber floor. But there was no Amee to help him this time. Only himself and his own hands, which were currently restrained behind his back. David spluttered once more, the blood now stinging his eyes.

'I'M GONNA KILL YOU! I'M GONNA FUCKING KILL YOU!' Roman screamed into the night.

David licked the coil. It was different this time, he could tell that much. He was awake, he was conscious, he was pretty sure of that. He licked again. He could taste it. He could taste the tang of dirty metal. Or was that his own blood? Without stopping to ponder it, David squirmed on the ground, taking the deepest breath he could before attempting to shuffle back and make the coil slip out. It didn't work. He moved back a few inches, but the coil remained, still inside, still tight. Roman Guild screamed in delight once again, and David swallowed, raging with the urge to simply rip it out. *God help me rip this thing out!* His heart clanged against his ribcage, and he spluttered again, more tears streaming down his face.

Then, as if instinctively, his feet replaced his hands. With a heave, he lifted them from the ground and placed them on top of the coil. He felt it tug down, jamming hard against his throat and cramming his tongue up against one side of his mouth. With a wince, he tried shuffling back again, this time sliding his arse against the ground with one big push whilst his feet remained clamped on the coil.

The coil jerked up in his throat. He shivered and twitched in pain. It was as if the coil was made of jagged glass, steadily cutting into his innards as it retreated up the tunnel. But it had worked. It had moved. He closed his eyes and pushed again. A clump of sick and blood began leaking onto his bottom lip, down his chin, and onto his chest.

SHIT! The pain was blinding, but David did it all over again. This time his vision went blurry, and his head began to wobble atop his shoulders. The coil was nearly out; he could feel it. It was clinging to his throat by a thread, and just one more jerk would dispel it completely. He spluttered, spat, repositioned his feet on the coil, and slid on his arse one more time. The coil flopped from his mouth and landed with a thud on the cold ground.

Then there was a wall of colour. David kept his mouth open, his lungs panting hard into the harsh autumnal air as the world around him attempted to put itself into an order. The stars came first, a whole cluster of them. Then the moon over the tree line, steadily swinging to stillness like a metronome. David blinked once, then twice, and the order was finally complete. Then came the first question: *What now?*

He looked up and saw the tall man continuing to attack the weed-kid, who remained motionless and bloodied on the damp grass. He took the beatings like a doll. Without life. Just a thing to be played with, a thing to be torn and broken. David spluttered again. He knew he had to act fast. He knew he had to do something, and he had to do it while Roman's back was turned. Any hope of escape would be over as soon as the tall man turned around. He had to do something now. *Right now!*

With a heave, David rolled himself onto his belly, wincing at the huge sting of pain which spiralled up into his hands like the bones were being crushed. *Let go, Charlie, let go!* But it wasn't Charlie. It was the restraints, plastic cuffs that were tied around his wrists, forcing them into submission. He tried to ignore them. He looked up, his eyes squinting against the blinding lights of the Lincoln. *That's it*, he thought to himself. The car. The car was his only hope. He didn't know how, and he didn't know why. But it was.

Without thinking, he pushed with all his might onto his knees. Then he stood up. The blood immediately rushed to his head, and he wobbled slightly, trying to divert his stumble in the direction of the waiting vehicle. He spat out another clump of vomit, and Roman's voice yelled out into the night.

'HEY!'

David didn't even turn. It was like there was someone else inside him at the controls, urging him forward, pushing him on, keeping David on his feet long enough to reach the door of the Lincoln. To his relief, Roman had left it open when he had gone to retrieve the coil, so all David had to do was fall into the car and shuffle across to the driver's seat.

'FUCKER!' yelled Roman, chasing after him.

David leant down and shoved out his elbow, nudging the car into drive. His foot hovered above the pedal and Roman Guild stopped in his tracks. He looked at David with wild eyes. Then there were moments again. Small ones. David stared at Roman, and Roman stared back at him. He raised his hands, but he wasn't surrendering; David knew that much. Roman was still in control.

'Here again, David,' he shouted over the rumble of the engine. 'You wanna escape like last time?'

David tried hard to ignore the speckles of white and black that were fizzing in his eyesight, blurring the tall man, then unblurring him, then blurring him again. He felt like he might pass out, but he couldn't do that. Not here, not now. He blinked and shuffled on the leather.

'You're not,' he spluttered. 'You're not gonna...'

Roman looked down at the coil. 'Guess I got ahead of myself. Didn't pay enough attention. You're tenacious, I'll give you that. You always manage to find it in yourself, if you're given the chance. Come out of the car now.'

'Why the fuck would I do that?' said David. His throat was hoarse and bleeding, and he only barely got the words out.

'Because your tenacity's got you, what, ten feet? It can't get you any further. Don't make it harder on yourself.'

'I'm not gonna do what you say.'

Roman laughed, then lowered his hands, glancing from left to right mockingly. 'What are you gonna do? Drive that thing all the way home with your hands behind your back?'

David panted, his right foot hovering over the pedal. 'No,' he replied. 'Just ten feet.'

David pushed his foot down on the accelerator, propelling the Lincoln forward at such a pace that his head fell back onto the headrest. The last thing he saw was Roman's smile fading faster than the spinning of the Lincoln's wheels.

In his dream, the water was fully out. The sand carried on into the distance, dull and grey, until it reached Derling. David sat up and stared. The back of his tweed jacket was wet with salty water, and he stank like the ocean, but he didn't mind that. He was looking at Charlie now, who was standing with his back to him.

'Guess you were right. Guess it does go all the way.'

David took a breath, getting his bearings. 'Not always. Only sometimes. It's like I told you, Charlie. When everything is in the right place. And the moon is with you.'

Charlie turned and looked down at him. 'Did you get out of there?'

'I'm not sure.'

'Are you going back?'

There was a moment, and then David nodded. 'Yes.'

'And then what?'

A gust of wind chilled David's bones, and he shivered, pulling his jacket close to his body as he looked into his son's eyes. He felt the tears beginning to form, his blood beginning to chill.

'I know what you're asking, Charlie. I know. You ask me every night. That's why I stopped dreaming. I just can't do it. Finding the person who killed you was the only thing left I could do for you, and I couldn't even do that.'

Charlie knelt down beside him. 'That wasn't for me; that was for you. That was always for you, Dad.'

David looked down at the sand, watching as the particles rippled beneath him, like they might form a hole and swallow him down into some other form of life.

Charlie continued, 'Punishing them was like punishing yourself. You kill them, you go to prison. Wasn't that how you hoped it would end?'

David winced at the words, but he allowed them to settle in the air. Because they were true, they were obviously true; he'd just never said them. He never could. 'Of course it was,' he said now. 'I am to blame, I wasn't there for you, I was a bad father. These dreams I have, the dreams I've been having since you've been gone, they're not real. They're lies. We never went to the beach. I didn't talk to you like this. You didn't talk to me the way you talk to me now. I never held your hand. I never called you kiddo. I wasn't there. I was someplace else. In a bar, with a woman, in my own head. I didn't care for you the way I should have. That's why you're gone. A dad should protect his child. That's his duty. But I had my time and I failed. I made it short. Too short.'

Charlie held David's hand again. 'Dad, there's still time. Amee's still out there.'

The sand started to move faster, swirling and spinning, and David felt himself sinking into it.

'Amee's out there, and she needs you. I think you're waking up now.'

Charlie let go of his hand, and then he was gone.

'ARGHH!'

The high-pitched howls echoed in the night, yanking David out from the warm blanket that was unconsciousness. His eyes flickered open, then closed, then open again. There was something cold running down onto the ridge of his nose, and just above it, where the cold seemed to go warm, there was pain. A lot of pain, in the middle of his eyebrows. He winced and went to feel it, but his hands remained stiff behind his back, clasped together by the unrelenting tug of plastic.

'ARGHH! ARGHH! FUCK!'

David lifted his head from the steering wheel, blinking to look out ahead of him. The bonnet of the Lincoln was crumpled, with two small streams of smoke leaking from underneath.

'Shit...' he murmured. With all his effort, he pulled his

legs up and stepped out of the open door. He tried to keep his balance, but it was hard. He was still dizzy, like it could all just be another dream. Another world that he would find himself in for a while before moving on to the next one.

'FUCK! ARGGH!'

Roman screamed again, and this time David could see him. He was crumpled up just ahead of the car, both hands wrapped tight around his right knee, which was twisted and bleeding in the white glare of the Lincoln's headlights. David approached him, peering down at the tall man as he writhed in pain.

'YOU GODDAMN...' The tall man didn't finish. Instead, he gritted his teeth and let out another long moan. His left knee was bleeding through the fabric of his trousers.

'I did that...' said David, like he was grasping what had just happened.

To his surprise, Roman Guild burst into laughter. It was pained, hoarse and sharp, but undeniably a roar of delight. It drifted up into the night sky to chill the hairs on David's neck and silence the hooting of the owls. He took a moment, shook his head, then approached the person he was more concerned about.

The weed-kid was lying a few feet from the fire, and he was in a bad way. Only one side of his face was showing, but David could see the damage Roman had unleashed upon him. His face had swollen up into a plum, dark purple, and a gash underneath his cheekbone was steadily seeping blood into his open mouth. Two teeth were missing, two fingers on his right hand were bent out of place, and David could see Roman Guild's boot mark imprinted fiercely on the collar bone and up onto his neck. If it weren't for the steady rise and fall of the weed-kid's chest, David would have gone so far as to say that the life had been beaten out of the boy's body. He knelt down beside him.

'Marty,' he whispered.

Marty's lips trembled. 'Hmmm.'

A cold anger spread through David. 'Why the hell...?' he started. Then he turned back to Roman. 'What the hell is this?'

The tall man laughed again, his whole body swaying on the ground. 'I couldn't resist.'

'You were gonna kill him. You wouldn't have stopped. You were gonna kill him. Why?'

'David...' Roman gripped his knee, blood seeping through the gaps between each finger. 'People like me don't have a reason.'

'Did she tell you to do this? That woman, Amee's mum, did she tell you?'

'No.' The tall man shook his head, then howled up into the sky again, finishing off the sound of agony with another long, and guttural laugh. 'She wanted you alive and scrambled, just like the detective.'

David looked down at the coil, the dark and wet metal shining vividly in the light of the dying fire. 'But you killed Alfie.'

'Yes, I did. Of course I did. An old man that no one cared about or contacted, depressed and alone, living out in the middle of nowhere. Like I said, I couldn't resist.'

David stood up straight and walked uneasily towards Roman. 'You mean you killed him for nothing?'

Roman squirmed on the grass again, his broken knee shifting up towards his chest as he hugged it tight. 'Not for nothing,' he panted through his teeth. 'I did it for fun. Because it gets me off. We all have weak spots. Yours is probably the normal kind. Tits, pussy, alcohol, drugs. Mine is murder. Mine's always been murder.'

David shook his head in disbelief, his anger burning so strongly that it was beginning to bring tears to his eyes. 'You're insane,' he said.

'Oh yes.'

'You're insane, and you're going to hell.'

'But I'm not. I thought I was, a long time ago.'

'You wouldn't have got away with it, you stupid fuck. The whole of Gealblath is looking for that boy.'

'And you along with him. Oh, it would have been the perfect story. Finding you lost and confused, with the boy dead at your feet. She probably would have thanked me for doing it my way. So much cleaner.' Roman grinned, then coughed, his body beginning to shake. 'She hates messy things.'

David took another step towards him. 'But it's not happening. You've lost. And now I'm coming for her.' He swayed, trying hard to keep himself rooted to the spot as a wave of darkness fluttered over his eyes.

'Coming for her?' said Roman. 'You can't come for her. You can't win this. A mother and a daughter is too strong a thing. Stronger than anything or anyone. Stronger than you, any day.'

'Bitch, I beat you with my hands behind my back.'

'Beat me?' The tall man glared up at David, his eyes flashing in the headlights. 'You've not beaten me.'

Without warning, Roman pulled himself from the ground and swiped at David's legs, pushing him over onto the wet grass and sending his vision into another hole of darkness. He felt Roman's hands wrap around his throat.

'I'M GONNA FUCKING KILL YOU!' he yelled.

David opened his eyes, the blanket of darkness rippling away, and he saw Roman's smile, delight and fury overwhelming his every feature. *You got too close. You idiot, you got too close.* David tried to struggle, but there was no struggling to be done. The tall man's full weight was on top of him now, crushing him into the ground.

'I'M GONNA LOOK YOU IN THE EYES WHEN YOU'RE DEAD!'

Spittle formed on his teeth, and Roman spat down onto David's face. David tried to struggle again, but his body wouldn't move. The air was entirely gone. The blood was slowing. It felt like there was something in his head that might explode if Roman were to squeeze any tighter. The wall of blackness was coming back too. David could see it rising slowly up into his body. But he didn't succumb to it. Not yet. If he succumbed to it now, he knew he wouldn't be coming back. It would stay forever. Tears trickled out from his eyes, and his head started to hurt more. Romans hands were growing harder, and colder, until... there was something else. Another pair of hands, holding onto his own. Softer, smaller, warmer. And Charlie's voice echoed in David's darkening world.

'If you let go, I'm here.'

But David didn't let go. Not because he didn't want to. But because he didn't have the time. There was a scream, Roman let go of his neck, and then David saw light again. It came in the form of Roman Guild and Marty behind him, yelling at the top of his lungs. The yell was one of pain, of adrenaline, but most of all, survival. He wrapped his arm around the neck of the tall man and shoved the coil deep inside his throat. Roman spluttered, and he tried to fight back, but his injured knee stopped him from turning. All he could do was squirm and struggle, his eyes staring up as Marty continued to scream, and scream, and scream, until he stopped and let go.

The absence of the scream left a painful ringing in David's ears. But soon it was replaced by another sound. A better one. A sound that flooded relief into David's heart. The tall man flopped onto his side with a thud, and David gasped, blinking at the sight before him.

'Ma... Marty...'

The weed-kid swayed, peering down vaguely at the now motionless Roman Guild. His face was bruised, bleeding and swollen. David could hardly even recognise it.

'We have to save her,' Marty mumbled. 'We have to save her, Mr Cooper.'

David breathed deeply, sucking in the clean, nighttime air. 'We will,' he replied. 'We will, Marty, we will.'

Then there was nothing. Quiet. Except for the breathy rumble of the coil, the growl from the butchered Lincoln engine, and the owls hooting on their branches. Simply quiet. And then the weed-kid collapsed onto the grass.

22

BLACK WATER

There were three knocks on the door, and Amee Florence came out from under the sheets. Her room was bright, and all the other children had gone. The beds were empty, unmade, except for two. Angus Campbell's and George O' Calloway's. But then, they were always the clean ones. The goody-goodies who made the rest of the children look bad. Amee had heard it far too many times.

'Why don't you leave your bed neat like Georgie does?'

'Why don't you clean your plate like Angus does?'

'Why don't you wash your face, clip your nails, flush your shit like they do?'

Those two boys were the beacons of light, the shining examples, and Amee hated their guts. But then, they hated hers too, of course. Especially when she would mess up their beds, scatter their clothes, and throw just about as many of their belongings out the window as was humanly possible. They found that decidedly unfunny. Amee, on the other hand, found it hilarious. So did her friend, Tabby. In fact, usually

Tabby was the one who put her up to it. Not that Amee had any way of backing that up.

'Now tell the truth, Amee, why did you do this? Georgie and Angus are very hurt, you know. It took Angus over an hour to find his shoe in the rose bed.'

Mrs Wilson was the head of the orphanage, a proper religious nut who might as well have worshiped the ground beneath George and Angus's feet.

'It was my friend's idea,' Amee would say.

'And which friend is this?'

'Her name's Tabby. She's my best friend.'

'Imaginary friend. Amee, I've told you before, the friends you have are here in the orphanage. They're your real friends –'

'No, not imaginary, she's very much real. She told me it would be a good idea, and she laughed when I did it.'

'But that's not true, is it, Amee? Only you can see this friend, and that makes her imaginary. Do you understand that? She's not real. And you can't blame someone who isn't real.'

At this point, Amee Florence would burst into laughter because Tabby Mayberry would be blowing raspberries right into Mrs Wilson's face. Then she'd get a cuff on the wrist, a disappointed tut, and the punishment of spending the rest of the day in her room with only a book on good behaviour to keep her company. Or so Mrs Wilson thought.

THE BIG BOOK OF GOOD BEHAVIOUR: HELPING KIDS BRING MANNERS INTO MATURITY.

The book was open now, but Amee wasn't reading it. For her, its only purpose was to hold noughts-and-crosses tournaments. Currently, she was beating Tabby thirty games to ten. Though to be fair, it was a little harder to concentrate in the mid-space, especially because Tabby was an avid reader.

'Amee, you know there are three simple breathing techniques to calm down a raucous child at the beginning of the day –'

'Three in a line – I win!'

'Damn it!'

Amee whooped for joy and punched the sheets above her. She and Tabby were tucked underneath them. The blue and pink sheets were tied to each corner of the bed, looming over them as if they were zipped into a tent out in the wilderness somewhere. She turned the page, and was already beginning to draw the next nine boxes as Tabby continued protesting.

'It's not fair, I pointed for my circle to go in the other box. You put it in the wrong one!'

Amee shook her head. 'Not true. I would never cheat.'

'You always cheat. You may as well have 'CHEATER' written on your forehead.'

'Yeah, well, the magic marker's been confiscated. Thanks to you.'

'Hey, drawing Mrs Wilson into the painting on her wall was your idea.'

'I thought it was a good likeness. And she really fitted in with all those other disciples.'

The two of them laughed, and Amee put her first 'X' into the left-hand corner. She liked times like these. Mrs Wilson would send her to her room, but she had no idea that the punishment was, in effect, a relief. It meant time alone with her friend. Time away from the other children, the living ones, who would push her around and make jokes about the way she talked to herself. She didn't like spending time with them. She much preferred her time with the dead. Tabby was more real, more truthful, and more worthwhile than anyone living in the orphanage. Only today, their time together was going to be cut short.

Knock, knock, knock. And Amee Florence came out from under the sheets.

'Who's there?' she called out.

Mrs Wilson's voice came through the cracks in the wood. 'There's someone here to see you, Amee.'

Amee sat up in her bed, and Tabby shuddered momentarily in the corner of her eye. 'Who?'

'Someone from the hospital. Someone who wants to help you.'

Two weeks ago, Mrs Wilson had threatened to call a doctor when Amee tore down the curtains and burned them in the garden outside. In all fairness, it was a bit extreme. But Tabby didn't like the dark when Amee was away. What else could she do? She felt she owed it to her, seeing as she was such a good friend to Amee.

'Is it the doctor?' Tabby asked her, but before Amee could reply, Mrs Wilson called out again.

'We're coming in...'

The door began to open, and Amee swung her legs over the mattress and rushed across the room to push the nearest bed in front of it.

'Amee,' Mrs Wilson hissed as the door slammed shut.

'I don't want to see a doctor.'

'Amee, open this door.'

'No! Go away!'

'Amee. I'm going to count to three. By the time I get to three, if this door isn't open, your *Ghostbusters* VHS is going in the bin. One –'

Amee pushed the bed away and pulled on the handle. Two women were revealed on the other side. One: Mrs Wilson, plump, cross, and warty, with a beehive-like nest sitting upon the top of her head. The other: pretty, but old, with a good posture, pouting lips, and long blonde hair.

'There now,' said Mrs Wilson triumphantly. 'That wasn't hard, was it? Amee, this is Mrs Nightly. She's a nurse. One who's very interested in talking to you.'

'Hello,' said Mrs Nightly politely.

Amee didn't respond. Mrs Wilson glared at her, then put on a fake and contorted smile.

'Okay, well, I'll leave you two alone, shall I?'

'Yes,' replied Mrs Nightly. 'Yes, if you would.'

'Right, well, be good, Amee. Be polite.'

Mrs Wilson gave the nurse a weird sort of courtesy, then she left them alone. Mrs Nightly walked into the room.

'Do you usually put a bed up against the door to stop people coming in?' she asked, closing the door behind her.

'When I don't want to talk to them,' replied Amee.

'You knew I was coming then?'

'I knew Mrs Wilson had called a doctor.'

'So why didn't you hide? That's what girls your age do, isn't it? You should have gone someplace else, some place secret. Perhaps the garden? It's a lovely summer's day outside.'

Amee took a step backwards. 'I don't want to talk to a doctor.'

'I'm not a doctor. I'm a nurse.'

'I don't want to talk to a nurse, either.'

'So talk to me then.'

'But you're a nurse.'

Mrs Nightly sat on one of the mattresses. 'Yes, I am. I am a nurse. But I'm not right now. You don't see the white

374

coat, do you? The stethoscope? I don't have any of those nurse-y things. Right now, I'm just a woman on a bed. That's alright, isn't it? You can talk to a woman on a bed, can't you?'

Amee creased her eyes warily. 'I suppose so.'

'So talk to me,' said Mrs Nightly. She patted the fabric on the mattress beside her in an effort to get Amee to sit down. But Amee didn't comply.

'What about?' she asked.

'I want to know why you didn't hide.'

'Because I don't like leaving the house.'

Mrs Nightly nodded. There was something in her eyes, Amee could tell, like she didn't quite believe her. Or something more than that. It was like she disbelieved the words but believed the person. It was strange. Amee had never seen that in a person before. She'd never seen that in anyone. It made her more relaxed, in a way. It was like there wasn't that same kind of wall, the one that was there with everyone else in the orphanage. That wall was already gone. Or it had never existed in the first place. Because of her eyes.

'You don't like leaving the house,' said Mrs Nightly.

'Well...' Amee pinched her shirt as she considered her next words. *You can't tell her about Tabby. If you tell her, she'll think you're crazy, like the rest of them. She'll take you away. She'll put you in one of those white jackets and masks that you see in the movies. You cannot tell her.* 'No,' she said. 'I don't.'

Mrs Nightly nodded again. She stood up and began pacing about the room, her eyes flicking from one bedspread to the next, taking them in silently, with interest, until she got to George's. 'This one's pretty tidy,' she observed.

'That's George,' Amee told her. 'He's really clean.'

'I can see that. Which one's yours?'

Amee nodded towards the bottom bunk beside her, and Mrs Nightly hummed in acknowledgement, her heels clopping softly against the carpet as she approached it. She laughed as she spotted the book.

'*The Big Book of Good Behaviour.* You need the manual, do you?'

'Mrs Wilson wants me to read it, but I never have.'

'Oh?' Mrs Nightly picked it up and spied the wrinkles in the spine. 'Seems it's been used quite a bit.' She opened the book onto the first couple of pages and stared at the markings, a slight smirk spreading across her face. 'What's this then?'

'That's just a tournament I've been having.'

'With a friend?' she asked. 'Mrs Wilson told me that you didn't have any friends. She said you didn't like the other children in the orphanage.'

'I don't.'

'So who's done this?' Mrs Nightly began venturing through the noughts-and-crosses tournaments that led her all the way to page ninety-five. 'Quite a friend. You must spend a lot of time together.'

Amee dipped her head. 'Tabby.'

'Tabby?'

'Tabby Mayberry. She's...'

'She's...?'

Amee allowed Tabby to reappear for just a second, before she blinked her away and focused again on the stranger.

'Imaginary.'

'Dead.'

They said the words at the same time, and Amee stared at the nurse in shock. 'I've... I've not told anyone that before.'

'But she is, isn't she? She's dead. And you can talk to her. Is that why you didn't hide from me? Is that why you don't go outside, because you don't want to leave her?'

Amee nodded, and Mrs Nightly did the same, her comforting smile still stitched between her cheeks.

'It's often the way,' she continued. 'They get attached to a particular place, so much so that they can never really leave it.'

Amee couldn't believe it. This person was actually talking to her about the dead people. Talking in a way that made her seem normal, sane, not at all crazy. That look in her eyes was there again. The look of belief, of trust, in her.

'I don't understand,' said Amee.

'Amee, I'm going to be honest with you. I'm not here for the reasons you think I am. I'm here because when I heard about you, I thought you could be someone quite special. They have no idea what you are. They think you're just another troublemaker. A child who needs to be put right, like the other kids in this orphanage.'

Mrs Nightly bent down to Amee's height, staring at her straight in the eyes. Pale ice blue meeting hard winter hazelnut. Amee couldn't look away. It was like there was a line between them, a tether that was tense enough to hold them still.

'You're a gift, Amee. What you have, what you can see, it's special. Really special.'

'You don't think I'm crazy?' asked Amee.

'Amee, I want to ask you if you would come with me. I can take you away from here. I can take you to a place where your abilities are accepted. Not only that – admired, cherished. You don't belong here with the other children.'

'But I have a friend here,' said Amee.

'You'll have friends there too. Lots of friends, far more than you could ever have in a place like this. Where we're going, there are more dead people than anywhere else, and they're all waiting to talk to you, Amee. They're all waiting to be your friend. Trust me.'

Amee bit her lip. She didn't want to leave. She had a friend in the orphanage. A good friend. But then, the thought of living somewhere she wasn't an outcast, somewhere the living understood her for what she was... It sounded good. It sounded like the best thing in the world. She would be an idiot to say no, surely. And yet she bit her lip.

'I... I don't know.'

'Amee, I'd like you to do things for me. You see, I'm very interested in the dead people. I can't see them myself, and I want to know more. I want to know lots about them, about all of them. And you could help me with that. You could be important. So important.'

'Yes...' Amee began nodding slowly. 'Yes, I could do that.'

'You'll come then? It won't be right away. There will be things that need to happen first. Things will need to be put in order. You'll be able to say goodbye to your friend, if that's what you're worried about.'

Amee took in Mrs Nightly's face. It was a nice face, comforting. Here was a person who finally understood. Not only that, who wanted to understand more. A living person who cared about the dead.

'I'll come,' said Amee, before she could think about it anymore.

Mrs Nightly beamed with delight, letting out a relieved cry before pulling Amee into a hug. Amee hugged her back, feeling her heart pumping fast and hard against Mrs Nightly's chest.

'Oh, that's wonderful. Thank you, thank you.' Mrs Nightly pulled away. 'Thank you, my darling. But don't tell anyone, not just yet, not until everything's finalised.'

'Okay,' replied Amee.

'You promise?'

'I promise. I don't speak to anyone anyway, only dead people.'

Mrs Nightly hugged her again, coming so close that Amee could hear her breathing against her ear. 'Alright,' she said. 'Alright, I should go. Yes, I've got to go. But I'll be seeing you soon, Amee. I'll be seeing you very soon.'

Mrs Nightly let her go and began navigating her way past the beds, but before she opened the door, she looked back.

'There is one other thing, Amee. Before this, before the orphanage...'

Amee's whole body tensed up, her skin rising in goose pimples. 'Yes?' she replied unsurely.

'I won't ask you now. But just so you know, I want you to be entirely truthful when I do. Is that okay?'

Amee felt tears form behind her eyes, longing to come out and stain her cheeks. 'Yes,' she replied.

'It's alright, Amee. It's all okay. When you're with me, everything will be okay. You can tell me everything. There'll be no need to keep secrets anymore.'

Mrs Nightly gave her one last smile. Then she pulled open the door, stepped out into the corridor, and closed it softly behind her.

Amee stood there uncertainly, controlling her breaths, slowing her heart. Everything had happened so fast. It had come out of nowhere, hit her like a storm. But a good storm. Potentially the best storm in the world. She sat on the bed, her fingers picking gingerly at her tights as she closed her eyes. When she opened them, Tabby was standing in front of her.

To her surprise, Tabby's face was dark and sad. She looked at Amee with vague disappointment. Tabby had heard everything of course, and now Amee would have to talk to her.

'Hello,' she said.

But that was it. There was so much more to say, but she didn't know how to say it. It was like she couldn't put it into a sentence. She couldn't explain it to Tabby because surely she could never understand. Tabby was dead after all. And Amee was living. So she sat there, staring at her friend, until Tabby finally opened her mouth.

'You're leaving,' she said simply.

And Amee nodded. 'I...' She tried desperately to find the words. 'I...'

A few seconds of silence passed. Then Amee closed her eyes, held, opened, and let the shape of Tabby fade from her view. She was replaced by the sickly yellow wallpaper behind.

* * *

The first time Amee awoke, she was in the car. Her face was on something cold and leathery, and when she lifted it, the fabric clung to her skin, making a funny sound as she unpeeled herself and took in her surroundings. Her head was dizzy, and things weren't quite as they seemed to begin with. Everything felt bigger, like it wasn't a car at all, and the walls were stark white, like there were a thousand bulbs on the ceiling. Everything felt wrong, and the feeling of disorientation made Amee feel sick in her gut. She tried to lift herself further, but she couldn't do it. The edges of what felt like Velcro cut into her chest and legs, and it wasn't until she pulled again that she realised they were tied down. That was when she opened her mouth.

'Help...' said Amee. 'Help me...'

The engine beneath the floor roared louder, and she blinked a few more times, trying to make more sense of where she was. It only took a few more seconds. She was in an ambulance, in the back, and it was slowing down.

'Marty? Marty, are you there? Mr Cooper? Marty?' Amee struggled against the straps. 'What's going on? Where am I?!'

The ambulance stopped. A door opened and closed, and then there were heels on the road outside. The rear door of the ambulance opened and someone stepped inside. It was a woman, tall and skinny, with a big tangle of frizzy black hair. She came up alongside her and placed a hand on her arm. A cold shiver swept through Amee's spine.

'Mum...' she said quietly.

The woman stared blankly back, stroking Amee's arm for a moment before producing a spindly needle and placing it just above her left elbow.

'No,' Amee rasped fearfully. 'No! Please, don't! I don't wanna go back, Mum, I don't wanna go!'

There was a sharp pain as the needle went in, and then a warm fuzz passed up through Amee's body and into her shoulders. The world started going black again.

There were no dreams this time. Only darkness. A darkness that became her, that wrapped itself around her being like that was all there had ever been. It was like she was sinking into something final, definite, hollow. Until she wasn't.

The relief came with a noise. A distant noise at first, but it grew louder and louder until it pierced the darkness like a hot knife, splitting it open to reveal the doorway back into consciousness. As soon as it did, Amee took her chance, allowing her body to soar out of the dark and back into the light, a voice following her as she went.

'Little fishy...'

Her eyes flickered open. There was no leather now. No straps. Just a soft mattress and a pillow beneath her head, cushioning it like a pair of soft and delicate hands.

'Hmm...' she mumbled, and then she focused on the nearest thing with colour. It was a poster on a wall, full of deep browns, light greens, and blue, a vast amount of blue, like an ocean. It dominated one corner, reaching out towards the horizon of a long and distant valley, which was actually just the edge of ripped paper. Amee blinked again and saw it properly. *The Land Before Time*. That was when she knew where she was. It was her room again. Room C19. And she was lying in her bed.

'Don't try to sit up,' said someone in the corner of the room.

Amee turned to see her mother. She was sitting in her usual chair, her legs crossed and her face blank. Blank enough for Amee to know that there was something beneath it, something that was ablaze with emotion, like a fire left to fume behind a brick wall. Amee stared into those narrow and motionless eyes. Her mother was breathing deeply, she could hear. Her mouth was closed, but her chest was heaving, panting so hard that her whole body was swaying back and forth. A few seconds passed before she spoke again.

'You disappointed me, little fishy. You really made me sad.'

'I'm sorry, Mum.'

The words were so quiet that Amee could barely even hear them herself. Her mother leaned forward.

'What did you say?'

'I'm sorry,' said Amee, a little louder.

'Say that again.' Her mother stood, her heels echoing loudly off the floor as she came up beside Amee's bed and bent down towards her. 'Say that one more time.'

'I'm sorry...'

Her mother lifted her hand towards Amee's cheek. It stayed there for a few moments, lightly tracing the outline of bone, circling about the flesh as if she was trying to calm Amee down, console her, show her everything was alright. But then her mum pulled her hand back and slapped her.

For a second, Amee's world went black again. She gasped, the sudden sharpness of pain making one side of her face tingle. She tried to process what had just happened, but it wasn't long before the hand came back and slapped her again. *KASLAP!* The sound of flesh on flesh rebounded off the walls, and Amee didn't move. She sat there dumbly and let her mother do it again. Another slap, and then another, and then another. Harder, and harder, and harder each time. The slaps collided Amee's world into spasms of darkness, like they were jostling around the drug that was still in her system, the same way you'd jostle a fuel pump for any last drop of fuel.

It wasn't until her cheekbones went numb that the onslaught finally stopped. Then Amee's mum pulled her into a firm embrace.

'Oh God, I was so scared for you. I've hardly been sleeping. Why did you do that to me, little fishy? Why would you do that?'

Amee didn't respond. She lay there, staring blankly at the wall until her mum let go.

'Look…' her mum said, tracing a finger down Amee's black hair. 'You look so much older. How did that happen? Was it him? The teacher? What has he done to you?'

'Nothing,' replied Amee. 'He did nothing. This was me. This was all me.'

Amee could feel her mother's stare piercing into her, her breaths coming harder from her nose, the fire still flickering behind that wall.

'Here,' her mum said, and she held her hand out, the same hand which had just crashed against Amee's cheek. 'Come with me.'

The hand in question led Amee to the bath in the adjacent room. The water roared out of the tap and Amee sat in the tub, her knees pulled up tight to her chest and her chin balanced on top of them. It took about eight minutes for the freezing water to reach her bare breasts, and when it did, her mum twisted the tap and pulled up a stool.

'Put your head in,' she told her.

Amee shivered. Both hands gripped the side of the tub and her cheeks inflated as she held her breath. A second passed, then another, then one more, and then Amee finally leaned forward to push her face into the rippling water. When it broke the surface, she felt pain, a lot of pain, and it forced her back almost as soon as she'd been submerged.

'All the way in, Amee,' her mum urged. 'I want your head all the way under.'

Amee spluttered, the water dropping quickly from her face. She didn't take the time to think about the pain. She clenched her teeth, tightened her grip on the bath, and went in again. For a few seconds, her world went numb, like the water had soaked into the skin and purged it of all feeling. It felt like she was somewhere else entirely, perhaps the ocean, weightless, like a stone amongst the waves. But then her mother pulled her hair so hard that it felt like she was attempting to tear it away from the scalp.

'OW!' Amee yanked herself back from the depths. 'That hurts!'

Her mother ignored her protests. 'It needs to be done. You don't want your hair to stay like that forever, do you? It will take a few washes. This is just the first.'

With a shudder, Amee reached up and touched her fringe. 'No, but...'

'But nothing. It needs to come out, Amee. Put your head back under.'

Her mother stared at her, both pupils unmoving, like a pair of black stones. Amee shuffled in the tub. Ignoring all her basic instincts, she took a breath, closed her eyes, and leaned forward all over again.

A whole half hour had passed before her mum finally stopped, by which point the water in the bath had turned black, with a few strands of long dark hair floating about in the midst of it. Amee remained in the same spot, her knees still up to her chest. She'd stopped shivering now. Her mother was tracing a finger up her arm, pivoting aimlessly about the goose pimples just like she had done on her cheek. For a few seconds, Amee thought she might hit her again, but the fire was gone. The whole process had cleansed her mum just as much as it had cleansed Amee. For the time being, anyway.

'Why did you do it then?' her mum asked softly. 'Why did you leave me?'

There was a silence. Amee didn't turn to look at her mother's face. Instead, she looked ahead, her eyes focusing on a long and crooked crack in one of the white bricks on the far wall. Some mites had made a home there. She watched one climb its way up the clay and slip into the dark opening.

'Because I wanted to help,' she replied eventually.

'Help who?'

'The dead people. The house on the cliff. I wanted to set them free. I wanted to set them all free. But I couldn't do it. Mr Cooper wanted to find the detective. He wanted to find whoever killed Charlie. That's why we were in Cornwall.'

Her mother shuffled on the stool, one hand holding the edge of the bathtub. 'What makes you think you could find the house?' she asked.

'Nothing,' said Amee. 'But I wanted to try. I wanted to set them free if I could, set them free before the green monster got them. They've been seeing it more. The dead people. They can hear it. They can sense it.'

'A story. I told you, Amee, that's just a story. They're imagining it. It's not real.'

Amee turned to her. 'Where are Mr Cooper and Marty?'

'They'll be fine, little fishy. Don't worry, they'll be fine.'

'You didn't tell me about him...'

'About who?'

'Roman. That's his name, Roman. Roman Guild. He found us, and he's like me. He can see dead people, like me.'

Her mother straightened her back, biting her lip slightly. 'Yes,' she said in response.

'But I didn't know that. Why didn't I know that?'

'Because you didn't need to know. It's not about him,

Amee. None of this is about him. It's about you.'

'That's not what I mean. Mum, that thing, the coil. That would never be used on me, would it?'

Amee had been holding the thought off for days now, but it couldn't be held back any longer. The words came out in one go, almost slurred.

'Why would you say that?' her mum asked unflinchingly.

'It's like there are things I've been remembering. New things, things that feel like memories. They've been coming back to me for days now. It started with the caravan park, and then there was the beach, and just now, in the ambulance, I remembered something else. I was in a place a long way away from here, and...' Amee stopped, the water around her rippling in small, dark waves. 'I don't understand it. I feel like there's two parts of me. One before and one after. It's like I've been torn.'

'How do you know these aren't just dreams?'

'Because they feel real. I know what dreams feel like.'

Her mother sighed. She lifted her hand to rest it on Amee's forehead, stroking her delicately. 'You think I would use the coil on you, Amee? Why on earth would I do that?'

'Not you. There was this... this woman...'

Amee swallowed back a lump in her throat. The image of the nurse floated before her eyes once more, and she closed them tight as she tried to remember.

'Listen to me, Amee,' her mum said in the darkness. 'You're tired, you're worn out, you're not thinking right. It's always just been the two of us here. Nothing else.'

'But there was someone –'

'No. I told you to listen to me. You're tired. You're just tired. You've been away a whole month. You've changed, and it's confusing you. Just stop '

Amee opened her eyes and saw her mum staring at her earnestly, pleadingly, so much so that Amee wondered whether she was actually right. Perhaps she was tired. Perhaps this was all happening inside her mind. The detective had been insane and disorientated; that had been her first instinct anyway. Maybe his ravings had put the ideas into her head. Bad ideas. Ideas that had overcome her since the caravan. Her whole body shivered. *But they all seem real*, she thought. *Too real. Real enough not to be just another lie.*

'Look,' said her mum. 'What you've been through, it would make anyone feel like they're not themselves. That's okay though. It will pass. It will all pass, and when it does we can continue our lessons. We can talk about Roman in the morning, if that's what you want. We'll talk about it if it will make you feel better. But I meant what I said before: this is all about you. You're the important one. That's why I was so upset when you went away. I'm nothing without you, little fishy. I hope you understand that. I hope you understand how special you are to me. I knew it as soon as I laid eyes on you. I knew you were a gift. A special gift. Just for me.'

At that moment, it felt like Amee's entire world stopped. Her mum's touch, which had once felt warm and comforting, suddenly felt like a stake of ice. *She said that. Didn't she say that? Didn't she call you a gift?* Her mother was still staring at her, and Amee stared back. *Gift.* That word. The memories had felt fractured, like images from lost dreams, but that word had remained constant. It had spun in and out of memory. Mrs Nightly had called her a gift. She had called Amee that lots of times. *And now she's calling you that once again.*

'Are you alright, Amee?'

Amee leaned back. *It's her. It's your nurse. Here, in front of you.* The image of Mrs Nightly had felt blurred in her memories, almost as if she was looking through a misted window, but Amee could recognise her now. The hair was different – it was black instead of blonde, curled instead of straight – but the face was the same. The voice, the words. *But that's your mother's face. That's always been your mother's face, for as long as you can remember.* Amee felt her head start to churn. *For as long as you can remember...* But how far back could she remember? What if things had been different before? What if Mrs Nightly had needed Amee to believe she was her mother? That was, after all, why Amee had obeyed her. Why she had stayed so long. Because there was nothing else. She would never leave the only person in the world she was supposed to love.

'Amee, tell me what's wrong.'

Amee blinked once, then twice, and then she glared at the woman who was actually Mrs Nightly. 'You...' she said.

And Mrs Nightly tilted her head. 'Yes, me. You're special to me. You're the only person I care about.'

'Really?'

All the memories were spinning in front of Amee now, a jumbled ball of string with every strand leading back to the woman in front of her. She remembered the orphanage, the park, the beach, that film she had seen flickering upon the wall, the girl on Christmas morning.

'What do you mean?' asked Mrs Nightly.

'Do you care about me, or do you care about someone else?'

'Who else would I care about other than you? You're my everything, you're my –'

'Grace.'

The light bulb above them flickered, changing the room from light to dark, and then to light again. Once the flicker was over, Mrs Nightly's face had changed entirely. She glared at Amee with that fire back in her eyes. Fiercer than ever. Hot enough to burn Amee alive. The look of a mother to a daughter was completely gone. The look of love wasn't there anymore. But now Amee realised it had never been there in the first place, not for her anyway. That love was for someone else. Another girl entirely.

Mrs Nightly stood up from the stool and wandered from one side of the room to the other. A few seconds passed. Amee half expected her to explode into a rage. But instead of exploding, the nurse simply sighed and spoke quite quietly.

'What was the trigger, I wonder?'

Amee gripped the tub harder. 'What are you talking about?'

'It must have been the caravan,' said Mrs Nightly, almost to herself. 'You told me you went to Alfie's home. That must have been the trigger. Returning to the same place with the same nerves, the same feelings. It's like a parallel.' She stood there contemplating, as if this was some kind of difficult equation.

'What did you do to me?' asked Amee.

'You wanted a mother,' Mrs Nightly replied. 'So I gave one to you.'

'But why did...? How could you...?'

'Why did I make you forget? Because this is what I do. Anything to get me closer to what I want. The end of all this, the person I'm fighting for. You are nothing compared to that. Everything I've done, I'd do again and again. Because it's right. And insignificant. Compared to her. That's all you need to know about it. Step out of the bath for me now.'

The nurse moved aside and watched Amee expectantly. But she didn't move.

'What are you going to do to me?'

'Just step out of the bath.'

Amee's whole body was trembling now. Fear, confusion, and anger were flowing through her in waves, making her chest hot. She took a deep breath, then she pulled herself up, the water cascading off her as she stood completely naked in front of Mrs Nightly.

'Amee. Step out.'

But Amee didn't step out. The water continued to *drip, drip, drip* from her skin. Some of it was still black with dye, a strange dark substance peeling off Amee's bare flesh, leaving her untainted, and new again.

Mrs Nightly came up alongside her and reached out a hand. 'Amee, you'll do as I say.'

Amee looked at it, her head still spinning. Everything felt so on edge, like she could tap the world around her and it would shatter. 'No,' she muttered.

'You will do as I ask,' the nurse replied. 'You will always do as I ask. Don't you understand by now, little fishy? You belong to me. Now take my hand and step out of this bath.'

The hand reached closer, and for the last time in her life, Amee Florence obliged. She grabbed hold of Mrs Nightly and fell backwards, her feet slipping from the tub as she toppled onto the hard floor and brought the nurse crashing down with her.

'ARGH!'

The impact of her head on the rubber sparked a ringing inside Amee's skull, but it didn't block out the sound that came from Mrs Nightly's mouth. It was unlike any sound Amee had heard before. It was a sound of pain, of fragility, like the mask of hardness had been stripped away, leaving nothing but the real woman underneath. She reached forward and pulled the curls on Mrs Nightly's head, and they grappled as if they were kids fighting in the school yard.

Mrs Nightly roared. 'AMEE! AMEE! LET GO!'

But Amee didn't let go. It was like she was on autopilot. Even she didn't know what she was doing. She held on, pulling harder, and harder, and harder, until she heard a hideous tearing sound, and she fell back with two clumps of curled black hair squeezed into her palms.

'ARGH!' Mrs Nightly reached out and grabbed Amee by the throat, gripping her so hard that it felt like the bones might snap. 'YOU LITTLE BITCH!'

She pressed her face right up close to Amee's, and Amee didn't think twice about taking her chance. In a flash, she jerked forward and head-butted Mrs Nightly on the nose, sending her flying backwards into the edge of the bathtub with a high-pitched shriek. Then she leapt up and charged towards the door, pulling it open to reveal the empty white hallway on the other side.

'Amee!' she heard Mrs Nightly shout. 'Amee, come back here!'

Amee started running, but something was wrong. Her head was throbbing, and tiny black specks were converging in and around the centre of her vision, making the corridor dark and blurry. She touched the back of her head and felt warm blood. Suddenly, she felt like she was going to be sick. She tripped before one of the doors and her naked knees thudded against the floor. Mrs Nightly stepped out into the corridor behind her.

'HELP ME!' Amee shouted. 'GET ME AWAY FROM HER! PLEASE! SOMEONE! ANYONE! HELP!'

The sound of a door-knob turning came from above her

head, and Amee turned as a child-like voice spoke from behind the wood.

'Hello? What's going on out there?'

'HELP ME! GET ME AWAY FROM HER!'

Mrs Nightly approached her and bent down. A streak of blood was running from her nose in a straight line. 'Quiet, little fishy.'

'Mrs Nightly?' the voice called again. 'What's going on? Who's out there? Hello?'

'HELP, HELP, SHE'S GOING TO –'

But before Amee could finish, Mrs Nightly had pulled out a clump of keys from her pocket and shoved one into the door. She opened it, revealing a young boy on the other side. He couldn't have been more than nine years old, with white-blonde hair and two buckteeth. The room behind him was almost identical to Amee's. There was a television, a bookshelf, a desk with two chairs, and movie posters on the wall: *The Muppet Movie* and *It's A Wonderful Life*. The only thing that was different was the second bed in the corner. An elderly man was sleeping there, his face covered in liver spots and his cheeks rippled with thick and hairy wrinkles.

'What...?' Amee whispered.

'It's alright, Peter,' said Mrs Nightly.

The boy looked at Amee's naked body, then the blood under Mrs Nightly's nose. 'Are you hurt?' he asked timidly.

'Everything's okay. I want you to go back to bed, Peter. Before you wake up the other patients. Can you do that for me?'

The blonde boy wavered, then nodded. 'Okay,' he said. 'But please don't be long. I'm seeing dead people again. More of them. And Willy too.' He gestured over towards the sleeping man.

'I said, go back to bed.'

The boy dipped his head. He nodded again, then stepped back, allowing the nurse to close the door and lock it. Amee looked at the number. Room C15. She turned her head to see the other doors along the corridor. All of them were closed; all of them silent. C14, 13, 12, 11... They went on and on and on until the bend, then beyond; Amee knew because Amee had seen them. She'd just never seen what was on the other side.

'But... but...' She stuttered, feeling the vomit churn inside her once again.

'How many times have you run from me?' Mrs Nightly reached into her pocket and Amee saw a flash of something long and silver.

'I don't understand,' groaned Amee. 'Those rooms, those patients. They're like me. But I thought –'

'Never again. This will be the last time, I promise you.'

Mrs Nightly reached down and dug her nails into Amee's arm. But Amee didn't run. She didn't fight back. Her energy had entirely gone now, her vision was still blurred, her legs had turned against her. She was beaten. She knew she was beaten. Her eyes filled with tears.

'Mum...' she said for some reason.

Then the nurse stabbed the needle into the bump above Amee's elbow, and that warm and fuzzy feeling swirled around inside her once again.

'That's right, little fishy.'

Amee felt the world around her blur. Darkness swept through the corridor, engulfing everything in its path, until nothing but Mrs Nightly's voice remained.

'When you wake up, you'll have a mother again. And this mother will make sure something like this can't happen again. This mother will have a little fishy that can't leave its home. Even when it wants to.'

The darkness became deeper, and for a moment, Amee thought about Marty. She thought about his face, his smile, his kiss.

'This is what you make me do,' said Mrs Nightly. 'It's on you, all this. What I'm about to do is on you.'

A second passed. Then Amee blinked, Marty disappeared, and her head fell fast towards the white dusty floor.

'When I think of you, I think of the ocean. I think of its blue waves, its mountains, made of coral, spiralling down the vistas until everything's black, and cold, and different, and new all over again. I think of the things that live there. Big whales, tiny shrimps, sharks with their long, sharp teeth, and lobsters with their thick red claws. I think about how long it might go on for. Miles and miles and miles, round and round the earth, over and over again until things meet once more, if things ever meet once more in a home like ours. And then I tilt my head back, like this, and I think...'

23

THE START OF A PLAN

The Lincoln spewed smoke into the cool blue morning air, staining the break of day with the hot stench of burnt fuel and rubber. It was thicker now, darker. Given its condition, the car wouldn't get much further, certainly not as far as it had already gone. Roman Guild's body had busted it pretty bad. The bonnet was warped and crumpled, with a thin slice of black metal hanging dangerously close to the front right wheel, and the headlights were knackered. It was a miracle it had got them this far, to be honest. But now Mr Cooper pulled on the handbrake, and the Lincoln made its final turn onto the kerb, the wheels crunching hard against the dirt.

Marty looked into the rear-view mirror. A different face stared back at him. Instead of his usual pale skin, his flesh had turned a vicious shade of brown, green, and blue. Crusted splodges of blood coloured the edges of every bruise. His eyes were almost double their usual size. They puffed out as if he'd been stung by a couple of hundred wasps, and blood vessels had turned the irises red, making him look like that kid from *The Exorcist*. The rest of his body hurt, too. He hadn't dared to look under his shirt to inspect the damage yet, but he was fairly sure the picture would be similar. His entire right-hand side hurt like a bitch, throbbing continuously and making him wince in pain when he took a deep breath. The fingers on his hand felt like a couple of blocks of ice, repositioned now, thanks to Mr Cooper, but still a continuous source of sharp pain. What's more, his groin felt like someone had been jumping on it for a couple of days; his teeth were missing two members, including the one that had been stitched a couple of months back; and the skin on his right palm had puss-filled blisters from when he'd tried to hit Roman Guild across the face with a burning log. Other than all that, Marty was doing fine.

He swallowed and turned away from his reflection, looking instead at Mr Cooper. He didn't look so great himself. The ridge of his nose was cut, with a long line of dried blood trickling down towards his bottom lip, and just below that, his neck was inflamed with two ginormous bruises that circled around the flesh, where Roman's hands had attempted to strangle the life out of him. He turned to meet Marty's gaze.

'You're awake,' he said.

'Yeah,' replied Marty.

'How are you doing?'

'I'm fine. I mean, I'm fine when I sit like this...' He shuffled onto his side. 'And lay my head back like this...' He craned his neck up into the headrest. 'Then it doesn't feel like I'm going to die in the next five minutes.'

Mr Cooper managed a small smile. 'Fair enough,' he said, peering back towards the windscreen.

The teacher's head dipped down as he noticed something

in the sky, and Marty looked with him, immediately seeing the sign around twenty feet in front of them.

WELCOME TO GEALBLATH: THE SUNSHINE COAST GREETS YOU

Marty let out a long, slightly agonised sigh. Not because of the absurd notion that Gealblath was anywhere near a coast that regularly experienced sunshine, but because of something else. Something that was stapled up and down the right side of the board. Missing person posters. Specifically, his missing person posters.

'What do you think?' asked Mr Cooper.

'They could have chosen a better photo,' said Marty.

'I mean we've got to get in there. If we're going to get Amee, we've got to go in. We need to think of how we're going to play this.'

'Play this?'

'We can't just go waltzing in, announcing our arrival. Every cop in the town's still gonna be looking for you. And me too. We've got to play it smart.'

'We might not have time to play it smart.'

'What do you mean?'

Marty pushed himself up on the seat. He instinctively reached for the pain in his ribs, only to retract his hand as the burn blisters met the fabric of his shirt. He held it still and waited for the pain to stop. 'I woke up in the boot of the car, back when Roman was driving us to the valley. He was talking to a woman about Amee, and I heard something.'

'Heard what?'

A voice. Rory's voice. My bully, talking to me, egging me on, willing me to rise above the danger until I fell straight into it.

'They were saying what they should do so this won't happen again. And Roman, he said something about snipping Amee's fins.'

'What does that mean?'

'I don't know. But I think it means we have to move fast, before something happens. We don't know what these people could do, how far they'd go. I mean Roman...' Marty felt his stomach start to knot, a fierce wave of anxiety sweeping through him. 'Amee was terrified of him, and I never knew why. She was so strong when it came to everything else. But that was the reason she couldn't be alone with you in the beginning. She didn't trust you, because of him. Whatever he did to her... I don't trust that she's safe at all.'

'Roman's gone,' said Mr Cooper. 'He's in the valley with that thing down his throat.'

Marty hesitated, remembering the moment he had stuck the coil in, feeling the tall man jerk uncontrollably against his grasp. Roman was gone now, or he hoped he was at least. He had no idea how the coil worked, or how long it could take to wipe a memory. Roman had been out cold, but what if he woke up? What happened then? Marty tried not to think about it.

'Even with Roman gone,' he replied, 'her mum could be even more dangerous for all we know. Just think about it. Roman Guild worked for her. If someone like him worked for a woman like her, then Amee needs to get as far away from her mother as possible. She needs to get out of the hospital before something happens.' Marty reached into his pocket and pulled out the keys they had found in the Lincoln. 'We've got the keys; that's all we need. We just have to do it now. Before it's too late. We have to be fast.'

'Okay, okay, but that still doesn't help us. I mean, even

if everything goes to plan. Even if we can evade the police and get Amee out of the hospital without anyone seeing, it still won't take long for her mum to realise she's gone. And the moment that happens, all she has to do is call it in and every officer in Gealblath will be blocking every exit out of town. Like I said, we have to think smart if we want to get out of there. We need to think.'

Marty huffed. Mr Cooper was right of course. Even though he didn't want him to be. The whole place was like a mousetrap. They could take the prize, but the walls were designed to collapse in on them as soon as they did. He placed the keys back in his pocket, then watched as Mr Cooper opened the door and stepped outside. Marty followed suit.

'How bad is it?' he asked.

Mr Cooper's eyebrows furrowed as he inspected the damage to the smoking vehicle. 'I don't know.'

'Aren't you supposed to lift the bonnet or something?'

'Then what?'

'And then, you know, look at the engine.'

'Probably. But I won't lie to you, Marty, I wouldn't know what I was looking for. I've never had one of these things. I've always been more of a bike guy.' Mr Cooper scratched his beard, then tapped the bonnet of the car twice. 'But then, that's why we're here.'

The teacher walked past Marty and over towards a weed-filled embankment beside the road.

'Where are you going?' asked Marty.

'You recognise this place?'

'No. Should I?'

'Maybe not. It was pretty dark the last time you were here.' Mr Cooper reached down and started pulling back the weeds. His bruised hands rifled frantically through the undergrowth. 'Come on,' he hissed under his breath. 'Be here, you bastard, be here.'

At that moment, something glistened in the sun, a flash of blue metal protruding from the grass. Mr Cooper peeled back the last of the weeds to reveal the Honda Shadow underneath, coupled with a black helmet.

'No shit,' Marty laughed.

'Yes shit. This is where we dumped it when we left town. Twenty feet from the welcome sign, two miles from the bus station. It's a little rusty, but it'll be okay.'

Mr Cooper picked up the helmet, then he foraged inside it and slipped out a small chain of silver keys, sticking one of them into the ignition. The engine choked into life, and the teacher let out a sigh of relief.

'You know, somehow I've actually missed this thing...'

He smiled as he gave the bike a weird sort of stroke. Then he turned back to Marty, scanning his face once again. His eyes narrowed at the bruises and cuts, and his smile disappeared almost as soon as it had come.

'You know, we should talk about that.'

'Talk about what?' asked Marty. 'The bike?'

'No, what happened back there. In the valley, with Roman. That's something we should talk about.'

'What, like a heart to heart?'

'No, that's not what I mean.'

Marty turned away. He knew what Mr Cooper meant. But the truth was, he didn't know if he actually wanted to talk about it. The adrenaline was still coursing through him, still soaked in the bones and in the blood, and the only thing he could think about was using it to his advantage. To get into Gealblath and get Amee out. If he stopped and talked about what had happened now, he might begin to understand it, and understanding something like that could be dangerous. He had no idea what it would make of him. In a way, he didn't want to know. He just wanted to keep going, with no time for reflection.

'Marty, what you've just gone through,' Mr Cooper continued. 'That's a big thing. It's a scary thing. It's messed up, and it shouldn't happen to a kid like you. A kid your age.' He fumbled over his words. 'Just, you know, I'd understand if you wanna talk about it, that's all.'

'Maybe. I don't know. Maybe after all this is over I'll want to talk about it. But not right now.'

'You won't though,' Mr Cooper replied abruptly. 'You think you might, but you won't. You'll keep it in. If I've learned anything in my life, it's that things shouldn't be kept in. After what happened with Charlie, I didn't talk to anyone, but I should have done. I ended up having dreams instead. Dreams where I'm out at sea with him, walking across the tide, saying things I should be saying out loud to someone else. That's what it feels like, in a way, when you keep it all in. It feels like you're out there. Like a boat in the ocean, just kind of drifting away from people. And the longer you keep it in, the longer you drift, until there's no going back. I'm just saying you can talk to me, if you want to. Whenever you want to, you can.'

Marty wasn't used to Mr Cooper opening up to him. When he had opened up back in Cornwall, he had been at his lowest. He was lost, vulnerable, cold, and completely detached. But this was somehow different. This moment was almost kind. Marty opened his mouth to respond, but just as he did so, the teacher's eyes widened.

'Boat,' he said simply.

Marty nodded unsurely. 'Yeah?'

'Boat.'

'Yeah, I get the analogy; it's clever. Listen, I –'

'No, I'm not talking about the stupid analogy. I'm talking about a boat. An actual boat. The police have the power to block off every exit out of town, which would really screw us over, unless...'

'Unless what?' asked Marty.

'Unless we don't take an exit out of town. At least not the one they'd expect.'

'What the hell are you talking about?'

'A boat. A boat to Derling. My girlfriend's father has one padlocked away on the beach, or my ex-girlfriend, I guess.'

'What, and you have the key?'

'The beach will be virtually empty this time of year, which means no one would see us. Plus, it's only around a mile from the hospital, which makes it far more convenient than any route out of town would be.' Mr Cooper nodded to himself. 'There's just one thing...'

'What?'

'The key.'

'Right, yeah, the key. You don't have one.'

'No, I have one. Only it's on the other side of town, in my flat.'

'In your flat? Are you kidding me?'

'No, don't shit your pants, Marty. In my flat.'

'So what? We just walk into your flat and get the key? I thought you said we would play this smart.'

'No. Not you. Just me.'

'What, and I go to the hospital?'

'No.' Mr Cooper stared at Marty intensely. 'Here's what we're going to do. We wait until nightfall. I'm gonna take you to the cabin on the beach and then I'm gonna get the key. You'll wait for me there. Once I come back, we can make sure the boat's ready to go, and then we can think about how we're going to get Amee out of the hospital.'

'But how long will it take you to get the key?'

'Two hours? Three at most.'

'No. No way. That's way too much time. It could be too late by then.'

'You got a better solution?'

'Yes,' said Marty bluntly. 'You get the key and I get Amee. You said it yourself, the hospital's right near the beach. I'll have enough time.'

'Yeah, enough time to get caught. You can't go by yourself, Marty. It's too dangerous.'

'You don't trust me?'

'No, I trust you. But you have to trust me. My way works, my way is smart, and my way is the only way we can all get out of Gealblath tonight. Amee too. You've just got to listen to me, Marty.'

Mr Cooper stared at him earnestly, and Marty opened his mouth to argue, but nothing came. There wasn't anything he could say that would sway the teacher; he could see that. Mr Cooper was dead set on his plan. Shut firm, with no leeway.

'Okay then,' said Mr Cooper, realising he'd won. 'We've been here long enough. Someone is bound to come along and see the car. We've got to dump it.'

And without waiting for a reply, he stepped away from the bike and began walking back up the embankment towards the smoking Lincoln.

It felt like forever before the sun began to set. It stayed hanging in the same spot for a lifetime, letting the blue blanket of sky continue on, and on, and on into the horizon. It elongated Amee's sentence in the hospital until Marty was sure the light would go on for an eternity, a wall between them and Gealblath, between him and Amee. He was just about to give up hope when the blue turned into red, and then pink, before all colour finally dispersed into a thick and wonderful darkness.

Then they were driving. Marty was at the back of the Shadow, his arms wrapped awkwardly around the waist of the teacher and his head covered by the biker's helmet. Mr Cooper had decreed that was the best option, seeing as Marty's face was the most likely to draw attention. He, on the other hand, was completely open to the elements, open to Gealblath. He rode on the outskirts, the roads closest to woodland or closest to the beach. Just in case a car got too close, or a glance lasted too long; then they would have somewhere to hide. But thankfully none did. The town was too dark for anyone to see clearly enough, and too cold for anyone to try in the first place. In the end, the drive was entirely without incident, and by the time they were pulling up beside the cabins on the beach, only thirty minutes had passed since they had first set off.

Mr Cooper turned the key, then pulled it out of the ignition, swinging his leg over the vehicle before holding it steady for Marty to dismount. He did so ungracefully.

'You alright?' Mr Cooper asked.

'That thing really digs into the arse,' Marty replied.

'Yeah, it's been doing that for a while.'

Marty turned away, peering towards the abandoned power plant which was just half a mile to the right. A rush of anxiety flooded through his chest. He remembered being there years ago. He remembered the screams, the fall, the eagles spiralling about the chimney, which now reached high into the clouds, gazing ominously onto the beachfront. Marty pulled up his visor and followed the chimney's gaze towards the waves, which were slowly creeping out from the shore.

'The tide's out,' he noticed with a frown.

'Going out,' replied Mr Cooper. 'Don't worry about it. The water will come back eventually.'

Mr Cooper rolled the bike and propped it up alongside the nearest cabin, craning his neck to look left and right along the road before he approached the door. Two long sheets of plywood were stapled along the windows, covering up the damage that had occurred on their last visit. Mr Cooper stared at them with a vague sense of regret.

'Sorry again,' he muttered under his breath. Then he leaned forward and kicked the lock, sending shards of wood and rusted metal onto the pebbles.

'Jesus Christ!' Marty shouted.

'That should do it. Just like old times, hey, kiddo? You can take the helmet off now. I'm gonna need it.'

Marty did as he was told. A wave of emotion hit him when he followed Mr Cooper into the cabin. This was the place where it had started. The last time he was here had been with Amee, on the day that he learnt who she was and what she could do. It was also the day he had decided to stick by her, no matter how far they went, and no matter how dangerous it got. And now he was back. The wooden hearts on the wall began to rattle in the breeze, and the teacher returned from his quick scan of the cabin.

'Alright, this should be fine. It's seven o'clock, so by the time the hand reaches nine, I should be back with the key. The boathouse is just a few huts along. Until then, you stay here, you stay quiet. No one should be around at this time of night, but if someone does come, just remember not to panic. Keep inside. Keep the door closed, keep your mouth shut, and wait for them to go. You understand me?'

Mr Cooper began walking towards the door, his fingers fiddling with the helmet strap.

'What about light?' asked Marty. 'I need light.'

'No light. You don't wanna draw any attention to this place. The moon's big enough anyway. You can see me alright, can't you?'

Marty stared with puffy eyes towards the moon, which hung shimmering in the sky directly above the water. In all fairness, it was big tonight. Bigger, in fact, than Marty had ever seen it before. Mr Cooper stepped back out onto the pebbles, his breath catching in the silver-glazed air as he pulled the helmet down over his head.

'And you're sure you're only gonna be two hours?' said Marty, running after him.

'I don't know. But I'll be back soon. You just have to wait here. It'll all be okay if you wait here.' Mr Cooper nodded reassuringly, then walked towards his bike.

'Mr Cooper!'

'What?' the teacher turned back.

'It's just, if we do it, if we save her, I just wanna know what happens then?'

'You seriously want to talk about that now? I thought you wanted to be quick.'

'No, I am serious.'

Mr Cooper wrapped his hand around the clutch of the Shadow. 'I suppose we go looking for this place. House on the cliff, wasn't it?'

Another gust of sea wind blasted Marty's hair, sharpening

the sting in the cuts on his face, making them pulse and throb.

'What about the detective? I mean, what about whoever killed Charlie? They're still out there.'

'It's like I said, Marty. The world doesn't give you justice, and I'm tired of trying to make it. The least I can do now is something I should have always done.'

'What's that?' Marty asked.

Mr Cooper's gaze flickered. 'Be a dad.'

At that moment, the breeze died down. The whistling began to quiet until there was nothing but the sound of waves on the shoreline.

'Get inside, Marty.' Mr Cooper pulled down the visor on his helmet and began walking the Shadow towards the road. 'I'll be back as soon as I can.'

'Mr Cooper,' Marty called out again.

The teacher yanked his visor up. 'What already?!'

'You stopped...'

'Stopped what?'

'You stopped calling me Weed-kid. You haven't done it since the valley.'

'Yeah, well, I suppose the nickname doesn't really suit a guy who took on Roman Guild and came out alive.'

Marty felt his face go red behind the blood and the bruises. 'I don't know a good nickname for a guy like that...'

Mr Cooper climbed onto the Shadow and sparked it back into life. The front wheel ground hard against the stones and onto the black road.

'How about Marty Evans?' he called out.

Then he pulled the visor down once again and propelled the bike forward. The engine choked out fumes and oil, and Marty watched as the teacher accelerated down the road, his eyes beginning to squint as Mr Cooper got smaller, and smaller, and smaller, until he went down a steep slope and disappeared entirely from view.

That was when Marty's face stiffened, and he breathed in the cold moonlit air. For a few moments, he turned back to the cabin. He wavered, like he might actually go back inside, like he might listen to Mr Cooper and follow his plan. But then he remembered that night one month ago. *What was the promise I made that night? That promise wasn't to Amee, it was to myself. Stick by her. Be the person she thinks you are. Be courageous and stick by her.* There had never been a moment that Marty hadn't intended to see that through. And this wasn't going to be one of them. With a deep breath, he turned on his heel, trod onto the tarmac, and began sprinting across the road in the opposite direction.

24

BEFORE THE NIGHT ENDS

He was wearing tweed in the picture. His head was cocked to the right, his face gaunt and unshaven. He wasn't menacing, but the camera film betrayed a glimmer in his eyes that would have humanised him. Anyone looking at the photo would see the monster, if they chose to, which of course they did, because it gave them an easy answer.

HAVE YOU SEEN THIS MAN?

The words were printed just above the photograph, followed by his name, 'David Cooper'; his age, 'forty-four'; his height, 'five-eleven', and then some text pointing him to the gallows.

Wanted for questioning in connection with the disappearance of Marty Evans (13). Last seen

28th September in Gealblath Hospital at 14:00.
If you have any information or have seen David Cooper
please contact the Gealblath Police Department
immediately or call 999.

David felt the anger swell through his chest. *Fucking hyenas.* This town had never trusted him since Charlie went. Not that he had ever cared before, but this was too easy. This was so easy that it actually hurt. Another kid had gone missing and Gealblath had judged him guilty with a few lines of ink, laminated and presented in every street, allowing everyone to nod their heads in agreement. *We were right. David Cooper is indeed a killer.* The town had been waiting to find him guilty for ten whole years. And now he was right in the centre of it.

David moved away from the rubbish bin and set his bike up against the wall, just where the shadows started to congregate. As far as rubbish tips went, he had never been more grateful for this one, stationed right on the edge of Eden Park Lane. All he had to do was stash his bike there, make the five-minute walk to his home, retrieve the key, return to the tip, and make the ride back to Gealblath Beach. Simple. One could almost say too simple, but then, David still had butterflies running rabid inside his stomach. What he was about to do was madness, after all. Of course it was madness. Yet he was still about to do it. It was the only thing that could be done if he was going to save Amee Florence before the night was over.

David took a deep breath. *Stay calm,* he thought to himself. *That's all you have to do. Just stay calm and act as if you belong.* A moment passed, then another, then one more, and then David Cooper walked out of the tip and onto the street.

The houses were lit behind curtains. Deep orange glows illuminated silhouettes. Some of the people of Gealblath were cooking, pacing about their kitchens, searching for the right sauce; others had accumulated in lounges, their bodies curled into each other and their eyes fixed on small screens. No one was looking outside. No one saw the ghost on their street, gliding silently across the pavement. David Cooper was walking through Gealblath unseen and unnoticed, just as he had done before the shit hit the fan a month ago. In a way, he had slotted right back into his role. Being a ghost suited him. So long as things didn't go bump, no heads should turn. Or at least, that was what he was hoping for. That was what he prayed.

It didn't take him long to get to number forty-seven, his old haunt. The lights were off inside so there was no one home. But David had expected that. There was no way Gerri was going to stay in the house of a child killer, especially with police sniffing around the place. He took a step forward, then stopped. The door looked bigger than usual. It loomed over him like a black hole, drawing him forward while pushing him back. This was the last place on earth he wanted to be, yet the only place he couldn't avoid. The black hole sucked him in now, wrenching him up the steps to the front door until his knuckles were quivering just inches above the knocker. *Open it*, he thought to himself. *Open it, you idiot, and get yourself out of sight.* David's pulse was roaring inside his ears, urging him to run back to his bike and leave Gealblath as quickly as he could. He was close to listening to it. At one point his fingers coiled and retracted, his feet tipping back on the last step. But then, like all black holes before and all black holes after, this one didn't let go. The door pulled him forward and David found himself placing the key firmly into the lock.

The ghost swept up the stairs inside, keeping to the shadows. *One minute*, he thought. *One minute. Get in. Get the key. Get out.* But by the time he had climbed the stairs, he couldn't help but stare. The last time David had been in this flat, he had been a different man. Full of rage and fire, wanting to save the girl, or rather, wanting to right a wrong in the only way he knew how. Running on instinct, with lines blurred and ethics forgotten. The flat seemed smaller now. It felt like his head could hit the ceiling. He found himself hating it. This home was a part of himself he wanted to forget, yet now he was inside it once again. It was a cruel joke. A lagging mirror. And David couldn't wait to leave. With a shake of the head, David turned away from the reflection.

He pulled off the helmet and threw it on the sofa. The counter tops were different to when he was last here, items rearranged, everything in the wrong place. The police would have turned the whole place over multiple times. Everything would have been swept and double swept in the search for a lead. Gerri would have been questioned too, but she wouldn't have told them about the key. She would have told them about the bathroom cabinet, she would have told them about his mood swings, his violent tendencies, the fight in the tavern, and the way he would wake up sweating from bad dreams. But there would be no reason to tell them about the key. *Oh God, tell me she didn't tell them about the key.*

He opened drawers, pushing aside piles of paperwork, pens, scissors, paperclips, and all of the other shit that had accumulated over the years. He pulled open cupboards, cabinets, and scoured in between the cushions of the sofa, all before coming to his senses and checking the key rack. That was when he spotted it.

A copper key dangling from the third hanger.

He took a deep breath. *Calm yourself down, you idiot. You keep on like this, you're gonna attract the attention of every neighbour on this damned street.* David grabbed the key and shoved it into his pocket. *Okay, you've got it now. Just go. Just turn around and get the hell out of here.*

He turned on his heel and marched over towards the door, but just as he did so, something stopped him in his tracks. *No.* He turned his head, staring into the kitchen on the other side of the room. *Leave it. I don't care why you've stopped, just leave it and go.* The kitchen door was ajar, revealing one of the counter tops. David took a step forward. *Don't. Just don't. I don't care, I don't. I don't care what you've seen. You've got the key, just go. Jesus God.*

He walked against his instinct into the kitchen before reaching out to flick on the lights. They came on quickly, instantly revealing the hot pot that was sitting half full on the oven. It was still steaming, with a half-eaten plate of salad and mince beside it. By the time David realised what he was looking at, Gerri had already started talking.

'I don't want you to do anything, I don't want you to say anything. Just sit down in the corner and raise your hands above your head.'

Gerri was stood in the corner. She was wearing silk pyjamas and her hands were gripping a small, short-barrelled handgun. Her finger rested on the trigger.

'Jesus, Gerri. What are you doing here?'

'Don't say anything. Don't do anything. I don't want to use this, so please just sit down in the corner.' She squeezed the gun tighter, her eyes wide and petrified.

David raised both arms above his head. 'Where the hell did you get a handgun from?'

'My dad told me you'd come back for me. He said you were dangerous and I should protect myself. Looks like he was right.'

'Gerri, I don't –'

'Sit down in the corner.'

'Don't panic, I'm not armed, I don't want to –'

Gerri cut him off with a scream. 'JESUS CHRIST, I DON'T WANNA USE THIS, BUT I'M FUCKING GOING TO UNLESS YOU SIT DOWN!'

David stumbled backwards into the kitchen cabinet. 'Alright, shit, I'm sitting down! Look, I'm sitting down.' He fell onto the floor, his heart now thumping beneath his weather-beaten leather jacket. *Why didn't you check? You fucking moron, why the hell didn't you scan the flat first?*

'Show me your pockets!' Gerri gestured at his trousers and David opened up his pockets.

'There's nothing, see? I'm not carrying anything. Don't panic.'

At that moment, his ex-girlfriend ran over towards the knife rack on the wall, the gun still pointed at David's head. She began retrieving the blades with her other hand.

'What the hell are you –'

Gerri opened the window above the sink and started to throw the knives out one by one.

'Fucking hell, Gerri, stop! I'm not gonna knife you, Gerri! I don't wanna hurt you! I don't wanna hurt anyone! I haven't hurt anyone. Gerri, you need to listen to me! I can explain everything!'

The last knife landed on the pavement below with a clatter, then Gerri turned towards him and gripped the gun in both hands again. 'What else in this room can hurt me?'

'Gerri, you need to calm down.'

'I'm not bullshiting! What else can fucking hurt me?!'

Without waiting for an answer, she looked across to the blender. Using her free hand to grip it, Gerri pulled out the blade and marched back to the open window, throwing it into the night.

'Gerri, would you calm the fuck down and stop losing your shit?! I can explain everything! Gerri!'

With frantic breaths, Gerri then ran over towards the microwave and tried desperately to pull it away from the plug. The gun swerved to and fro, aimed at David's torso.

'JESUS CHRIST, GERRI, I'M NOT GONNA TRY TO KILL YOU WITH THE MICROWAVE!'

Gerri stopped, both hands coming to steady the gun. 'I don't want you to fucking move!'

'I'm not gonna move. Okay? Are you listening to me? I'm not gonna move. You've got me on my arse, and I'm gonna stay on my arse. You just need to stop. You just need to stop and breathe.'

David spoke as soothingly as he could, trying to portray an image of calmness. After a few seconds, Gerri managed to pause and reflect him.

'Okay... okay...' She swallowed. 'Tell me where the child is.'

'Can you lower the gun first?'

'Fuck that! Where's the body?'

'Jesus, Gerri, there's no body. The child's not dead, he's alive. He's hurt. But that wasn't me –'

'What the hell are you talking about, not you?'

'It was someone else.' With a wince, David lifted his neck up to show her the bruising around the windpipe. 'You see?'

417

Gerri squinted at it, her eyebrows furrowed and her skin starting to grow even paler. 'Just... just tell me where he is...'

'Gerri, I can explain everything, but it's gonna be hard to believe.'

Gerri let out a weird and panicked laugh. 'No shit it's gonna be hard to believe. I don't believe a word that comes out of your mouth. It's all been lies from the beginning, David, hasn't it? Everything. Everything's just been one big lie.'

'Okay, you're right, I've lied. But not for the reasons you think. Not for the reasons anyone thinks.' David's tone was higher now, his voice shakier, like a child's. 'You're gonna think I killed my son. You're gonna think I'm some crazy serial kid killer, but I'm not, okay? I'm not. Marty Evans is alive. Please understand that. The child is alive. I swear.'

'But you took him.'

'Look, I get that this is hard to understand. I get that this is difficult. But this is all about someone else. That girl, you remember that girl? The new girl from school. The one I was talking about. She can do things, Gerri.'

'She can do things...' Gerri mimicked him distrustfully.

'Yes, she can do things. Things that you would have to hear about from her to believe. But the point is, she created a way to reopen the case. Charlie's case. That's where I've been. I've been with her and Marty, trying to find the detective, to find Alfie.'

'Can you hear yourself?' Gerri laughed again, and she lifted the gun towards David's head once more.

Her hands were visibly dripping with sweat. Any second now they might slip, David knew. They might slip, and the finger that was curled around the trigger might pull. He raised his arms higher.

'Gerri, please listen. If you come with me, you can hear it all from Marty. You can hear the exact same thing. It won't be me trying to talk my way out of –'

'You want me to come with you? What, so you can shut me up? So you can take me somewhere quiet and kill me? Do you really think I'm that stupid, David?!'

Her hands slipped, causing the finger around the trigger to whiten as she tried to gain control of the weapon.

'Shit!' David yelled out. 'Please don't fire! Please take your finger away from the trigger, Gerri!'

'I'M NOT GONNA FUCKING LISTEN TO YOU!'

'You've got to listen to me, because the girl is in trouble. That's why I'm here. That's why we came back. She's in the hospital right now. Gealblath Hospital. She's with someone who could hurt her. That's where we're going, me and Marty. We're going to get her. But we need to be quick, and you have to believe me!'

David went to push himself off the floor, but before he could, Gerri closed one eye and aimed down the barrel of the gun.

'You take your arse one inch off the floor, I swear I will shoot you!'

David lowered himself back down and let out a moan. 'What do you want me to say?'

'I don't want you to say anything. I just want you to sit there and shut the fuck up.'

'Okay... okay, that's fine. But let me just ask you something first. After the two years that we've been together, after all that time, all those days, everything we did and everything we shared, do you not think there's the slightest chance that I could be telling the truth? That maybe everybody is still wrong about me, like you believed they

419

were back then? Because if there is that chance, if you find that chance, then you should come with me. You can bring the gun, you can hold it up to my head for as long as you want, but come with me and hear it from Marty Evans himself.'

A few seconds passed. Gerri dipped her chin, tears starting to drop onto the kitchen floor.

'I don't trust you anymore, David. I did once, but not now. Never now. Not after all this.'

'Okay, but you did once. You trusted me once. It's a mistake, Gerri. All of this is a mistake. And I've made lots of those, even before this happened. I've been so in the wrong. But I'm trying to be better. I was a bad person, but I'm not anymore, I believe that. I really believe that.' David lowered his hands and placed them on either side of him. 'Gerri, if you could trust the person I was back then, if you could find it in your heart to trust that person, then you can trust this one now. I promise you that. Let me take you to Marty.'

'Take me to him?'

'Yes. Take you to him. I'll take you to him, and you'll see then. You'll see that I'm telling the truth. He'll tell you.'

'I'm not...' Gerri shook her head. 'I can't...'

'Gerri, I know there's still trust here. I can see it. I can see it's still in you. Otherwise, what are we doing? You would have called the police by now. You would have called the police and there'd be no reason for you to hear me out.'

Gerri began to pant harder. She started to lower the gun. 'I... I...'

'You're hearing me out. I think you wanted me to explain, and I've explained. Everything I've told you is true, and if we don't go now, it will be too late for the girl. Just let me take you to Marty. Please just let me do that.'

With his heart still thumping in his chest, David slowly pushed himself up from the floor. Gerri swung the gun back up.

'Don't! Don't or I swear I will –'

'No,' said David gently. 'No, Gerri, you won't.'

He took a step forward. But then, from out of the silence, there came a sound. It was distant at first, but it soon grew louder, fiercer. Sirens that rose and fell in a sort of pattern. David turned to the window to see the blue and red glares piercing the cold night sky.

'What?' he muttered dumbly. 'What is that?'

Gerri was staring at him with wide eyes. 'I want you to sit in the corner.'

'Gerri, what is that?'

David marched towards the open window.

'Don't move,' screamed Gerri suddenly. 'Don't fucking move. I'm telling you, David, I will shoot!'

But David ignored her. His hands curved around the sink, and he looked out into the night, immediately spotting the three police cars swerving quickly onto the kerb. 'You called the police?!'

'I called them as soon as I heard you. They're going to take you in, David. They're gonna take you in.'

'You fucking...'

The doors of the cars outside opened, and David watched as the officers ran across the road and towards the front door.

'I'm sorry, David,' said Gerri. 'But you have to be taken in. They have to do this. Please just get back in the corner.' Gerri jumped in shock as the door below them burst open. 'Please! Please just get back in the corner! It'll be better for you if you get back in the corner!'

421

'I'm not giving myself to them, Gerri.'

'Armed police!' a deep male voice called from the top of the stairs.

'PLEASE, DAVID!' Gerri began screaming at the top of her lungs. 'JESUS GOD, PLEASE JUST GET BACK IN THE CORNER! HE'S IN HERE! OFFICERS, HE'S IN HERE!'

But before she could get another word out, David jumped up onto the sink and pulled his legs out onto the ledge. Gerri ran forward, her finger whitening on the trigger one more time.

'NO! DON'T MOVE! OFFICERS! OFFICERS! I'M GONNA SHOOT!'

David saw the leather boots of the cops rush into the kitchen. He closed his eyes, braced, then pushed himself off the sink and out of the window. He heard the gun shot first, and then the wind, hissing against his face as he fell. His muscles tensed before his shoes touched the ground and every inch of him spiralled into a hot and darkening pain.

25

COMING HOME

Marty's ears were ringing. The pain. The pain was doing that. It was churning through his system, gnawing about the edges like a mole. It burrowed its way up, then down, then up once more, right into his head. He stopped running and waited for this bout to pass. He was on Oaking's Close now, which meant he'd been running for nearly half a mile. There was only half a mile more to go. Marty waited for things to align properly again. The road shifted into a straight line. The sky climbed its way upwards towards the stars where it belonged. Then he straightened his back, took a deep breath, and spoke into the cold night air.

'This is a pain I've felt before. Rory's pain. It doesn't mean anything now. Keep going. Come on, you know you can. Just keep going.'

And then he was running again.

A whole hour passed before he finally reached his destination. It was a suburban neighbourhood, lit up dimly by yellow overhanging bulbs that were smattered with small droplets of salt water. Marty had been there before. Whenever his own house got too awkward to live in, a house on this street would be the designated bunker for the weekend. In a way, it felt like a second home. Coming back to it now, after a whole month, it was the first time he could stop, and look, and breathe in that air, the same air that he'd breathed before he went away. And despite everything, he could smile.

Number three. Mike's house. Marty peered up the driveway, looking immediately towards the bedroom window on the far side, above the gutter of the garage. It was glowing brightly. He remembered one Halloween when the three of them had been in that room. He'd left to go to the toilet, but he'd actually ended up leaving the house, climbing up onto the garage, and knocking ominously on the glass of the window outside. Mike had screamed. Teddy had cried. Marty, on the other hand, had nearly pissed himself laughing. Things were a lot different now. He felt almost like a different person. He took a moment, exhaling through another bout of crippling pain, before jogging towards the bin beside the garage door.

The tiles were slippery, but Marty just about managed to grip onto them. He crawled up towards the window, then shimmied onto the ledge. As usual, Mike's room was a mess. Warhammer figures were scattered on the pale-blue carpet. On the desk by the door, half-eaten plates of food and crumpled cans of Irn-Bru ran amuck. In the corner, where the carpet met the wall, layers of unwashed laundry lay on top of each other like a sweaty, ketchup-stained Leaning Tower of Pisa. Teddy Kowalski was sitting just beside the tower painting a goblin warrior.

Marty's heart fluttered in his ribcage. In that moment, it felt as if he'd been reunited with a loved one after years away from home. Like he'd come back from a war overseas and was touching a past life for the first time. But of course it hadn't been years, there had been no war, and Teddy was his best friend, not a loved one. All the same though, the feeling remained. After everything that had happened, everything Marty had been through, it was just nice to see Teddy painting Warhammer figures again.

Okay, he thought. *Enough shmooshy stuff. Snap out of it. You need to hurry; you need to be fast. You've already been an hour. A whole hour where anything could have happened to Amee. You need to get in there and get out as quickly as you can.*

Marty reached up to the window and tapped twice on the glass. Teddy jumped with a 'Shit!', and Marty dipped his head, keeping his body low upon the tiles before reaching up and tapping again. He heard Teddy's voice call out from the inside.

'Mike? For shite's sake, that's not funny. You said you needed the toilet.'

Marty gave the glass another tap, his knuckles hitting the window harder.

'Oh shitting hell, Mike, I'm gonna shove this goblin up your arse, I swear to God!'

Marty listened as Teddy's footsteps crossed the room and the window began to slide open. At the same moment, Marty lifted himself back up, and Teddy's jaw dropped halfway towards the floor.

'What. The. Hell.'

'Shh.' Marty put a finger to his lips, as if it might keep Teddy calm. It didn't work.

'WHAT THE HELL?!'

'Teddy, shut the hell up. Seriously, be quiet.'

'IT'S YOU! IT'S ACTUALLY YOU!'

Marty pulled himself into the house, trying desperately to ignore the pain in his ribs. 'It's me. Okay, it's me, but you need to shut the hell up.'

'But how...? Your face... Your hair... Why... What...?!' The questions rolled off Teddy's tongue like a malfunctioning conveyer belt, jumbling together and clogging the system.

'You need to calm down,' Marty told him. 'You just need to take a breath, and chill out, and shut up.'

Teddy's skin turned whiter and whiter until it looked like all the blood might just drain out of it entirely. He took a long gulp of air. 'Marty. You're alive.'

'I'm alive.'

'But how? Mr Cooper. Everyone at school was saying he killed you and ran away to Mexico. Me and Mike, the cops were talking to us and everything; it was like something out of a film. Oh.'

'Oh what?'

'Mike.'

The sound of a toilet flushing resonated from beyond the walls, followed swiftly by heavy footsteps down the hall, a slight sneeze, and a high-pitched squeal.

'HOLY SHITE!'

Mike stood gawking in the doorway, and Marty immediately pushed his finger up against his lips again.

'No, please be quiet!'

Mike's mother called up from the floor below. 'Michael Torford, what have I told you about your language?'

'MUM! IT'S –'

'No! Be quiet!' Marty grabbed his friend by the shirt, pulling him inside the room before slamming the door shut behind him. 'I'm back, I'm alive, I know it's crazy, I know you're confused, but you've got to be quiet. No one else can know I'm here.'

Mike and Teddy stood together. Teddy with the half-painted goblin still clasped rigidly in his hand, Mike with a face that suggested he had just seen a ghost risen from the grave.

'I don't understand,' he said after a few seconds.

'I don't blame you.'

'Everyone thought Mr Cooper had killed you and run away to Mexico.'

'I know, Teddy told me, but that's not what happened. I could explain everything, but... Wait, why Mexico?'

His two friends stared at him dumbly.

'I dunno,' replied Teddy. 'That's just the place everyone said he went.'

'Why is it always Mexico?'

'Who gives a shit?' said Mike. 'You're alive, Marty. I can't believe it. This is awesome.'

Marty shuffled uncomfortably. Despite the situation, he cracked a nervous smile. 'You didn't count me out that quickly, did you?'

Teddy went to nod, but then swiftly reconsidered his decision when Mike did the opposite.

'Of course not,' said Mike confidently. 'I mean, some people did. I mean, well, kind of everyone did. Everyone but us. We always believed in you.'

Marty took that in. It was strange to think of everyone believing he was dead. He couldn't even begin to consider what his parents must have been going through for the last month. His mum, certainly, would have been distraught. But he hadn't meant for all this to happen. He couldn't have helped it. He couldn't have helped any of it. It had just happened. And that was the way it was. He was fully prepared for the consequences. But not yet. He couldn't face them yet. Not while Amee still needed help.

'OUCH!' he yelped as Mike prodded him with a finger.

'What happened to you, Marty? Your eyes, they look like they're bleeding.'

Marty pushed him away. 'I got beaten up.'

'By who? Mr Cooper?'

'No. Everything you've heard about Mr Cooper is wrong. He's not a bad guy; it's all bullshit.'

'So he didn't kidnap you?' asked Teddy.

'No. Well, it was kind of a mutual decision.'

Teddy turned to Mike. 'Is it just me or does that not make any sense?'

'No, Teddy,' replied Mike. 'I mean, you're right, it's usually just you. But right now, that doesn't make any sense to me either.'

'That's fine.' Marty paced back towards the window. 'I don't think there's much I can say to make you guys understand, and there isn't time to say it anyway.'

'What about your hair?' asked Teddy.

'What about it?'

'It's all blonde. Was that a personal choice?'

'No, Teddy, it wasn't. Listen, none of that matters right now. The point is, I need you.'

'You need us?' said Mike.

'Yes. Everything that's happened, where I went, why I left, none of it's about me. It's not about Mr Cooper either. It's about Amee.'

'Amee?' Teddy repeated the name, like he was tasting a long-forgotten memory. 'Isn't that...'

'The girl,' Mike finished for him. 'The new girl. The one Marty thought was in the hospital.'

428

'Thing is, I was right. She was in the hospital. But she got out. Since then, I've been with her, but you can't know why.'

'Why not?' asked Teddy.

'Because there's no time to explain what happened, and there definitely isn't time for you to try to believe it. She's in trouble, and we've got to go now. All three of us. She needs my help, and I need you guys.'

Marty slid the window up towards the ceiling, but just as he did so, Mike marched over to him and slammed it shut.

'No way.'

'What do you mean, no way?'

'Five minutes ago, we thought we'd never see you again. You can't just come in here, explain nothing, ask us for help, and expect everything to be gravy.'

'Mike, seriously, you don't understand. There's no time. Amee –'

'No, I don't think *you* understand. You've been gone for a whole month!'

Teddy nodded. 'That's, like, twenty years in dog years, Marty.'

'Okay, but what dog's counting?'

'That's not the point,' Mike continued. 'We're your friends, Marty. We're your best friends. You can't just do that to us.'

Marty looked between the pair of them, and the pair of them looked back at him. Their faces were pale, lost, and confused, but relieved. Definitely relieved. Marty could see that. They were happy that they were looking at him, and he was happy too. He sighed. Mike was right, of course. Mike was always right.

'Okay, I can explain, but...'

'But what?' asked Mike.

Marty hesitated. 'Best friends, right?'

Mike and Teddy nodded back. 'Best friends,' they said together.

'It's gonna be hard to believe –'

'Marty.' Mike cut him off abruptly. 'We were the only ones to believe you weren't dead. The only ones.'

Marty gave him another smile. He knew what that meant. *Why are you doubting them?* he thought. *You called this place a home, but it's not. They're your home. And you can trust a home. A home is all you can trust.*

'Okay,' he said. 'Okay, I'll explain. But we can't just be standing here in your bedroom while I do. I'm serious when I say time's running out.'

'What do you mean?' asked Teddy. 'Where are we going?'

But Marty was already climbing out the window.

The hospital was only a quarter of a mile away from Mike's house. Marty knew that because he'd been round there at least five times when Mike's hay fever got so bad it brought on severe asthma attacks, and on a night like tonight, he thanked every single one of them. There was hardly enough time to get through the entire story before they had reached the outskirts of the car park, but Marty just about covered the crucial parts. The strange message in the shoebox, that night in the cabin, the caravan park, the dead detective, Roman Guild, and, of course, Amee's ability to see dead people. Mike and Teddy took it all in silently, their eyes wide, their mouths hanging so low you could fit a whole fist neatly onto the tongue. Even after he finally finished, it took about a minute for one of them to actually say something. It was Teddy who had the first word, and it was a predictable first word at that.

'So you kissed Amee Florence?'

Marty had to laugh, but he immediately regretted it when a burst of pain punched his ribs. He stabilised himself against the parked van they were hiding behind.

'Really?' he wheezed. 'That's the part you're having trouble with?'

'That does seem a bit unlikely,' Mike piped up.

'It's true!'

'No, yeah, I believe you. I dunno, it's just unlikely, I guess.'

'Oh, you guess?' Marty shook his head in disbelief. 'And you're completely fine with the other parts?'

'Oh yeah, those parts I believe, one hundred per cent.'

Mike gave him a smile, his chest still heaving from the run. There wasn't anything in his eyes that suggested he didn't believe him. Those eyes were full of trust, and something else. Something Marty hadn't seen before. Admiration, he guessed. Admiration of him. It felt strange in a way, like Mike was looking at someone else now. He'd been gone for a month, but somehow Marty felt like he was years ahead of both of them.

'So how does she do it?' asked Teddy.

'Do what?'

'How does she see the ghosts?'

'They're not ghosts.'

'They sound like ghosts. In fact, they sound exactly like ghosts.'

'She doesn't like that word. She just calls them people. And I don't know how she can see them. She doesn't either. But she could always do it, for as long as she can remember.'

'Oh, right, okay.'

Marty turned towards the hospital. The outside was glowing white. Three pillars were arched in front of the doorway, tall and domineering, like the entrance to some kind of fortress.

'Okay,' he said, 'I've explained. Now we've got to get in there. We need to save Amee.'

Mike followed Marty's gaze nervously towards the white building. 'So what did you say her mum was going to do to her?'

'I don't know,' replied Marty. 'But nothing good.'

'It's just, I'm not really... I don't know if I can...'

'What?'

'Marty, I couldn't even stand up to Ross and Rory.'

'What are you talking about? You threw a knife at Rory's head.'

'Yeah, a school knife. It might as well have been a spoon.'

Teddy patted him on the shoulder. 'You took on Ross, didn't you?'

'Yeah, if taking on Ross means lying down and letting yourself get beaten into oblivion.'

Teddy shrugged. 'Still took him on.'

'Listen, I'm not brave. Not like you, Marty. Everything you've just said, everything you've done, that's not me. That's not me at all.'

Mike wiped at one of his double chins. His face had turned as white as the hospital. His chest was still heaving, but it wasn't from the walk anymore, that much was obvious. Marty knew how he felt. He had thought the exact same thing once. Before everything had happened, before Roman Guild had tried to kill him, he had thought courage meant something entirely different. He had thought courage was about being strong, being fearless, being the winner, but it was never that. Courage wasn't about prevailing against adversity; courage was about looking for it in the first place.

432

The search. That was what Amee had told him. That time she had talked to him beside the fire, that time he had opened up to her just before the kiss. She had told him he was courageous from the moment he had decided to stick by her. That was the point, Marty realised. True courage was the search for courage, regardless of the consequences. Mike would find that too, if he was to take the opportunity. He would find that just as Marty had found it.

'It's not that I don't want to come with you,' Mike sniffed. 'I do, but...'

'But what?' said Marty. 'Mike, after everything I've just said, you still want to go in there. That's what bravery is. I mean, that's what I think it means. Doing things even though you're scared of them. Looking for courage even though you're worried it's not there. That's what makes you brave. That's what makes you really fucking awesome.'

Mike looked at him. The colour returned to his cheeks, filling them in like someone was dabbing them with a wet paint brush. 'Really?' he asked.

Marty smiled. 'Mike, you've painted warriors your whole life. Now it's your chance to be one. And trust me, you walk through that door and you will be. You will be.'

A small yellow car swerved onto the lane just ten feet in front of them and pulled into the car park before cruising towards the hospital. The three of them watched it from the shadows.

'Okay,' Mike said under his breath, as if he was gearing himself up. 'Okay, I can do this. We can all do this. We're warriors, all three of us.'

'That's the spirit,' Marty whispered back. 'We should be fast though. We've already been here too long.'

'So what's the plan?' asked Teddy. 'Do we just walk in?'

Marty shook his head. 'I can't do that. Not when everyone in town knows who I am. There are posters of my face everywhere.'

'But it's not really the same face, is it?' said Mike.

'What?'

'Your face now isn't the same face as it was before. It's all busted up, swollen and disgusting looking.'

'Thanks, Mike.'

'No, but you know what I mean. It's different. Your hair's different too.'

'And it's a hospital,' Teddy added. 'There's probably loads of busted up faces in there. You'll be right at home.'

Mike nodded. 'He's right. It's amazing, but he's right.'

'But I can't just walk in. I'm gonna draw attention. We've got to think of something else.'

Another car past to the right of them, and the three boys gathered together in the darkness once more. Marty watched the wheels turn and a thought popped into his head.

'Mike, the last time you were here you were in a wheelchair.'

'Yeah well, actually, it's pretty hard to remember. I was very concussed at the time.'

Marty nodded, scanning through the plan in his head, making sure it wasn't crazy. 'Right, okay, that's what we need then.'

'How does a wheelchair solve anything?' asked Teddy.

'Think about it. All I have to do is sit in a wheelchair, cover up my face with one of those blankets, and you guys can push me the rest of the way. All they'll see is blonde hair, completely different to all the posters.'

'What if someone looks closer?'

'I pull the blanket up more.'

434

'What if someone asks you to pull it down?'

'I'll pretend I'm asleep.'

Marty looked between Teddy and Mike hopefully, waiting for one of them to tell him it was a good idea, but neither of them did.

'I don't know,' said Mike. 'I mean, it's not really a plan they'd conjure up at MI5, is it?'

'Who's asking for that? You've got a better idea, have you?'

'Well no, but –'

'So that's it, that's what we've got, that's what we're gonna do. We get in there quickly. We get Amee out. Then we meet Mr Cooper at the beach. It can work.'

Mike and Teddy stared at Marty unsurely.

'And you're sure Mr Cooper will meet us at the beach?' asked Mike.

'Of course I'm sure. If Mr Cooper says that's gonna happen, then it's gonna happen. Like I said, I trust him.'

A silence ensued. It was a brief silence, an awkward one. The three friends stood together in the shadows apprehensively, their breaths catching in the air, illuminated by the low-hanging moon, until Teddy finally spoke, breaking them out of their trance.

'Alright,' he whispered. 'So who's getting the chair?'

26

THE KILLER ON THE STREET

David searched for the bullet wound. It felt like he was leaking, spurting out blood like a faulty water main, but his fingers couldn't find the wetness. *In your head. It's in your head, you idiot. There's no wound because she didn't hit you.* So why was there so much pain? David stood and winced in the night air. It was originating in his thigh, he could feel that now. It was in the thigh, but the pain snaked up his whole left side until it reached the breast, culminating around his nipple before fading away. *You just jumped from the window. You've hurt a muscle, or maybe you've sprained something. It's not a bullet wound. Not life threatening. You're okay. You're fine. Now get back into it, David, into the now, before it's too late.*

'DOWN THERE! DAVID! THE KILLER! HE'S DOWN THERE! I SHOT – BUT I – I DIDN'T MEAN TO – HE WAS TRYING TO KILL ME – HE'S ARMED – THE

KILLER IS DOWN THERE!'

David turned to see Gerri in the window above him, her silhouette aglow from the orange hue of the lights and her eyes wild and petrified.

'OFFICERS! PLEASE GET HIM!'

'ARMED POLICE!'

David heard the cop's voice again, resonating loudly from the stairs of the apartment. *They're coming down. They're coming down to get you. Run. Fucking run. Now!* He began sprinting across the pavement, passing the patrol cars that were still illuminating the street with the colours of panic and urgency. The neighbours were peering through their windows, some of them staring out from the cracks in their doors or the gaps in their letterboxes, watching as the police exited David's flat one by one.

'Shit,' David panted against the pain. 'Shit, shit, shit!'

'STOP!' another officer yelled out from behind him. 'GET YOUR HANDS IN THE AIR!'

But David kept running, so fast that the soles of his shoes only just gripped the tarmac.

'STOP!' he heard again, this time from someone younger, his voice higher, potentially a new recruit on his first time out.

His gun finger could be itching. Right now, at this very moment, he could be squinting an eye as he aims for the kill. Something to tell his peers down the station, something to boast about at the pub. 'David Cooper. One look, one touch. BAM! He fell like a sack of shite! That's one for the trophy collection.'

David turned a corner, his heart pumping against the pain in his hip, squeezing at his insides, begging him to stop. But the adrenaline allowed him to ignore it. The adrenaline allowed him to ignore everything. All he could think about was the rubbish heap, the bike propped up by the bin, his only escape route. It wasn't that much further now. If he could just keep going. If he could just avoid getting shot. Maybe he could get there.

'HEY!'

A door opened five feet in front of him. Two residents appeared on the steps of their home.

'David,' one of them said, recognising him. 'That's David Cooper, the child killer. I'm gonna get my knife!'

'No, for Pete's sake, Jason!'

David dipped his chin down, wishing he could go faster. Everyone on this street wanted him dead; he realised that now. He was a killer running from the law, and they wanted to make sure that this time the law would catch up. That was what they wanted. That was what they craved. A new day, with no strings attached to the old one. And so David knew he had to keep running, he had to sprint faster than he'd ever sprinted before, lest the dawn begin to appear on the horizon.

'ARMED POLICE!'

David turned another corner, the pain on his left side feeling like it was about to gnaw its way out of his flesh, to split him in half and leave him a bloody mess on the tarmac. But just as the pain became too much to bear, he finally came up alongside the entrance to the foul-smelling rubbish tip. He slipped into the darkness.

'HE'S IN THE YARD! COVER THE ENTRANCE!'

David ran towards the back of the tip, clattering into the bins before pulling on the vehicle beside them. The Shadow was cold, and it stung his flesh as he grabbed it. He swung his right leg over the seat and another bout of pain shot through him. To his relief, the police hadn't entered the yard yet. They were swarming around the entrance, their backs pressed to the fence and their gun arms visibly hovering beside the opening. *Hold on*, David thought then. *Gerri told them you're armed. They think you were going to kill her. That's why they won't come in. They think you've backed yourself into a corner, ready to fire.*

'GIVE YOURSELF UP,' one of them screamed. 'DO IT NOW! WE'VE GOT YOU SURROUNDED!'

David shoved the key into the ignition.

'ARMED POLICE! WE WILL FIRE!'

He watched as their firearms came into view, and then, almost patiently, he waited for one of them to take the first leap. *Come on. I want you to do it. One of you do it, one of you make the first move. Just inch a bit closer, that's right.*

A few more seconds passed. Then one of the officers took the step. A head appeared momentarily around the edge of the fence, just long enough for David to kick himself into action. With his left hand, he pulled on the throttle, revving the engine up to its maximum, before shoving his thumb down on the kill switch. The loud *CLAP!* of the backfire echoed out from the rubbish tip.

'SHIT!' the officer screeched and jumped out of view, and like a repelling magnet, the others followed suit. Without wasting any more time, David twisted the key once more and kicked off, letting the wheels propel him forward.

'SHOTS FIRED! SHOTS FIRED!'

Okay, David thought. *This is it. Might get shot. Might get killed. Hope I won't. Come on, Fate, give me something good for once!* He pulled the front wheel to the left and screeched onto the open road, keeping his spine down and his head ducked low. The police dispersed from the fence.

'HIT HIM! HIT HIM!' he heard one of them shout.

There was a shot. It rang out into the night air, but David didn't feel the impact. All he could feel was the rush of the world around him, pushing him forward, willing him on, until he reached the first turn and swerved the bike out of sight.

The moon was lighting his way, so he kept the headlamp off. He travelled along the road at seventy, constantly keeping his ears pricked for the roar of engines, the screech of sirens. Because they were coming. David knew they were coming, so he had to be quick. He had to go fast.

We can't go straight to the hospital now, he realised. *It's too dangerous. Amee will have to wait. She'll have to wait, and hope, and pray. All I can do now is get to the cabin unharmed. I just need to get there. Please God, let me get there.*

He pulled harder on the throttle, squinting against the wind. The Shadow choked bitterly beneath his grip, and David checked over his shoulder. There was something on the air, he realised. A siren. He could hear it in the distance, rising and falling. For a moment, he wondered whether it could be in his head. But then he turned back to the road, and in the distance, he spotted the source. Coloured lights were approaching fast, merging together in a huge ball as if there were just one beam. Really, there must have been about ten patrol cars in total, and each was heading towards David.

'Shit!' he yelled, and he swerved to the right, pulling as hard as he could until the wheels began to screech.

Ahead of him, another three patrol cars appeared in the distance. *Okay*, thought David. *Don't panic. Get off the road. That's all you need to do now. You just need to get off the road. Find a place and lie low. They're congregating here, but they'll pass. They'll all pass eventually.* David squinted again, his head spinning from left to right as he tried to find another way out, another exit perhaps. It came in the form of a small building, grubby and unkempt. A petrol station with only two empty cars parked askew on the verge outside. *That's it,* thought David. *That has to be it. That's your out.*

David revved the engine, then pulled into the garage and braked amidst four large rubbish bins. He propped the Shadow alongside one and crouched. The whole corner was hidden from the glow of the lights, so David sank deeper into it, staring at the road through a gap between two of the bins. The sirens got louder, and louder, and louder, and then David saw the first car. It passed across the entrance at about fifty, but any sense of relief was short lived, because it didn't take long for the next two to arrive. These ones slowed at the kerb, turning into the petrol station and stopping in front of the pumps.

The sirens switched off. David watched as a slightly overweight officer stepped out of one of the cars. *Don't look over here. Please don't look over here. God, please don't let him look over here.* A moustached policeman climbed out of the other car, and the two exchanged words. The fat one turned, grabbed the fuel pump, and jammed it hard into his vehicle. David took a breath. *They didn't see you. They don't know you're here. They're just filling up. You're fine. Don't panic. You're fine.* But despite thinking this, he felt his heart racing at one hundred miles per hour.

He watched as the fat officer finished filling the tank, then entered the shop. The other officer waited for him, leaning up against his police car. He began scanning the station and focused in on the area nearest the bins. *Get back,*

David told himself. *Get back. Further into the shadows. Make sure he can't see you.*

David pulled himself deeper into the darkness. His leg hit a stray rubbish bag and a can of dog food rolled out. Despite the sacks of rubbish around him, it managed to miss every obstacle and came to a stop about five paces away. The officer turned. *No*, David thought. *Don't come over here. Please don't come over here.* But the policeman was already walking. His boots landed heavily on the tarmac, a bony hand coming to rest atop his belt as he stared towards the can. He rested his foot on top of it, rolling it forward, then back, then forward again, until he pushed it back towards David. He felt his body begin to tremble. The officer sniffed, his moustache quivering a bit under his nose, the bristles stretching.

'Hey,' he whispered.

David felt a lump inside his throat.

The officer stepped closer. He pursed his lips, sucking back on some air to make a funny kissing sound. 'Come on,' he muttered. 'Come out.'

David stayed still.

'Heard you rustling in there. You looking for food or what?'

The officer made the same sucking noise with his lips, and that was when David finally understood. *He thinks you're an animal. A cat, or a fox, or something. Not you, not David Cooper; he's not seen you. Don't panic.* There was a small moment of relief, but then the officer took another step.

'I'm not going to hurt you...'

He peered deeper into the shadows, and David nudged himself backwards. *Shit. He's not backing off. You fucker, why don't you just back off?* His arse scuffled against the tarmac. *He's gonna see you, he's gonna see you, and the first thing he'll do is go for his gun.*

David turned his head, searching for something, anything, to defend himself with. It took a few seconds before his eyes finally landed on a bottle. It was broken at the bottom, sharp and jagged, thick enough to make an impact. *Could you do that though?*

His hand curled over the neck of the bottle as the officer took another step. *Yes. Yes, if I had to. I could.*

'Come out,' the officer said, his voice far closer now.

David took a breath and gripped the bottle harder. *I could do it. If he makes the first move. If he raises the gun, it could be the only way.* Sweat dripped down David's nose, the glass bottle beginning to quiver. He closed his eyes, but despite his conviction, his fingers loosened.

What are you doing? he riled against his own actions. *This is your only defence. You could do it, of course you could do it. It's you or him. Make it him.*

The officer placed his hand on one of the bins and bent down, making that sucking sound once more.

But what if I don't want to? What if I don't want to hurt anyone anymore? What if that's not me?

A slight wind rippled the rubbish bags. The officer turned his head.

Then you'll be taken in. Or worse, you'll be killed. You'll leave Marty alone in that cabin, and Amee alone at the mercy of her mother. That house may never be found, and Charlie might never be able to finally rest. That's what will happen.

The officer snapped his fingers. 'Come on...'

David placed the bottle on the ground. *Then I'm sorry,* he thought. He took another breath, raised his head, and

443

then prepared himself to surrender. There was a noise. A voice coming over the officer's radio.

'Calling units two to ten, this is Alpha one-fifty. Be advised, the suspect's destination could be Gealblath Hospital. He was attempting to abduct the witness on Eden Park Lane and he admitted that area was a possible target. Repeat, units two to ten be advised the suspect is headed to Gealblath Hospital –'

'Received and understood.' The moustached man clicked off the radio at his shoulder and turned away from the rubbish bins.

The fat officer stepped out of the shop. 'Gealblath Hospital,' he called over to him. 'You get the dispatch?'

'Yeah.'

'Units two to ten. Jesus Christ, how many men do we need to take this bastard down?'

The two of them returned to their cars. Before David even had time to breathe a sigh of relief, the wheels were churning and they were gone. David stood, the sweat clinging to the strands of his beard.

'Gealblath Hospital,' he said to himself. *Gerri must have told them. She must have told them that's where I'm heading, and now that's where they're going. Units two to ten.* David didn't know how many police officers that was. Judging by the cop's reaction, it was probably a lot. But still, he wasn't at the hospital. And neither was Marty. Not yet anyhow.

He took another breath, watching as the moisture from his lungs travelled up towards the full moon. It still hung low amongst the darkened clouds on the horizon. *That was a bullet dodged,* he realised. *No. Not even that. It was a touch of fate.* David didn't normally get those, and he

444

certainly wouldn't be getting many more this night. He was pretty sure they were all but spent.

He straightened the kink in his back, then walked back over to the Shadow. *Okay, shake it off. Back to it. All you have to do now is get back to the cabin. Get back to Marty. If you can do that, then you won't need another touch of fate. It'll be back in your hands, back in your control. All you have to do is get there. That's it. Just get there. And pray that Marty Evans has stuck to the plan.* He grabbed the bike's handlebars and began walking it out of the shadows of the station.

27

THE HOSPITAL AGAIN

'Okay,' said Marty, pulling the grey cotton blanket up towards his nose. 'Let's go.'

The wheels rolled forward, and he leaned back into the torn leather. The reception of the hospital was full, relatively, for a Sunday evening, but that was good. It had to be busy. That way there was less chance the boy in the wheelchair would stand out. He must have been a sight, after all. The blanket covered most of his body. The only part it didn't cover was cunningly hidden behind some dark sunglasses that Teddy had found on one of the seats by the desk. Mike pushed the wheelchair into the nearest corridor. Marty watched as nurses, doctors, and patients bustled past them obliviously.

'Slower,' he said then. 'Mike, go slower. It's gonna look strange.'

'Sorry, yeah. Slower, slower, yeah.'

'Which room is it?' asked Teddy.

Marty felt about in his pocket. 'Room C19. I remember.'

His hand came up against something hard and cold. The keys gave access to every room on that floor, but Marty only needed one. Amee's door. Amee's room, where she would surely be waiting for him. *Please*, he thought to himself. *Please let her be waiting for me*. The chair turned a corner, and Marty spotted the stairs at the end of the corridor.

'Stairs, Mike. Stairs. Over there.'

Passers-by started glancing down at them. Teddy smiled in response. They were beginning to stand out, Marty could tell. Now that they were heading into quieter territory, they were getting noticed.

'Don't smile, you idiot,' Marty hissed. 'Don't look back.'

'Where am I supposed to look?' said Teddy. 'It's alright for you, you've got sunglasses to hide behind.'

'Yes. I have. That's the idea –'

At that moment, a nurse stepped away from a water cooler and turned towards them.

'Oh, hello' she said.

The three of them kept walking, but the nurse followed them.

'What do we do?' Mike whispered. 'Marty, what do we do?'

'Stop,' Marty whispered back.

Mike complied, halting the wheelchair before turning slowly towards the woman.

'Michael, what are you doing here?' the nurse asked. 'You're not getting into any more fights, I hope?'

She came up behind the chair and Mike gave an unconvincing laugh.

'Hello Miss Redford. No. No more fights.'

'It's good to see you looking so well now. How's your mother?'

'My mother is fine, Miss Redford.'

'Oh good. Listen, I heard about that boy. Marty, I think his name was? The one who went missing. I know you were friends with him. I remember he was with you, before it all happened.'

Marty's heart began throbbing into overtime.

Mike cleared his throat. 'Yes, Miss Redford.'

'Are you doing alright? Are you coping? You know this hospital doesn't just patch up cuts and bruises. There's counselling if you need it. If you wanted it, that is. It's there for you. Both of you.'

The nurse beckoned towards Teddy, and Marty squinted up towards his friend. He responded with another one of those big beaming smiles. Marty restrained himself from slamming a palm into his face.

'Who've you got there, by the way?' the nurse asked. She took a step closer to the wheelchair.

'Nobody,' replied Mike.

Marty clenched at the blanket, pulling it back up to cover his nose.

'Well, I can see it's somebody.'

'No, no, it's...'

The nurse came around Marty's right side, so he flopped to the left.

'Hello?' she said unsurely.

'He's sleeping,' said Teddy. 'He can't talk to you because he's sleeping.'

'I gather that. His eyes look swollen behind those glasses. Is he alright?'

'He's fine,' Mike responded a little too quickly.

'Yeah. He's just having an allergic reaction,' said Teddy. 'He ate some yoghurt, and he's allergic to yoghurt.'

'Oh? And what about this cut above his eyebrow?'

'He fell down the stairs. That's why he's in a wheelchair.'

The nurse paused for a second. 'Was that before or after he ate the yoghurt?'

'Before. He fell down the stairs before.'

'Yeah,' Mike confirmed. 'And then he ate the yoghurt to cheer himself up.'

'I see.' The nurse straightened her back again. 'Are the glasses really necessary?'

'He gets embarrassed when his eyes go big.'

'It happens a lot then?'

'Well, he eats a lot of yoghurt. He keeps forgetting. It's a thing.'

Marty slipped further into the chair, fighting against the urge to give the game up right there and then. *Yoghurt. Bloody yoghurt. Where's Mr Cooper when you need him?*

The nurse sighed. 'Boys...'

'Listen,' Mike cut in. 'He's really tired, and we need to take him to his ward. We only went to get some fizzy drinks. His mum's been waiting for a while, and she'll start to worry any minute now. We don't want her to worry.'

Marty opened his eyes half an inch, watching as the nurse bit her lip. Her gaze flickered between his two best friends.

'Alright, fine. Do you know where you're going?'

'Yes,' said Mike confidently.

'And you'll get him back to his mother okay?'

'Without a doubt.'

The nurse smiled, then placed two fingers upon Marty's shoulder. 'Alright then. I'll let you get him back. But remember what I told you, Michael. There's always counselling. Someone to talk to if you're struggling.'

'I'll be sure to do just that.'

Another few seconds passed. Then Marty heard the nurse walking in the other direction.

'You're both idiots,' he muttered.

And even Teddy, who rarely doubted his aptitude to think on his feet, couldn't disagree.

The rest of the journey to Amee's floor was without incident, other than the fact that Mike was close to melting by the time they'd lifted the wheelchair up the last stair.

'Sweet... Jesus... I... thought... everyone called you Weed-kid... they should change your nickname to... "Surprisingly Fucking Heavy"... or... or something.'

To save his friend from an almost certain heart attack, Teddy took over the pushing from that point on. He rushed Marty past rooms C1, C2, C3, on and on and on, until Marty pulled the keys out of his pocket and jumped out of the chair for room C19. Before he could stick the key in the lock, however, Mike grabbed his shoulder.

'Hold on, Marty. What if her mum's still in there?'

Marty turned to look at him. A river of sweat stained his collar, and his chins appeared to have swollen to twice their usual size, but instead of a fierce red, Mike's face was deathly pale.

'Well, we've just gotta hope that she isn't,' Marty replied earnestly. 'This is the hoping part, guys. When the plan ends and there's not much else you can do about it other than hope things go alright.'

'And that normally works, does it?' asked Teddy. 'Just hoping? I mean, is just hoping gonna be enough?'

Marty placed the key into the lock. 'Let's hope so,' he said. Then he pushed on the door to reveal the dimly lit bedroom on the other side.

It looked exactly as Marty remembered. The bed was in the same place, the posters on the wall, the table, the bookshelf, the television in the corner, just as old and broken. Another familiar thing was the dread in Marty's stomach. Because once again, there was someone missing.

'Amee's not here.' Marty stepped slowly into the room. 'How can she not be here?'

Teddy and Mike followed him.

'Why were you so sure she'd be in this room?' asked Teddy.

'Because this is her room. When she was in the hospital, she told me she was hardly ever allowed out, not unless there was a reason.'

'Well, maybe there is a reason.'

'Yeah, that's what I'm scared of. Why isn't she here? Where have they taken her?'

Marty started pacing, his eyes scanning from left to right, searching for something, anything, to give them a hint of Amee's whereabouts. But there was nothing. Just that same old room. Nothing had changed. Not even the sheets on the mattress. He let out a long and hopeless sigh.

'What do we do now?' asked Mike. 'I mean, we can't search the whole hospital for her, can we?'

Marty turned to look at him, and that was when he saw it. A small silver camera fixed where the wall met the ceiling. Its lens was pointed towards the table in the middle of the room.

'What are you looking at?' asked Mike.

'There's a camera here,' said Marty. 'But there weren't any downstairs. Think about it. When we were here a month back, in our own rooms, did you see any then? No. Because they don't have cameras in the rooms. They're not allowed to have cameras in the rooms.'

451

'So what's your point?'

'My point is, there's a camera in this room. This place, this ward, it's different to the rest of the hospital. What they were doing to Amee here, the tests they were doing, maybe they needed to record it.'

'What good does that do us?' asked Mike.

Marty retrieved the keys from his pockets once more. He rifled quickly through the tags. 'That footage has to go somewhere.' His fingers hit upon a thick key with a purple tag which read 'CONTROL ROOM C30'. He lifted it up. 'Here! On this floor! Every hospital has a control room! They're like a surveillance thing, right? I'll bet you anything the tapes from this camera will be in there. If we can find the footage, we can find out what happened to Amee. We can see where they took her.'

'You don't think we should just get out?' asked Mike nervously. 'You know, think things over, maybe come up with a new plan –'

'No.' Marty's response came out fast and blunt. 'We're not leaving. We're finding Amee. Right now. Tonight.'

His two friends took a few seconds. Despite their blatant reluctance, they eventually nodded.

'Fine,' said Mike solemnly. 'Get back in the chair.'

A few minutes later, and the three of them were pacing down the same corridor again. Marty was beneath the blanket, staring through his thick shades as they passed each door. He tried to catch the numbers. C20, C21, C22. He could hear Mike panting behind him, his shoes making funny squeaks against the hard rubber floor. C23, C24, C25. The corridor was still empty. Still silent. C26, C28, C29. The wheels started to pick up even more speed.

'Okay, Mike, slow down.' Marty spoke to him sternly,

but his friend didn't listen. Teddy started to jog next to them. 'Mike, I'm serious, slow down!'

Marty heard Mike's cheeks flubber from behind.

'This... one... it's this... one.'

The next thing Marty knew he was colliding with the wall at the end of the corridor. 'Jesus shite, Mike!'

'Oh... sorry... sorry about that... it's just... I wanted to be quick... it's too quiet.'

Marty looked around the place and immediately understood what he meant. So far, they had met no one on this floor, but that wasn't necessarily a good thing. Everything was too quiet, too still, too easy. It felt like they were being set up for a fall, like those moments of peace before a hard storm hits dust off the road. Marty knew those moments well. He was an expert in them. This felt no different. And that scared him. But there was no time to feel fear now. He pulled the keys from his pocket again.

'Wait,' said Teddy.

'What?' asked Marty.

'Shouldn't we knock first?'

'Given the circumstances, Teddy, I think we can forget our manners.' He placed the key into the lock and turned it.

'But anything could be in there. We don't know what's behind that door.'

'It's a hospital control room, Teddy. It's not MI5 headquarters.'

With a push, the door creaked open, and the room on the other side was revealed. It took a few moments to take it in. The bulbs flickered on, as if automatically, and the walls were steadily illuminated in a soft yellow hue. The room may as well have been the headquarters of MI5. Despite an immediate sense of chaos, the place was in fact immaculately organised. Two tables lined the left and right walls, with dozens of VHS tapes stacked neatly on top of them. Sticky notes had been stuck from folder to folder, with even more travelling up two box-like television monitors, which were perched beside an old projector. The centrepiece of the room was displayed on the far wall, an intricate mass of information cluttered amongst the bricks. Like a crazy detective's wall, there were newspaper clippings, documents, pictures, pins, numbers, maps, great big words written in red, other big words written in blue, drawings, X-rays, birth certificates. It seemed like anything and everything had been placed on there, and all of it revolved around just one thing in the centre. A black-and-white photograph of a girl. Young, blonde, a nice smile, pretty eyes. She stared at Marty, Mike, and Teddy from across the room.

'What the hell?' said Mike.

The three boys stepped inside, and the door swung closed behind them.

'Is this normal for a hospital control room?' asked Teddy.

'Take a guess,' responded Marty.

'No?'

'There you go.'

They came up to the wall and Marty gaped up at it. Along the top were photographs, seven of them in a row, starting with an elderly man and ending with a middle-aged woman. Each one had a pin stuck in the corner, with multiple threads splaying out underneath, connecting every picture to a mass of information. Marty fingered one and followed it down to a newspaper clipping. The word

FRACTURE

was written in blue above it. The column was dated back to the second of June, 1984, with the headline:

MP WARNS OF MORE POWER OUTTAGES
AS HUGE STORM WHIPS COAST:
Locals unimpressed with police efforts amidst worst storm in decades

Marty stared at it for a second, then followed the thread back up to its specific photograph. It was of a young woman, potentially in her twenties. Her hair was dark red, her eyes a pretty hazel. Her teeth were stained somewhat, and her skin was dabbed to death with freckles, some small, some large. Beside the picture were two more sticky notes. One read:

PRIORITY

and the other read:

ASPERGERS

'Who is she?' Mike was standing beside Marty now, his own gaze set firmly on the blonde girl in the middle.

Marty glanced at him, then he turned towards the television in the corner. 'Start looking through those tapes, Mike. Amee's room has to be here somewhere.'

'Yeah.' Mike took a step back, seemingly struggling to take his eyes away from the wall. 'Right, okay, the tapes.'

'Teddy, you keep an ear to the door, see if you can hear anyone coming.'

Teddy nodded. He turned quickly and rushed back to the exit.

'What do you suppose it all means?' asked Mike as he started rifling through the video tapes.

But Marty didn't answer. His gaze had returned to the wall. He reached up towards another thread. This one was connected to an elderly man, potentially in his seventies. He was sitting in an armchair, his arms cradling what looked like a cropped-out baby and his eyes staring just left of the camera. He was dressed in a jumper, rolled up at the sleeves. His skin looked worn and patchy. His hair was all but gone. Once again, there were two sticky notes beside him. One read:

VULNERABLE

and the other read:

ARTIST

Marty followed the connected thread to an X-ray of the human skull. He peered at the words scrawled just beside it:

R. F. D. Blood clot / stroke. L. O. D. Collinson Gardens Care Home

Below was another sticky note, which read:

Fracture still unknown but see thread to 3

Marty scanned about the threads, his eyes finally landing upon a piece of paper which was tagged:

DRAWING 3

The drawing was of a jagged spiral, long, black, and big enough to engulf the entire page. Marty shook his head in confusion.

'Got anything yet, Mike?'

'There aren't any dates, just random numbers.' Mike continued looking, his face almost buried in a mass of VHS tapes now.

Marty tapped his foot impatiently, then his gaze caught something else. He spotted it on the far right of the wall, just underneath a small picture of a house in flames. Another newspaper clipping. This one had a single headline:

CHARLIE COOPER DISAPPEARS:
Search begins as Charlie Cooper, thirteen,
goes missing in seaside town of Gealblath

'Charlie...' muttered Marty. He followed the thread from that clipping, arriving momentarily on another column:

POLICE ADMIT LACK OF RESOURCES
TO FUND SEARCH

Then another:

DETECTIVE PERCIVAL, HEAD OF
COOPER INVESTIGATION, QUITS

Then one more:

SEARCH FOR CHARLIE COOPER OFFICIALLY
DRAWS TO A CLOSE

Then the thread landed finally on one photograph: Amee Florence, her hair that familiar mousy grey, her lips pale and frowning. Beside her picture were two sticky notes. One read:

MOST IMPORTANT

The other read:

LITTLE FISHY

Just beside them there was something else. A sheet of pink paper that read:

CERTIFICATE OF ADOPTION: This is to certify that WINONA NIGHTLY has officially, and by law, adopted AMEE FLORENCE on 19th FEBRUARY 1991.

Marty touched the photograph. 'Adopted...'

'Huh?' said Teddy from the back of the room.

'Amee. It says here... She never told me she was adopted.'

'Here she is!' said Mike suddenly.

Marty turned back towards him. 'You found it?'

'Yeah. Well, no. I gave up and just shoved one in. It had the number seven on it. But I'm pretty sure that's Amee.'

Marty came up beside him. The television was indeed displaying Amee's room in fuzzy black-and-white.

She was sitting at the table, with her mum sitting opposite holding a notebook and pen. *Not her mum*, Marty corrected himself. *Winona Nightly. The woman who adopted her.*

'Open your eyes.' Winona's voice crackled. 'How do you feel?'

'Fine today, Mum.' Amee Florence's voice was small, almost inaudible.

'Did you sleep?'

'Yes.'

'Did you dream?'

Amee nodded. 'The ocean.'

'Why did you dream about the ocean?'

Marty's ears pricked up at the sound of footsteps behind him. He turned to see Teddy peering over his shoulder.

'I don't know why,' Amee responded.

'When you dream about the ocean, are you inside it, or outside? Like a bird, are you looking down? Or are you submerged?'

'Neither. I'm not anywhere. It's just the water. It's like I *am* the ocean, I don't know...'

'What is this?' asked Mike.

Marty shook his head. 'I don't know, but it's not good.'

'What do you mean?'

459

Marty looked back towards the wall, his eyes narrowing in on Amee's picture, the information underneath, the news clippings, the threads.

'She told me they were looking at the dead people. She told me that's what they were doing here. But this...' Marty refocused on the footage. 'What if she was wrong? What if all this time she thought they were examining the dead people, but they were actually examining her?'

The tape continued rolling on, the picture going distorted, then normal, then distorted again, until Winona spoke once more.

'Close your eyes again. Then open them and tell me what you see.'

Amee closed her eyes. Then, after a few seconds, she opened them. She flicked her hair back behind an ear and looked into the corner of the room.

'Just the room, Mum.'

'Amee...'

'It's true.'

Winona hesitated, the pen hovering above the notebook. She twitched slightly, like she was itching to write something down. Then she laid the pen on the table and straightened her back.

'Three days now,' she said impatiently. 'Three days and no dead people. Why is that?'

'I don't know.'

'No, I think you do know. I think you know perfectly well.'

Marty felt a knot begin to tighten in his stomach.

'I've been lenient with you, little fishy. Yesterday. The day before. But three days...' Winona leaned closer. 'You're not seeing them, but it seems to me you're not looking.'

'I am looking.'

'No, I don't think you are. I think you're lying, and you know what happens when you lie to me.'

'No,' said Amee suddenly, the fear immediately evident in her voice. 'Not him. Please, Mum, I don't want him.'

A shiver flooded through Marty's system. He watched as Amee rose up from her chair. Winona rose with her and walked towards the door.

'Just a few minutes,' she said softly. 'Then we'll try again. We'll see if you don't look harder.'

Winona opened the door, closed it, and Amee Florence was left on her own.

'What's happening?' asked Mike, but Marty couldn't answer.

Amee scampered towards the corner and fell into the wall, her hands covering her face. Quite slowly, the door opened again, and a tall man stepped forth to fill the frame. Marty's breath caught in his throat.

'Roman...' he said gravely.

The tall man began walking, a smile spreading across his face. 'Little fishy,' he said excitedly.

Amee Florence started to yell, her screams getting louder, and louder, and louder, until Marty reached forward and stopped the tape. Then there was silence. The three of them stood still, their bodies rooted to the spot and their bones shaking. It took about ten seconds before one of them could even attempt to form words.

Mike shook his head. 'I don't... I don't understand...'

Tears were beginning to swim in Marty's eyes. He felt the anger rise inside him again. The hatred for Roman Guild. The hatred for Winona Nightly. They couldn't get away with this. He and Mr Cooper had to make sure of that. What

461

they had done to Amee, what they had put her through, they would pay for it. Marty pulled himself away from the computer. *It begins with saving her,* he thought. *You know that. It begins with getting Amee out of the hospital.*

'What are we going to do now?' asked Teddy.

And then a ball of ice sank deep into Marty's stomach. Because Teddy was still beside him. He had left the door unmanned, unguarded. He wondered how long Teddy had been there for. He wondered how long they had been watching, their backs to the door, with their ears tuned in to the television. Then, all of a sudden, there was no need to wonder. Because a voice confirmed it for him.

'I can tell you what we're going to do....'

The world shook beneath Marty's feet. It felt like he was dissolving into some kind of nightmare, where the horrors from the tape had merged into his own reality. Winona Nightly was standing in the doorway, her black, frizzy hair illuminated underneath a flickering bulb. She walked forward slowly.

'You're going to step away from the television. And then you're going to explain to me, very simply, what it is you are doing in my hospital.'

28

THE BIG MOON

David brought the bike to a halt. His feet dragged on the wet grass, and he turned his head in search of anyone trailing him. Thankfully, there was no one. There hadn't been a single siren since the petrol station. There had just been the wind, the rumble of the Shadow's engine, and now the silence. It felt good. Silence was usually a curse, making him sink into unwanted thoughts, where Charlie was front and centre. But right now, silence had never sounded sweeter, and David's thoughts were exactly what he needed. Coherency. Rationality. That was the only way he'd survive this town one more time. David jumped up onto the verge and pushed his bike into a gap between two cabins.

'Damn it,' he said as he tried to move the vehicle deeper into the shadows.

The moon was still bright tonight. It was low and overhanging like a nuisance streetlamp, following him wherever he went, trying its best to keep David in the spotlight. *He's here! Gealblath, get your arses in gear! The killer's here! He's on the street!* It felt like nothing was on his side right now, like even the moon itself was attempting to screw him over. But screw the moon, because David had done it. He had made it to the beach, he had got out of the mousetrap. And all he had to do now was get the boat. David felt about in his pocket. The key was still in there; it was still safe. *Okay*, he thought. *So what are you waiting for?*

Despite the pain in his ankles, David walked as fast as he could onto the beach. The adrenaline was still coursing through him. It straightened the veins and numbed the muscles, ensuring that one leg followed swiftly after the other. The walk was contact free, but that didn't ease his fear. It didn't stop David glancing behind himself every two seconds, or curling his fists into balls every time a breath of wind bit against his neck. Every part of him remained on edge, expecting another ambush, anticipating the next fall. It was an instinct; a horrible lingering dread that it wasn't over. He wished he was wrong. He wished the instinct was uncalled for and unwarranted. But, as ever, the depths of David's fears spilled out into his reality, and he stopped as soon as the boathouse came into view.

The ambush came initially in the form of a smell. Distant at first, but then growing and thickening into something more pungent, until it became unmistakable. He slipped into the shadows of one of the nearby cabins and watched as a small dot of amber appeared twenty feet ahead, slowly burning, then not burning, then burning again. The couple were sitting close together, their backs against the very door that David was heading to. *Junkies*, he thought bleakly. The drug-users would often make their way down to Gealblath Beach at this time of year. It was like it was their season. When the beach was cooler and the stones were left untrodden, they would while away their time taking hits and spouting empty words into a void where no one was listening. But David was listening now. His left ear was dipped into the wind, trying desperately to pick something up. But their voices were low. Just vague and distant mumblings in the glowing darkness.

He cursed and tried to think. He could wait, of course. He could wait for them to leave, but that could be hours from now, and every second spent out in the open was just another second waiting to be caught. But then, what option did that leave? Approaching them? Telling them to get lost? He bit his lip, tasting the salt that was already clogging the pores of his skin.

They might not recognise you, he considered then. *It's dark and you look different. Plus they're probably high out of their minds. They might not be able to recognise their own shit. Just go over there and tell them to bugger off. It's only a couple of drugged-out teenagers, after all. It's not the entirety of the Gealblath police force.*

David stalled. No. It was too risky. Too abrupt. He knew he could never have planned for this, but improvising his way out of it felt wrong. Dangerous even. If he wanted to save Amee, he had to –

'Hey!'

The call cut off his train of thought. David looked over at the couple again and saw that one of them was standing. The amber dot of his spliff hovered just underneath his chin. They had seen him. Somehow they had seen him, and now all chances of concocting a new plan had been stolen.

He took a step forward. 'What's the problem, pal?'

'What are you doing skulking in the shadows? Trying to pull a fastie?'

'What if I am?'

The teenager shifted. His features were hard to see in the darkness, but David could just about make out his dark red hair, shaved right up close to the scalp and buzzed to bits around the ears. He swayed on his feet, like there might be something more in his system than just a bit of cannabis.

'You a rozzer?' he asked, his voice cracked and nasal.

The girl stood up along with him. She was smaller than her boyfriend and far rounder at the waist. Her belly button was displayed under her shirt and her lips were smothered with black lipstick.

'No, I'm not a rozzer. I'm not here to pull a fast one either. I'm just a concerned citizen.'

The boy shrugged his bony shoulders. 'We're doing okay.'

'I'm not concerned for you. I got a head's up about some teenagers causing a nuisance. They didn't want to call the police on you, so they called me instead.'

The boy took another drag of his spliff, then passed it to his girlfriend. 'What are you, the patron saint of this beach?'

David straightened his back in an effort to make himself seem taller. 'You could say that, Ginger.'

The girl turned towards her boyfriend. 'Let's go...'

David's heart did a little leap in his chest. *Yes, that's right. Don't stick around to chat with the bald, bearded guy threatening you in the darkness. Use the sensical part of your brain and get the hell out of here.* But the boy stayed put.

'What are you doing around here at this time of night anyway?' he asked. 'You a dealer?'

'Jesus,' replied David. 'You got plant life growing up there in your skull? Let me make it clear, Ginger; either you get off this beach or I'll make you get off it. And trust me, you don't want that.'

The teenager frowned, his hand reaching down towards his pocket. 'You know, I really don't like people calling me names.'

His girlfriend grabbed him. 'Don't, Reggie. Let's just go. It's freezing out here anyway.'

Reggie stopped. His fingers stayed put.

'You got a boner or something?' asked David. 'What is it, you gonna wank off in front of me? I think you should listen to your girlfriend, Reggie. She's a smart girl.'

'Hold on a second,' said Reggie. 'It's you...'

'It's me what?'

'I thought you looked familiar. Look at him, Emma. He's the guy. The guy who stole that kid. The guy who killed his son. I recognise him from all those posters. From the news, all that. Don't you recognise him? Look.'

There was no fear; that was the worst part. The two teenagers now looked at David with a strange sort of admiration, like the weed had taken the edge off, making him more of an experience than a threat.

'Jesus,' he replied unconvincingly, 'what the hell are you kids smoking?'

'It is, isn't it? He looks different, but it's him.' The boy tilted his chin, examining every inch of David's face through the shadows.

'There are two possible answers to that,' David growled back at him. 'One. No, I'm not him, and I'm gonna bend your nose out of shape if you don't back the hell away from me. Two. Yes, I am the kid killer, and I'm going to do a lot more than just bend your nose.'

Reggie grinned, and David saw his teeth: yellow, cracked, and bleeding around the gums. The teenager reached into his tracksuit pocket and removed a short red pocketknife.

He flicked out the blade with a soft press of a crooked thumb.

The girl called Emma gasped. 'Reggie! What the hell are you doing?'

'Yeah, Reggie.' David felt his heart beat in his throat. 'What the hell are you doing?'

'I reckon you're David Cooper.'

'I reckon you're fucking blind.'

'I reckon you're David Cooper, and I reckon there's a juicy price on your head.'

David smirked. 'Are we in a western right now? What is it, you wanna kill me and get your bounty?'

'Oh, I'm not gonna kill you. I'm not like you.'

David swallowed, his eyes flickering down to the knife. It glinted in the glare of the moon. Reggie lifted it to his face.

'But I still reckon there's a price on your head. People want you dead, my man. They want you dead for what you did to that boy.'

For a moment, David considered retaliating. Telling them his story, the truth. But then he stopped. He knew there would be no point trying to convince this guy. If he couldn't get Gerri to believe him, then Reggie would be even more of a lost cause.

'All I would have to do,' said Reggie, 'is give you a stab in the gut and run to the nearest payphone. I'd be a hero.'

Emma tugged a little on his sleeve. 'Reggie...'

'But the thing is,' Reggie continued, 'I don't give a shit about being a hero. Why should I help the rozzers after everything they've done to me and my family? I care more about real rewards. What can you give me in return for us walking away?'

'What?' replied David. 'You wanna rob me or something?'

In a flash, Reggie rushed towards him and pressed the knife up against David's neck. Blood trickled into the threads of his beard.

'SHIT!' Emma screamed.

'You want me to call the police?' Reggie spat at David through gritted teeth. 'I can do that. Like I said, I don't give a fuck! I want what you've got. As much as you've got. I reckon that's fair for what I could do for you.'

The knife pressed hard against David's skin, and every time he breathed, another trickle of blood fell into his beard. Reggie's face was so close that David could smell the weed still lingering on his breath.

'What do you think I have?'

'I don't give a shit what you have. I just care about what I can sell.'

'You fucking junkie.'

'We've all gotta find a way to pay the bills. Emma, help me out here.' Reggie turned towards his girlfriend. 'Take what he's got. I'll make sure he doesn't try anything. Come on, empty your pockets!'

David didn't need to be asked twice. He began to withdraw the contents of his trousers, placing all of them in the waiting hands of Reggie's girlfriend.

'A wallet,' she said softly.

'How much?' asked Reggie.

Emma opened it up and flicked through the notes. 'I don't know, a few hundred?'

David had to stop himself from wincing. *A few hundred. Damn it. You should have treated yourself more in Cornwall.*

Reggie's eyes glanced down to the key in Emma's hand. 'What's the key?'

'Key to the flat,' answered David. 'But it's not just mine; my girlfriend lives there.'

'When's she out?'

'Never, apparently.'

The blade pushed deeper, and David felt another droplet of blood fall from the skin.

'You're still playing smart, even with this blade on your windpipe? Where do you live?'

'Eden Park Lane. Other side of town.'

'And the other?' asked Reggie, looking at the small, chainless key which Emma was inspecting with squinted eyes.

David let out a long and entirely false sigh of despair. 'My motorbike. Honda Shadow.'

Reggie's grin stretched wider. He licked the cracks of his teeth, clearly enjoying the idea of such a hot prize on a cool, autumnal night. 'Where is it?'

'It's beside the cabin,' David stuttered. 'Number twenty-two. Please don't –'

'Shut the hell up. Remember, this is the deal. We take your shit, and you get out of this alive.'

David bowed his head again, trying hard not to crack a small smile of victory. *That's alright, Ginger. You've done me a favour taking the butt-fucker.* But still, David acted distraught. *Make them think they've taken enough. Make them think they're winning.*

'Okay,' he said then. 'So you've got my bike and the key to my house; that's got to be it. What more could you want?'

The teenager jammed his knee into David's groin. 'That's for me to decide.'

'His hand,' said Emma. She was staring down at David's fist, her eyes wide and curious, just as hungry as Reggie's were now. 'What's in his hand?'

470

David had been hoping they wouldn't notice that. He'd been praying they would miss it.

'Why are you clenching like that?' whispered Reggie.

'Sorry, when a druggie's got a knife to your throat, you go a little tense.'

'Open your hand.' The knife pressed harder. 'Open up, or I'll open you up.'

David winced against the blade, then he let out a sort of defeated whimper, his fingers slowly peeling back to reveal the small copper key.

'It's for the boathouse,' said Emma excitedly. 'That's why he's here. That's what he was trying to get into. He wasn't called over here; that's bullshit. He wants to get into the boathouse.'

'Oh, that's too good...' Reggie took the key from David's hand. 'We can get the boys down tomorrow, make them bring the van. I reckon we could get a few hundred from –'

David struck before Reggie could finish the sentence. It was just a small window of opportunity, but as soon as Reggie's gaze turned towards his girlfriend, David reached out for his throat and clutched him hard around the windpipe as his other hand went for the knife. But Reggie was quick, quicker than David had assumed a junkie teenager could be. The blade retracted, then returned, piercing David's abdomen before pushing him backwards into the wood of the boathouse.

'SHIT!'

David heard Emma shriek into the cold night air, and he let out a thick and agonised groan.

'You fucker!' yelled Reggie. 'You think you can mess with me?' Reggie's voice was hoarse, broken up and squeezed by David's hand, which remained tight around his throat. 'Let go,' he told him then.

But David didn't let go.

'Let go, or I push deeper.'

'Fuck...' David breathed desperately.

'LET GO!'

The knife was pushed deeper, eating into David's flesh so hard that it felt like his whole body was screaming.

'Oh fucking hell,' he moaned.

With a shudder, he let go of Reggie's neck, and his knees gave way beneath him. He fell to the ground and Reggie pulled the knife from the wound.

'Jesus!' Emma came up alongside her boyfriend.

'You arsehole.' Reggie kicked David in the gut. 'You wanna kill me like you killed those kids?'

'Leave him now,' Emma yelped. 'Reggie, just leave him.'

'This arsehole wanted to fight back!'

'I know, I saw, but we should go now.'

David pulled his knees up to his chest, curling himself into a pitiful, crumpled ball. Reggie grabbed him by the beard and spat hard onto his face. Emma took Reggie by the arm, pulling him up from the pebbles. He obliged, stepping backwards before stuffing the key into his pocket and pushing the blade of the knife back into its hilt.

'You're lucky my bird's with me. That's not punishment for what you did.'

'We should be quick.' Emma shivered. 'Before someone comes, we should go.'

Reggie nodded. Whispers of clouded breath were steaming from his nose. 'Stay where you are, David Cooper. Bleeding out on the ground is the last decent thing you can do for this town.'

He spat one last time, then he and his girlfriend disappeared into the night.

'Fuck,' David coughed. 'Fucking hell...' He pulled his hand up towards the moon to see the blood dripping down onto his wrist. He watched it for a few moments, trying to filter out the shock. He rolled onto his back and rested against the boathouse. The blood formed a thick circle on the stones.

He stabbed you. That's what happened. The bastard stabbed you, and now you're bleeding out.

David slowly unzipped his jacket and felt around for the wound. It was in his abdomen, just above the hip. He supposed that was both fortunate and unfortunate. Fortunate because another inch to the left and his stomach would have been skewered. Unfortunate because another inch to the right and the blade would have missed him entirely. *He was faster than I thought. And stronger. You moron, why did you fight back?* A blast of salty wind stung his eyes, and he closed them for a moment, trying hard to steady his breaths.

'You're okay,' he whispered. 'You're okay, calm down.' His finger touched the opening, prodding against the flow of blood. *It can't be too bad. The blade can't have gone in that far. You would be screaming if it had. You would be in agony.* But the pain wasn't excruciating. It wasn't overcoming him like other pain had done before. *That could just be the shock. The adrenaline. It could be worse than it feels. You idiot, you could be dying.*

David shook his head, biting down on his tongue. *Either way, you've got to get up. You've got to move. You can't stay here. You've got to get back to the cabin, back to Marty. He's waiting for you. Marty's still waiting for you.* With a deep breath, David pushed himself forward, then fell back, wincing painfully at the sting in his side. *If you stay here, you'll die, David. If not from the wound, then from the cold.*

Come on, get your arse up. Get up, while you've still got the adrenaline.

'Come on...' he muttered. He pushed himself forward onto his feet. *Okay,* he thought to himself. *First part done. Now it's just the step. Just take that first step, and then the rest will come. They will come. I know they'll come. Just do it. Do it, do it, do it.*

'Do it.'

His words came out in small, icy waves, and he watched as they dispersed and dissolved in the silver glow of the moonlit night. Then he started moving.

Five minutes passed before the shock began to recede, and in its place came the pain. It started growing, culminating in taking over the entire right side of his body. It wasn't overbearing, however. It didn't feel like a pain which would kill him or take him out of action. It was just there. A presence that he was having to deal with. A demon he was having to fight. The problem was the blood loss. It was coming out faster now, staining the shirt beneath his jacket. David had to get stitched up before it was too late. Somehow, someway, he had to try to close up the wound without any external help.

How the hell are you going to do that? And even if you can, what then? Where do you go? Your bike is gone, the boat is gone, and there's no way across the shore. You've fucking failed. What the hell are you going to do?

The questions hit him one after the other. None of them were answered, because David couldn't answer them. All he could do was walk, one foot in front of the other, over and over again, until the curve of the beach began to incline and the door of the cabin finally blurred into view. Then David breathed out a long and exhausted sigh, the small victory momentarily relieving the anxiety in his chest. He approached the cabin and wrapped his cold and bloodied hand around the door. It swung open with ease and he stepped inside.

'Marty,' he called out. 'Marty? Are you there?'

He waited for a moment, but there was no reply. There was just the quiet. Nothing other than those old, useless hearts that tapped incessantly upon the walls.

'Marty?' David called out a little louder, and another bout of pain stabbed his abdomen. His eyes began to adjust properly now, the cabin around him becoming clearer, revealing nothing but the furniture inside. 'Oh shit,' he muttered then. 'Oh...' He turned and stepped back out onto the beach. 'Marty?!'

His voice rang out in the cold, empty air. But there was no reply except the echo, distorted by the wind. *No. Please no. Please tell me no.* A slight sweat began to trickle down from his temple, and David squeezed harder against the bleeding wound. *He couldn't have. Surely, he wouldn't have. Please, Marty, tell me you didn't go to the hospital alone.*

But David already knew it. His prayers were in vain. Marty had gone. He had gone to the hospital, he had gone to get Amee, and now the police were going to find him.

'No,' he said to himself. Then he said it louder, and louder, and louder once more, screaming out into the night before falling to his knees in desperation. 'NO!' he roared. 'NO! NO! NO!'

David closed his eyes and held his head, his blood leaving a wet print upon the scalp. There was no way out now, he knew. And Marty was as good as caught. *How could this go so wrong? How could this go so terribly wrong?*

His eyes opened and he stared helplessly at the moon. It was low in the sky still. Where the water would usually reflect it, there was nothing but sand and rock, stretching out towards Derling. David squinted at it. Then, for a moment, it felt like everything inside him stopped. The pain, the frustration, the hopelessness. It all stopped. And David Cooper cocked his head. *How far does the tide go?* He had seen it earlier, but he hadn't looked, hadn't taken it in. But he did now. *How far could it go under that moon? Under that big moon?* David swallowed, sliding both hands down his scalp to place them lightly on the stones. *Didn't it go all the way once? Wasn't that what you told Charlie? Or was that just a dream?*

He shook his head. *What does it matter now? What does it even matter?* But his eyes kept staring, following the beach from the stones, to the sand, and off towards Derling. There was no water in sight. *What was it I said? When everything is in its place? When everything is in its right place?* David pulled himself upright. *Everything,* he thought, peering up towards the moon. *Everything in the right place. And the moon is with you. But it can't be.*

At that moment, a noise erupted from behind him. It started off distant, but soon grew louder, a high-pitched whine that rose and fell in tone, piercing David's eardrums like the knife had pierced his side. He recognised the sound immediately, but he didn't turn. He didn't look for the source, because he knew what it was already. The dark world around him began growing lighter, the stones beneath his feet illuminated with blue and red, blue and red, blue and red. Wheels screeched beside the beach and David felt tears begin to sting the corners of his eyes.

'Over...' he said to the moon. 'I'm sorry, it's over now. I'm beaten. I'm done.'

Another harsh gust of wind whipped up the salt from the stones, and David dipped his head, both hands rising up into the air as he waited for the siren to stop.

29

WINONA'S DEAD WARD

'I... we... what...'

Mike spoke first, but the words were simply warm air. They came without purpose, without intention, and they lingered in the room like a bad punchline. Winona Nightly was waiting patiently by the door. She looked different to the last time Marty had seen her. She looked thinner, and her cheeks were gaunt. She looked like she hadn't slept in weeks.

'I'll ask again,' she said quietly. 'What are you doing in my hospital?'

'I... it's just... we're not...' Mike tried again, but this time Marty helped him finish.

'We're here to find Amee.' He took a step forward, into the light. 'We're here to save her.'

'Marty,' said Mrs Nightly slowly, like she was only just recognising him. 'Marty Evans.'

'Yes,' he replied.

Winona straightened her back. 'Save her from who?'

'Save her from you.'

He heard Mike gasp, but Marty ignored him. There was no use in lying now. Lies couldn't help them. Only the truth was left. And Marty was going to use it.

'We're going to save Amee before you hurt her.'

'Hurt her...' Winona repeated slowly.

'I know you. I know the sort of person you are, and Roman too. You're bad people; you're dangerous.'

Marty tried to keep his voice from shaking, but it was hard. His entire body seemed to be trembling now. The floor felt like it was swaying beneath his feet, just waiting for him to crumble, but he held firm.

'Where is Roman?' asked Winona.

'He's gone,' said Marty. 'And that coil too. He tried to kill us. Me and Mr Cooper.'

'I should never have left him alone with you.'

'You're just as bad. You let someone like him be alone with Amee. You used him as a punishment, I saw.'

Winona began to approach. Her eyes flashed underneath the deep-yellow lights.

'Marty,' she said again. She stopped in front of him and reached out. For a moment, it looked like she was about to slap him, but she didn't. Instead, she cupped his bruised cheek. 'I'm sorry this happened to you. I'm sorry any of this happened. Truly, I am.'

Marty pushed her hand away. 'You're not sorry. You're only sorry we got away. You gave Amee to him, I saw. I saw on the tape. You gave Amee to him, and you left him alone with her.'

'You think you know me? You think you know what we do here?'

'No. But I know Roman. I know the sort of person he is. What he did to Amee...' He trailed off, trying desperately to form the right words. 'It's no wonder she was so afraid.'

Winona bit her lip slightly. She turned on her heel and stepped towards the television. Marty watched as she bent over and poked the play button on the VCR player. Amee's yells pierced the room again. They surged about the walls so loud it was a wonder the paper notes and news clippings didn't fall from their pins.

'Watch,' said Winona.

'I turned it off because I didn't want to watch.'

'Watch.'

The screams continued. The three boys looked over at the tape, watching the tall man loom over Amee with that wide and sickening smile. Marty swallowed, wanting to turn away, to look around and never look back, but before he could, something on the tape made him stop. Instead of approaching Amee, Roman Guild reached out for one of the chairs beside the table and sat down. He stayed there, retrieving that large antique lighter from his pocket and using it to light up a cigarette.

'NO!' Amee screamed, but Roman Guild did nothing. 'STOP! STOP IT! STOP IT NOW! MUM, MAKE HIM STOP! COME BACK AND MAKE HIM STOP!'

The tall man leaned forward, the smile still plastered on his face, his chest rising and falling, faster and faster, as if the girl's scream was the most invigorating thing he'd ever heard. Then, after about a minute, the door opened and Winona Nightly stepped back into the frame.

'Okay,' she said firmly. 'That should be enough.'

Amee Florence stopped screaming. Roman Guild stubbed out his cigarette.

'Enough, little fishy,' he said teasingly. 'Enough for now.'

There was a click and the tape crumbled into static. Marty, Mike, and Teddy were left in confused silence.

'He never touched her,' Winona said quietly. 'You think I would let him touch her?'

She waited for a reply, but nothing came. Marty didn't know how to respond to what he'd just seen. He didn't understand it. *He must have touched her*, he thought. *She's lying, you idiot. Of course she's lying. Forget the tape. She is who she is, you know that. You know who she is. Don't let her fool you.*

Winona squinted, as if she could read what Marty was thinking. She reached into her jacket pocket and pulled out a burgundy notebook. It was messy, with paper hanging out in places and just a single black band to hold it all together. She held it out towards him.

'This, Marty, this is Amee. This is what she has done for me. Every lesson. Every dead person we have traced and examined. Hundreds of them. All that work. You think I would hurt her, after she's given me this? Not once have I hurt her. Not once have I allowed her to be hurt. You and that teacher want to turn this into something it's not. You took her away from me, do you understand that? You and David Cooper took Amee away from her home, and you want to blame me for what's happened to her?'

'How can a hospital be a home?' questioned Teddy.

'It's not a home,' said Marty. 'What you're doing here is wrong, all of it's wrong. It's not normal. We didn't take her away; she wanted to go. She still does.'

'Wrong?' Winona repeated the word, making it sound harsh and sharp upon the tongue. She put the notebook back into her jacket. 'Have you ever lost someone? Someone you cared about? Someone you loved?'

'What are you talking about?'

Winona fixed her eyes onto the picture of the blonde girl

in the centre of the wall. 'She was just eight years old.'

'Who was?'

'Grace. It was a Volkswagen Beetle that did it. Bright yellow. She was just outside the house, looking for the birds. She liked to wait for them to come to the feeder. She'd chase them and see if she could catch one, but she never could.' Winona walked over towards the girl in the picture and traced her cheek with her finger. 'This particular morning, she chased one too far. I only saw the blur. The blur and the sound of the engine. And my story isn't like the others, Marty. I don't go in the ambulance, go to the hospital. I don't sit by her bedside, hold her hand, pray that she pulls through. I don't do that, because she gets hit hard. She gets hit so hard that I see the police picking skull fragments from the cracks in the tarmac.'

Tears started to swamp Winona's eyes now, flooding the fire that had been there before, quenching it.

'*That* is wrong, Marty. What happened to my girl was wrong. And I've spent the rest of my life wanting justice. But it was an accident. She ran out onto the road herself. It was her fault. It was her mistake. What justice is there in the world for a thing like that?' Winona looked Marty right in the eyes. 'I can tell you. Justice. From the world. That's what I deserve. That's what we both deserve. The world needs to give us justice for what happened, and I know that it can.'

'Is that why you adopted her?' asked Marty. 'Amee, I mean. Because you knew what she could do?'

His gaze glided over to the adoption paper, and then another photograph just beside it caught his eye. A grainy image of a middle-aged man. Slightly sinister looking, with a long, crooked nose and dark shadows underneath his eyes. Marty recognised him as Roman Guild. Beside him was a thread leading to a newspaper clipping.

TWO DEAD IN QUARRY STABBING:
Suspect caught in the early hours as police chief reassures public of their safety

'They could all help me,' said Winona. 'Amee most of all. But it was her choice. It was all their choice. I didn't force any of them to do this.'

Her lip began to tremble a bit, but she held it firm. Marty could tell she was trying to recover from her moment of vulnerability, like it had been a defect, like it was something to fix and put right.

'I was there for them like no one else was. I understood what they could do. I cherished it. I loved it. And in return, they could help me find my daughter. They could help me save her.'

Marty glanced between Teddy and Mike, trying to ascertain whether they had just heard the same thing. Judging by their reaction, they had.

'What do you mean, save her?' he asked.

Winona peered down at him coldly. 'Marty, you don't need to know what we're doing here. What I want you to know is why we're doing it, where it all starts. It starts with her, with Grace, an innocent girl who was taken away. What we're doing here is not wrong. What we're doing here is trying to make things right.'

'Why are you telling me this?'

'Because I want you to understand that I'm not a bad person. And because I want you to have a choice. Leave Amee and me alone. Here in the hospital. Knowing that what we're doing is good. Or continue in your efforts to take her away from me. And understand that by doing so, you're stopping me from being reunited with my daughter.'

The hum of the bulbs above their heads began to get louder, the lamps inside the room growing strained. Marty took a deep breath and clenched his fists.

'Where is Amee?' he asked.

The words came out quiet, but strong, and that was good. Marty wanted them to be strong. He needed them to be strong. Mike and Teddy turned to look at him, their eyes glistening with fear.

'I want you to think about this, Marty,' said Winona. 'I really want you to think. I'm giving you a choice. This isn't just about you; this is about your friends too. The consequences will fall onto them as well, make no mistake. Your answer to this is important.'

Marty stiffened. 'Where is Amee?' he repeated.

'You really want to know?'

'Where is –'

'The theatre.'

Marty faltered, staring at Winona in confusion.

'Do you understand now?' she continued. 'That's what you've made me do, in order to ensure she can never run away again. There was no choice anymore. She was past having a choice. But I'm giving you a choice. You can leave here or –'

'You won't just let us go,' said Marty. 'You want to use the coil on us. You want to make us forget.'

'The coil –'

'The coil is gone. It went with Roman. You won't be able to use it on us, so what happens then? You're gonna just let us walk? You're actually gonna do that?'

Winona curled her lip. 'Making you forget. You think that would have been bad? You think you've escaped some kind of horror? I don't think you understand. The coil wasn't

483

my evil. That was my grace. My mercy. Without it, keeping people quiet requires a far more severe intervention.' Winona reached her bony fingers into her jacket and pulled out a long silver syringe.

'What the hell?' Teddy gasped.

'Just a small dose.' Winona took a step forward. 'That's all it would take.'

'All it would take for what?' asked Marty.

'To ensure that no one would believe your story. And why would they, when you won't even believe it yourself?'

Marty stared at the needle, his heart beating faster and faster within his chest, urging him to surrender, pleading with him to simply hold up his hands and admit he was beaten.

'You won't die,' Winona continued softly. 'I want you to understand that. None of you would be the boys you are now, but you would have a life. That's more than my daughter could have if I allow you to get in the way.'

'Marty...' Mike's meek voice arose from beside him.

Marty turned, but just as he did so, Winona Nightly struck. With a furious roar, she grabbed Marty by the shoulders and pushed his neck into her chest.

'SHIT!' Teddy grabbed Marty's arm and tried to pull him back.

Winona screamed. 'DON'T TOUCH HIM! DON'T TRY TO TOUCH HIM!' She pushed Teddy away and then pressed the needle hard against Marty's skin. 'I gave you a choice! There's nothing else I can do, Marty, you've got to know that. There's nothing else.'

Mike and Teddy yelled out in unison. 'NO!'

The needle shook, wavered, but then it stopped. Something quiet but loud came from the other side of the door. Voices at the other end of the corridor.

'I don't understand. Do you think we're harbouring him or –'

'We've just been told to search the hospital.'

'Do you have a warrant? Surely you need a warrant to search this place. Not even us nurses are allowed to come up here...'

The voices trailed off into the distance as if they were moving away. Before they disappeared completely, however, Marty screamed at the top of his lungs.

'HELP! I'M MARTY EVANS! HELP ME! HELP ME! POLICE! I'M MARTY EVANS!'

Winona pressed the needle tight against Marty's skin. 'NO!'

Teddy jumped forward and clasped his hands around her neck. He pulled her down so hard that her head gave a sickly *kathump!* when she hit the floor. The burgundy notebook slipped out from underneath her jacket.

Marty twisted from her grip and Mike bent to pick up the needle.

'Stay down,' he squealed, brandishing it towards Winona as if it was a weapon. 'Don't move or I'll needle you!'

Marty looked frantically about the room. 'Teddy!' He grabbed his friend and pushed him towards the floor. 'The notebook!'

'What about it?'

'Winona's notebook, grab it!'

Teddy reached over and stuffed the notebook quickly under one arm. 'Okay! Now what?'

'Now run!'

Without a second thought, the three of them sprinted fast towards the door, Winona screaming after them.

'STOP!'

With a cry of relief and fear, they pulled the door open and rushed into the harsh white light of the corridor. Marty blinked against it, his lungs panting and his head spinning. He went to grab the keys from his pocket.

'Marty Evans!'

A voice called out, and the boys turned to spot three uniformed officers staring at them about twenty paces away.

'Oh,' Mike muttered.

They watched as one of the officers slowly reached for his radio. KRRCHH! The radio flicked on, and Marty sprang back into action.

'Run!' he screamed again, hightailing it in the opposite direction.

'HEY!' one of the officers shouted. 'HEY! WAIT! STOP!'

'This way!' Marty charged down the stairwell, descending so quickly that he wasn't sure he touched any of the steps at all.

'Where are we going?' yelled Mike.

But Marty didn't answer. He had no idea where they were going. All he knew was that they had to keep running. They had to be fast, faster than they'd ever been in their lives. He hit the floor for Ward B, ran out of the stairwell and sprinted towards the nearest door he could find.

'In here!' he called out, and his two friends fell into the room with him. Marty pulled the door shut.

'Oh shit! Oh shit! Oh shit!' Teddy panted.

'Calm down.'

'OH SHIT!'

Marty grabbed the burgundy notebook from under Teddy's arm and stuffed it into the waistband of his trousers. Every part of him was on fire. His ribs felt like they had been stabbed with hot glass, and the pus inside his blisters felt like boiling water. He tried to ignore it all, but it was hard. It felt like at any second he could just curl into a ball and cry. He took a moment and tried to stay on top of things.

'Did that really just happen?!' asked Mike dazedly.

'Yes,' said Marty bluntly.

He scanned about the room to see whether they were alone or not. They weren't. An elderly woman was sitting up in bed, a pressure pad wrapped around her arm and a small drip attached to the top of her hand. She gaped at the newcomers.

'Are you my visitors?'

'Uh, yeah, I suppose, for a bit.' Marty turned back to the door, opened it a little, and watched through the crack as the police began to file along the corridor.

'How many are there?' asked Teddy.

Marty craned his neck, attempting in vain to count the number of officers on the other side. He gave up after seven and closed the door again.

'No idea.'

'Why did they come? How did they know we were here?'

'I don't care. I don't wanna care. All I care about is how we're going to find Amee.'

'Where is she?'

'The theatre. That's what Winona said. She's in the theatre.'

The elderly woman spoke up. 'Oh, just my luck. I've been due to go to the theatre for three weeks. I can't tell you how many times I've been pushed back. If I have to eat one more grape or do one more crossword, I swear I'll replace this darned hip myself.'

Marty tried to tune her out, but Teddy didn't.

'Sorry, lady, when you say the theatre, do you mean like the West End?'

Mike gave an irritated moan. 'No, Teddy. She means the operation room. That's what a theatre is.'

'Operation room?' Marty repeated.

'Yeah,' said Mike.

Another kerfuffle of boots and radio transmissions sounded from behind the door, and for some reason Marty ducked down, his gaze now fixed on the elderly woman.

'Do you know where this theatre is?' he asked frantically.

'Ground floor, I believe. Do you need to go there yourself? You look awfully hurt.'

Marty shoved his ear against the wood of the door, listening as the muffled radio communications grew distant.

'Then that's where we need to go,' he said firmly.

'We can't,' said Mike. 'There's a thousand police officers outside that door. We can't just walk right up to them. You're gonna get us caught, or even worse, bring us back to that woman.'

Teddy raised a hand, as if he was asking a question in a school classroom. 'Hey, you guys?'

'We're in a messed-up situation,' Mike continued. 'There's no way to get Amee out, and you've got to accept that. I think we should go.'

Marty felt a spike of anger begin to bubble along with the pain. 'You want to just give up on her?'

'I'm not giving up on her. I'm just being realistic.'

'Hey, guys?' Teddy called out again, but Marty was too angry to acknowledge him.

'She's in the operation theatre, Mike. That's the reality right now. The reality is, she's in there, and we're the only ones who can get her out before –'

BRRIIIINNNNNNGGGGG!

The bell cut him off, and Marty turned to see Teddy with one elbow lodged through the safety glass of a fire alarm.

'WHAT IN THE WORLD?' the elderly woman yelled over the noise.

'Teddy, what did you...?' Marty trailed off, hearing shouts and shrieks on the other side of the door. He opened it and watched as people started running.

Teddy shouted over the ruckus. 'I'm sorry, was that stupid?'

Marty shouted back. 'Teddy, that was actually the smartest thing you've ever done.'

'What on earth are you playing at?!' the woman yelled.

'Don't worry,' Teddy reassured her. 'There's no fire.'

Marty watched as the last of the officers vacated the corridor. All that was left were the doctors and nurses, all of whom were in the process of evacuating patients, their backs turned and their attention diverted.

'Okay, guys,' Marty turned back towards Mike and Teddy. 'It's now or never.'

Mike opened his mouth again, that glint of fear still deep set within his eyes. 'But I... I...'

'Can do it,' Marty finished for him. 'I know you can, Mike. You're scared, I get that, but that doesn't mean you're going to leave. You wouldn't even if I asked you. And you know that.'

There was a moment. Mike shivered, straightened, and nodded his head. 'Okay,' he said quietly.

'Is anyone going to tell me what in God's good name is going on?!' the elderly woman shouted.

Teddy turned towards her. 'Sorry, we're saving a girl with supernatural powers from her evil mum so she can help dead people get into heaven, or something like that. It should free up the theatre for you.' He gave the elderly woman a sympathetic smile, and Marty grabbed him by the arm.

'Let's go!'

And then they were running again. By the time they got to the ground floor, the hospital was full of activity. Doctors and nurses pushed wheelchairs and beds while the fire alarm blared loudly above their heads. They worked fast, but there was an order to the evacuation. An order that ensured a raging fire could not divert their focus, let alone three boys slipping along the sidelines.

'Operating theatre,' Marty murmured to himself as they hid beside one of the vending machines.

'Anyone got any cash?' asked Teddy.

Marty ignored him. Another burst of doctors bustled past them, and Mike pointed towards some double doors at the end of the hallway.

'There!'

Above the doors, the words 'OPERATING ROOM' were plastered in big bold letters. The three of them jumped up again and shoved their way through the crowd and towards the entrance. To Marty's relief, the doors weren't locked. The hinges swung open, allowing him, Mike, and Teddy to step inside. To get to the theatre itself, there was a contamination corridor, this one empty, which led them all the way to a large, dark room with a sharp smell of antiseptic. Marty pulled the doors closed behind him.

'Jesus,' panted Mike. 'This is more running than I've done in my whole life.'

Marty stared. Despite the darkness, he saw a large leather bed in the centre, beside which stood a trolley full of medical tools. Around the walls there were counters, each one stacked with equipment, tubes, bandages, plastic tubs, and cardboard boxes. But there was no Amee. For a second, Marty felt his heart sink into his stomach, but before it could get all the way down, Teddy called out behind him.

'Over there,' he said.

'Where?' Marty replied frantically, but he saw it just as soon as he'd asked the question. On the other side of the room, a pale-blue curtain was camouflaged against the blue walls. 'Nice spot, Teddy!'

'And you thought I was the stupid one.'

'Well, you distinguished a curtain from a wall,' said Mike. 'I wouldn't say you're out of the woods yet.'

Marty rushed to the curtain and held out a hand to pull it back. He could feel the bones inside shaking, trembling each finger like a thousand volts of electricity was spreading through the veins, and he knew why. This was it now. The final shot. If Amee wasn't behind this curtain, he had no idea what they'd do next.

'Okay,' he said, and then he grabbed the fabric and tugged it.

The new girl was lying asleep in bed on the other side. She was flat on her back, attached to a drip which was taped to her left hand. One pyjama leg was rolled to the knee, and Marty saw a circle of X's etched around her shin. He leaned down and cupped her head.

'Amee? Amee, can you hear me?'

She didn't budge.

'If the alarm didn't wake her up...' Mike started, but then he stopped.

Without warning, the ringing above them cut out. A high-pitched tone replaced it for a few moments, and then there was silence.

'They know there's no fire.' Marty glanced over at the door, then back at Amee. 'They'll be looking for us now. We have to get out of here as quickly as we can. Mike, help me with this.' He started tearing back the tape from Amee's hand, pressing his finger hard on the tube.

'What are you doing?' asked Mike, his voice beginning to shake again.

'Taking out the drip. Go see if there's any bandages in here.'

Mike scanned the room, then ran to one of the boxes on the counter. He came back with a long roll of wound dressing. 'This will work, right?'

'Fine. Now all you have to do is wrap that around her hand when I take out the needle. Otherwise, she's gonna bleed everywhere.'

Marty clutched Amee's wrist in one hand and the cannula in the other.

'Is there actually gonna be blood?' asked Mike. 'It's just, blood isn't really my thing.'

Marty ignored him. 'You ready?'

'Uh, yeah, sure.'

With one swift motion, Marty yanked the drip away from Amee's flesh. He stepped aside and let Mike wrap the dressing around her hand.

'I did it!' he exclaimed. 'I did it – you see that, guys? I did it – I – SHIT!'

In a split-second, his relief transitioned into terror. Amee lunged up and grabbed his wrist, causing Mike to pull away and tumble backwards. Her eyes flickered open, then shut, then open once more, her head lifting slowly as she took in the room around her.

'Mum,' she mumbled, and then she focused on Marty. 'Is this a dream?'

Mike climbed back to his feet, his face as white as the sheet on the bed.

'Amee.' Marty clasped her hand. 'It's me.'

'You're a dream?'

'No, Amee, I'm not a dream. We're gonna save you, Amee. Do you understand? We're here to save you.'

Amee's eyes shut again, and for a moment, it looked like she had drifted back to sleep.

'She won't walk,' said Teddy.

'No,' Marty agreed. 'We'll have to push the bed.'

He pulled on the bed and rolled it away from the curtains.

'Have you gone mad?' said Mike. 'We can't just march her through reception. What about all the cops?'

'I'm not gonna march her anywhere.' Marty came up alongside a box of medical equipment. He reached inside, pulled out some surgical masks, and threw two of them over towards Mike and Teddy. 'Here, put these on.'

'Masks?' Mike gaped at him. 'That's your plan? Masks?'

'You got a better one?'

'Marty.' The name came out of Amee's mouth quietly, almost like it was just another breath. Her eyes were open, but they swayed in her skull and she blinked groggily, fighting unconsciousness.

Marty held her hand again. 'What is it?'

'Ambulance. In the station. There's a way out.' Her words were mumbled, but clear enough for everyone to get the picture.

'She wants us to take an ambulance?' asked Mike.

'At the back of the hospital,' replied Marty. 'If we can find an ambulance, we could get out of here without being seen. Amee, that's –'

'Completely stupid,' Mike finished for him. 'Unless we all suddenly know how to drive.'

'I've driven *Crazy Taxi*,' said Teddy confidently.

'Shit,' replied Mike. 'I forgot that's how you get a driving licence.'

'Well, no, but it's good practice though.'

Marty looked into Amee's eyes. 'Do you know the way?' he asked.

Amee nodded. She reached out and prodded Marty on the cheek, a deep frown settling across her face. 'What happened to you, Marty?'

Marty gave her a comforting smile. 'Don't worry about it.'

'So what if she knows the way?' Mike protested. 'We can't just leave. There are police around every corner, and Winona, she's still out there!'

'No...' Amee cut him off, pushing herself up the bed until her head was resting against the rails.

'No? What do you mean, no?'

'It doesn't have to be that way. I can help. If I can see, I can help.'

There was a brief silence. Amee closed her eyes again.

'What does she mean?' asked Teddy. 'Is it dead people, Marty? Is she seeing dead people?'

'Trying to see them,' Amee replied. 'If I can see them, then we don't have to leave this room blind. They can guide me and I can guide you. If I just...' Amee opened her eyes, staring into nothing. 'I just need to see them, but it's hard.'

'Okay,' said Marty. 'Just try, Amee. All you can do is try.'

Mike spluttered. 'But even if we can get to the ambulance, what happens after that?'

Marty stood upright, pulling his mask over his mouth and nose. He took hold of the bed posts again. 'How many levels did you get through on *Crazy Taxi*, Teddy?'

'You're joking...'

'I dunno,' replied Teddy. 'Two? Maybe three? I'm pretty sure I hit a wall after that.'

Mike groaned in despair. 'Please don't hit any walls.'

'That's good enough,' replied Marty.

'Good enough?!'

'It'll have to be. Like I said, Mike. This is the hoping part.'

A second passed. Mike looked between Teddy, Marty, and finally Amee. 'Oh Jesus Christ,' he muttered.

His forehead was dripping with sweat, but it wasn't from fear anymore. It was everything else. The situation around them, the question of how he had gone from painting warriors in his bedroom to being here in this hospital, fighting Amee's mum and evading seemingly hundreds of cops. Marty knew because Marty had experienced it before. It was that change, that sudden change before a recognisable life became an unrecognisable one. The shock to the system, the adrenaline, the dread. The urge to shut it all down and awaken from a wild and ridiculous dream. But there was no awakening, because it was real. And you could either adjust and survive or sink into dark, wet quicksand. Mike wasn't sinking now, at least. None of them were sinking. And in a few minutes, this could all be over. It could all be done. Marty smiled reassuringly at his friends from behind his mask. Amee blinked and then looked at him.

'I can see them,' she said.

And for a moment, it looked as if her eyes had turned a lighter shade of blue.

30

ACROSS THE SILVER ROAD

It was Monday and the morning fog was just starting to clear, revealing the mark that the night's storm had left upon Gealblath's streets. From one road alone you could tell. Instead of the usual greys, blacks, and blues, there were deep greys, dark blacks, and bright blues. They glistened in the morning like the rain had given the town a cleansing scrub. It did that sometimes, David considered, as he stared out of the upstairs window. Sometimes a storm could reverse the years of a cracked and pale postbox. If it was powerful enough, and if the rain hit long, and hard, and kept focused, sometimes a storm could rejuvenate a whole town. Perhaps that was why there was such a calm immediately after. When everything started again, renewed and reborn. The morning after was like a first breath of new life. A moment, just before the day, when everything was back to where it had begun. And everything felt good.

David took a drag on his cigarette. This morning did feel good. But then, mornings tended to after a night with Natasha. She was lying in the bed behind him, her soft and knotted brown hair resting on the feather pillow. Her left breast was just about visible in the gap between the duvet and the sheets. She was breathing heavily, sleeping. David took a long look at her. It was funny, in a way. With her eyes closed, she looked just like his wife. The brown hair, the curved body, the slightly tanned skin. It was only when she opened her eyes, and the green shone through the irises, that the difference was easy to discern. He took another drag in contemplation, then he shook his head and turned away. It wasn't a thing he liked to think about. Especially in the morning, after the deed was done. It wasn't a thing he understood. But then, perhaps that was why he didn't like to think about it. In some strange way, being unable to comprehend something made it far easier to rationalise, simply because it made it irrational. When things were irrational, they were impulsive, and David always followed his impulses. He didn't have many, anyhow. Especially in married life, when things were so mundane and routine; he had to cling to the few impulses he had in order to survive the life he'd been dealt. Natasha was one of the few. Natasha was survival, in every respect. Gorgeous, familiar, dangerous, and most of all beautifully irrational.

David turned back towards the window to continue his admiration of the storm's work. They were on the edge of Gealblath, on a street called Berwick's Place. Natasha's best friend had owned The Sea Cabin for seven years before she had run out of money, and since then, the inn had become an empty block on a quiet corner. An empty block that Natasha had a spare key to. In a way, it felt like David was sat in his own little bubble, hovering above the world and looking down, without taking part. People were beginning to line the streets now, with jacket sleeves rolled up to their elbows, enjoying the September air as if the storm hadn't just marked the finite end to 1988's long summer. He watched them with a scowl, then the sheets rustled behind him.

'Hmm...' Natasha opened her eyes to the dark and dusty room.

'Hmm...?' David mumbled back.

Natasha frowned, as she usually frowned in the mornings, like the night before had been in its own separate realm, where consequences didn't exist and life was just another bad story in the back of a distracted head. Natasha pushed herself up on the mattress.

'When did the storm stop?' she asked, her throat dry and hoarse.

David peered at the clock. The hour hand was just starting to hover above the number seven. 'A couple of hours ago. Give or take.'

'You were awake?'

'Mmhm.'

'Did you sleep?'

David tilted on the chair, bending over slightly to press his cigarette into the ashtray. He watched as the last embers of light flared, then fizzled and burned themselves into something grey.

'Mostly,' he replied.

He joined her in bed again, taking another packet of cigarettes from his nightstand before slipping one onto her lips. He lit it and she breathed out a plume in thanks.

'God must be angry,' said Natasha.

'Hmm?'

'The storm. God must be angry at someone, don't you think?'

David lit another for himself. 'I think it got humid.'

'I don't think so. I think a storm like that is God's work. Like he's punishing someone. That's what my dad told me when I was small.'

David shrugged. 'Well, if God's punishment is a few extra inches of rainwater in the gutter, tell him I'll miss another sermon.'

'You're missing the point,' said Natasha, scolding him, but David knew the point just fine.

Natasha wasn't quite like him. Her reasons for adultery were less cut and dry, more askew. She was very religious, almost to the point of delusion. More importantly though, she had a husband, whom she loved, and she had three kids. Amelia, the eldest, age fifteen. Max, her middle child, who was twelve. And then Archie, a mistake, but a happy one, turning three in November. Natasha would give them the world. And she did, everyday, which was more than David could say for him and his family. But every now and then there would be these moments, these falls from grace, where Natasha would ring David and invite him to The Sea Cabin. Then they would spend a night entangled in a life of their own, out of breath and out of their minds, until the morning came and regret fuelled the absence of pleasure once more. Natasha, unlike David, would agonise in her attempt to work it out. She would think about it until the thinking started to hurt, and then she would start anew. But she would never find an answer. And three weeks later, she'd be calling him again. Her weakness was a circle, sewing back over itself, the same end always in sight and the same regret always destined to repeat.

'Don't you think about punishment sometimes?' Natasha rested her head on David's shoulder. 'True punishment?'

'I don't think about those things,' replied David honestly. 'You don't need to be punished. Neither of us needs to be punished.' He took another drag of his cigarette, feeling the pulse from a vein in Natasha's neck thump lightly against his shoulder.

'How's your son?' she asked him then.

David frowned at the question. 'Don't,' he responded.

'I'm just asking. I want to know how he is.'

'And I don't want to talk about him. I don't want to talk about any of them.'

'But I just –'

Natasha went to say something, but before she could finish, David leaned up and pressed himself into her cheek. He kissed her vigorously before moving down to her jaw, and then her neck, until she opened her mouth and spoke once more.

'Max got onto the football team.'

David pulled away. 'What?'

'Max got onto the football team. He's playing left wing. That's what he wanted.'

'Natasha, I just said –'

'What? So we can't talk about our families?'

'Why do you want to talk about them?'

'I don't know. I just thought you might be interested. I thought you might want to know something about my life.'

David gave a sigh of exasperation. 'You don't need to talk about that now. You don't need to think about them.'

Natasha pushed herself up the mattress and pulled the sheets to cover her breasts. She looked at David like that was the worst thing he could ever say. 'Can you hear yourself sometimes?'

'What?'

'Are you telling me you don't feel wrong about this? About any of this? What we're doing, you don't...' She faltered, flicking her burnt-out cigarette onto the floorboards beside the wall. 'You don't go home at night and cry about it?'

David shook his head. 'I don't torture myself.'

'Well, I do,' said Natasha. 'I do all the time.'

'So why do you keep calling?'

Natasha looked at him, her tears beginning to draw a silky white curtain over the green of her eyes. 'Don't ask me that, David. Don't. It's not fair.'

David stubbed out his own cigarette, then began kissing her neck again. 'I'm sorry,' he whispered.

'Stop,' she said faintly, pulling her head away from him.

But David didn't stop. He slipped a nicotine-stained palm under the sheets and squeezed her right tit.

'David, stop...'

'What are you doing today?'

'Why do you care?'

David kept rubbing, his fingers dipping slightly under the breast. He felt the sweaty moisture from the night before. 'We can stay in bed a little longer.'

'You've got school.'

'No, I don't have anything when I'm with you.' David pressed his lips up against a freckle on her shoulder. 'Everything else can go to hell.'

'You can't...'

'I can.' He squeezed her breast again. Then, in one fluid motion, he sprang from the sheets and lay down on top of her. He pressed his lips down hard on her neck and her breaths started to get heavier and longer, until her heartbeat began to vibrate beneath his chest.

501

'I just worry,' she whispered sadly.

'So stop.'

'True punishment,' Natasha continued, dipping her head back to stare up at the cracks in the ceiling. 'How long would it last? For pushing a family aside, how hard would it be? Can a debt like that be crossed, do you think? Can you get to the other side of it? Or does it wash you away like that storm outside? And if it does, can you sew up your wounds before you meet God's judgement?'

'Natasha.' David lifted himself up again. 'Stop...'

'These mistakes of ours are wounds,' she mumbled. 'They're cuts in the soul. I can feel them.' She rubbed at her chest, her lip trembling a bit. 'I just want to know whether they can be healed.'

'We're not wounded. And you haven't pushed anyone aside.'

'No...' Natasha responded. Her voice was shaking now, every word quivering on the tongue, perhaps out of arousal, or perhaps out of fear. 'It's not like I'm absent. I'm there for them when they need me. I'm still their mother.'

'You see?' David replied.

'A mother's what I have to be. A mother's all I have to be.' Natasha nodded at her own words.

'Yes,' said David nonchalantly.

Outside, the world continued to wake up. Cars started busying the streets, people talked louder and faster, about the storm, or about something else entirely.

'Do you want another cigarette?' asked Natasha.

'No,' replied David. 'I want you to go down on me.'

Natasha took that in, and for a moment, David wondered if she might scold him again. But then she smiled, and with two fingers, she pinched him slightly on the arm.

'Oh, you're bad,' she said as she turned David around and placed her thighs on either side of him. 'You're so bad. How can I resist someone who's so bad?'

Natasha began mirroring David's actions, kissing quickly down his skin as if their conversation hadn't just happened, like she'd lost all regret and had been overcome by a sort of wild greed. She bit his abdomen, and David squirmed.

'Too hard?' she asked.

'Just a bit,' said David.

'I'm sorry.'

She dipped lower and filled her mouth in apology, sending a flush of wetness and warmth up and down every nerve in David's body. He smiled. Then he raised his arms above his head, his eyes closing as he collapsed into every inch of it.

* * *

'Come on then...'

David Cooper stood with his back to the vehicle, his teeth chattering from the wind, the pain, the adrenaline. He was still bleeding, he could tell. The blood rushed from his abdomen, dripping steadily down his clothes and onto the rocks beneath his feet. His hands were halfway above his head, and when he looked at them, he could see blood illuminated in blue, then red, then blue again. The high-pitched siren pierced his ears. David spoke once more.

'Come on then...' The words had become weaker, resigned. David hated their taste in his mouth. 'Come on...'

The moon still hung low in the sky, lighting the path that led all the way to Derling. It meant nothing to David now. The white beams bounced off a wave-less ocean, painting the sand, turning it into a silver road which led to safety, and yet a silver road which was now entirely blocked. David was too late. His only road now was to a prison cell, dark grey, windowless, and quiet enough to let him contemplate how everything had gone so badly wrong.

'Do it!' shouted David, feeling his eyes start to well up. 'Come on, do it, just do it, you fuckers. Get it over with.'

There was a noise. A car door opened, and the siren cut out.

'Mr Cooper?'

The voice was quiet, young sounding, and David turned to see Marty leaning out of an ambulance door. He lowered his hands, gaping in shock.

'What the hell? Marty? What are you doing here?'

'Don't panic, Mr Cooper. Everything's under control.'

Another kid spoke up from behind the windscreen. 'I did it! I actually did it! Mike, did you see that? I did it!'

The driver's door burst open, and David saw a lanky teenager bouncing up and down in front of the wheel. A fatter, Asian kid was scrunched up into a ball beside him.

'You can look now, Mike,' the lanky one said happily. 'It's over now. We didn't crash!'

'I'm not looking.'

'Mr Cooper...' Marty jumped out of the ambulance, his busted-up face illuminated by the red and blue flashing lights. He was staring at David's abdomen. 'Is that blood? What happened?'

'You tell me. What the fuck is going on?'

The lanky kid hopped down from the driver's seat. 'You swear?'

'Huh?'

'That's weird. I've never heard a teacher swear before. Hello, sir!'

He held out a hand. David glared at him.

'Marty, would you mind telling me who the fuck this is?'

'That's Teddy. Teddy Kowalski. Don't shake his hand. It's best to ignore him.'

Teddy's hand was still poised for the shake, but David didn't take it. Instead, he grabbed Marty by his bruised and bony shoulders.

'Marty, I'm being serious. What is –'

'We did it!' the fat kid cried out. His hands were now hovering on either side of his face. 'I can't believe it; we actually did it!'

'*I* did it,' Teddy corrected him. 'I told you those games of *Crazy Taxi* would pay off.'

Marty pulled himself away and walked across the pebbles to the back of the vehicle. 'I don't think we were followed,' he said. 'At least, I'm pretty sure we weren't.'

'You were supposed to be looking behind us,' Teddy told him.

'No, that was Mike.'

'Mike, were we followed?'

Mike jumped down onto the beach. 'I have no idea. I wasn't looking.'

'Are you kidding me?'

'What? I was scared. Your driving wasn't exactly the most calming experience.'

'Marty.' David came around the ambulance. 'You've got to tell me what the hell is going on, and you've got to tell me now.'

With an impatient sigh, Marty Evans pulled open the back door of the ambulance and revealed the bed inside. A young, pale girl was lying asleep in its sheets. It only took a second before David recognised who she was.

'We went to the hospital,' said Marty. 'We went to save her.'

'That wasn't the plan.'

'There wasn't time for the plan. If we had waited any longer, we would've been too late, and I'm not even fucking sorry.'

David went to say something back. But then he stopped. Because he realised he wasn't sorry either. 'What happened to her?' he asked as Marty climbed into the ambulance.

'She's just weak,' he said. 'What happened to you?'

'The plan didn't work out.'

David pressed his hand against the wound, tightening the skin as it started to throb harder. It needed to be tended to quickly, he could tell. It needed to be closed before the pain overcame him and sent him into a long and black sleep.

'It looks painful,' said Marty.

'It's fine,' David lied. 'It just needs to be stitched, that's all.'

Marty let out a little laugh, and David frowned at him. 'What's funny?'

'Well, it's lucky for you we're here then, isn't it? Maybe you *should* shake Teddy's hand.'

Marty's two friends appeared around the corner.

'What do you mean, lucky?' asked David.

'Well, listen, I don't know what happened on your end of the plan. But I guess it's lucky that Teddy's just parked a huge first-aid kit on your doorstep, isn't it?'

Teddy held out his hand to David again. 'Hello, sir,' he repeated with a smile.

A burst of wind crept up from behind them, and David looked out into the darkness, the hairs on the back of his neck standing on end. He could have sworn there was another siren resting somewhere in that wind. Any minute now, a police car would be swerving down that road. Any minute now, he could be back in the town's grasp, in the depths of defeat. With a deep and painful breath, he jumped up into the back of the ambulance.

'What are you doing?' asked Marty.

David picked up a suture kit and began rifling through the contents. 'You don't think you were followed, but we need to act like you were.'

'How d'you mean? You got the boat?'

David pulled out some dressing and placed it on his wound, biting off a few inches of tape before sticking it down to stem the blood. He swung the kit around his shoulder and turned towards the sleeping girl. 'Don't have the boat,' he said. 'But we don't need it. The tide should be low enough.'

'Low enough?' asked Marty. 'What do you mean, low enough? Low enough to swim?'

'Low enough to walk. The moon's taken the tide out all the way. If we're quick enough, and if we're lucky enough, we could get to Derling before the water comes back.'

'That's crazy.'

'You got another idea?'

David stared at Marty, and Marty stared back at him. His jaw shuddered up and down as he attempted to form an answer. Nothing came except another gust of wind, which blew loudly into the back of the ambulance, carrying – David could have sworn – that same high-pitched siren.

'What about you?' asked Marty, glancing once more at the blood above David's waist.

'I'll be fine once we get to the other side.'

David placed a hand on Amee's shoulder and gave her a heavy shake.

'She won't get up,' said Marty. 'Getting out of the hospital took everything out of her. She's been like that ever since we got to the ambulance.'

'Okay. I'll carry her.'

'Carry her?'

David leaned over and picked Amee up in his arms, lifting her over his shoulder while simultaneously trying to ignore another huge bout of pain.

'But Mr Cooper, you can't –'

'I can sew myself up once we cross. That's all we need to do now, Marty. But we need to be quick. We need to be fast.'

David turned and jumped out of the ambulance.

'What about us?' Mike questioned, looking up at David expectantly.

'Yeah,' said Teddy. 'We're coming too, right?'

'Wrong. There's no way I'm putting two more children in danger. You've got families to think about.'

'But we –'

'He's right.' Marty climbed down from the vehicle. 'You've done enough. You've helped save Amee. That's more than I could have asked for.'

'But we can help,' Teddy urged him.

'No,' said Marty. 'You can't.'

'Actually, you can,' David realised out loud. 'If the police find the ambulance here, then it's not gonna be hard for them to guess where we went. We need to move it.'

'Hold on.' Teddy's mouth popped open in disbelief. 'Are you telling us to drive this thing out of here? You? A teacher?'

'A teacher and currently Gealblath's most wanted. Yes, I'm telling you. Come on, you can't be that far off your first driving lesson anyway. What is it? One year? Two?'

'Four.'

'Okay, well, consider this early practice. You don't have to go far, just away from the beach. And go slowly.'

'Remember, it's not actually *Crazy Taxi*,' said Marty.

'Oh, don't worry about that,' replied Teddy. 'I'm miles better at this. I think I suit the real thing better, when you don't have to keep collecting coins and stuff.'

David turned towards the sea, pulling on Amee's thighs to balance her properly on his shoulder. 'Okay, Marty. We've got to go.'

But Marty lingered. The three boys stood in silence for a few seconds.

'So I guess this is goodbye?' said Mike.

'Yeah,' said Marty. 'I guess it is.'

'At least we know you're coming back this time.'

Mike held out a hand, but instead of taking it, Marty pulled his friends into a big, tight hug.

'I'm coming back,' he told them confidently. 'I don't know when, but I'm coming back. In the meantime, this is another section you can file in the bro code.'

'What section?' asked Mike

Marty let go, smiling at them. 'Being there when you're asked to be. Staying even when you're afraid.'

Mike shook his head. 'I'll file it under "not leaving your friends for a girl". You're still not very good at that.'

'I'll get better.'

David turned his gaze up towards the moon. It was touching the horizon now. The last freckles of its white light were scattered vaguely about the sand, which was splayed out in front of them like the ugly spine of an ominous, sleeping beast. He swallowed as he stared at it.

'Marty…'

And Marty nodded. With a deep breath, he turned away from Mike and Teddy and came up alongside David.

'Are you sure we can actually cross this thing?' he asked.

'No. But we can try. That's all we can do.'

Marty gave his friends one last look and held his hand up in a salute. Then the two of them stepped onto the first mound of sand and David heard the water squelch beneath his feet.

* * *

Simon Le Bon was crooning at David when he finally stopped. The voice was coming out of the Thorntons' open window, reciting lines about saving prayers and morning-afters as if he was giving some kind of musical sermon. David tried to block it out. He cut off the Shadow's engine, yanked up his visor, and stared across the wide, windswept street.

A police car was parked just beside his house, swerved aggressively onto his driveway. Vanessa was standing on the doorstep. Her soft brown hair was fluttering in the wind, and a cigarette was held tightly between her teeth. She took it out when she spotted him. Then, with a last breath of smoke, she flicked it onto the grass and walked back inside.

'Okay,' David said to himself, feeling his heart begin to thump hard in his chest. He trod solemnly towards the house.

Two officers were waiting for him there. One was plump, with blonde hair. The other was tall, and just about old enough to be on the wrong side of good looking. They stared at David awkwardly as he unzipped his leather jacket.

'David Cooper, I believe?' the tall one said.

David observed his face, wondering briefly if he was the kind of person he didn't like the look of. His features were handsome, but he'd kind of let himself go. His chin sagged, his stubble was unkempt, and there were bags under his eyes. It was a shame, because a face like that should have been well-kept. A face like that should have been cherished.

'Yeah,' David responded.

'Do you mind sitting down?' the officer asked, and he gestured towards the sofa where Vanessa was sitting.

No, David decided then. *I don't like the look of this one.* He took a few seconds, then stepped into the lounge and sat beside his wife.

'What's going on?' he asked.

'Your son didn't make it into school today. We've been trying to call you on the school's number, seeing as that's where Mrs Cooper said you'd be.'

'Where the hell have you been?' Vanessa glared at David with furious eyes.

'I've been sick,' he lied. 'I didn't make it to school.'

'Your wife said you were at the range yesterday evening,' said the blonde officer. 'Were you with a friend?'

'Yeah.'

'And this friend can vouch for you?'

David nodded. 'Of course.'

'Good.' The tall officer took out a small notepad and started to scribble something down onto the paper. 'That's good; that helps us.'

'Helps you with what?'

'With the search for your son.'

'What? He's actually gone missing or something?'

'He didn't make it into school this morning. He left for the bus, but he never got on it.'

511

Vanessa let out a slight moan. She cupped her head with her hands. 'I should have gone with him,' she cried. 'He's so young. Why didn't I just walk with him?'

'It's not your fault, Mrs Cooper. There's no reason –'

'The bus?' David interrupted. He glared at the tall officer. 'What's your name again?'

'Alfie,' the officer replied. 'Alfie Percival.'

David turned and pointed out of the window. 'The bus stops on this street, Alfie. The stop is literally at the bottom of it. You're telling me he got lost on his own street? The kid's thirteen; he's not three.'

Alfie eyeballed him. 'We don't think he got lost.'

'So what? What do you think –'

'Oh, use your head David,' Vanessa hissed at him. 'They think someone's taken him. They think someone's taken our boy; that's why he's missing.'

'Bullshit. There's no way that happened.'

The two officers glanced at each other.

'What do you mean by that?' asked the blonde one. 'What do you mean, there's no way?'

'You're telling me someone took him on this street? You don't think he just ran away? Every kid bunks off school every once in a while. Why is this any different?'

'Because it's Charlie,' said Vanessa. 'Charlie wouldn't do that.'

'How do you know?'

'Because he's our son. Jesus Christ, David, do you even know him?'

There was a pause. The blonde officer shuffled uncomfortably, his mud-caked boots staining the yellow carpet.

'You said you were ill, sir?' he asked.

'Yes.'

'You don't look ill,' Vanessa snapped through gritted teeth.

'No, I'm pretty sure it's flu. Not leprosy.' David glared at her, then looked up towards Alfie, watching as he flicked over another page in his pad. 'Hey, job's worth. What are you writing there, *War and Peace*?'

Alfie flicked David a small smile. 'Just a few notes. Helps me remember. Your friend, what did you say his name was?'

'What, are you running low on characters? It's Ethan. Ethan Reed. He's a colleague of mine.'

'And he'll definitely tell us you were with him last night?'

'Is my word not good enough?'

'Mr Cooper, if everyone's word was good enough in a missing person investigation, then no one would ever stay missing.'

'Jesus,' David responded scornfully. 'Missing person investigation. Can you guys hear yourselves?'

Vanessa stood and turned to the two officers. 'Is that everything?' she asked.

'Sure,' replied Alfie, keeping his eyes fixed on David. 'We'll be in touch as soon as we get anything. In the meantime, it's best to stay here. We'll have officers around in about an hour.'

'He's skiving, for shit's sake,' said David. 'He's a thirteen-year-old boy. It's only been a few hours and already Starsky and Hutch are on my doorstep – give me a bloody break.'

Alfie closed his pad, then stuffed it into the upper pocket of his coat. 'We're just doing our duty, sir,' he said.

And with that, the two officers exited the house, leaving David and Vanessa alone and in silence. Vanessa swayed a bit on the carpet, her breaths small, uncontrolled. She was just a second away from breaking down completely, David could tell. He stood up himself.

'Jesus...'

'Where were you last night?' asked Vanessa.

The words came out quiet, but they had a weight to them which lingered in the room. Outside, the police car began to rumble, and David turned to watch it cruise past the window.

'Jesus,' he said again.

Then he walked into the kitchen.

* * *

The big moon shimmered off the waves. The salt water was biting David's wound now, causing him to bite hard on his tongue in response. He didn't know why. It didn't cancel anything out, it didn't stem the agony, all it did was add another bout of pain on top. A different pain to rival the old one, for a little while, until his tongue started to get numb and the old pain took control once again. Amee wasn't folded over his shoulder anymore. The waves were too high, and so David held her up to his chest like he was holding a baby. By this point, it felt like her weight had tripled, but David kept going. The lights of Derling were getting closer, flickering in the breeze like a beacon beckoning them home, and David was sure they would get there. Any moment, or any minute, they would find the shore, and they would have made the crossing. They just had to keep going. They just had to be strong.

Marty moaned from alongside him, the water now kissing his collarbone. 'Jesus...'

'Not far now, Marty. It's not far.'

'We won't get there.'

'Are you swimming?'

'No, but –'

'Then you're alright. We're both alright, Marty. We're fine. Just a bit longer. Just hold on for a bit longer.'

Marty took a breath. David could tell that he wanted to turn around and make his way back towards Gealblath, but he didn't. Instead, he looked at David, and found a similar resolve.

'Okay,' he said. And the two of them kept going.

It took them another twenty minutes before they reached Derling. The waves crashed hard on the beach, frothing all the way up to a thick wall of crumbled sandstone. Beyond was a steep forest that seemed to go on for miles, climbing so high into the sky that it left shadows on the moonlit water. David and Marty walked through those shadows and their legs buckled underneath them as they made it onto the sand.

'We did it,' panted Marty. 'We actually did it.'

David let out a pained groan in response, laying Amee down on her back. Marty kneeled beside her immediately.

'Is she okay?' he asked.

'She'll be fine. We need to keep her warm. Get wood and make a fire.'

Marty nodded. 'Are *you* okay?'

But David didn't answer. He grabbed his stab wound, then pulled the suture kit from his shoulder, removing some supplies before walking back over towards the waves.

He'd never sewn himself up before. He'd never had to. The last thing David had stitched was an emblem onto his shirt, back when he was a kid playing orcs and warriors with his best friend, Kevvy. That wasn't exactly good experience, but it was experience all the same, he supposed. David sat and dabbed the needle into the waves of the rising tide. The moon was even lower now, but it was bright enough to see the wound, a small 'V' shape on the left side of his abdomen. The blood flow had been mostly stemmed by the bandage. The skin beside it was softened and wrinkled by the salt. David held a shaking needle over it. Then, quite slowly, he pushed the needle into the upper layer of flesh and threaded it into the bottom. *Okay*, he thought. *The pain's okay. The pain's not too bad.* He bit his tongue, taking another breath before pushing the needle through and going again. He was just starting to believe he was getting the hang of it when a voice spoke up from behind him.

'Does it hurt?'

David stabbed the needle into an entirely irrelevant patch of skin. 'SHIT!' he hissed.

'What's wrong? Is it that bad?'

'It wasn't.'

With some effort, Marty sat down and pointed up the beach. 'Fire's going,' he said. 'Not sure for how long. The wood's a bit damp.'

David placed the needle back over the wound and pressed it down again, his eyes flickering briefly towards Gealblath. It was strange to see the place from here, he thought. Like Derling had been for so many years, the town was just lights now, with the huge power plant chimney just a vague silhouette in the middle.

'I can't believe we actually crossed,' said Marty. 'I mean, I heard people had done it before. Like there was that story of a cricket game back in the sixties. But I thought that's all it was. A story.'

'Cricket game?' said David. 'That *is* a story. But who says some stories can't be true, right? I guess the moon is just with us.'

516

'The moon and you.'

'What do you mean?'

'Well, the moon can clear the road, but you're the one who took it. You're the one who got us here. Thank you, Mr Cooper.'

David shuffled uncomfortably. 'I'm just doing what I can. Or what I should.'

'Yeah, that's why I'm thanking you.'

There was a moment then, short and quiet, with nothing but the waves to soundtrack the night. Then Marty spoke once more.

'What happened back there?'

David's finger slipped slightly on the thread, but he regrouped and closed up another half-inch of flesh. 'Oh, I ran into some trouble. And half of Gealblath's police force. Turns out walking into town as Gealblath's most wanted wasn't the best idea after all.'

'Whose idea was that?'

'Some total ass. Wait till I get my hands on him.' David winced, his fingers covered in blood. 'What about you? What happened out there?'

'I saw Winona,' said Marty quietly.

'Winona?'

'Amee's mother. Her adoptive mother.'

David hesitated for a second, looking back towards Amee, who was lying peacefully beside the fire. 'I didn't know she was adopted.'

'Neither did I,' said Marty. 'She never told me. I think there are a lot of things she's not told me.'

A wave landed upon David's lap. They were getting bigger now. They would continue to do so as the night went on. Brick by brick, the wall between Derling and Gealblath would re-form, until an ocean separated them once more. David leaned over and peeled some seaweed from his heel.

'So what happened?' he asked.

'She tried to talk to me. She tried to talk me out of saving Amee, talk me out of all of this. It was like she was pleading. There's this girl...'

'Girl?'

'Her daughter, I think. The thing is, it's not just Amee and Roman. Winona has more patients in that hospital, patients who can see dead people. And she's using them to find her daughter. I think that's what this whole thing is about.'

David took that in for a second, pushing the needle through the last inch of flesh. 'But that doesn't make sense...'

'What do you mean?'

'If she's doing all of this to find her daughter, then what were she and Roman doing in Cornwall? Why would they go there? What makes Alfie a part of this?'

Marty looked out to sea, squinting at the blurry lights of the faraway chimney. 'I think they're interested in Charlie,' he said. 'When we got into the hospital, we found this room. Winona's room. And there was this wall. You know those walls that cops have in the movies, with all that information which kind of connects together? Well, she has a wall like that. And there was this girl, this old guy, and Roman, and Amee was there too. I saw what Winona had connected to her...'

'What?' asked David.

'Charlie,' replied Marty. 'The case. There were newspaper headlines, clippings, articles that dated back to his disappearance. And each one of them led back to Amee.'

David tilted his head, removing his hand from the wound. It remained clamped shut. No blood. No tear. 'But...' he said randomly, only he couldn't finish the sentence.

'It's like I said, Mr Cooper,' said Marty. 'I think there are a lot of things she hasn't told us.'

A gust of wind kicked up the water around them, and out of the corner of David's eye, he saw Amee lift her head in the flickering light of the growing flames.

* * *

Four p.m. and the sun was entirely covered now. The clouds lingered in the sky like dark smoke, discharging wisps of rain as if to threaten a new storm. Bigger this time, and longer, like it might overcome Gealblath entirely and never relent. David Cooper stood in the kitchen and watched it gather from the nearest window.

'We can't stay in this house,' said Vanessa from behind him. Her hands were shaking violently around a large coffee mug.

'We were told to,' replied David. 'So that's what we have to do.'

'You can stay in this house?'

'Yes.' David turned and watched as Vanessa stared at the kitchen tiles, then up at him, her face just about as dark as the world outside. 'You look tired,' he told her.

'No shit.'

'You should get some rest.'

'How do you expect me to do that?'

David took the coffee mug from her and set it down, taking both of her hands in his.

'An hour. Or two, if you can manage it. Standing here torturing yourself isn't going to do you any good; you know that. You need to lie down. I'll be here if the police come back and I can tell you if they've found anything.'

A single tear escaped Vanessa's eyes. She sank into his arms, her head trembling against his chest.

'Where is he, David?' she moaned. 'Where is our son?'

'They'll find him,' David assured her. 'I promise, they'll find him.'

He leaned forward and kissed the top of her head with dry lips. Then he waited a moment and pulled himself away. Vanessa took a few breaths. After a few seconds, she turned and began walking down the hall towards the stairs.

David watched her go, his ears pricked up as her weary footsteps creaked up the stairs one by one. He took a breath himself and then marched towards the telephone beside the fridge.

'Come on,' he whispered as he dialled a memorised number. 'Come on, please.'

'Hello?' Ethan's voice crackled over the line after just two rings.

'Ethan, it's David. Listen, the police haven't talked to you yet, have they?'

'What? No, pal. Andrew just told me your son didn't make it in today. I'm really –'

'Okay, I need you to do something for me. They're gonna ask if I was with you last night, and you need to tell them that I was.'

'You met with Natasha?' he asked.

'Yeah,' replied David. 'I need you to do me this favour.'

'Shit. I kind of wish you'd told me.'

The floorboards above David creaked as Vanessa crossed the bedroom.

'Why do you say that?' he asked.

'Juliet came round last night. We had dinner at Hamish's.'

The words came out distorted and muffled, but David heard them. He thumped his head painfully on the wall. *No. Please. Don't. Don't tell me that.*

'I'm sorry, David, I can't say you were with me. I can't do that. I was with so many people. If the police ask me, I wouldn't be able to –'

'Thank you.'

David slapped the phone back down onto the hook, a wash of panic and anxiety gnawing its way into his gut. This was bad. This was really bad. He paced into the centre of the kitchen, then back again, trying to work out what he was going to do next. If Charlie didn't come home, then David knew this investigation would get real. The police would be searching for suspects and David had already told them a lie. A terrible lie that would be discovered as easily as it had left his mouth. Once Alfie discovered that, then he would come back, and he would ask David the same question. He couldn't lie again. This time they would need an answer.

David clenched his fists into balls before turning on his heel and heading over to the phone once more. This time it was Natasha waiting for him on the other end, her two-year-old kid shrieking beyond the fuzz of the line.

'Hello?'

'Natasha, it's David.'

'David, I told you not to call me here –'

'Listen, there's been… Something bad has happened.' David stumbled over his words, trying desperately to form the events of the day into a sentence. 'Charlie's gone,' he said eventually.

'What do you mean, Charlie's gone?'

'My son, Charlie. He left for school this morning, but he never got there. He's gone.'

'You mean he's missing?'

David leaned his back up against the fridge and closed his eyes for second. He was still trying to adjust to the situation. None of it had sunk in yet. The whole day just felt like a blur, a kind of terrible dream that had crept out of the dark and overtaken his reality. He wiped at his face and nodded.

'He's gone. Yes.'

'Oh shit. David, that's...'

Her two-year old's happy cries twisted suddenly into wails, cutting Natasha off before she could finish the sentence.

'Shh, shh, shh,' she whispered. 'Shh, shh, shh.'

'Natasha, they asked where I was last night. The police. They wanted to know where I was.'

'Oh shit.'

'I told them I was with Ethan. But I hadn't... I didn't... Ethan went out last night.'

There was a pause. David was left with nothing but the child's cries, shrieking over and over, until Natasha spoke again. Her voice was hard and cold as ice.

'Are you joking me?'

'I know.'

'You told me it was okay. You told me you had already talked to Ethan, that he could cover for you if anyone asked, like you normally do –'

'Yeah, well, I didn't.'

David listened as Natasha appeared to yank on the cable and pace across the room. The whines of her toddler grew ever more incessant as she did so.

'You reckless arsehole. Why not? Why didn't you –'

'I just didn't, alright? That's not the point. The point is that he can't vouch for me now. They'll go to him. They'll know I was lying. And if Charlie's not found, which...' David trailed off, peering out towards the sky. The world outside was continuing to darken, the day was getting closer to night. 'If he's not found soon, they'll come back. They'll ask me again.'

'No,' said Natasha, as if she knew what was coming. 'No, David, don't...'

'Natasha, I have to tell them.'

'No, you don't.'

'I've lied to them once already, and I don't have any other place to turn. You know how these officers are. If they can't find Charlie, they'll wonder why I lied. They'll start looking at me. I don't have any other choice –'

'I'll tell them you're lying.'

David heard Natasha's breaths crackling through the speaker, and he shuffled his feet on the tiles, twirling a finger nervously around the cable.

'What?' he said shakily.

'You can't do this to me, David. I have a husband. I have a family. I'll tell the police you're lying. I swear, if you do this, I'll tell them you're lying.'

'Natasha, this isn't about us. This is about Charlie. This is about my –'

'YOU'RE NOT TAKING MY FAMILY AWAY FROM ME!'

David jolted against the wall as Natasha yelled at the top of her lungs.

'I WON'T LET YOU DO IT! YOU THINK I WOULD JUST GO ALONG WITH THIS?! I'LL TELL THEM YOU'RE LYING, DAVID! I'LL TELL THEM YOU'RE A FUCKING LIAR!'

Natasha's child began to wail even louder, the cries piercing David's ear like a razor blade was being driven deep into his skull.

523

'Natasha,' he tried to say. 'Calm down, I'm telling you, I –'

'YOU'RE A FUCKING LIAR! YOU'RE A FUCKING LIAR! DON'T CALL ME AGAIN!'

'Natasha –'

But before David could finish, the phone line cut out, and there was nothing but a low, electronic hum in response. David listened to it. His heart began beating faster in his chest and the kitchen around him fell into a weird kind of blur.

'No,' he said quietly. 'No, shit, no...' He dragged his hands across his head, every inch of his body feeling like it was about to cave in, like the world was pressing him down into a black hole of panic and anxiety.

'NO!' David picked up the phone and slammed it down on the cradle, spit flying onto the wall as he roared: 'NO! NO! BITCH! FUCKING BITCH!'

'What's going on?'

David turned to find his wife standing beside the stairs, her hand clutching the banister.

'Is it Charlie?' she asked. 'Is it something about Charlie?'

David swayed on the spot, his mouth opening, then closing, attempting to form some sort of response. But he couldn't do it. Without thinking, David walked out of the kitchen and towards the front door.

'Where are you going?' Vanessa cried. 'David, what's happened?'

But David didn't answer. He stepped out onto the rain-sodden porch, then he slammed the door and began running.

* * *

The fire roared brightly and David squinted into the depths of it. The side of his body was throbbing harder than ever before. Every stitch felt like a saber-tooth that had been jammed deep into his abdomen. He winced at the spasms, but he kept quiet, because Amee Florence was awake. And she was talking.

'I don't know,' she said faintly. Her head was resting against the sandstone and her hands shivering violently on the sand. The wind had died down now. The waves were calmer, the air warmer. But still, she shivered. 'There's a whole part of me that's been missing for a long time, and now it's waking up. She made me think she was my mum, when she wasn't. She made me think I'd been in the hospital my whole life, but I hadn't. I feel like I... It feels like my head is burning up...'

'You don't know why they would be looking at Charlie?' asked David. 'You don't know why you're connected?'

Amee sniffed, staring at him in the light of the fire. She shook her head, and David sighed.

'The important thing is, you're out,' said Marty. He was sat beside Amee, a hand clenched to her shoulder. 'You're away from her; you're safe.'

Amee shook her head again. 'We won't be safe. Not while she's still looking for us. And she won't stop. She'll never stop.'

There was a silence. The waves rolled up the beach smoothly, the moon now a vague sketch behind the clouds. The dim red lights of Gealblath's shoreline flickered almost as frequently as the fire beside them. David inhaled its smoke.

'What about you?' he asked. 'Are you feeling better yet?'

'Still sick,' said Amee.

David knelt forward and placed his hand on her forehead.

She flinched, but not too badly. 'Your temperature's not high. That's good. We'll keep the fire going, keep you warm until the morning. You should be okay by then. It's probably just the anaesthetic.'

Amee looked back at him with a frown. She turned towards Marty, her eyes wide and confused, as if she couldn't quite understand what had just happened. Marty appeared to agree.

'I know,' he said.

'What about you, Marty?' asked David.

'Me? Oh, I'm fine. I mean, it feels like my insides are gonna explode and my face is about to fall off, but other than that, I'm fine.'

'Good. Like I said, let's keep you warm and I'm sure you'll feel better in the morning.'

'Thanks for the kind thoughts, sir.'

'No problem.'

'What was she going to do to me?' asked Amee suddenly.

David clutched his side and reclined back down onto the sand. 'Don't think about it,' he told her.

But Amee's face appeared to crack, like a wave of emotion had crumbled the foundations and sent her tumbling into despair. 'I hated her. I hated her, but she was my mum. I feel like I've lost someone. She was my mum, but...'

'But she wasn't,' David finished for her. He leaned forward, catching Amee's gaze through the fire. Her tears looked silver in the moonlight. 'Amee, how far does your memory go back?'

'I remember the orphanage. My friend, Tabby. And my caregiver.'

'Do you remember anything before? Do you remember your real parents?'

At that moment, Marty began rummaging around his waistband.

'It's... it's hard to remember. Sometimes the memories just return. Other times there's a trigger, like a place, or a book, and then a whole day of memories. Or a whole week, or a month. They just sort of appear in my head like a hallway of doors. Some of them are open, and some of them are closed. I just –'

'Bernard Hill Community Orphanage.'

David turned to see Marty holding what looked like a burgundy notebook. It was soaking wet, dripping. David recognised it as the notebook that belonged to Winona Nightly.

'Your first lesson,' Marty continued. 'Winona described you before you started. Amee Florence, mousy hair, white skin, blue eyes. Found at the approximate age of eleven years old in Eden Park Lane. Date of birth unknown, previous residence unknown –'

'Give me that.' David leaned over and snatched the notebook from Marty.

'I took it from Winona in the hospital. She said it had everything about Amee in it, so I thought it might say something –'

'That can't be right.'

'What do you mean it can't be right? I was there. I heard her say it –'

'I'm not talking to you, Marty. I'm talking to Amee. Eden Park Lane. That can't be right.'

David stared at the new girl, watching as her hair blew in the wind, landing in front of her left eye. She didn't respond.

'That's where she was found,' Marty answered for her.

'You were found on this street and sent to the orphanage. Is that what happened?'

Amee shook her head. 'I don't know.'

'Can you remember?'

'Why are you asking her this?' said Marty.

'Eden Park Lane. That's my street. My home. Or it was once.' David held the notebook up to Amee, the pages just inches from being burned by the fire. 'The street where you were found is the same street where Charlie went missing. The street he disappeared on ten years ago.'

Amee stared back at David darkly.

'Is that something you remember?' he asked.

And another silver tear fell down her cheek.

* * *

'CHARLIE!'

The road had fallen dark, and David sprinted across it, without any awareness of what was in front or behind, to one side or to the other. He simply ran across it and screamed into the void.

'CHARLIE!'

But Charlie didn't show himself. There was no Charlie on this street. Charlie had gone, leaving nothing but the cars and the bins and the houses and the eyes that were watching through semi-drawn curtains.

'CHARLIE!'

The name echoed out across the road, and the heavens opened once more, rain falling hard on David's face. He slid to a halt and glared up into the clouds.

God's punishment, a voice said then. *That's what this is. God's punishment.*

'Bitch,' he said back. Then he screamed, just like he'd screamed his son's name: 'FUCKING BITCH! WHAT HAVE YOU DONE?!'

He started running again, his eyes darting frantically about the street, as if Charlie might appear, as if all of this was just a stupid game and his son would simply jump out from behind a shrub and yell, 'BOO!' But he didn't. This was real.

'CHARLIE!' David called out once more. But there was no sign, no answer. Apart from the voice in his head.

How's your son?

'Oh, just fuck off, you no-good, lying bitch.'

Max got onto the football team. What team did your son get into? Did he get into a team? Have you asked him? Will you ever get to ask him again? David?

David stopped running. He let out a weird little moan as he looked back down the other end of the road. The rain smacked the tarmac, dimly lit by the vague orange fuzz of the streetlamps.

'Charlie, come on...' he pleaded desperately. 'What is this? What the hell is this?'

There was a gust of salted wind, and David's bones shivered in the midst of it.

True punishment, Natasha replied assuredly. *But that's not what you should be asking, David, because you suspected that already. What you should be asking is how long does true punishment last? Can a debt like yours be crossed? Ever? Can you get to the other side of it and sew up the wounds before the end? I think not. But that's just me.*

'NO!' screamed David. 'NO!' He clasped his head in his hands and fell to his knees. 'No, no, no. No, no, no.'

Just to the side of him, a window opened, and David turned to see a woman watching from the darkness of her kitchen. She was old. Very old. Her eyes were wide and curious. He recognised her as June Forsythe, a woman who had said hello to him several times, but with whom he had never had a conversation. She looked at him strangely, like she wasn't really seeing David Cooper on the street, but rather something else. A remnant of last night's storm which had returned to disturb her.

'Yeah?!' shouted David for no reason. 'What the fuck do you want?!'

She pulled the window closed and yanked on the curtains, leaving David alone on the road with nothing but the echoes of his own screams for company. Echoes that would stay with him for a long time, he had no idea.

31

THE SECRET BOOK

When Amee Florence opened her eyes, the street was the first thing to hit her. It was long and wide, quite overwhelming from a kid's perspective. The houses seemed to loom over her, with windows like eyeballs, staring at her like she was an intruder.

'Where am I?' she asked no one in particular. Perhaps the houses. None of which replied. She winced slightly at the pain in her feet, and it was then that she realised she wasn't wearing any shoes. In fact, she wasn't wearing much at all. Just a nightdress, with a slight tear around the hem which caused goose bumps to prickle her thighs. She tried to ignore the jagged cement against her feet and began walking down the street.

'Where am I?' Amee asked again. But the street ignored her. There was just the silence. She broke into a run. 'Someone? Anyone?! OH!'

Pain erupted in her right foot, and she fell to the ground, feeling the fabric of her nightdress tear further. Amee turned and saw a stream of blood seep from her split toenail.

'Little girl?' a voice called out from behind her.

She looked up to see an elderly woman standing in her front garden. She was dressed in a faded pink dress, with two rubber gloves pulled right up to the sleeves.

'Are you hurt?' the lady asked. 'Do you need help?'

'I'm...' Amee responded quietly. 'I'm...'

* * *

The breeze lifted the hairs on the back of Amee's neck, and she turned to see Mrs Nightly walking across the road. Two hands were locked behind her back, and her spine was jolted upright in that familiar uncomfortable pose.

'Lost,' she said simply. Then she bit her lip, curled it, and swivelled back on her heels. 'And this is where you were found?'

'Yes, Mrs Nightly.' Amee scratched slightly at her mousy hair.

Mrs Nightly picked up the burgundy notebook which had been resting on the bonnet of the parked American Lincoln. 'Do you remember where you saw it?' she asked.

Amee pointed over to some dustbins on the pavement, some with their lids hanging open, others with their lids firmly closed. Beside them were cartons from Saturday mornings, empty lager bottles from Sunday afternoons, half-eaten ready meals, torn-up cereal packets, waste paper, toilet rolls – anything and everything that implied this neighbourhood had never strayed far from absolute normality. Only Amee knew that was a lie, because Amee remembered.

'The fracture,' she said. 'It was over there, where the bins are.'

A deep male voice came from behind Amee, causing the hairs on her neck to stand on end again, although it had nothing to do with the wind this time.

'A little fishy lost, a little fishy alone.' Roman Guild stepped out from behind the car, stroking his thumb over his antique-looking lighter, flicking the lid off, then on, then off again. 'You must have been terrified. But don't worry, you never have to be alone again. Not while I'm around.' He grinned at her, and Amee turned away from him. 'What's that?' he mocked. 'Little fishy not grateful?'

'Quiet, Roman, I'm trying to think.' Mrs Nightly stood him down with a single line. She was staring about the street now, her head tilted and her nostrils flaring. 'I recognise this place,' she said after a few seconds. 'Don't you recognise this place?' She inclined her head towards Roman, who shrugged his shoulders in return. 'I recognise this place. Eden Park Lane. I've seen it somewhere before.' Mrs Nightly squinted down at the notebook, then looked up again. 'Where did that boy go missing?'

'What boy?' asked Roman.

'Cooper. Charlie Cooper. It was here, wasn't it? Eden Park Lane. I'm sure it was here. I remember seeing it in the papers.'

Roman pocketed his lighter. 'Does it matter?'

'They never found him. It was a long investigation, but they never found that boy.'

Mrs Nightly looked Amee in the eye. There was something different written across her face now. An urgency, for sure, but also an excitement. A wild sort of excitement which seemed to have turned her into something else entirely. Amee found it difficult to recognise the woman in front of her.

'Amee,' she said slowly. 'Tell me what happened on this street the day you were found.'

'I've told you already,' said Amee.

Mrs Nightly nodded, reaching for the pen in her jacket pocket before hovering it over the burgundy notebook. 'So tell me again.'

* * *

The waves kissed the shore like a mother finally reunited with her lost child. One kiss, then two, then three. Then a slight pause, and the kissing repeated. One, two, three. Amee leaned her head against the rock, her eyes closed as she let herself fall into the ongoing rhythm. One, two, three. Then a pause. And then again. The sand embraced the water, and the water embraced the sand. Moulded it, positioned it, like everything might stick, before another kiss turned it into something new once more. One, two, three. The mother and child carried on, as a mother and child would carry on, with no idea of when they might part. One, two, three. They cherished their time together, like the waves were a promise, like no matter what happened, they would always come back. One, two, three. And Amee Florence opened her eyes.

'Were you with me? Were you always with me, even when I couldn't see you?'

Charlie Cooper was standing on the beach in front of her, his light-blonde hair entirely still in the breeze, his dark-blue eyes staring sadly.

'I was with them,' he replied. 'My dad, and Marty. I had to stay with them. I wanted to be there if they crossed.'

Amee stared across the beach, watching Marty as he slept beside the smoking bundle of twigs and leaves. He had been passed out for about thirteen hours now, but Amee was letting him sleep. Mr Cooper, on the other hand, had trudged off into the woodland in the early hours of the morning. He hadn't returned yet, but Amee wouldn't worry until later. They would all have their separate ways to come to terms with everything that had happened. If Mr Cooper needed to be alone, then he needed to be alone.

'It was bad,' Charlie continued. 'They won't talk about how bad it was, but what happened to them that night was bad. And I think it changed them forever.'

Another wave kissed the shoreline, and Amee felt a lump swell in her throat.

'It's my fault,' she said.

'No.'

'If I hadn't –'

'No. None of this is your fault.'

A few seconds passed. Amee nodded, peering back out towards the power plant chimney on the other side of the sea.

'It's not real, Charlie. None of it was real. Everything she told me was a lie.'

'But you know now,' Charlie replied. 'That's good at least.'

'Good? She made me a part of her story. But now the story's gone, I don't know what I'm left with. I have no idea who I am.'

'I know who you are. You're Amee Florence.'

'But who is that?'

Her tone was hard. A little too hard for Amee's liking, so she took a breath and calmed herself. If this was going to make her anything, she couldn't let it make her cold. Not to her friends. Not to the people who truly cared about her.

'It's like I'm just a memory I'm struggling to remember. It's like Amee is on the other end of a rope, and I'm only just holding on.'

'At least it's back in your hands now,' Charlie responded. 'At least there is a rope. Maybe if you keep holding, eventually she'll come back to you. Maybe if you keep holding, eventually you'll remember.'

Amee looked up at her friend, blinking slightly in the glare of the sun that illuminated the sky behind him. Charlie always knew what to say, she had to give him that. Of all the dead people she had talked to, Charlie was the only one who had managed to maintain a grasp on life's complexities. Its realities and their solutions. She didn't know why. Perhaps it was just his character. It made it all the sadder that he had been snatched away from life before that character could grow. God only knew the size of the shoes he would have been able to grow into.

A rustle of branches sounded from across the beach, and Amee turned to see Mr Cooper walking out of the forest.

'He's back,' she said.

The teacher jumped onto the sand, looking up and down the beach until he spotted Amee. He began walking towards her. Amee turned back to watch his son start to disappear into the ocean behind.

'You're leaving?' she asked in surprise.

Charlie smiled. 'Guess you don't need me. You haven't needed anyone for a while.'

'No,' she replied slowly. 'No, I guess I haven't.'

Charlie disappeared and Mr Cooper took his place.

'How are you doing?' he asked, his face pale and sagging behind his beard.

'I'm fine,' replied Amee. 'Where have you been?'

'There was a boat. It came quite close, so I wanted to see where it was going. There are tracks up into the forest. I guess the owners have a house up there.'

'Why did you want to see –'

'You washed it off.'

Amee followed the teacher's gaze down to her legs, where the black X's had been faded by the sea and the salt.

'Yeah,' she said quietly. 'It's like you said last night: it's best not to think about it. There's so much I want to remember, but more I want to forget.'

'You won't forget,' Mr Cooper replied firmly. 'The pain you feel will be there forever. But it won't make a mould of you. That's what people think. That's what I thought once, but it doesn't. You make a mould of it. You use the pain, shape it into what you want it to be. You'll get better from here, Amee. I'm sure of it.'

He flashed her a comforting smile, but Amee kept her face stern and rigid.

'I already know how to use it. To find the house on the cliff. To set them all free.'

'I believe you,' said Mr Cooper earnestly. 'And we will. We'll find it.'

A couple of seconds passed before Amee actually took those words in.

'You're going to let me?' she asked.

'I am.'

'Why?'

'Because it's my road,' he said. 'I've been trying to find the right one for a long time now. This is the only road with light. I think I've been on the dark ones long enough.' He touched his stitches briefly. 'But it's also a road that can wait.'

'What do you mean? We can't wait. If the green monster is –'

'For you.'

'For me?'

Amee stared at the teacher blankly, watching as he sat on the rock beside her. His wound was still hurting him; she could see that. His entire left side seemed to curve uncomfortably into his body, as if one corner of his ribcage had been twisted out of shape.

'Amee,' he said through a dry throat, 'my responsibility isn't just to Charlie now. It's to you as well.'

'What do you mean?'

Mr Cooper stared harder into her eyes. 'Eden Park Lane. What were you doing there?'

'I told you last night. I don't know.'

'You don't know as in you can't remember?'

'I remember the street. I just don't know why I was there. It feels like I had just woken up, like I'd been having a really long dream. A dream where I was...'

'Where you were what?'

'In the water. I dream about that sometimes, being in water. It's like I'm living in it, feeling the waves as they swirl around me, like I'm part of their makeup. If I try to think of anything before Eden Park Lane, I'm left with that. Just the dream. The dream of water. Before I woke up.'

Mr Cooper took that in, his lip folding over the hair on his chin. 'But there was something,' he said, his voice lighter than it had been before. 'It might seem hard now, but Amee, your life can't be that complicated. You had parents. You had a mother. You had a father. You had a life before that hospital and before the orphanage. A life that you've just forgotten. Finding that should be my first duty.'

'But you don't know how quick we might have to be,' said Amee. 'The green monster. The one the voice talks about. If it's real, it could –'

'If it's real,' repeated Mr Cooper. 'And how sure are you of that? The whole thing sounds more like a fairy tale than anything real. The green monster, the house on the cliff. It all sounds like a story.'

'But they've seen. So many of them have seen it and –'

'Amee, if you tell a child there's a monster under the bed, they'll hear it. If you tell them it exists, they'll see it in the dark. They'll sense it in their dreams. This is no different.'

'So you don't want to help.'

'I do. I want to help in any way possible, but you have no idea what this voice means, what it's saying. You're acting like it's the answer to everything, but you don't know anything about it. No one does.'

Mr Cooper swivelled on the rock and pulled out the thick burgundy notebook from beneath his jacket.

'What are you doing with that?' asked Amee hesitantly.

'I spent most of the night reading it...' He flopped the notebook open in one hand. 'This survey. That's all it is. It's just one big survey of dead people. Occasionally, the voice comes up. The house on the cliff. But every time it does, the conversation stops as soon as it starts. Winona wasn't interested in knowing more about the voice. All she cared about was the dead. Don't you see? That leaves us with nothing.'

He placed the notebook down on the sand, and as he did so, Amee spotted a purple page protruding from the white ones. She paused for a moment, then she took the notebook in her own hands and pulled it out. The purple page was actually many pages, all bound together and stapled into the notebook. THE HOBBIT: COLOURING AND ACTIVITY BOOK. She frowned as Mr Cooper continued talking.

'I'm not saying it's hopeless. That's not what I'm saying. But we know where to start with you. The orphanage must know something, or the people who found you on the street that day. There'll be connections; there'll be contacts. There's a place to begin.'

Amee kept looking at the book, brushing her thumb against the cover. A funny sensation came over her as she did so. It had been a long while since she'd last held this book in her hands. It wasn't anything special, just something to pass the time in the hospital. When the days got too boring, too uncomfortable, or too dark. It was something she could lose herself in, even if just for a few hours. So what was it doing in Mrs Nightly's notebook? Hiding away, secret. Amee hadn't touched the book since her memories were taken, so why was the book taken too? Amee unclipped it from the staple before turning it over in her hands.

'Amee, are you listening to me? Your parents could still be out there. For all we know, your parents could still be alive. Do you understand that? You could have a family.'

Amee looked up at him. 'Family?'

'Yes. Family. I owe it to them, Amee, if they're still alive. I owe it to them to bring you home.'

'Home,' she repeated again, tasting the word on her tongue as the pictures in her book began to sparkle in the sun.

It was fully out now. The clouds had dispersed and the sun lit the world around her, making pretty, glinting patterns on the ocean waves. She squinted at them. *Family. Home.* Both of those were prospects Amee had never really considered, and the temptation to drop everything to find them was almost crippling. After all, to find them would be to find herself, and that was something Amee wanted more than anything. But then she blinked, and those patterns in the sky turned into another sort of pattern, almost like a person, standing alone against the blue. She frowned, then turned back to Mr Cooper.

'I owe them that too,' she said.

'What?'

'The dead people, that's what I owe them. Home.'

The waves crashed harder onto the beach, and a gust of ocean wind rippled over the surface, making Amee shiver. Mr Cooper sighed and took back the burgundy notebook.

'You're cold,' he said. 'We should get you out of the wind and find you something to eat.' He placed a hand on her shoulder, then he stood up and walked crookedly towards the smoking campfire.

Amee shuffled and stared once more towards the open water. She contemplated whether to see Charlie again, but she didn't. Instead, she simply sat, kept her eyes shut, and felt herself sink into another sodden memory.

* * *

Amee sat on one side of the desk. Winona Nightly sat on the other. Her bony hands were clasping her notebook. The camera above the door was making the room hum.

'It's the voice again, Mrs Nightly. He's talking about the voice again.'

The boy in the corner was nice to look at. He had thick brown hair that stuck up in clusters, like he had applied some gel that very morning, and his jaw line was lean, almost perfect, if it hadn't been for the unfortunate dabbles of acne which ruined his skin. He and Amee had been getting on well until he'd started hearing the voice.

'Ask him if he can continue to help us,' said Mrs Nightly. 'I want to know when he died, and I want to know how it happened.'

Amee swallowed. 'Can you tell us when you died?' she asked.

'I told you. Christmas, 1979.' The boy placed a hand on his hair. 'My head. My head got so hot –'

'And where was it? It wasn't far from here, is that right?'

'The green monster is coming,' the boy recited the line once more. 'I saw it again last night. Why is it always at night?'

Amee leaned back on her chair. 'The voice,' she said to her nurse. 'He's talking about the voice again.'

Mrs Nightly tutted. 'Then I believe we're done for the day. It's a shame. He was giving us a lot before now.' She stood, holding the notebook tight to her breast. 'Another lesson. Tomorrow morning. We'll see if the dead are a little more helpful.'

'Mrs Nightly...'

'Yes, Amee?'

'Do you know why...? I mean, do you ever think...?'

'What is it?'

'The voice. Why do they all hear it? I mean, why do they all hear this one voice?'

Mrs Nightly stared at her with a slight frown. 'I'm not sure,' she said. 'We don't understand a lot about the mid-space. It isn't a world we know. We don't know its walls, its boundaries, its lines, like ours. Perhaps whatever lines there are, some things can transcend them. Things like this. That wouldn't surprise me. That wouldn't surprise me at all. But we don't think about it, Amee. Isn't that right? We don't think about it.'

'No, Mrs Nightly,' replied Amee. 'We don't think.'

With a slight smile, Mrs Nightly opened the door and walked into the hallway, leaving Amee alone in the room.

She took a moment, then began to let the patterns form again in the dark. She watched as the good-looking boy appeared in front of her.

'The voice,' he murmured hesitantly. 'The voice is –'

'What does it sound like?' Amee cut over him. 'Tell me what it sounds like.'

'I don't know. It's not a bad voice. It's sort of...'

'Sort of what?'

'Warm.'

The word came out quiet, almost too quiet to hear above the ongoing bustle beyond the walls of her room. But Amee caught it. A rush of nostalgia and happiness seemed to flow through her. It was like electricity, whistling through her veins. Good. Definitely good. So good she quickly became sad.

'I wish I could hear it too,' she said, and with a few blinks she batted the image of the boy away. Above her, the buzz of the camera dissipated into silence, the red light dimming down, dimming down, until it was gone. Amee craned her neck towards her bed, spotting her colouring book on the pillow. 'I wish I could,' she said again. Then she stood up and began walking towards it.

* * *

Amee shielded her eyes against the sun, watching as Mr Cooper placed two hands sensitively around the bruises on Marty's neck.

'Turn your head,' he said lightly.

Marty turned, looking off in the direction of the woodland.

'Other way,' said Mr Cooper.

Marty tried to turn to the left. His cry of pain made Amee jump.

'I can't,' said Marty, wincing. 'It hurts. I think it's broken.'

'Your neck's not broken. Try again.'

'No, I can't. It's over. I'll never be able to passively disagree with anyone ever again.'

Marty pulled himself from the teacher's grasp, and Mr Cooper smirked.

'If Roman took away your ability to passively disagree, I'd say he's done your overall personality a favour. But don't worry, you'll be shaking your head at me in no time. It's just gonna hurt for a bit.'

Marty held his windpipe, rubbing his hand up and down as he leaned against the sandstone wall. 'You'd better be right, teacher.'

'Or what? You'll passively disapprove? Good luck with that.'

'Damn it. Just kill me.'

'Hang in there, kiddo.'

Amee took a step forward, a ball of anger rising in her chest. 'I'm sorry he did this to you.'

Out of instinct, Marty went to shake his head, but he regretted it almost immediately. 'Shit!' He winced again. 'No, it's not your fault.'

'I know it's not,' Amee came up alongside him and sat on the sand. She placed the small purple colouring book beside her. 'I'm just sorry. Roman was my responsibility. He was my demon to fight, not yours.'

The two of them stared at each other. There was a moment, still and quiet, and Mr Cooper whistled awkwardly.

'I'll be back in a minute,' he said then.

'Where are you going?' asked Marty.

'To get wood.'

'You've got wood.' Marty pointed at the ample bundle of twigs and logs beside the already roaring campfire.

'To get more wood.'

'Why do you need more wood?'

Another beat passed. Marty gawked at Mr Cooper, and Amee shuffled closer to him.

'I think it's a hint, Marty,' she said.

Marty looked at her. Then the penny dropped. 'Oh...'

'Want more wood?' asked Mr Cooper.

'Yeah, on second thoughts, the bundle looks awfully light.'

'That was my instinct as well.' Mr Cooper bent over and grabbed his bag. 'I'll be back in a few minutes,' he said, and then he began pacing up the beach.

Marty smiled at Amee, and she felt a tingle of heat in her cheeks. She turned away, desperate not to let Marty see any kind of hint that she might be blushing. With the amount of red and brown bruises scattered on his own features, it was almost impossible to tell if he was blushing too. For her own sake, Amee hoped he was. After all, they were both in the same situation. They both wanted to say and do the same thing, without either of them having the nerve to actually say or do it. Surely he must have been. *God*, Amee thought, *please let him be blushing too.*

'I dreamed about you,' Marty said then. 'In the valley, when Roman was...' He stuttered, swallowing against the words that had landed him back in the memory. 'I dreamed of you. You made me feel warm. When everything else was going cold.'

'I dreamed about you too,' replied Amee. 'Back in the hospital, back when I was alone. I dreamed of your voice. Of your face.'

Amee placed her hand down upon Marty's. He started to blush and Amee could see it. She gave an invisible fist pump.

'So,' Marty said after a few seconds. 'Did Mr Cooper tell you the plan?'

Amee frowned. Clearly, Marty wanted to move the conversation onto something less awkward. But she didn't. She didn't want to do that at all. Nonetheless, she cleared her throat and responded.

'He wants to look for me,' she replied plainly. 'My past, I mean. He wants to find out where I come from.'

'Oh. Well, you want that too, right?'

'I want to find the house on the cliff. That's all I've ever wanted to do. You know that.'

'But maybe this'll be good. Maybe answers are what you need. I mean, we don't know how long it'll take to find the house. Maybe it's best to know who you are, how you fit into the world, before committing to something like that. That way you know what you're coming back to when it's over.'

'I already know something I'm coming back to,' said Amee softly. She squeezed his hand tighter.

'You won't come back to me,' said Marty. 'You'll never come back to me, because I'm gonna be with you. From now on, Amee, through everything. I'm gonna be there.'

Marty's face had suddenly turned very stern. The smile had disappeared, the blush dissipating in the darkness of his skin. He was serious, Amee could see. He meant every word of what he said. He stood by it, like a promise that could never be broken.

'In fact,' he continued, 'there's a thing I've been meaning to ask. I've been meaning to ask it for a while now, only I've been too scared.'

'What?'

'If Roman didn't kill me, and if I ever got to see you again, I wanted to ask if maybe you wanted to be my girlfriend?'

Amee felt her heart jump in her chest, and Marty must have sensed it, because his confidence seemed to drop in one fell swoop.

'Maybe,' he said. 'I mean, definitely maybe. You know, I just thought I should put it out there. I just thought I should have the courage to ask, you know, if I survived everything. I mean, I like you a lot. We like the same kind of movies, and we've been to Cornwall. That's a thing couples do when they get old, but we've done that already. The circumstances weren't ideal, but...' Marty grabbed his head and moaned. 'Oh shit! Just forget I ever said it, okay? Just forget it. I didn't mean it. I said maybe!'

Amee leaned forward and put him out of his misery. 'I want to be your girlfriend,' she told him.

Marty peered gingerly through his fingers. 'You do?'

'Yeah, I do. Definitely.'

And with that, Amee took the initiative. She pulled his hands away from his face and planted a soft and delicate kiss onto his lips. Marty kissed her back. He returned her kiss with so much vigour that it was a wonder he didn't send her flying into the ocean. She held his shoulder, every inch of her feeling like it was floating in mid-air, like Marty's embrace had taken her away from the beach and everything else entirely. It felt right. It felt like everything that had happened so far, everything in her life, it had all been leading her to this moment. This kiss. This was her story, and she loved the ending. Only the curtain didn't fall. After a few seconds, Marty pulled away.

'Thank you,' Amee said randomly.

'Thank you for what?' said Marty.

'Thank you for saving me.'

Marty took her hand and smiled at her once again. 'Always, Amee.'

Amee had another urge to kiss him, but just as she did so, the sun disappeared behind the clouds and a gust of wind fluttered the colouring book towards the fire. She leaned forward and grabbed it before it caught the flames.

'Hey,' Marty muttered. '*The Hobbit*. Where'd you get that from?'

'It was in Winona's notebook. It used to be mine, but she took it from me.'

'It's your colouring book?'

'It's not just for colouring,' Amee replied defensively, turning the book around in her hand. 'I could draw in it too. I like drawing. There wasn't a lot to do in the hospital, so it was just a way to pass the time. Trust me, you would have done the same if you were as bored as I was.'

'Do you remember what you drew?'

'Not really.'

'Can I see your drawings?'

'No.'

'Are you embarrassed?'

'No.'

'You're embarrassed, aren't you?'

'Not as much as you'll be when I break up with you.'

'Oh bloody hell, that was fast.'

With a peck on the cheek, Marty leaned over her and went to grab the book. But then there was a noise. A loud noise, erupting from out of the trees.

'HEY!'

Amee dropped the book and looked up to see Mr Cooper sprinting towards them. He was waving his arms hysterically towards the waves.

'BOAT!' he yelled. 'BOAT!'

Amee turned to where he was pointing. The boat was about fifty metres from them, the chugging of its motor just about audible over the wind.

'What the –' Marty began, but before he could finish, Mr Cooper was by their side. He stamped down hard on the fire, then pulled the pair of them up over the sandstone wall and into the forest.

'Shh!' he hissed as they fell behind the trees. 'Get down here!'

The three of them pressed themselves onto their bellies, then watched as the boat moved slowly to the left, the foam of the ocean breaking against the hull.

'Why are we hiding?' asked Marty, but Mr Cooper didn't answer him.

A glint of fear flashed in his eyes. The sun broke through the clouds once again.

'Is it the same one as before?' asked Amee.

'Definitely,' said Mr Cooper. 'Two blue stripes on the hull.'

Marty turned his head towards him and winced a little. 'You've seen it already?'

'They're hovering.' Mr Cooper kept his voice low, as if the driver of the boat might hear them. 'They're hovering like they're interested.'

The engine of the boat choked and it bobbed violently on the waves.

'Police?' asked Amee.

'No,' replied Mr Cooper. 'It's not a police boat.'

'Coastguard?'

'No, this is civilian.'

'So why are we hiding?' asked Marty.

'Did you say you weren't followed last night?'

Marty hesitated. 'I said we might have been. I don't know. Mike wasn't looking.'

'You said you might have been?'

'Well, you said it wasn't police.'

Mr Cooper's gaze remained on the boat. It swayed on the ocean breeze, its engine now emitting a low and guttural hum. It felt strange to look at it, Amee thought. It felt almost like the boat was looking back, like it was searching amongst the tree line, scouting out the beach for any sign of life.

'Winona,' Mr Cooper whispered. 'Could she have followed you?'

'Jesus, how paranoid are you?' said Marty.

'Answer the question.'

'No. She was hardly conscious last time I saw her.'

'But conscious.'

'Hardly.'

The boat's engine coughed back to life, and it began cruising across the waves once again, passing steadily across the backdrop of Gealblath.

'If she believes Amee is crucial in finding her daughter, then she's not going to let her go without a fight. She'll try everything in the world to get her back. It's not paranoid to suggest that could be her.'

Marty shook his head and winced again. 'It could be anyone.'

'How many boats do you see around here, Marty? This can't be fishing territory, so what's that boat doing hovering around this beach all day?'

Amee looked out across the ocean. He was right, of course. There were no other boats. Just that one, prowling around the waves like a lonely predator.

'We're gonna have to leave,' said Mr Cooper. 'And fast.'

'What?' Marty gasped. 'No way, I'm not leaving. I can hardly move. I need rest. Amee needs it too.'

'We can't risk it, Marty.'

'But maybe the boat belongs to someone nearby. Maybe there's a house.'

'The tracks,' Amee realised out loud.

'Huh?'

'Mr Cooper, you said there are tracks in the woodland, going up the hill. Maybe there's a house at the top?'

Mr Cooper frowned at her. He pulled on his beard.

'There you go,' said Marty. 'There's a house. And the people who live in the house have a boat. Simple.'

'You don't know that.'

The engine of the boat made an oily splutter, and then it disappeared around the curve of the beach, leaving nothing but a trail of shimmering white foam in its wake.

'But I could find out,' Marty said then. 'If I follow the trail, I can find what's at the end of it.'

The teacher shook his head. 'Don't be stupid; we have no idea how far the hill goes. Trust me, that thing's steep. It's basically a cliff. And you said it yourself, you can hardly move.'

I moved from the campfire to here, didn't I?'

'Hardly.'

A few seconds passed. The teacher bit his lip, staring towards where the boat had been. He *was* paranoid, Amee could see that from a mile off, let alone a few inches from him. He was sweating and his eyes were wide, his pupils dilated. She could almost see the throb of his heartbeat in his neck. He was scared. But not for himself. None of this was for himself. He was scared for her. Mr Cooper was protecting her like a father would protect his child. She felt a sudden rush of warmth towards him. The teacher turned back to Marty.

'Are you sure you could do it?' he asked.

'I just asked Amee Florence to be my girlfriend. I could take on a mountain right now.'

'Okay, fine. Amee and I will follow the boat around the beach. You see if there's a house. But if you start hurting, come straight back. Don't be a hero. You've done that already.'

Marty stood up. 'Show me where it is.'

Ten minutes later and Marty was already heading up the woodland trail. Amee and Mr Cooper were back on the beach, preparing to make the long hike around the forest to find the boat. Before they got going, however, Mr Cooper pressed his hand to his stab wound and gave a small whimper.

'Okay,' he whispered. 'Okay.'

'Do you need a moment?' asked Amee.

'No. We don't have a moment. Let's go.'

He took a step forward, but Amee could see his face growing pale. The run had taken it out of him. He was panting like a dog that needed water.

'We *do* have a moment. Just take a few minutes, sir. Get your breath.'

Despite himself, Mr Cooper obliged. He sat down against the sandstone wall, his teeth gritted and his eyes shut. Amee sat along with him. She suddenly realised that she was still holding his arm, and there was not a hint of fear at doing so. She remembered over a month ago, when she could hardly be left alone with him without cowering in a corner in fear. So much had changed since then, Mr Cooper more than anything. She sat for a couple of minutes, then she turned to the forest.

'Why couldn't I go with him?' she asked.

'Because we can't take chances anymore,' Mr Cooper breathed. 'If he wants to go, that's fine. He's right; we don't want to move from here if we can help it. We're not ready. It has to be done, but I'm not risking you too. You need to stay with me.'

Amee shuffled, tracing her left hand delicately on the sand beside her. It still felt warm from when Marty had been holding it, and for a second, she allowed herself to crack a slight smile. Mr Cooper opened his eyes and frowned at her.

'Why are you smiling?' he asked.

'No reason,' she replied quickly.

'It's not like you to smile.'

'I'm not.'

With an awkward cough, Amee leaned over and picked up the colouring book which was still sat on the sand. She opened it up and held it in front of her face in an effort to hide her blushing.

A mess of colours hit her as soon as she looked at the pages. Greens, blues, and reds invaded, colours that were just as vivid as the day they had been applied. They swooped across the page so spectacularly that for a moment it was hard to tell what she was even looking at. But after a few moments, she worked it out. The cliff came first, and then the ocean, laid out across the middle of the page like a great blue carpet, stopping only when it clashed with the beautiful red sunset in the upper quarter. Around the picture were her own drawings. The house, standing tall on the cliff edge, and the figures just beside it. A small girl holding hands with a woman in a dress, and a large man coloured in green, with vivid yellow eyes set deep in his face. Above him, the ocean spanned out into the sunset. Two huge eagles soared above it, heading to the other side of the water, where there was a skyline, like a silhouette, not dissimilar to how Gealblath looked from Derling. And much like Gealblath, there was a tall landmark in the middle. The chimney. Looming large above the water like a watchtower, keeping the waves in check, ensuring that they didn't travel too far from home. Amee lowered the book and stared at the chimney in real life.

'What's wrong?' Mr Cooper caught her look.

Amee took a moment, her heart thumping faster than ever in her chest. 'The drawing,' she said dumbly. 'My drawing.'

Mr Cooper grabbed the book. He did a double take and looked up at the skyline. 'What am I looking at?' he asked.

'Can't you tell?' Amee replied. Her body had gone into a sort of shock. A rush of memories flooded through her. She remembered holding the crayon in her hand. She remembered her skin, stained with colour, her fingers dabbing blue holes into the ocean. She remembered her nurse peering over at her work, her smile flickering.

'Tell what?' said Mr Cooper.

'A house,' said Amee. 'The house on a cliff.'

'I don't understand.'

'It's my world. I used to draw my world into the pictures, before I forgot. Before Mrs Nightly took the book away from me. Before she took my memories.'

Mr Cooper hesitated. He looked up towards the trees that climbed into the afternoon sky, and his jaw dropped open. 'Oh...'

And at that moment, the sun reappeared from behind the clouds, causing tiny little stars to reignite upon the ocean's surface and twinkle gingerly below the horizon.

32

THE HOUSE ON
THE CLIFF

The wind whistled through the trees as Marty climbed higher. His ribs were hurting now; his entire right side throbbed harder than it had ever throbbed before. Yet he carried on, pushing himself further and further, until his regret grew stronger and stronger, and every part of him wanted to fashion a small sled from the trees and slide all the way back down towards Mr Cooper and Amee. *Why did you suggest this?* he asked himself miserably. *What in the world made you think it was a good idea to suggest this?* He went to pinch his thigh and felt a stab of pain in his arm. He yelped and a nearby squirrel fell out of its tree in shock. *Great*, he thought bitterly. He was in so much pain, he couldn't even scold himself properly.

Marty bent over, using his blistered hands to clear a small ridge on the incline of the hill. He sat there for a moment. He must have climbed at least half a mile already. The ocean was splayed out far below, with the chimney casting a long, other-worldly shadow over Gealblath. It looked quite beautiful from up here, he realised. It didn't incite the same sense of fear that it had before. There was no anxiety flooding through him. There was no feeling of worthlessness. Marty was clean of his insecurities. He looked at himself differently now, and so he looked at the power plant chimney differently too. It was something good. A memory in the making of him.

He smiled to himself and immediately felt a little better. In all truth, his injuries didn't feel as bad as they had yesterday. That meant they were getting better, which meant his bones were probably not broken. And if he had it in him to rescue Amee Florence from Gealblath Hospital *and* ask her to be his girlfriend, he knew he had the willpower to climb a simple hill. Marty took a few breaths. Then, with a heave and a wince, he twisted himself back around and renewed his climb up the trail.

It took another twenty minutes before he finally felt the hill begin to level out. As soon as it did, the trail disappeared, replaced instead by an intense mass of greenery. Untended grass and wildflowers lay out in front of him, green, pink, and yellow, flickering from side to side in the salted air. The air itself felt humid, more humid than anything he'd experienced before, even when he had gone to the south of France on holiday with his parents. It was stifling, and it caused small droplets of sweat to trickle from his hairline.

Marty looked to the left, immediately spotting a gate which stood at the end of a tunnel of apple trees. It shimmered vividly in the glare of the sun. Two small, crumbled brick walls were on either side, and there was a house standing beyond it. It was big, almost medieval looking. A proper old

Scottish country home, only its time in the sun had been and gone. The house was stark black, charred right down to the bone, like some great fire had gutted it and left nothing but the shell. The windows were broken and splintered, the door was hanging loose on the hinges, and the roof looked like it could cave in at any moment. The ghost of a place, standing alone in the wind. It lay right at the end of a long lawn, and just behind it, the grass began to slope down steeply to a jagged cliff edge.

Marty approached the gate and looked more closely. The house couldn't be inhabited; he knew that almost immediately. And that meant the boat couldn't possibly belong to anyone up this hill.

'Shit,' he muttered under his breath.

Mr Cooper was going to have a field day now. Marty could just hear him raving about how it *must* have been Winona, how she *must* have followed Marty from the hospital, and how they *must* now pack up and leave the beach as fast as they could. Only Marty didn't want to go. If anything, Marty wanted to stay on that beach for as long as possible. Where it was just him and Amee, away from the rest of the world – apart from Mr Cooper, of course, but they could just send him to get firewood whenever they wanted to be alone. That sounded like bliss, as far as Marty was concerned.

And yet he had to tell them the truth. If Amee was truly in danger, he had to let them know. Marty kicked at one of the clumps of flowers by his feet. He went to turn, and that was when he heard it…

KASLAM!

The first petal landed, and a flock of birds flapped out of the long grass and into the cloudy blue sky. Marty felt his heart jolt in his chest. The sound of a door slamming had come from beyond the gate, but the door of the house remained open, hanging halfway towards the charred porch, motionless and untouched. Marty looked up towards the windows, all of which were vacant. Black as night. He swallowed. Then he opened his mouth and called out.

'Hello?'

Marty's voice echoed and he waited, watching as the grass rustled in the wind. There was no reply. *Of course there's no reply. There's no reply because there's no one there. Obviously there's no one there.* And yet the sound of the door replayed in his head. It resounded over and over, eventually changing from something scary to something a little more hopeful. Of course, if that *was* a door, if someone *did* live in this house, then Marty could take that information back to Mr Cooper. Perhaps they wouldn't have to leave that beach so soon. Perhaps they could stay a little longer.

Marty grabbed the black metal bars of the gate. *Come on*, he thought to himself. *You can at least check. A sign of life, that's all you need.* With a slight push, Marty opened the gate and began walking carefully towards the porch. The door hung just a few inches from the steps. It was held in place by rusted hinges, but the maze of fluffy cobwebs made it look like it had been suspended in mid-air by some ginormous spider. Marty peered gingerly into the depths of the house. A tall and crumbled entrance hall awaited him. Wooden beams lay on the ground, two chandeliers dangled dangerously from the ceiling, and in the centre, a twisted staircase climbed to the first floor, ruined, with splinters circling around the bannister like a coil of barbed wire. Marty held his breath before calling out again.

'Hello?'

He heard his voice rebound off the scorched walls, but once again there was no reply. Only a seagull returned his call, squawking in Marty's general direction as if to say, *What's wrong, pal, you believe in ghosts?*

Marty frowned. Nowadays, he *did* believe in ghosts, and he was sure this house had plenty of them. But ghosts weren't what he was worried about. Ghosts couldn't open and close doors, so what had? With a deep breath, Marty pushed past the cobwebs and stepped tentatively into the dust. That heat hit him again. Sharp and stinging, it seemed to bite his flesh as if he was standing in the fire that had gutted the building itself. But judging by the ash and the cobwebs that filled every crevice, the building must have been ablaze years ago. There was no way anyone could stand living inside here. And even if they could, Marty wasn't sure he wanted to meet them. An urge to return to Amee pounded inside him, and Marty came to his senses. He turned towards the door, but then, once again...

KASLAM!

His body turned as rigid as a statue. Marty looked back across the hallway, watching as the ash swirled in the streams of sunlight. At first, there was nothing to suggest any noise had even occurred, but then a rustle came from the corner. A large and blackened fireplace stood underneath a section of peeling plaster, and when the rustle came, the dust in the hearth shifted, dancing up towards the mantelpiece.

'Hello?' Marty whispered nervously. But again, there was no reply. He swallowed and approached the fireplace, sweat dripping from his forehead. He came up to the hearth and slowly looked up the flue. Then, quick as anything, it exploded in a flash of white.

'CRAWCH!'

The seagull flew into his face and sent him tumbling backwards. It soared up to the ceiling, flying from corner to corner and pecking desperately at the panels before shooting out of a broken window. Marty sat on his backside and watched it climb into the clouds. Relief flooded through him in a wave. *A bird*, he thought to himself scornfully. *It was a bastard bird. This whole time, it was just a bird.*

'You pussy...' Marty laughed. He climbed to his feet and patted the ash off his trousers. Then something else caught his eye. A glint of gold. He looked at the floorboards, where a picture frame was lying face down, one that must have been knocked from the mantelpiece when the seagull took off. Marty went to pick it up, but at the same moment, another sound came. It was soft this time. And quiet. But it was enough to make Marty's bones shiver.

Kaaslip, tap. Kaaslip, tap. Kaaslip, tap.

The noise reverberated off the dark walls and Marty twisted on his feet. *That was no bird*, he thought to himself. *That sounded nothing like a bird. That sounded almost...* He wavered. The noise sounded once more.

Kaaslip, tap. Kaaslip, tap. Kaaslip, tap.

It was louder this time, coming from the door on the left of the stairwell. *There*, thought Marty. *It's coming from there. Whatever it is, it's coming from behind that door.* He hesitated, then took a few steps towards it.

Kaaslip, tap. Kaaslip, tap. Kaaslip, tap.

The sound got louder as Marty got closer, and pretty soon he found his hand hovering just above the door knob, more beads of sweat trickling fast from his fringe. He pushed the door and it opened with a loud and agonising creak.

On the other side was a kitchen, old looking, and charred like the rest of the house. A broken window gazed out onto the lawn, and underneath it lay a vintage oven, the doors tattered and burned. On the floor were cooking instruments, semi-cooked themselves, scattered about the tiles all the way around the room until they got to the table. There, the tiles seemed to crumble away into rubble, before being replaced by a big pair of leather size-fifteens. Marty looked at them, then he looked up, his heart almost stopping as he saw a man sitting reclined on a chair. His green eyes were glaring at an antique-looking lighter nestled firmly within his grip.

He flicked it alight. *Kaaslip*. Then he jerked it shut again. *Tap*.

'Marty,' said Roman Guild without looking at him. 'Good of you to join us. Will your friends be long?'

'I...' Marty tried to form words, but no more came. Someone grabbed him from behind and wrapped a hand around his jaw. His head was yanked back, and Marty found himself staring into the cold and steely eyes of Winona Nightly.

'Tell us where they are,' she hissed.

And then Roman stood up from the table, and Marty felt his legs turn to jelly.

33

THE PHOTOGRAPH

The waves crashed forcibly upon the shore, spraying the sand with foam and seaweed. David looked into the icy blue eyes of Amee Florence.

'Amee, talk to me. You have to talk to me now. Talk to me.'

'I don't know what you want.'

David grabbed her wrist, and with his other hand, he lifted the colouring book up in front of her.

'The house on the cliff. Was this your life? Before the orphanage? Before all this? Amee, I need you to talk to me. I need you to cooperate.'

Another wave, harder this time. The wind picked up. The ocean grew as frantic as David's own heart, mirroring his panic, pounding the shore in a desperate effort to get the sand to budge.

'I don't know,' Amee cried. 'How am I supposed to know anything if nobody's told me the truth?!'

'Think!' David squeezed her wrist. 'Remember!'

'GET OFF ME!'

Amee ripped herself from David's grasp and David stared down at her.

'We need you to remember,' he said, his voice lower. 'It's important that you remember.'

'I can't.' Amee shook her head. 'I need time. I just need time to –'

'Amee, we don't have time! If Winona took this book from you, it's because she knows what's inside. She knows what the house is, and she knows where to find it. It's a map. A map Winona didn't want you to have.'

'No,' Amee responded desperately. 'She doesn't know! Neither of us knew!'

'But what if she does? What if you knew too, before she took your memories?'

The waves continued to smash against the sand, causing the trees on the hill to sway and creak. David looked up towards them. Then he leaned over and grabbed his backpack from the sand, the pain of his stab wound now entirely gone.

'What are you doing?' asked Amee.

'You want to find the house on the cliff? Your book says it's up there.'

'But it can't be. It doesn't make sense. How would I know about it?'

'I don't know! All I know is, we need to be fast. If Winona thinks we've found the book, she'll be coming. You want answers, don't you? Whatever is up there, whatever it is, it's an answer. And that's what we need now, Amee. We need answers.'

Amee glanced up at the trees, her body now beginning to shake. 'Marty's up there,' she said gravely.

'Yes,' said David. 'But if we're fast, we can catch him. And we need to be fast. Are you ready to do this?'

Another moment passed. Then Amee took a deep breath. 'Okay,' she said. 'I'll do it.'

It took them a full hour to get to the top. By the time they did, the sun had begun to dip in the sky, causing a strange strip of pink to line the horizon. Amee and David had been silent for the journey – it had taken almost everything out of them, and they knew if they were to talk, it would have been wasted breath.

They finally spoke when they reached what looked like an overgrown, wild orchard.

'A garden...' they said together.

And then, almost consecutively, they turned and spotted a house sitting just twenty feet from an open gate. It was black and charred, the wood peeled back like blisters on the skin, unhealed and hardened after years of wear.

'That's not the house,' Amee muttered when she saw it.

'How do you know?' asked David.

'It's just a feeling.'

'Or a memory.'

The two of them looked at each other. David saw a bead of sweat trickle down her forehead, but he knew it wasn't from the climb. The heat was almost overpowering up here. It was a thick heat like Gealblath's, only stronger, wrapping around his body like an oversized blanket. He turned and walked towards the house, trying to shake it off.

Amee came up alongside him as they past by the open gate. 'What happened to this place?' she asked.

'Fire,' replied David. 'A long time ago.'

He felt the stitches twitching inside him, each one of them bending, then straightening, attempting desperately to keep the blood from pouring through. They wouldn't last much longer, he knew that. The blood would soon come, and his world would soon crumble. But not yet. *Not yet*, he thought.

They reached the porch and stopped for a few moments, taking it all in.

'This isn't the house,' Amee repeated adamantly. 'This place can't be where they cross. It's not right. It's wrong. All of this feels wrong.'

David went to look at her, but as he did so, he spotted something. A set of footprints, embedded like ghosts in the ash which covered the floor of the porch, two inches deep. One, two, one, two, one, two, until they passed the hanging door and entered the house itself. David peered into the blackness.

'Marty?' he called out.

No answer. Amee stepped past him.

'Marty?' she shouted. 'Are you in here?'

Again, no reply. David walked into the entrance hall and almost gasped. If anything, it was even hotter in the house than it was outside. The warmth rippled about the place as if the fire had just been put out that very morning and the last of its heat remained trapped within the walls.

'Do you recognise any of it?' he asked Amee.

'No. It's like I told you, Mr Cooper, the memories are triggered. I can't help when I remember. It just happens.'

'But how are they triggered?'

'It happened last night, remember? All you said was the name of that street, and then it all happened at once. The feelings I had, the road I was on, the person who found me. That was the trigger. It started all blurry, but then became clearer. In the morning, I even remembered her name, the person who found me. She was called June. I remembered how she bandaged me up; I remembered the feel of her sofa, the smell of her kitchen. Things become so vivid, even though they begin so small. But here there's nothing. If it was going to give me a memory, if it *could* help, then it would have done so already. But there's no trigger, no blur, no anything. It's just...'

Amee trailed off as she looked at David. He was standing as still as a statue now. It felt like a wave of electricity had rippled through him, stopping him in his tracks, gluing his feet to the floor. All he could do was stare at her.

'What did you just say?' he managed to get out.

'The trigger,' Amee repeated. 'It's not –'

'No, not that. The woman. What did you say about the woman?'

'I just said that she became clearer. Just like all the memories.'

David unfroze himself and took a step forward. Amee took a step back. Her foot crunched on something that sounded like glass, but David ignored it.

'Her name, you said her name was June.'

'Yeah. So what?'

David continued to stare, his own memory going back, and back, and back. For the first time in years, he remembered June Forsythe. She'd spent almost all of her time in her front garden, planting and replanting, tending and re-tending, her long skirt stained by grass and her bony fingers covered in thick, wet soil. She had smiled at David sometimes, but he had never smiled at her. He didn't talk to his neighbours. He didn't talk to anyone. But that didn't mean he was ignorant. He'd had a wife, and he knew June's story, even if she never knew his.

David took another step towards Amee Florence. 'Was she dead?' he asked, quite seriously.

'What?' replied Amee.

'June. June Forsythe. Was she dead when you saw her?'

'No. I know who's dead and who isn't dead. The woman cleaned my cut, she fed me, she took care of me before I was sent to the orphanage. She was alive. She was definitely alive.'

A silence broke out across the hall. The space between them was filled with nothing but the squawking of birds, the whistle of the wind, and the small and distant sound of breaking waves.

'Mr Cooper, why is it so important?'

'Because June Forsythe died nine years ago,' said David finally.

The words lingered in the room, swaying with the dust. David watched as the girl in front of him soaked them in.

'I don't understand,' she said simply.

'She was already ill when Charlie disappeared. She only lasted around a year after he went. That makes you, what, three years old when you were found? And yet you remember all that, down to the name.'

Amee stared back at him, her ice-blue eyes sparkling as they caught a gleam of light through a shattered window.

'How old were you when you were discovered, Amee?' David asked her then. 'How old are you now?'

'I'm thirteen,' replied Amee. She clenched her jaw, her confusion replaced by a look of defiance. She stood there, resolute. 'I'm thirteen years old. I know I am.'

'But Amee, you –'

At that moment, a large clatter echoed from inside the house, and the two of them spun towards a door beside the twisted staircase.

'Marty?' David called out.

But there was no reply. Just the silence, and the sounds of birds, wind, and waves that clung to it. David looked down and spotted the footprints again, different to his own and heading towards the source of the noise.

'Stay here,' he told Amee, leaving her by the mantelpiece as he walked across the hallway. 'Marty?'

He pushed on the door and entered a large, blackened kitchen, empty but for the oven, the fridge, the table, and its chairs, all of them ruined from the fire. He looked again at the footprints in the ash. There were a lot of them now, circling, sweeping, as if there had been a scuffle. One set was small, another was thin, and the last set looked like they belonged to a couple of huge boots. David frowned at the dust.

'Who could...' he began, but before he could finish, someone kicked the door closed behind him and a pair of thick hands grabbed him by the neck. They slammed him so hard into the wall that he felt a huge splinter of wood pierce his arm.

'FUCK!'

David twisted around to see the tall figure of Roman Guild looming over him.

'Did you miss me?' He grinned and flung him to the floor. 'You cocksucker, you left me to die. Don't you realise you can't kill me? No one can kill me!'

The tall man wrapped his hands around his throat and started to squeeze, and David turned over, desperately searching for something – *anything!* – he could use to fight back. Just when he felt the bones in his neck might snap, his fingers wrapped around a rusted fork and he lunged forward, driving it as close to Roman's eye as he could get.

Roman cried out and loosened his grip, and David slid

out from underneath him, climbing to his feet before sprinting towards the door.

'AMEE! AMEE, GET OUT OF HERE!' He ran into the entrance hall, feet sliding across the dust as he spotted Amee standing still by the mantelpiece. A golden frame was held tightly in both hands. 'AMEE, WHAT ARE YOU DOING?!'

Amee looked up at her teacher, her face ghostly white. She looked like she was in a trance – like she was out of her mind entirely.

'David...' she muttered.

And then those big hands were around David again, wrapping around his neck and pulling him into a headlock.

'Little fishy doesn't want to run.' Roman laughed. 'Little fishy's too brave.

'WHAT ARE YOU DOING?!' David cried. 'JUST RUN, AMEE! RUN AS FAST AS YOU CAN! I'LL FIND YOU!'

'Find her? You stupid fucker, you think you're ever gonna leave this house alive?'

'He'll leave it alive...'

The voice came from the porch, and David turned to see Winona Nightly standing in the doorway, one arm around Marty Evans and a long, sharp needle placed against his neck.

'They all will. But when they do, they won't be the same.'

'Marty...'

There was a new gash on Marty's face. A fresh streak of blood trickled from his forehead and down his cheek. He looked at David with dead eyes.

'I'm sorry, sir,' he said quietly.

'You see?' said Winona, her voice shuddering with rage. 'This is what you make me do. When you try to stop me from taking back my world.'

'Let him go!' David screamed, and Roman squeezed his neck so hard, he felt the muscles spasm.

'I'll let him go,' replied Winona. 'I'll let you both go. And then I will take Amee back to the hospital, where we will continue our work. And you will never find her again.' She lifted the needle from Marty's skin. 'I can do that, you know. The coil was my kindness. Too kind, as Amee has already proven. I won't make that mistake again.' Her eyes flashed towards Amee. 'How much does she remember now?'

Amee remained rigid by the fireplace. She was still deaf to the world around her. Still deathly pale. It looked as if she was going to pass out at any moment. Roman gave another laugh.

'Little fishy looks like she's about to faint. This is too good. I've never made her faint before. Hey, look at me, little fishy. Eyes on me. It's been a long time since you've looked into these eyes. They've missed you.'

Amee looked up, but she didn't look at Roman. She looked at David. Her entire body began to lean back and forth, left to right, like there was an earthquake going on inside her.

'David,' she muttered again. 'David, I remember...'

Roman's arm gripped tighter, and David felt his heart leap into his throat.

'Yes, that's right,' said Winona bitterly. 'That's right, Amee, you remember. But by the time you leave here, you will have forgotten. And believe me, you're lucky. These two will suffer something much worse. I'll make sure of that. No more chances.'

'So what are you waiting for?' said Roman.

Winona stared at him, the look in her eyes a mixture of wildness and serenity, like the two were interlinked, working together to make her hand clench around the needle with a belief that what she was doing was absolutely necessary, and undyingly right.

'Nothing,' she replied simply.

And with that, she pressed the needle into Marty's neck, and he let out a terrible and blood-curdling scream.

'NO!' screamed David, watching as Marty collapsed into the ash at Winona's feet.

'Roman, bring him to his knees.' Winona yelled the order, and the tall man sent a knee into the back of David's leg, crippling him so that he fell towards the floorboards.

'AMEE, RUN! FOR GOD'S SAKE, RUN!'

But Amee didn't run. Instead, she simply fell forward, sending a cloud of dust into the air as she thumped against the floor. The frame slid out of her grasp and across the wood. It stopped a few feet from David, the glass shattered. He only caught a glimpse of it before the swirling ash covered it from view, but a glimpse was just enough. He saw a woman first, with curled black hair and a warm smile, standing beside a man, who was large and fierce looking, with a hand clasping the shoulder of a girl, Amee Florence, with her mousy hair lying in tangles on her shoulders and her eyes looking slightly left of centre. Below her, a few words were engraved on the frame.

TO THE FLORENCE FAMILY.
HAPPY THIRTEENTH BIRTHDAY TO YOUR
BEAUTIFUL GIRL. 8th JULY 1978

David blinked at the words hopelessly, and then he felt Roman twist his neck, and his entire body felt like it erupted into a ball of pain and fire.

34

THE GREEN MONSTER

"'When I think of you, I think of the ocean. I think of its blue waves, its mountains, made of coral, spiralling down the vistas until everything's black, and cold, and different, and new all over again. I think of the things that live there. Big whales, tiny shrimps, sharks with their long, sharp teeth, and lobsters with their thick red claws. I think about how long it might go on for. Miles and miles and miles, round and round the earth, over and over again until things meet once more, if things ever meet once more in a home like ours. And then I tilt my head back, like this, and I think, my little fishy, I think of you.'"

The bed creaked as Amee's mother leaned over and stroked Amee's hair. Amee looked out of the window and sighed. The sun was setting over the horizon now. The great chimney of the town on the other side of the ocean was drenched in shadows, and its red lights were just beginning to become visible and shine.

'Mum,' she said. 'Don't you think I'm a little old for this story?'

'What are you talking about? This one used to be your favourite. Besides, you were the one who wanted to read with me tonight.'

'*Used* to be my favourite. I'm thirteen now.'

'So what? I'm thirty-five and I still like it. Come on, one more time.' She reclined on the bed and continued reading, making sure to mimic the different animal voices. '"*But why do you think of me?*"'

'"*Why? Because this ocean is where I live and breathe. It's bigger than anything, and more wonderful than words could describe. Without it, there would be nothing, so don't you see?*"' She cleared her throat. '"*You are my everything, little fishy. You're my ocean. And I will always come back to you. Otherwise I wouldn't be able to breathe.*"'

Amee's mother pulled her hand from behind her head and flicked the book onto the last page. '*And so the two of them swam out into the great blue distance, singing about their love so loudly that every fish in the sea took notice once more, and every fish in the sea smiled, reciting the words back to them until the entire ocean was filled with a loud and glorious song.*'

'The end?' said Amee impatiently.

Her mum closed the book. 'The end.'

'I never realised how stupid the ending was.'

'What's so stupid about it?'

'She finds the little fish just by singing to her.'

'Yes, and the entire ocean sings along.'

'Exactly,' said Amee. 'Stupid.' She laid her head on her mother's shoulder, revelling in the smell of summer herbs and flowers that was infused into the silk.

'I think it's nice,' her mum replied. 'The singing is like a rope. It guides the little fish back to her mum when she can't see her in the dark water. I don't see what's stupid about that.'

'Maybe the fact that the entire ocean sings the song at the same time.'

Amee's mum smiled, her warm eyes twinkling. 'Here, read the title.' She turned the book over and tapped the front cover.

'*A Song About Love*,' Amee read aloud. 'So what?'

'Oh, Amee, so everything. A song about love is a song that can ripple throughout the entire ocean. It doesn't matter who hears it. Shark or whale. They all understand. And they all sing it back.'

'All just for one fish.'

'But one fish can be the most important fish in the world to someone who loves them. And, if someone loves them, do you know what that makes that one fish?'

'What?'

Her mother pressed her nose right up against Amee's face. 'The most important fish in the world.' She gave her a big, wet kiss, and Amee jammed her fingers into her armpits.

'HEY! HEY! GET ORRRFFF!'

Her mum pushed her away, and Amee crashed back onto the white, silky pillow, her skin flushed red and her grin wide enough to create dimples on each side of her face.

'I think it's time you start reading me real stories,' she suggested proudly.

'Pfft,' her mum scoffed. 'Real stories.' With a flourish, she leaned over and grabbed Amee's hair comb and held it under her nose. 'Our next story is *Great Expectations*,' she said in an over-the-top English accent. 'The most realest story of them all, don't you know? Spiffing! What for, what for!'

'Shut up! I mean stories that aren't for kids.'

Her mother dropped the comb, climbed off the bed, and gave Amee a quick peck on the forehead. 'Then you can read them,' she whispered. 'I like stories that make me happy. Even if they're not real. Now, get to sleep. I've done my job; it's time for you to close the deal.'

Amee yanked the covers all the way up to her chin. 'Fine. Goodnight, Mum.'

Her mum smiled at her. 'Goodnight, little fishy.'

She kissed her once more, then headed over towards the door, her heels making the floorboards bend and creak despite the lightness of her step. She put her hand on the knob, but before she turned it, Amee called over to her.

'Mum?'

'Yes, little fishy?'

Her mum looked at her with a playful grin, but Amee didn't grin back. A horrible thought had rushed through her head in the last few moments. It was something that she had been meaning to ask for a while now, only she hadn't found the strength.

'Is he back soon?'

The trace of that smile faded quickly from her mother's face. 'Tomorrow,' she replied.

And Amee Florence felt a stone sink deep into her belly. 'Oh...'

'It's alright, Amee. Just get some sleep for now. Dream happy things.'

A silence passed. Amee put on a false smile, then watched as her mum turned the handle and stepped into the corridor. The last rays of sunlight disappeared when the door closed, sending Amee's room dark and cold.

She dreamt that night of the green monster chasing her through the forest, shrieking her name maniacally from behind, getting closer, and closer, and closer, until his hands were around her throat and the air was being choked out of her lungs.

By and large, whether it be winter, spring, summer, or autumn, Amee Florence's life in Derling was a simple one. She woke up to the smell of her mum's cooking, which could either be the worst or best smell in the world, depending on whether it was savoury or pudding. She wandered outside in the afternoons, either in the forest or all the way down to the beach. She was homeschooled, so she had no other friends besides her mother, and she was a kid, which meant she was never bored so long as there was a tree to climb or water to swim in. That fact was especially true today, when Amee found herself halfway up one of the orchard trees, looking down at her mum as she collected apples and placed them into a big plastic tub.

'How many have you got, Mum?' she called down.

'Just twenty,' her mother replied. 'I'm thinking of doing a cranachan. Or maybe some kind of cheesecake. Which do you think?'

'So long as it's a pudding, I'm happy.'

'Yes, but which would you choose?' Her mum kept her eyes on the apples, her flowery dress blowing slightly in the breeze.

'I don't know. Would apples really work in a cheesecake?'

'Oh yeah,' her mum said nonchalantly. 'Yeah, I think cheesecake. Good call, Amee. An apple cheesecake with peanut butter. How does that sound?'

Amee rolled her eyes. 'Sounds great.'

'Great.'

Her mum set down the tub and began pulling some weeds out near the roots of an apple tree, talking quietly to herself about how she would have to collect some more peanut butter in town the next day. This was a conversation she had almost weekly. She used peanut butter in nearly every pudding, and sometimes in the mains too, which was part of the reason Amee hated them. She'd had better starts to the day than waking up to the smell of brisket and peanut butter.

'Three jars,' she heard her mum contemplate below. 'Or maybe just two. Yeah, three jars is too much. Three jars is weird.'

Amee laughed to herself, remembering the time her mum had bought fifteen jars during an outing to Prescott, which was their local town. She had fretted all the way home about how the man at the till had glared at her.

'Why was he looking at me like that? Have I just broken some kind of law? Oh God, I hope they let me back in. I'll need some more for Anna's party next weekend. I'm doing a peanut butter carrot cake.'

For the record, they had let Amee's mum back in. But the manager made sure to guard the baking aisle while she loaded her basket.

Amee looked over towards the ocean, watching as the waves frothed and foamed over each other from afar. The surface of the water had turned so blue that she had an urge to jump down from the tree and sprint as fast as she could into its depths. *Maybe later*, she thought. *If he isn't back yet.*

She hadn't told her mum that the dreams had started again. They tended to come back when Amee knew a job was coming to an end, when she knew he was close. It was like he was reaching into her head, grabbing her dreams by the collar, shaking them, spitting at them, making her as scared as he possibly could, like it was practice. No matter how hard Amee tried, she couldn't get rid of him. He infected her nights, just as he would infect her days, and the only relief she ever got was her mum. Her soft, funny, peanut butter-loving mum. Amee swallowed a ball of anxiety, then looked down at her.

'How soon is it?' she asked before she could help herself.

'How soon is what?' her mum replied, but judging by the sound of her voice, she already knew what Amee was talking about.

'How soon until he's back?'

Her mum wiped her soiled hands upon her skirt. 'Have you been dreaming about him again?'

'No.'

'Amee, please don't lie.'

'It's not my fault. He comes to me, and I can't help it.'

'When you say he comes to you, what do you mean? He's hurting you? Amee, you have to understand that what he did, he did a long time ago. He was different back then. He was...' Her mum stopped. Perhaps because she didn't believe what she was saying, or perhaps because, for just a moment, she felt that he was watching them. Listening. And he would make her pay for talking about him behind his back. Amee got that feeling too. She got that feeling lots of times.

Just at that moment, a sound arrived on the wind. A rumble that was distant at first, but then grew into something unmistakeable. Amee turned towards the driveway to see a grubby, rusty van passing around the corner. It spluttered to a stop beside the porch and the engine cut out with a sharp *clang*.

'He's home,' Amee said gravely. 'The green monster's home.'

'I wish you wouldn't call him that.'

579

Her mum picked up her tub of apples, and Amee watched as the man stepped out of the truck and began to dust himself down. He was a woodsman, so he was nearly always covered from head to toe with moss and grass at the end of a long job. His skin seemed permanently stained by a dark and sickening green.

'I wish you wouldn't call him that,' she heard her mum say softly. 'He's not a monster. He's your father.'

Amee shuddered, clinging so hard to the branch that she felt splinters of wood stick into her palms. 'I know,' she said.

Her mum left the orchard and embraced her husband in a quick and unfeeling hug. Then they walked into the house together. Amee stayed in the tree for another twenty minutes before she followed.

That night, she had the dream again. The green monster was behind her, the twigs and branches snapping under his feet as he ran. He screamed her name so loudly that every bird scattered from their nests.

'AMEE! COME BACK HERE!'

But Amee kept running, sliding fast down the forest slope, trying desperately to reach the beach.

'AMEE, COME BACK HERE! I WANT TO HUG YOU! THAT'S ALL I WANT TO DO! I JUST WANT TO GIVE YOU A BIG HUG!'

'No!' Amee cried, because she knew he was lying. She knew what had happened the last time he went to hug her. Their argument was over, and she thought he was making it up to her, but he was still angry. She could feel his fury through his fingers, through the squeeze, the spittle, those eyes, mad eyes, staring into her as she struggled to breathe. 'No!' she cried again.

'WHY WON'T YOU LET ME HUG YOU?!'

'Leave me alone! Just leave me alone!'

But her dad was fast. Pretty soon Amee heard his big boots coming up behind her.

'I JUST WANT TO HUG MY DAUGHTER!' he screamed.

And then Amee felt his hands close around her neck, and she sprang up in bed, hot sweat trickling down her temples.

Her room was silent at first. The world outside was completely black, apart from the chimney on the horizon, which was lit up in red, just as it always was. After a few seconds of staring at it, Amee began to hear crying. It was coming from the floor below. The sobs were small, but recognisable.

She leapt up from her mattress and crept towards her door, making sure to tread as quietly as she could on the creaky floorboards. *Mum*, she thought as she pressed her ear to the wood. It was her mum's voice, her mum's sobs. Amee knew, because she had heard them before.

She opened the door and crept to the top of the stairs, peering down to see her mother curled up on the rug in front of the fireplace. The flames were flickering beside her, illuminating one side of her tear-stained face. Amee had witnessed this scene lots of times, but never this soon after the green monster had returned. Ordinarily she would go back to her room and try to forget she'd seen anything, but this time, she didn't turn away. She crept down the stairs, walked over towards her mother, and lay down beside her. She placed both arms around her shoulders until she felt her mother hold her back.

'My little fishy,' her mum whispered.

The two of them cuddled into each other, watching the fire as it spat and flickered behind the grill. Tiny sparks and embers twirled up and down, up and down, as if they were performing some kind of dance. It was like they were partners playing off each other. Some went this way, others went that. Some congregated, twisting around until they split apart. Some disappeared, others remained. The dance promised to continue for the rest of the night, or for as long as the hearth was warm. Amee leaned over and spoke against her mum's ear.

'Why don't we go away?' she asked hopefully.

She felt her mother shudder against her touch. 'I wish that we could,' she responded.

'But why can't we?'

'Because it's my duty to stay. I'm somebody's wife, Amee. That means something. I can't just run away when it gets hard. And things get hard, that's just what things do. One day you'll learn that.'

'But I don't like to see you like this.'

A crackle of warmth sounded from within the hearth.

'I'm alright. I have you. When I think of you, I think of the ocean.'

Amee pressed her face so close to her mum that she could smell her. The orchard, the soil, the fruit. Everything was once again embedded in the fabric of her clothes.

'You'll always have me, Mum,' she said softly.

'And you'll always have me. I promise you that.'

Her mother squeezed Amee tightly, and then they were silent once more. They remained that way until dawn, staying warm in each other's arms even when the flames had died and the hearth went cold, and there was nothing but the darkness and the two of them alone in its midst. They stayed warm until the sun came up and they were awoken by the birds' morning call.

When autumn ended and winter came, it floated by slowly, as slowly as winters tended to pass on the cliff, and the green monster had several more jobs. This was good news for Amee, who hated the thought of being locked up with him, with his cold, lingering stare and his hoarse voice. The man was winter personified, and she would have preferred to take on the elements outside. But thankfully, she didn't have to do that. Amee stayed indoors. She loved art, so she would draw pictures while listening to *Rocky's Rocky Radio*, which crackled out of the radio every Monday through Thursday. She started reading real books (her mum got her *Great Expectations* for a not-very-funny Christmas present), she cooked a lot, and her mum cooked with her, which meant that peanut butter was used in nearly everything. Most importantly, she slept well. The bad dreams had gone, just as the green monster had gone, and they were replaced with other dreams, nicer dreams. Dreams that made her want to stay in bed forever. But of course, as with all nice dreams, they didn't last.

On the final day before spring, the green monster came back, and when he did, he was worse than ever. He would shout at things that didn't need to be shouted at, he would hit things when he got angry, throw things, sometimes at the wall, sometimes at Amee's mum. One afternoon, he threw a full glass of gin and tonic right at Amee, and she ran from the house, sprinting as fast as she could towards the orchard before climbing to the top of an apple tree. She didn't come down for the whole day, and when she did, it was only because of her mother, who stood by the gate singing the words from *A Song About Love*, urging Amee to come home and get warm by the fire. Amee eventually obliged. Her mum was already upset enough. There was a look she carried in her eyes now. Something worn down, something resigned, and something beaten. Amee couldn't quite understand what it meant, but come one windy night in February, she finally worked it out.

The time was 9:21 p.m. and the voices had started in the kitchen. At first, they were normal. Her mum and dad often had a fight late in the evening. But usually that fight would fizzle out and disintegrate. Her mum would go one way, and the green monster would go the other, and then everything would be over. For a while, anyway. But this time, the argument carried on. The voices got louder, and harder, echoing through the cracks in the floorboards so that Amee could hear them.

'Get out of your head for one second. I'm not against you –'

'Big fucking joke. You've been against me for years now. I know it. I've seen it. You've just been waiting for an excuse to leave and take the girl away. Now I've lost my job you're –'

'Stop it, just stop it, you're deluded –'

'Call me that again!'

'Get away from me. Don't touch me –'

'I'll do what I want; this is my house!'

'This is *our* house, we built this house together. Don't –'

'And now it's a house you want to tear down! You want to take everything from under my feet! Well, I can tell you, you're not gonna do it! You're not gonna fucking do it, you psycho bitch!'

At that moment, there was a yell, the sound of glass smashing, and Amee's heart leapt into her throat. She heard feet bounding up the stairs, then her door opened and her mum fell desperately into Amee's bed. Her face was covered by her hands, and Amee could see tears falling through the cracks.

'Little fishy,' she whimpered. 'Little fishy, little fishy.'

Downstairs, Amee could still hear the green monster raging. Cabinet doors were flying open in his search for something else to drink. Drawers were being pulled, cutlery was falling everywhere, and all the while, he was still shouting at the top of his lungs.

'BITCH! BITCH! FUCKING BITCH!'

Her mum held Amee, and Amee held her back, stroking her skin in a small sort of spiral.

'He's not going away again, is he?' she said. 'He's staying forever...'

'Yes,' her mum replied after a few seconds.

'Then I want to leave. I want to go. I can't stay with him, Mum. I can't.'

'I know, Amee, I know. We'll leave. I promise you. We'll leave. We've had enough, we've had enough now. Both of us.'

Amee gave in to the tears. They spilled onto her mother's dress as she sobbed, but her mum didn't mind. She let her cry, holding her so tight that Amee could hear her mother's heart beating beneath her chest.

'When?' she sobbed.

'Soon,' her mum whispered. 'I promise you, it'll be soon. We'll be together. It'll just be you and me. And maybe a few jars of peanut butter.'

Amee looked up into her mother's brown eyes. 'But how do I know you're telling the truth?'

Her mum smiled at her, then she turned on the bed and pointed towards the window. 'Look out there...'

Amee looked. The chimney was sparkling in red, the ocean underneath it, and the moon was reflected delicately upon the waves. It was bigger than usual. It hung low in the dark night sky, its craters like a face smiling down upon the two of them.

'When I think of you,' her mother said, 'I think of the ocean. Do you remember what that means? It means you're my everything, you're my world. I would never lie to you. That's a mother's promise, Amee. A mother never breaks her promise, do you understand? A mother always tells the truth.'

'I understand,' replied Amee.

She pulled her mother into another hug, trying desperately to cut off the noise downstairs. She didn't want to hear the green monster anymore. Right now, he didn't exist to her. It was just her and her mother, breathing alone in the room together.

'Whatever life throws at us,' her mum whispered, 'I'll always be here for you. And I'll always find you again. If you forget that, if you get lost, then just remember. When I think of you, I think of the ocean.'

She kissed her on the forehead, and then the two of them lay down, holding onto each other until the green monster went quiet. By then, Amee was already half asleep. She watched with semi-closed eyes as her mum got out of bed and left the room, and listened as her footsteps crept slowly back to the entrance hall. Amee wanted to go with her. She wanted to stay awake, just to make sure everything was okay, to make sure the green monster wouldn't start fighting again. But the night was too dark. The sleep was too close. And pretty soon, Amee found herself drifting into another dream.

This time, however, she didn't dream about the green monster. This time Amee dreamt about the ocean. She was with her mother, swimming through the water as if they were flying, soaring through foam and waves, against the currents and over the coral. They swam far and wide, hand in hand, until the smell started. It filled Amee's nose with something other than the salt of the ocean. Something harsher, harsh enough to sting her nostrils, and gnaw unpleasantly at the back of her throat. She let go of her mum's hand, grabbing her neck as she choked on it, but doing that only made it worse, and when she turned to grip her mum's hand again, it was gone. She had disappeared in a thick and ugly fog, which was drifting through the water as if it was on fire, like the coral itself was burning and engulfing the ocean in a cloud of impenetrable smoke. Amee called for her mum, but there was no answer. She called louder, peering desperately through the water as she choked harder, and harder, and harder, until everything went black, and she finally awoke upon the cold and sweaty sheets.

The smell of smoke was still strong in Amee's nose. That was the first thing she noticed. It was surging up through the floorboards, making her lungs burn and her eyes water.

'Mum?' she called out nervously.

But just like in the dream, there was no reply. Amee jumped out of bed and ran out of her room, racing to the top of the stairs and looking down to see the smoke spilling out from the kitchen. She coughed, then spat, and turned as if instinctively towards the fireplace. That was when she spotted the bundle. Her mum was lying there, in the spot she would usually lie, just underneath the mantelpiece.

'Mum!' Amee ran down the stairs and came up towards her. 'Mum, wake up, there's smoke. There's smoke, Mum, there's a fire!'

But her mother didn't move. She didn't even flinch. Amee tilted her head, then knelt down beside her and shook her by the shoulders.

'Mum? Wake up, you have to wake up – there's a fire!' She shook again, then again, and again, but her mother didn't wake up. Her eyes didn't open. She remained fixed in her position, her face unchanged, as if moulded in stone.

It was then that Amee felt something wet on her hands. She pulled her mum over, immediately seeing the red liquid that stained her dress. She shook her again, so hard that her head thumped against the floorboards. But there was no response. No quick smile, no eyes opening. She held her by the armpits, but no laughter met her in return. No sparkle, no prank, no surprise. Just the blankness. Her lips were pursed, but she wasn't going to kiss. Her fingers were curved, but she didn't want to hold. There was nothing. An emotionless face. A summer dress that she couldn't smell, but for the stench of blood. Everything about her mum was gone, and yet Amee was holding her in her arms. The two things didn't add up, and it made her want to scream, but instead, all she could do was stare. And disbelieve. Utterly disbelieve.

'Mum? Mum, stop it. Just stop it now. There's a fire in the house, and you've got to wake up. You've got to be here. You can't leave. You promised. Hey. You promised me. You can't leave, Mum, you promised. Please don't leave me alone.'

'Amee…'

The voice came from behind her, and Amee turned to see the green monster standing on the other side of the room, a long kitchen knife clenched in one hand.

'She's gone, Amee. She's gone. I'm sorry. I'm so sorry. Come here, let me help you understand.' He held out both arms, standing with his back to the smoke as if he didn't even know he was inches from the flames.

Amee stood. 'No,' she replied shakily.

'Amee, I told you I was sorry. I didn't want to kill her. I didn't want to kill anyone. Just come here. Let me help you understand. Let me comfort you. Let me give you a hug.'

The green monster stepped forward, his eyes bloodshot and dark, with a glint of madness dancing amid the flames that were reflected there. 'Amee, this is what she made me do. This is what you both made me do. Now come here and hug me, before I lose my patience!'

The last word came in a high-pitched shriek, and Amee stumbled, watching as the green monster raised the knife in one hand.

'No!' she screamed.

And then Amee was running, sprinting fast towards the front door and out into the garden. She heard her father shout from behind her, but she didn't listen. She had to run. That was all she knew. She had to get as far away from the green monster as possible, before he caught up with her, before he grabbed her and didn't let go. She had to run fast.

'AMEE, COME BACK HERE!'

Amee reached the gate and swivelled. The house was almost entirely engulfed in flames now, and the green monster was silhouetted in front of it, the knife raised threateningly above his head.

'DON'T RUN FROM ME!' he roared.

All of a sudden, Amee thought of the dreams she'd been having. She'd been running in them, too. She had been sprinting through the forest with the green monster behind her, getting closer, and closer, and closer, until his hands were around her throat and the life was being throttled out of her. She never got away. She never escaped her dad's clutches. So why would tonight be any different? *Don't go*, a voice in the back of her head told her. *Don't go into the forest. Don't do it. He'll catch you, he'll be sure to catch you; you saw it in your dreams.*

The green monster started running towards her, and Amee didn't waste any more time. Instead of opening the gate, she turned to the left and sprinted along the wall and off into the tall grass.

'AMEE, COME BACK HERE! YOU BITCH! YOU FUCKING BITCH! COME BACK HERE NOW!'

She ran fast, her shins slapping against the grass as it grew longer, coming up to her waist as she disappeared into its midst. The smoke was rising high into the sky now. It cut out the light from the moon, and the further she got from the house, the darker the shadow became, until there was absolutely nothing to light her path.

'I can't see,' she cried to no one but herself. 'Please, someone help, I can't see.'

Just keep going, keep running – he's behind you. Quick!

'AMEE, COME BACK HERE!' the green monster screamed.

Amee felt the hands of the phantom in her dream close around her neck. She felt the squeeze, the snap; heard the scream of terror. She gasped and ran faster, desperate not to make that her reality.

Don't let it happen again. Just run. Run, run, run. And keep running.

'The cliff edge,' Amee panted. 'There's a drop somewhere close to here. There's a drop. What about the drop?'

But almost as soon as she asked herself the question, she was given an answer. Amee felt her feet hit nothing but air, and she tumbled forward, spiralling through the darkness and feeling the wind hit her face.

'AMEE!'

The scream of the green monster echoed into the night, and Amee closed her eyes, feeling herself fall, and fall, and fall, onwards, and onwards, and onwards, until it seemed like she would never, ever land. But she did land. Her lips only managed to part once before the end. She called for her mother, and she imagined holding onto her, clutching her tight, breathing in her brilliant-smelling summer dress, scented with basil, hogwood seed, and blossom. Then her body hit what she assumed was the ocean. And everything went quiet.

35

THINKING OF THE OCEAN

The wood beneath her cheek was warm. Amee Florence shuffled against it. She pushed herself up, watching as the room around her swayed, slowly but surely coming back into focus, along with the people who were standing in it.

'Wake up,' said Roman Guild. He was about ten paces away, holding Mr Cooper in a headlock. 'Wake up, dead girl. It's time to wake up.'

Amee took a deep breath. 'I died...'

Winona stepped out of the blur. She was beside the old and blackened fireplace, a fierce look on her face. 'So she remembers,' she said.

'What do you mean, she remembers?' Mr Cooper wheezed.

'Like you don't know.'

'I died,' Amee said again, feeling a rush of something cold hit her spine. 'I remember...'

The image of the green monster flashed before her eyes.

The raised knife, the mad glint in his eyes, the spittle, the fury. Her mother, the blood. The image of the ocean too. Not a dream. Never a dream. She had stayed in the waves for a long time, holding on to her own body, until the big storm drove her to the distant shore.

'But you're alive,' she heard Mr Cooper say. 'I'm looking at you, Amee. You're alive.'

'How is it looking at me, broken man?' Roman drove a knee up into Mr Cooper's spine. 'Do I look alive to you?'

'What the hell are you talking about?' Mr Cooper winced in pain.

'They're both dead,' said Winona, the words dropping out of her mouth like stones. 'Everyone in my ward has been deceased for a long time. That's how they see the dead people. They came back from the mid-space. Them.' She glared back down at Amee with that look of hatred.

'We're the chosen ones.' Roman laughed, twisting Mr Cooper's head so that he could look him in the eye. 'We're the ones allowed back to the world of the living, to do as we please. Didn't I tell you, David? You can't kill me. No one can kill me. Hell is a place for the weak, and I spit at its door.' He spat into Mr Cooper's face, and Amee turned away.

Dead. I'm dead. She tried to process the information, but none of it could even start to sink in. It wasn't real. It couldn't be real. *But the memory is real. This is my home. I know this is my home, I remember, but...*

A form appeared. It was just a silhouette at first, but then came the blonde hair, the warm smile, and Amee recognised the form as Charlie Cooper.

'She's still here,' he said in a small voice.

Amee shook her head. She was about to ask what he meant, but Winona spoke before she could.

'Do you get it now?' she hissed. 'That's all I've ever wanted to understand. Why do they come back? Why do the others stay? That's what I have to know if I want to save Grace. If I want to bring her back too.'

'Amee, she's still here,' said Charlie.

'What do you mean?' asked Amee, and her nurse answered as if Amee was talking to her.

'I mean that it's about you, Amee Florence. It's about you, and the others in my ward. Every one of you is going to help me save my daughter.'

'Except you'll never save her.' The words were muffled and breathless, but Mr Cooper just about managed to get them out as he pulled against Roman's grasp.

Winona's face twitched. 'What did you say?'

'Would you like me to eat his tongue, Winona?' asked Roman.

Winona walked over to Mr Cooper. 'You want to come between me and my work? You want to stop me bringing Grace back into the world?'

'Your daughter's dead,' said Mr Cooper. 'She passed away years ago, and she can never come back.'

'But she can.' Winona pointed towards Amee. 'If this girl can bring herself back to the living, then I can bring my daughter back too. I just have to find her first. That's all I have to –'

'But you haven't found her,' said Mr Cooper with a cold and dead certainty.

'What do you know about this?' Winona spat. 'Nothing. You're just a drunk and washed-up nobody, who's so ignorant of what it means to be a father that you lost your own son. You know nothing about me and my daughter. All you know is what you've heard from the girl.'

'No. Amee's told me nothing. But you have. Thanks to Marty Evans.'

Mr Cooper nodded over to a bundle on the floor, and Amee felt her stomach do a somersault as she recognised Marty lying motionless in the corner. His fingers were curled in the ash and his mouth hung half open, as if frozen in a scream. *Dead*, she thought bleakly. Then she closed her eyes. *No. Not dead. If he was dead, he would be here, but the only one here is...*

'I can hear her,' said Charlie. He was standing closer now, staring at Amee with an intensity that she had never seen in him before. 'The voice. This is it. I think this is the place.'

'He took your notebook,' Mr Cooper continued. 'I read it all last night. Front to back. All those lessons. Everything you did with Amee in order to understand the dead people and work out why they stayed. But you never actually found your daughter.'

Winona was visibly shaking now. She glared at the teacher with a trace of spittle dripping from the corner of her mouth. She was frothing like a threatened snake, just waiting for an opportune moment to spit the venom.

'Maybe you can't see it,' Mr Cooper said, his voice choked. 'Or maybe you don't want to. But the answer is there. The answer has always been in the pages. It took me just a few minutes to realise –'

KASLAP!

The echo of flesh on flesh rebounded off every pane of shattered glass, every board of splintered wood, around and around the hall until it faded into oblivion. Everyone in the room seemed to hold their breath. Winona had slapped the teacher so hard there was blood trickling from his cheek. She hissed out her next words carefully. One at a time.

'You. Know. Nothing. You. Cretin.'

'I know you'll never get your daughter back. And I can show you why, if you'd let me reach into my pocket.'

Winona swayed on the spot, her eyes flashing. It was almost as if she couldn't quite believe the teacher hadn't stopped, hadn't cowered down on the floor in fear and pain. Mr Cooper stood there like he wasn't bleeding, like he wasn't close to a fate that might be worse than death. A beat passed. Winona slid her hand into Mr Cooper's jacket and pulled out the familiar burgundy notebook.

'You realise how many times I've examined these lessons? You think there's some kind of answer that –'

'Pick a page. Any page.'

There was another moment, even more cutting than the last. Amee stared, unable to take her eyes off the pair of them. Winona too, it seemed, was oddly taken in by the teacher's persistence. She removed the band and opened the book somewhere around the middle.

'Gealblath Beach. One year ago. A boy who had died from drowning.'

'Date of death.'

Winona's lip curled. The muscles in her cheek twitched. She looked down and searched for it. 'Summer, 1981.'

'Another page.'

Winona looked like she was about to slap him again. But instead, she flicked to another page. 'Elia Marshall. Died twentieth of November 1991.'

'Another.'

'Why the hell are you letting this guy talk?' Roman Guild squeezed Mr Cooper's neck tighter, and he let out a yelp of pain.

'I'm asking myself the same question,' replied Winona. She slapped the notebook shut.

'The pattern,' Mr Cooper breathed. 'Didn't you ever wonder why Amee saw so few dead people?'

'Of course I wondered. That's what I'm trying to find out,' replied Winona, an almost desperate pleading in her voice now. She sounded like an adamant child terrified of being proved wrong. And Amee knew why. 'I'm trying to find out why they don't cross. What makes people like her so special?'

'Nothing makes them special,' Mr Cooper said quickly, as if he knew his time was running out. 'Kevvy wasn't special.'

'Who's Kevvy?'

'He was my friend. He died in Gealblath Hospital, back in 1968. But Amee never saw him. That's when I started to wonder. And the dates helped me: '79, '83, '87, '94. A whole notebook full of dead people, and yet every death happened within the last two decades.'

Winona shook her head. 'What are you trying to say?'

'I'm a maths teacher; I notice numbers. I don't know what stops the dead people crossing over, I don't know what caused all of this, but there's always a source. Cause and effect. Whatever it is, it happened on a specific date, at a specific time. I would guess thirty years ago.'

Amee blinked, then Charlie came back into her line of vision, bending down towards her as she pushed herself onto her knees.

'Amee, he's right. It's here. The house on the cliff. This is where it started.'

At the same moment, a voice spoke inside Amee's head. *Little fishy*, it said. *I missed you.*

'So when did your daughter pass away?' said Mr Cooper. 'Like Kevvy, it was more than thirty years ago, correct?'

Winona was just an inch away from Mr Cooper's face now, her teeth bared and her fingers trembling. She dropped the notebook onto the ashy floor and grabbed Mr Cooper's chin. 'You're telling me my daughter's gone?' she said.

'I'm telling you she crossed,' said Mr Cooper. 'I'm telling you that everything you're doing in that ward, with Amee, it's all for nothing. She crossed years ago, and you'll never find her.'

Amee watched as a tear fell down her nurse's cheek. Winona was crying. She was actually crying. Amee had never seen her cry before. She had always been stone cold. Dead set in her beliefs, in her purpose. But now that purpose had crumbled, and she was staring at the man who'd destroyed it.

'Why don't you stab him already?' growled Roman.

'No.' Winona shook her head, wiping away more tears as she looked Mr Cooper up and down. 'I don't want him gone. Not yet. I don't want him asleep. He can't feel any pain if he's asleep.'

'Winona...' Mr Cooper writhed against the tall man's grasp. 'Don't...'

Roman grinned at her. 'I love you,' he said.

Then, as quick as a flash, he stuffed one of his hands in his pockets, retrieved his lighter, and flicked it up against Mr Cooper's neck. Mr Cooper screamed as the giant flame caught his beard, and Amee gasped, turning back towards Charlie. His eyes were still fixed on her, like he had just realised something.

'You lived here with your mum and your dad,' he said urgently. 'Amee, did they die too?'

'My dad. My dad killed my mum. And he chased me off the cliff. The green monster.'

Mr Cooper's cries seemed to make the house rattle. Roman lifted the lighter further up his neck, his body rocking as Mr Cooper tried desperately to pull away.

'Then maybe this is about you,' said Charlie. 'Maybe this was always about you. The house on the cliff, the ocean, the green monster. The voice that talks to all of us is connected to you, Amee. It's talking to you. It's...' He stumbled on the last word. 'Your mum, Amee. What if she came back? What if she found a way back from the warmth?' Charlie stepped towards her, more alive than Amee had ever seen him before. 'Maybe... maybe she came back from the warmth. And maybe that stopped others from crossing. If it *is* all connected, then maybe that's what happened. Amee, if you join her now... If she finds you, we could end this.'

Mr Cooper's screams pierced Amee's ears again, but they didn't obscure the voice. Amee heard it loud and clear, clearer than anything else in the world, almost like it wasn't in her head at all.

Little fishy. When I think of you, I think of the ocean.

And this time, Amee replied. 'Mum?'

Winona Nightly turned towards her. 'Don't think you'll get off easy this time, little fishy. I still intend to punish you. You'll wish you never ran away from me and my daughter.'

But Amee ignored her. Amee ignored everything. Only the voice in her head remained.

When I think of you, I think of the ocean.

It was even stronger now. Like it was speaking right in this room.

Amee thought back, *Tell me. If you're here, please, just give me a sign.*

A flash of red appeared in the corner of her eye, and she swivelled towards the hearth. Sparks of light were pulsing from the ashes, like a fire trying desperately to breathe its way out into the open.

'It's time to cross,' said Charlie. 'That's what the voice is saying. But it's not talking to us. It's talking to you, Amee. It's always been talking to you. She wants to cross, but she won't do it –'

'Unless she's with me.' Amee finished for him.

The light in the hearth flickered, the ashes brightening, then fading, from red and back to black.

How do I do it? Amee asked, *I want to hold you again, I want to find you, but I don't know how.*

The dust rose and fell, and Amee thought of the words, thought of the voice.

'The warmth,' she said to Charlie. 'She came back from the warmth for me; that's what you said.' She peered over at Mr Cooper. His beard had been completely burnt off now. His skin was red and entirely warped by Roman's bright flame. Amee remembered the night she died. The flames had been bright then too, swirling about the house like an infection, a plague, engulfing the walls and burning the windows. The entire place had disappeared into a bright-orange glow, and Amee had seen it. That fire. That big fire. *But who started it?* The question came as a surprise to Amee, almost as if it wasn't even her who'd asked it. *A fire as big as that should have burned this place to the ground. But it didn't. The fire roared, but the house is still here, still standing, still intact, still...*

'Warm.'

Amee stared at the tall man. She watched as the flame blasted from his lighter, blue at the bottom, red at the top. Charlie faded slightly from her vision, and his voice became small and distant.

'Amee. Whatever you're thinking of doing...'

The words echoed into nothingness, and Charlie

disappeared, replaced instead by Winona, who stepped into the spot Charlie had been standing.

'Little fishy...'

She went to grab Amee's arm, but Amee was too quick. With a yell, she lashed out and pushed Winona aside so that she fell onto the floor. Then she climbed to her feet and sprinted fast towards the two struggling men.

'ROMAN!' cried Winona.

The tall man turned as Amee pulled the lighter from his grasp, a mixture of rage and amazement on his face.

'No way...' He gaped as Amee lifted the lighter and threw it towards the hearth, watching as it swirled through the air, almost in slow motion, before landing with a thump in the tiny mountain of old and blackened ash.

Then everything happened at once. Winona screamed and the hearth exploded with light. Flames spilled over the grill, engulfing the entire house like it had been covered in oil, spreading over every crack, every splinter, every beam, until the whole place was shining with hot orange flames.

Amee ducked down and covered her head with her hands. Everyone else in the room disappeared in a whirl of smoke. The heat was strong, but it didn't burn, it didn't kill. The flames weren't really flames. The flames were Amee's mother. The essence of her, the remnants of the warmth, returned from the next life. Amee watched as they twisted around the house, and then gathered in the place where her mum had been lying on that night thirty years before. A bright white light appeared there, and Amee felt it beckoning. A hand clasped her shoulder.

'AMEE!' yelled Mr Cooper. 'AMEE! QUICK!' His eyes were wide with pain and confusion, and he tried to pull her towards the door, but Amee didn't move. She stayed rooted to the spot.

'No,' she responded over the roar of the fire.

'AMEE, WE NEED TO GET OUT OF HERE!'

'Save him.'

She gestured over towards Marty, who was lying still amongst the flames, his body coming into view as the smoke started to thin. Roman and Winona were nowhere to be seen.

'I NEED TO SAVE YOU TOO!' cried Mr Cooper. He grabbed her hand, but Amee pulled away.

'It's too late for me. But you can save Marty. Go! Go now!'

Another burst of light rippled through the hall, and one of the chandeliers collapsed from the ceiling, landing just beside Marty and causing fire and splinters to shoot into the air. Mr Cooper yelled, then sprinted towards Marty and pulled him up from the floor, holding him close to his chest.

Amee called out to him. 'I'll remember who you are, David Cooper. You're a good person. I know you're a good person.'

A gust of sparks started falling between the pair of them, and Amee looked back towards the fireplace, her head tilting slightly as she saw the white light morph into a shape. She didn't know why, but she knew the shape was her mother. She could feel it in her bones. In her heart. Every instinct told her to go to it, but before she could, Charlie's voice vibrated close to her ear.

'It's time, Amee. It's time to cross.'

'Is that what I have to do now?' she shouted fearfully. 'Am I dying again?'

Charlie shook his head. For a moment, it looked like his hair was moving in the whirling flames, like he was in the room with her. Just for a moment. 'Not dying,' he said. 'Not this. Dying is going cold, but that's not where you're going.'

He lifted his hand towards hers, and Amee felt like she could touch it. Like he was finally with her, properly, now they were at the end. And she knew he was right. She could feel he was right. Everything had happened so quickly, but at the same time, everything had happened so slowly. She was always meant to return here. For years and years, she had been on her own, but now she and her mum had been reunited again. There was just one more step to take.

Amee turned back and saw Mr Cooper standing in the doorframe, with Marty cradled to his chest, a desperate look plastered on his face.

'Goodbye, Marty,' Amee whispered, and for a second, it looked like Marty's eyes opened and locked on to hers.

She wiped the tears from her cheeks and walked towards the hearth. She didn't know what to expect. All she knew was that she was walking towards her mother. And walking towards her felt like the most right thing in the world. She took one last breath as the white light gathered around her. Then she closed her eyes, and the warmth, like arms, embraced her.

36

THE WARMTH

Marty Evans, the weed-kid as they called him, was smiling at Amee awkwardly on the other side. He had a red plastic tray in his hands. His lips were pursed in a funny sort of fashion, like he was halfway through a whistle, and his fringe was still sticking out from the night before, giving the impression that he didn't really care what he looked like to other people. Amee Florence stared at him for a few seconds, wondering what the hell had just happened. She had been in the house. She had been standing in its flames, its warmth, and then she had walked forward towards the hearth and been engulfed in a white light. And now she was here. She watched Marty as he swayed from one foot to the other, waiting in line in the lunch hall, evidently eager to get something to eat. Then a voice came to her, whirling through Amee's head, as warm and pleasant as a song.

Thought you might like to say goodbye...

Amee turned around, but her mother wasn't there to meet her. It was just the lunch hall, and all the children and teachers bustling around in it.

Goodbye? she thought.

Marty Evans huffed, then took a step forward.

Isn't this where you first met? Don't you remember?

Amee realised her mum was right. This was the first time she'd met Marty. She had just been teased and bullied by three other girls. They had thrown her shoes up onto the changing room lockers, and then she had met Marty while standing barefoot in the lunch hall. Amee turned on the spot and saw herself. Or rather, she saw the back of her head.

This is where Marty Evans meets me, she realised. *But why am I here?*

Her mum's voice returned. *We're leaving soon, and I thought you might want to say goodbye. So? Will you say it?*

Marty scratched his nose, then looked up awkwardly at the girl in front of him again. He was whistling the *Ghostbusters* tune, about halfway through the rendition.

I do want to say goodbye, she thought. *But how do I do it when he can't even hear me?*

He wants to meet someone like you. You want to meet someone like him. Who's to say he's not listening?

Amee shook her head. There was no way he could hear, and even if he could, hearing a girl he hadn't met yet say goodbye would be so weird he'd probably run off and never meet her in the first place. No. She couldn't say goodbye. She couldn't do that. But she could watch him for a while. She didn't know how, and she didn't know why, but for one last time, she could watch this boy and remember the time they had spent together. She remembered all the conversations they'd had. Little ones, about movies, and big ones, about courage. She remembered their time in the forest, their time on the beach. She remembered the look on his face when she agreed to be his girlfriend, and she remembered the way his lips felt when she kissed him. She remembered Marty Evans. And, one last time, she smiled back at him.

He was coming to the end of the tune now. The *Ghostbusters* theme was entering its grand finale, and as it did so, Amee decided to join in. She whistled the tune along with Marty. Then she stopped. Because Marty was staring at her now. His fingers twitched on the tray, and he reached forward, his arm travelling through Amee's torso. She moved to the side, realising that he was in fact tapping the Amee Florence in the line in front of him.

'Hello,' he said simply.

Amee watched as she let out a terrified yelp and flung her tray high up into the air, spilling the cutlery down onto the lunch hall floor. Then the world around her started to spin, and once again everything dissolved into a bright white light.

She was swirling now. Her life was flashing before her eyes vigorously, violently, swarming past her in a hurricane. There was the house on the cliff, the green monster, her mum picking apples in the orchard, she was up a tree, she was in bed, there was blood, and death, and fear, and water, lots of water, until she was on the street, at school, in the hospital, with Marty, in the forest, in the caravan, the inn, the hospital again, the house on the cliff, fire, flames, red, orange, over and over and over again, everything and anything she had ever known, flying around in front of her like a storm of thoughts and memories. Eventually only one thing made sense. A white light in the centre, with two arms bringing her into an embrace that felt like the warmest hug in the universe.

Little fishy, said her mum.

Amee Florence relaxed into her. *I don't understand,* she managed to think. *I don't understand what's happening.*

It felt like her mum stroked her hair. *Don't worry. These are just the parts of you. Things have to be wrapped up before the end, like sending off a gift in the post. You remember when we used to do that? I could never work out the bow.*

Amee watched her life spin faster, like hands on a clock spiralling out of control, round and round and round, with no rhyme or reason at all. It just kept going, and going, and going, and Amee held her mum closer.

I don't understand what just happened.

I thought you'd like to stop off at one particular memory. I thought you'd like to linger, so you could say goodbye.

Amee shook her head, or what felt like her head, watching as the visions started to spiral into random colours. *But I didn't say goodbye. That was our hello. That was the first time we met.*

The colours converged into a tunnel, and Amee felt herself spinning quickly towards it, both hands (or what felt like hands) clinging harder to her mum, like she was worried she might fall if she let go.

Well, her mum said. *Saying hello is saying goodbye. Eventually.*

The tunnel seemed to swerve. It sent Amee this way, then that, before it seemed to incline and Amee went faster.

But he heard me, she replied. *Marty heard me whistling. How could...*

She trailed off, waiting for her mum to give her some sort of answer without hearing the end of the question.

Perhaps he did, she said. *Or perhaps he didn't. He'll probably hear you lots of times for the rest of his life. Who's to say which times are real and which times aren't?*

The tunnel rippled, the colours sparkling, fizzing. Amee spoke over cracks of soft lightning.

How did you do it, Mum? How did you come back?

I made a promise on that night. I couldn't leave you. I wouldn't leave you. If you were going to cross, then you weren't going to do it on your own. I promised that it was just going to be me and you. That was all that mattered.

The tunnel swerved again, and it felt like everything was starting to slow. Like a raging ocean at the end of a storm, the sun had come out, and the wind had begun to soften.

But you realise what you did? thought Amee. *You stopped everything. No one could cross. They were all stuck in this mid-space.*

Her mum hummed in response. *Oops.*

Another incline, steeper, like they were going up, and up, and up, gradually, comfortably, into something new.

But Mum, this was all you. Why?

Like I said, I made a promise. A mother's promise. If you're asking me how I did it, then I couldn't tell you. If you're asking me why I came back, then you should know. The real question is...

The two of them began to spin, and Amee saw the tunnel of colours spiralling into something else. Some other colour that she had never seen before. She gaped at it in wonder.

The real question is, her mum continued, *would you like peanut butter cheesecake for dinner?*

Amee let out a yell of emotion and held the light even tighter than before, so tight that it felt like she was stuffing her nose into a brilliant-smelling summer dress

I love you, Mum. I love you more than anything. I missed you. I didn't know it, but I really missed you. I'm sorry about everything.

She felt her mother squeeze her back. *I'm sorry too. I'm sorry about everything that happened. But you're here now. I've found you, and you've found me. I love you, little fishy. When I think of you, I think of the ocean.*

The strange colour was getting nearer, and the more Amee looked, the more it seemed to widen. Like a great big mouth, it sucked them in closer. Amee took what felt like breaths, and then she forced herself into a sort of acceptance. She figured she had to be ready for whatever was coming. She had to be strong, to be brave, to be courageous. But she was all of those things now. Her life beyond death had given that to her and then some. All that was left for her to do was hold her mum's hand and be thankful she was there with her, by her side, and they were facing it together.

Mum, she asked then, *is there peanut butter where we're going?*

Her mum's voice didn't respond. Instead, Amee felt hands cradle her like she was a baby, and the two of them crossed into the strange and new-looking colour. Amee didn't know what was happening now. She didn't know where she was. All she knew was that her mum was there, and there was warmth. A lot of warmth. The nice kind of warmth. The warmth that love brings. She felt herself nestle into it, like it was a raft on a strange ocean. Built well, secure, unsinkable. She floated out into some other place and smiled.

'I'll think of you in the night, in the daytime.'

37

AFTER IT ALL

The nail clung loosely to the skin, but Marty continued to pick at it, turning it red and chipped before his mum slapped his wrist.

'Stop it.'

She was sitting with a magazine in one hand, reading about the five best techniques to avoid dark roots after applying blonde hair dye. It seemed to include herbal tea, yoga, and a weird salon method called 'double processing', which Marty didn't really want to contemplate. His mum, on the other hand, had bookmarked the page by folding the upper-right corner.

'With you in a moment,' a male voice grumbled at them.

Marty looked up to see an officer staring at him from behind a desk. He was looking at Marty like he was an anomaly, or some kind of zombie who had returned to enact vengeance on Gealblath. It had been two months since Marty had returned from Derling, and since then everyone had done nothing but gawp. The town had thought him dead. They thought Mr Cooper had kidnapped him in the same way he must have kidnapped Charlie, and they assumed that he must have been ten feet underground, with maggots curling out of his eyes and rats gnawing at his fingernails. Apparently, a few kids at school had even made a bet on it.

'Ten pounds says he's dead.'

'Twenty pounds says he's not.'

'Forty pounds says Mr Cooper's taken a plane to Mexico, where he's living undercover as a car salesman.'

That last one was Teddy's. The other day he'd begged Marty to at least say he'd visited Mexico while he was on his travels, but Mike told him not to cave. Teddy clearly didn't have forty pounds to hand out, and according to Mike, this was the only way he'd learn.

The truth was, they were all wrong. None of them knew what had happened. Even the police didn't have the slightest understanding, despite having heard the story countless times by now. But then, they could never understand. So long as they believed him, that was the most important thing, and Mr Cooper had made sure of that. Marty was confident they would have flung him in prison if he hadn't brought back some sort of evidence to back up story. And the evidence he had brought back was pretty definitive, Marty had to admit.

He shuffled on his chair, glancing towards the clock again. A door opened and a moustached man with gelled hair stepped through. A thick white document was held tight under his armpit.

'Okay,' he said simply.

And Marty and his mum stood.

The room itself was small, the walls so tight that Marty felt like they were closing in, one by one, until they were inches away from crushing everyone inside. In a way, Marty often hoped they did. Anything to save him from answering another question.

Malcom Herrington was leaning on the back legs of his chair, twiddling his pen between two fingers. His eyes were fixed directly on Marty as he walked him through the first night on the beach. The night all of it had started. The story was short, and it had hardly any trace of Amee, nor any of Marty's reasons for going with her and Mr Cooper in the first place. As always, the detective had noticed. He bit on his moustache, then he tilted forward and grabbed the document in front of him.

'You remember the timeline?' he asked.

'I remember it was night,' replied Marty.

'Which part of the night?'

'The dark part.'

The detective flashed him a smile, and Marty's mum nudged him with an elbow.

'Be polite, Marty.'

'I don't understand why it's so important,' Marty snapped back at her.

The detective had asked for the timeline in every interview, from the first night in the cabin to the last day on the cliff, and each time Marty had answered as best he could. Yet it was never enough. The detective always pressed him for more. More locations, more numbers, more facts. That was just the way of it. Facts. None of them understood what had happened. None of them understood at all.

'We just need to know,' said Malcom, wiping a finger across his now saliva-stained moustache. 'I'm sure you can understand that.'

Marty slumped down in the chair. 'Midnight,' he said. 'Just past it. That's when I left for the castle.'

He heard his mother reposition herself beside him.

'And David Cooper met you there?' the detective questioned.

Marty nodded. *You know he did.*

'But David Cooper didn't send for you?'

Marty nodded. *You know he didn't.*

The detective flicked over another page in his document, landing upon a black-and-white picture of a young and pretty girl. She had mousy hair and eyes that glistened even without colour. Marty glanced at her. There was a silence in the room, but for the low hum of the security camera perched just above the doorway.

'Do you want to talk about her?' asked Malcom.

'Not really.'

'I'm going to have to ask you to talk about her.'

'So ask me.'

The detective leaned forward. He was trying to be subtle, but the creak of the chair leg betrayed him. They were all interested in Amee, of course. She was like a fossil to them. A relic from the past that they were intent on learning more from. But she was gone now. Amee was dead, and Marty was the only one left to elaborate.

'If I ask, will you tell me?'

'Probably not,' Marty replied. 'But you can still ask.'

Malcom smiled, scanning Marty up and down, like he was trying to find the way in. He saw Marty as a puzzle, he could tell. It was all about working out how best to crack him. But Marty wouldn't make it easy. He was resolute on that. The camera above the door clicked, and the red light flickered, then returned, like the tape was being renewed, and Marty gave a little smile. *I can do this all day,* he thought. *You don't have enough tapes for me.*

'You know...' The detective leaned back. 'I've been in this job eight years. I started back in Auld Reekie. Bumped up from a desk job when I was just twenty-four. Skinny little guy, still had pimples on both cheeks, but I was ready for anything. I had my notepad, had my pen – all they needed to do was throw the case on my desk and I was gonna dig in to it like Nana's Sunday lasagne.' He picked up a notebook beside the document. It was blue leather, worn at the corners. 'You know what's in here?' he asked.

'Paper?' Marty guessed.

Malcom gave him that smile again. 'Truth,' he responded. 'Every part of it. From every case I've had for the last eight years. And I mean every case. Murder, homicide, sexual assault, all the stuff that would twist the mind of any skinny twenty-four-year-old if they didn't have this. You see, the cases that come to me are a mound of rubble and fallen bricks. My job is to stack those bricks, build them into a structure that I can understand. If that structure crumbles along the way, well, then I know I've got a problem. But I need those bricks first.' He flapped the book about in his hand, then laid it back upon the table. 'So I need you to give them to me, Marty. With something like this...' He trailed off, shaking his head. 'I need the truth. In all its parts.'

Another silence filled the air. Around it there was dust, floating gracefully in the same way it had done in the house on the cliff.

'So,' Malcom finished. 'Can I ask you to talk about her?'

Marty straightened his back and clicked both wrists. 'I'm really looking forward to it.'

The detective's smile faded. He closed the document in front of him, hiding the picture of Amee Florence back in the midst of words and information that he had been struggling to comprehend for two whole months now. *Never*, Marty thought to himself coldly. *You will never understand.*

'Perhaps some other time then,' the detective grumbled. 'I mean, you don't mind coming in again, do you? It's not like you're busy?'

Marty felt his mother's glare cut into the side of his head. He didn't bow to it, however. He didn't do anything at all.

'Let's move on,' the detective said,

And the light in the camera flickered anew.

When the interview had finished and they'd left the station, his mother's glare remained. She was sitting in the driving seat, her eyes going from the road, to Marty, from the road, to Marty, over and over again until he was sure her neck would suffer some kind of sprain. Meanwhile, the town of Gealblath flittered past them. The houses stood in just the same way they had stood before Marty had left. The gardens, the fences, the tarmac. Everything about the town was exactly the same as he remembered. Only Marty had changed. He had left the flock and come back as something else, something different, and the town knew it. The people glared at him like his mum did, like he was an invader to their usual, familiar life. Marty wasn't familiar anymore, and for that reason, he knew he would never fit back in. Of course, he'd never wanted to fit in anyway, but he'd never felt like an outcast before. He'd never felt homeless.

They cruised past Gealblath Secondary School and Marty saw the old castle, wiped clean now, with nothing but a slight discolouration where his name had once been painted in red. <u>MARTY EVANS IS DEAD!</u> The words had gone, but their resonance still lingered. The boy who had read them on that overcast morning had died. Now he was something new. Now he was something *other*.

His mum glared at him again, then she pulled on the steering wheel and brought the car up onto the kerb. She turned the key in the ignition and the engine went silent.

'Why don't you talk to him?' she asked after a few uncomfortable seconds. There was emotion in her voice, making it tremble slightly, only slightly, but enough for Marty to notice. 'Is it the same reason you don't talk to me?'

He didn't answer. Outside, rain began to patter against the window, distorting Marty's reflection as he peered out of it. He shivered a little. The day was cold and wet, just like it always should have been. That was one thing that had changed about Gealblath, he supposed. The warmth that had taken hold of the town had gone, disappeared at the same moment Amee and her mother had crossed. And now the days were normal. Cold when they were supposed to be cold. Warm when they were supposed to be warm. Everything was back on track.

'You know,' his mum continued. 'That month you were gone was the hardest month of my life. But these two months come a close second. I just want you to talk to me, sweetheart. I want to understand why –'

'Why does everyone want to understand?' Marty snapped again. The rain began to hit the car harder, clanking against the metal like tiny stones. He glared at his mother. 'You will never understand.'

His mum nodded, tears beginning to swell upon her lashes. 'No, I understood the morning you were gone. I understood it was my fault. I understood I'd gone wrong somewhere in the last thirteen years. I became absent. And I paid for that. I know that's not why you left. I know you say that it's not why you left –'

'It's not.'

'But it is for me. That's what I understand. Every day I woke up and thought about how it ended. With a fight, another stupid fight. It burned me up inside that I didn't even get to say goodbye. There was just a fight, and then you were gone. That was my fault, I knew that. It was my doing. As a mother, I'd brought it on myself. And I had to deal with that.'

Marty felt the anger in his chest pivot into something different, something that made him want to bend over and fall into his mum's arms. But he didn't. He stayed rock firm.

'Would you ever have dealt with it, do you think?' he asked. 'Losing me without saying goodbye?'

The castle disappeared amongst the rain, and Marty's mother leaned forward again. Her eyes searched him up and down, as if she had only just discovered what was happening on the inside. The puzzle had been rattled, and somehow some of the pieces had come together.

'You're thinking about her, aren't you? That girl. That's why you don't want to talk to him. To me. It still hurts.'

Marty tried harder to keep his emotions from bursting out of him. 'Would you ever have dealt with it?' he whispered.

His mother placed her thumb on his cheek. 'It's a crazy thing, Marty. It's a thing I never would have believed if Mr Cooper hadn't...' She trailed off, shaking her head as if she was attempting to understand the last two months all over again. 'The thing is, that girl was already dead. She died thirty years ago. Everything that happened, well, it was never meant to happen. She was never meant to come back, and you were never meant to meet her. You should never have met her.'

Marty dipped his chin into his chest, his eyes closing momentarily. Amee Florence flashed in front of him. The pale skin, the blue eyes, the tangles in her hair. He remembered the time he watched her walking like she was barefoot on the grass.

'And yet you did,' his mum continued. 'You did. And that's wonderful. That girl had time. More time. And she got to spend it with you. Think about what you gave her. Think about what she gave you, and be happy that it got to happen. No one else gets a chance like that, Marty, no one else in the world.'

Marty felt the tears begin to fall. They streamed down his face as fast and hard as the rain outside, and his mother caught them as they did, letting him fall into her shoulder.

'But you can't let it define you,' she said to him. 'It happened, and that's good. But you can't lose yourself over lost things, Marty. You have to find a way of letting go. You have to find your own goodbye.'

Marty sniffed into her clothes, feeling the tears sting his eyes. 'My own goodbye,' he breathed.

The two of them held each other in silence, listening to the rain until it began to calm. The fleeting downfall left an imprint with puddles in the park, like footsteps, glistening momentarily in the light, before disappearing into the grass to meet with the roots.

When Marty dreamed, he was back in the house. The walls were black. The ash was falling. There was pain, a lot of pain, stinging his neck like a snakebite. Sometimes there was fire too. Bright-orange flames licked across his vision, engulfing him in a pit. And there, in the centre, was Amee. She was staring at him from afar, a white ball of light wrapping around her body as if it was a coat of silk. He wanted to save her, but he couldn't move. It was like he was paralysed, useless, just a dead weight watching her fall into a misty haze.

When he awoke, there were tears. In the hospital, he had been given his own room due to his tendency to wake up the ward every night, screaming and crying for Amee to step out of the fire and save herself. The nurses would come to comfort him. Mr Cooper, too, would hold his hand and swear that everything would be okay. Marty hadn't been harmed in the house. Winona's threat had been empty, and the substance in the syringe was hardly more than a tranquiliser. But at times, Marty wished there had been something more, because once he was out of the hospital, there was no one. No nurses. No Mr Cooper. Marty would wake up in the middle of the night, sweat pouring down his face, screaming out to his empty room, a yearning feeling within his chest. He'd call out Amee's name over and over again, as if he was fighting for it not to be forgotten. Because how could he never say that name again? How could that name not be part of his life forever? He would lie there in despair, and then he would have to go back to sleep, where the house on the cliff was waiting for him. And Amee too, disappearing into the blur of white flames. She always had a sad look on her face, like she wanted to tell him something, like she wanted to say goodbye.

Goodbye. The word spiralled around Marty's head. *Make your own goodbye.* But how could he do that? There was no funeral, no body. There was no final resting place, or a grave he could visit and tell her everything he would have said if he had been given the chance. There was nothing. All that was left of Amee were bones in the ocean, but he couldn't feel them, he couldn't hold them. He couldn't touch her death or look it in the face and come to terms with the fact that she was really gone. He just had memories, each one coming back to him in dreams, spiralling him all the way back to that blazing black house. The ash, the wood, the dust, clung to, the hearth, denser than night, like a paintbrush had painted it in the darkest colour it could find. All of it flashed into his head constantly, swirling around and around, until...

'Needs more. Around the edges, there are unfilled cracks. Why do you never do the cracks? Come on, the whole thing needs to be black.'

Marty opened his eyes and saw Mike snatching the model from Teddy's fingers. It was the day after the interview, and the three of them were sitting in Marty's bedroom.

'I was doing it,' Teddy protested.

'Yeah, and now I'm doing it.' Mike splodged his brush into the black paint, then began swishing it up and down the model of a small graveyard filled with undead figurines.

'I was leaving those bits on purpose,' said Teddy. 'It makes it look atmospheric.'

'No, it doesn't. It makes it look unfinished.'

'Atmospheric.'

'Unfinished. Marty, who's right? Me or Teddy?'

Mike raised his eyes hopefully to Marty, who glanced briefly at the graveyard.

'Yeah,' he replied.

'Yeah what?'

'It looks good in black.'

'That wasn't the question.'

'Oh right. No then.'

Mike let out a huff, then looked back towards his model. 'Still, I'm right. Teddy's wrong. Why don't you paint some of those bones there?'

621

Marty watched his friends distantly, remembering the night they had driven Amee out of the hospital. He thought then that it would be ages before he saw them both again. But now here he was, back with them, in the same room, with the same sort of conversations. Granted, the two of them had spent a lot of time talking about Teddy's driving skills, but even talk of that had petered out and the conversation had returned to normal things. Life had gone back to the way it had always been. Yet Marty had not let go. Could not let go. Not without finding the ending. *Goodbye.*

'Do you want to do a bit too?'

Marty saw Teddy looking up at him earnestly.

'Oh yeah,' said Mike. 'You can help us with the trees if you want. I'll mix a dark shade of brown. That should make them pretty ominous.'

He went to pick up one of the tubs of paint, but Marty waved him down.

'I'm good, thanks,' he responded.

Mike looked at him strangely. 'You're thinking about her, aren't you?' he asked after a few seconds.

'I'm always thinking about her,' replied Marty.

'You miss her,' muttered Teddy.

Marty gave a snide smile. 'Yes, Teddy. I miss her.'

'We miss you.'

'What?'

'We miss you,' Teddy repeated. 'It's been two months now, and it still feels like you never really came back from Derling.'

Marty felt the tears begin to sting once again. They teetered on the brink of falling, but he held them back, kept them at bay, the same way he did every time the conversation turned to Amee.

'It's hard to come back when she didn't.'

'But she did,' Teddy replied hesitantly.

'What are you talking about?'

'She did come back. She came back, and she met you, and she was happy. After everything that happened to her, she got the chance to be happy again. But now it's your chance to come back. She'd want you to do the same, wouldn't she? She'd want you to be happy.'

Mike shuffled forward. 'I think what Teddy's trying to say is –'

'I know what he's trying to say,' said Marty. 'You said it well, Teddy. I know I have to come back. I know I have to say goodbye. My own goodbye. But it's hard to do that when she's not…'

Marty trailed off, unable to formulate the words. He dipped his head so his friends wouldn't notice the tears, staring at the model set where Teddy's paintbrush still hovered over a pile of bones. He tried to stop himself from breaking down, focusing instead on the ribcage, the legs, the spindly skeletal hands, and the skull, with its dark black eyes staring emptily back at him. Then Marty blinked. And a strange sensation came over him.

'Marty?' Mike murmured, noticing the sudden change. 'Marty, are you okay?'

'I…' Marty continued to stare, his body starting to tremble.

Teddy stood and waved his hand in front of Marty's face, stopping only when Mike slapped it away.

'Marty, what's wrong?'

And Marty snapped out of his trance. 'I've got to go.' He sprang up from the bean bag and sprinted towards the door.

'Go where?' his friends called out in unison.

But Marty was already gone. He slammed the door behind him and ran quickly down the stairs, taking them three at a time before skidding across the floor and turning into the lounge. His mum was sitting and snipping out a page from another hair magazine, and his dad was asleep on the sofa beside her, his glasses lying lopsided on his nose.

'Mum,' Marty panted, adrenaline squirming inside his chest.

'Yes, sweetheart?' his mum replied. 'If this is about Mike, for the third time, tell him I've put the pie in the oven –'

'Mum, I've been thinking about what you said. About saying goodbye.'

The scissors stopped mid-snip and his mum looked up at him.

'What I said?'

'I think I know how to do it. I think I know how to say goodbye, but I have to go somewhere first.'

Marty felt his heart thumping hard within his chest. He watched as his mum bit her lip, then placed down her magazine to clasp Marty's hand firmly.

'Where do you need to go?' she asked.

Mike and Teddy arrived behind him, the heavy pounding of their shoes causing Marty's dad to splutter awake with a cough.

'Cornwall,' answered Marty.

His dad glanced between the four of them. He readjusted his glasses and swallowed hesitantly.

'What about it?'

38

EVERY OTHER SUNDAY

The road looked like it had been carved with water. The tarmac was glossed in sunlight that drifted in and out of the clouds timidly, the light reflected in the rain that had settled just a half hour before. David walked with his hands stuffed deep in his tweed jacket. He'd slept well last night. It was the first time in a long time and this morning he felt fresh, rejuvenated, like he had closed his eyes for years and opened them onto a nicer kind of world. A couple of children cried out in their front garden three doors down. One of them had a rugby ball in one hand and the other one had his arms out to catch it. Their eyes drifted towards David as he walked past. He acknowledged them with a slight wave. The skinnier kid went to wave back, but his friend shut him down before he could.

'What are you doing? You know who that is? You wanna disappear?'

The waving kid wimped out and lowered his hand.

'Don't worry,' David called over with a smirk. 'I know I started too big. These days I'm just doing rabbits.'

The skinny kid gasped in shock and dropped the ball, and then the two of them sprinted inside. They slammed the door behind them as David let out a long and hearty laugh.

He was still chuckling to himself when he climbed the steps to number 247. The wood of the door was black, the paint peeling around the hinges, and the brass knocker had turned green with rust. David looked towards the windows. They were smudged and dusty, and the view inside was blocked by slats of white plastic blinds. It looked like no one lived there at all, but David knew that wasn't the case. He knocked and waited for a minute. Then, with a slight click, a bolt slid out of place and the tired face of Winona Nightly peered around the half-open door. She hovered for a moment, looking David up and down. Then, without saying a word, she turned sideways and allowed him to step onto the carpet.

It felt strange at first. David had never associated Winona with a home of any sort. A home was too normal, too safe, too familiar, and Winona wasn't any of those things. Winona's life had been the hospital, Amee, Roman, what she had done, what she had intended to do. All the things he couldn't bear thinking about. Yet here she was, walking through a floral-wallpapered corridor and into a kitchen, flicking on a kettle with a bony finger. She was like any other person, only she wasn't. David was like any other guest, only he was not. He followed her silently, watching as she poured hot water into two cups of coffee granules, stirred them with a spoon, then placed them on either side of the table. She sat, staring at David with a look of contempt. Her eyes drifted towards his neck, which was still red and warped by the skin graft. The pain was still there, but it had lessened now. David sometimes forgot how bad the injury really was, but he would always be reminded by the stares, the looks, the grimaces. And then he would feel the fire all over again.

'You didn't ask how I take it,' he said. His voice was low, but it was loud enough to rip through the silence which had clearly been resting in this house for some time.

Winona sighed and pulled her gaze back to his eyes. 'How do you take it?'

'Black's fine.' David sat down on the chair in front of her.

'Good,' replied Winona, 'because I've run out of milk.' She swirled her cup once, then twice, then tipped it back and took a sip.

Her skin looked darker now, David thought. It looked ragged, like a set of un-ironed clothes worn for a little too long. Her eyes were blacker too, like the pupils had overspilled and stained the bags underneath. It was almost sad to look at her. There had certainly been no sleep in this house. There was nothing rejuvenated about her.

'I suppose you've had a long two months,' said Winona, as if she had been thinking the same thing as David.

'Throat's a bit sore.' He took a slurp of coffee, still hot. 'But they're coming around. Thankfully, I had more than words alone to convince them. If convincing is even the right word.'

'When you say *them...*'

'Everyone who needs to know, knows. No secrets.' David leaned back, remembering the relentless domino effect that had come with the telling of his story. It had gone from the police to the government, around and around and around, over and over again until it felt like his tongue had gone grey with repetition. But it was over now. Or at least, he hoped it was. His tongue was brittle, and he knew it would struggle to wrap itself around those words again.

'You're leaving, aren't you?' said Winona.

'I can't stay here,' replied David. 'Not now. It wouldn't be fair.'

'So why am I still here?'

'I told you to leave the hospital.'

'And I've done that.'

'Correct.'

Winona faltered, eyebrows furrowing to add more wrinkles to her forehead. She scratched her frizzy hair, which was still easing back to its natural blonde colour.

'You didn't tell them about me?'

'I had to tell them about you. Because I had to tell them about Amee. They know you adopted her. They know what you were trying to do.'

'So why am I still here?' Winona repeated.

'Well, adopting a dead girl and using her for your own benefit has turned out to be a bit of a grey area in ethical law. I think it hurts their brains to work it out.'

'You didn't tell them everything,' Winona realised out loud. 'Why not? After what I did to you. After what I did to her, to Marty, to –'

'What you did was wrong. What you did was evil, in every respect.'

Something flashed in Winona's eyes, and her top lip curled. Her next words came out in a hiss that David found only too familiar.

'So tell me, why am I still here?'

There was a moment of stillness, like the house had returned to its default condition. David stood and walked across the room until he got to the photograph frames that were set neatly upon the windowsill. There was a young girl in each of them, about eight years old, with beautiful blonde hair and a wide, full-toothed smile. She stared at David with bright eyes. He picked up one of the frames and tipped it towards the light bulb above him. The girl was sitting in a plastic car. One hand was holding the steering wheel, and her other held a half-eaten bar of chocolate, some of which was smudged over her lips and cheeks. There was a laugh on her lips, David could see. A laugh that had since gone silent in this house. The only person who could still hear it was sitting behind him. But she only heard the ghost of things, David knew. The bones of a laugh. Not quite remembered, not quite forgotten. The laugh haunted Winona, as Charlie's laugh had haunted David.

'It was her mother, you know,' he said then. 'Amee's mother created the mid-space. Stopped all of them from getting through until she was reunited with her daughter.' He held the frame tighter and tapped it a few times, frowning. 'Hard to believe a connection like that could be so strong.'

David placed the photograph back on the sill, but Winona kept her eyes on it, tears beginning to teeter on the lashes, making them sparkle in the light, carving her into something softer in the same way the rain had carved the street outside.

'I don't find that hard to believe,' she whispered.

'No, me neither.'

'I understood her mother was looking for her. Amee recognised the voice before I made her forget, but I never believed...' Winona shook her head. 'But that's why they came back. That's why there were fractures in the first place.'

'Yes,' said David. 'If fractures appear during an earthquake, then Amee's mother was the earthquake, and the house on the cliff was the epicentre. The cracks appeared around it.

Didn't you ever wonder why of all places the dead were returning to life in Gealblath?'

'Maybe I did. Maybe you're right. I didn't want to see, but it was always there. It was always in front of me. I wanted to believe there were reasons Amee and the others came back, but really, they were mistakes. Mistakes that had simply fallen through the fault lines.'

'You saw what you wanted to see,' David replied as he returned to his chair. 'You saw what would help you, help your daughter. That's why you were so interested in Amee.' He sat down again, finishing the last of his coffee in one big slurp. He wiped his face and looked Winona straight in the eyes. 'When did you know about my son?'

It looked like Winona had been waiting for this question for a while. She hesitated before speaking.

'When I visited the street. I realised it was the same place Charlie had disappeared. Amee was found there on the same day, at the same time. All those years ago. That's why we went to the detective. We wanted to know how much he had. Traces, leads, anything that suggested abduction. Or murder. Only...'

'There was nothing,' David finished for her. He felt a shiver rush up his spine. It was still hard for him to get his head around it. The fact that there was no murderer, no abductor. The fact that the shape Charlie had seen, that faceless shape, was the shape of Amee Florence herself, stepping through the fracture between life and the mid-space. No matter how hard David tried, it still made his body go numb and his heart go cold.

Winona nodded. 'That's when I knew. That's when I realised. Not only could the dead step out of these fractures, but the living could step into them. I thought then that I had a chance to save my daughter. A real chance.'

'And you never told me.' David felt his fists begin to clench under the tablecloth. The whites of his knuckles pushed against the skin, until he stopped them, and uncurled his fingers, taking a deep and lingering breath. There was no point in anger, he had to remember. There was no point at all in that.

'This was only about my daughter,' Winona responded firmly. The tremor in her voice disappeared, like the thought of her daughter made her strong, resolute, assured in everything she was saying and everything she had done. 'Nothing else mattered.'

'And what about Alfie? I guess he didn't matter either?'

'You think I could control Roman? You think anyone could control that man? He was a killer brought back to life. He had no respect for it. No fear for consequences. He just had a hunger. You can't control a person like that.'

'You didn't have to. You didn't need him.'

'But he was the first to come to me,' Winona explained. 'He came to me. He loved me. He was the first to bring me hope. And he was loyal, he was always that.'

The tears were gone from Winona's eyes now. Her face was hard, hard like a stone, and she spoke with strength and assurance. She was set in her ways, David could see. She was unsalvageable. But then, he'd never wanted to salvage her.

'Roman was loyal,' he said. 'And dangerous. And you liked the mix.'

'It kept the rest of them controlled. Amee too, Amee most of all. He never hurt her, but everyone has a weakness. When she saw him, she saw her father. She could hardly be in the same room with him. If you left the two of them alone, it was like an explosion. Absolute fear from a forgotten memory.' Winona took another sip of her coffee, as if what she had just said was the most normal and sane thing in the world.

David sighed sadly. He remembered the first time he had talked to Amee. He remembered her scream, her fear, her rejection. And then he remembered the last time. The bravery. And the acceptance. He felt another shiver up his spine, and for a moment, he felt like he might break down. But then Winona brought him back to the present.

'But he's gone now,' she said. 'They're all gone now.'

'Yes,' replied David, straightening. 'When Amee found her mother, the dead went home. The abnormalities were corrected.'

Winona stared at him. 'Every abnormality...'

David looked back, and in her bloodshot eyes, he saw the hatred sparkle.

'When are you leaving?' she asked then.

'In a fortnight,' answered David.

'And your ex-wife?'

'Staying in Perth. I'm moving close. On the coast, I think, so I don't miss the water. It's a strange thing to prepare yourself for. A new life. I've stayed in this town so long, just lingering, like a damn ghost. I'm still trying to get my head around it.'

'I'm happy for you.'

'No, you're not. Nor should you be.'

'Why do you think that? Because of what I did? That wasn't me. None of that was me. That was a mother desperate to save her daughter, willing to do anything to bring her back, to keep her safe. That's who you were dealing with.'

'I know,' David responded calmly. 'And I know you would

do it all again, if you thought that it could save her.'

'Yes.'

David stood up from the table and smiled sadly at Winona. 'Yes…'

'So what happens now?' Winona asked.

'Now…' David yanked up his sleeve and squinted at his watch. Twelve thirty p.m. There was half an hour to go. 'Now I've got to get to the beach. I'm saying goodbye to a few people there, and I don't want to be late.'

'I mean me. What happens to me? Why am I still here? Where is my punishment for what I've done?'

David craned his neck and looked at the photographs again, finding the girl staring back at him in the exact same positions, the exact same manner, her mouth open in the same soundless laugh. He imagined hearing that laugh for a moment. The pitch, the tone, the excitement. He heard the laugh and then he shut it out, staring distantly at Winona.

'I'm going to go now,' he said simply.

Winona jumped to her feet. 'David, I know what I deserve. I know I deserve punishment for what happened, and I know you're here to give it to me.'

'I don't need to give you punishment. No one needs to do that.'

'What are you talking about?' Winona glared at him. There was a note of desperation evident in her voice now. 'You said it yourself. What I did to find my daughter was wrong. It was evil. I need punishment.'

'You do. But not my punishment. Not anyone's. This house is empty enough. Every house will be empty enough. I know how that feels.'

The tears were back now. They filled Winona's bloodshot eyes and trickled down towards her lips. They erased the stone from existence, and David saw a mother then. A mother without a child, a mother without hope, but with evil, down there in the pit of her gut. An evil to find her lost daughter by whatever means necessary. He didn't hate her, David realised at that moment. He felt sorry for her.

'Please,' she whispered.

David turned back down the corridor, ignoring Winona as she cried at him.

'David! David! I need punishment!'

He reached the door and opened it onto the grey and cold Sunday afternoon.

'PLEASE,' Winona shouted. 'DAVID! PLEASE! PUNISH ME! PUNISH ME!'

David walked out onto the street and shut the cries away in the house behind him, where they would stay indefinitely, with no answer but the silence of rooms, photographs, and even the memories themselves. That would be punishment enough, David believed. That would always be punishment enough. He choked back some tears and began treading down the road, the last echoes of Winona Nightly disappearing with every step.

When he got to Gealblath Beach, the sun had begun to permeate the rain clouds, forming a hopeful glaze on the horizon. Years had passed where David had never really appreciated how beautiful this beach was, but he appreciated it now, as he stood on a small grassy knoll just beside one of the cabins. There were three stages to it, he could see. Stones turned to sand, sand turned to water, and water turned to another place, far out in the distance, beautiful now that it twinkled in the fight between sun and cloud. Derling stood as a hopeful silhouette. A reminder that, eventually, life could return, and the purgatory between two beaches could be crossed. David looked down towards the beach itself. The tide was out far, and on the sand Mike and Teddy were kneeling beside a big stone and reaching to turn it over.

'There's a crab under this one!' yelled Mike.

'Woah, Nelly,' Teddy responded. 'It looks like an egg with legs.'

'Yeah, not unlike yourself, Teddy.'

'Shut up.'

The two boys pushed each other, and David smiled. The pebbles began to crunch loudly beside him.

'Late again, David,' said Vanessa as she walked up onto the knoll. Both of her hands were stuffed inside a crimson coat pocket, while the wind blew her brown hair prettily across her face.

'I wanted to walk,' replied David. 'I like walking these days. It clears my head.'

She looked at his neck, then stroked it slightly, her finger trembling briefly above the nooks in the skin graft. 'It used to be the drink that did that,' she said.

David lifted his hand and held it out. It was still, unwavering, and as stubborn as the new stone Mike and Teddy were attempting to turn over in the sand.

'I don't need it,' he told her. 'I drank to blur things, but I don't want things blurred anymore. I want days like this to be clear. I want to feel them. Remember them. Like I didn't before.'

'I'm happy to hear that, David. I'm really happy to hear that.'

Out on the beach, Teddy abandoned the heavy stone for an easier one. He lifted it up, then reached down and removed another egg-shaped crab from the bed of sand. He dangled it above Mike's head.

'Hey!' yelped Mike. 'Don't do that! I told you, I don't like crabs!'

'Oh?' Teddy dropped it and picked up something else instead. 'How about this eel then?'

'NO!'

Vanessa laughed at the two of them, and David stared at her, his heart catching in his throat.

'What's that look for?' she asked

'Nothing,' David replied after a few seconds. 'It's just...'

He didn't say it, but David was remembering the photograph. The look in Grace's eyes. The smile, the laugh, trapped in paper and memory. Vanessa had a nice laugh too. He had heard it many times before, but when Charlie went, it had faded from his life, as so many other things had faded. He hadn't realised how much he'd missed that laugh.

Vanessa nudged him. 'Just?'

'It's just nice that you're here.' David swallowed. 'I appreciate it. I'll always appreciate it.'

Vanessa looked at him in a way she hadn't before, like it wasn't even David she was looking at. Or at least, not the David she had last set eyes on. There was something new in her gaze, he noticed. Like some love for him had suddenly been rekindled. It wasn't the same love that had been there when they first met, or when they had first kissed. It wasn't a love that would make her take him back or change anything at all. But it was a love all the same. Small and quiet. But there. And that was really something. After all, David could remember the last time she had been in Gealblath. Back when they had buried Charlie's box in the ground. He could remember the vacant look in her eyes. He could remember the hopelessness; remember the void. But today, that hopelessness was gone. It had been replaced with something else. Something small, yes, but something all the same. And that was all he needed. A recognition that the tide could change, and David could resolve to follow it.

Beyond them, Mike and Teddy started screaming again, and David peered back out towards the beach.

'Where are they?' he asked.

Vanessa pointed out to where she had just approached from, and David turned to spot two kids coming the same way, their hands in their pockets and their clothes rippling in the sea breeze. He smiled as they got closer, and then he jumped down from the grass and wrapped one of them in a warm hug.

'How are you doing, kiddo?' he asked.

Charlie Cooper squeezed him back. 'I'm doing good, Dad.'

They held each other for a few seconds. Then Charlie let go and beamed up at David, his cheeks red and wind bitten and his smile brighter than anything David had ever seen. His son stared with a glint of new life sparkling in his eyes.

'Good,' said David happily.

Beside him, Marty Evans shuffled on the pebbles. He was clinging to a worn backpack, the strap hung loosely on one shoulder.

'Okay,' he said. 'I've got it. Are you ready?'

David stared down at him. Marty had been waiting a long time for this, he knew. They'd all been waiting.

'Yeah,' replied David. 'Where do you wanna go?'

And Marty looked out towards the tide. 'As far as we can,' he said.

Ten minutes later and the three of them were walking in water. David squinted at the backdrop of Derling as the

637

clouds began to part. Beams of light shone, then disappeared, then shone again. The sunlight was dropping in and out like rain. The smell of the air was packed with salt, seaweed and ocean. That smell would always bring him back to Gealblath, David knew. Even when he eventually got far away, and the memories grew old, that smell would awaken them all again. But that was okay. David needed those memories if he wanted to remain the man he was. Because even the worst memories could create good things. And David was good now. He was sure that he was good.

Marty and Charlie stopped walking when the ocean reached their shins, and Charlie looked down, smiling.

'It still feels weird,' he said. 'The water, I mean. It's like I'm feeling things for the first time again. It's like I'm something new.'

'You'll feel normal again soon,' David told him. 'I'll make sure of it, Charlie. You'll be a kid again.'

'No, I won't be the same. None of us will be the same. But that's alright, isn't it? New is alright.'

A gust of wind blew Charlie's hair, and Marty cleared his throat beside him.

'It's still life, right? That's more than Amee gets.'

'How do you know?' asked Charlie. 'This is life now. But how do you know that what comes next isn't a different kind of living? One that we can't understand until we go there?'

'You can't know that.'

'No. But nothing that's happened so far has told me I shouldn't be optimistic. The warmth that I felt on the other side, it didn't feel like nothing. It felt like the opposite. It felt like everything good about life now. It felt like everything that makes this life worth living.'

'I hope that's true,' said Marty simply.

Charlie nudged him on the shoulder. 'So keep hoping. Things meet again, Marty, even when they seem like they're lost. Things survive. Just look at me. I'm living proof. I've always been.'

Despite his tears, Marty nodded back. After a few deep breaths, he shrugged off his backpack and reached inside.

'You ready?' asked David.

Marty took a few moments. 'To say goodbye,' he whispered. Then he pulled out something small and white and cracked along the top.

David felt a pang of sadness as he looked at the skull. It had been part of his life for so long. A constant companion and yet a relentless reminder of lost fatherhood. He remembered finding it, he remembered hiding it away, and he remembered the day he'd left it behind. That forest in Cornwall had been cold, but the eyes of the skull had been colder. They had stared at him emptily, in the same way they always did when they looked at the man who had failed them. Only David hadn't failed them. It had never been Charlie who had washed up on this beach. It wasn't Charlie who had arrived with the storm and found his way onto Eden Park Lane, where the fracture had merged the dead with the living and changed the world of those in Gealblath forever. That had never been him; David knew that now. It was someone else entirely. Someone who had died a long time ago.

Marty stroked the cheekbone with his thumb, like the skin still remained and might just flush red at his touch. 'Amee,' he muttered.

And David bowed his head.

'I thought a lot about how I'm gonna say this,' Marty continued. 'The truth is, we shouldn't have said anything to each other, you and me. We should never have met. But we did. We did meet, we did talk, and I want you to know that I'm happy for that. I'll always be happy for that. I promise you.'

The clouds dispersed once more. And like rain, the light pattered against Amee's skull, making it glow white and sparkle. Marty's voice shuddered.

'I'll think of you, Amee,' he said through the tears. 'In the night, in the daytime, I'll think of you. That's all I can say. I'm sorry. I can't say anything else. That's my goodbye.'

Charlie put his hand on Marty's shoulder. 'For now.'

Marty wiped his cheeks and lifted the skull towards David.

'You did well, Marty.' David smiled at him, then took the skull and looked down into the blackness of its eyes one more time. *I'll think of you too*, he thought. *Whenever I'm by the ocean. Whenever I smell the salt, and the water, and I feel the wind on my face, and hear the waves in my head. I'll think of you.*

The skull remained silent. David placed it delicately in the water, until just the top remained exposed to the breeze. The waves lapped around it, dipping into the cracks, filling them, engulfing the darkness with something blue.

David heard the shouts and screams of Marty's friends draw to a halt, and he turned his head, spotting the pair of them standing alongside Vanessa in the distance. They all looked tiny from where he was standing, and smaller still in the shadow of the power plant chimney behind them. David waved, and he saw Vanessa wave back.

'I wonder where the ocean will take her,' said Marty, staring out into the distance.

David stared along with him. It would take her to the same place the ocean took anything, he supposed. Somewhere new, and somewhere the same. Some place different, and some place so familiar. Years would pass, and Amee's skull could return to this spot, beneath the same waves, amongst the same stones. In many ways, it was impossible to tell where a road would lead. David knew that the best thing anyone could do was trust the tide and be ready for the moon's direction. His tide had taken him back to Charlie, and onwards to someone else. He was a new man, but an old man. A new father, yet an old father. He was in the same place, with another chance, and he would always be thankful for that.

Another gust of wind cut into the three of them, and David took hold of Charlie's hand. He felt the warmth of his son's skin against his. That warmth would be there forever, he realised now. Even when the skin went cold, and disappeared to bone and water. That warmth would remain, into a beyond that was waiting for them. There was a comfort in that, David thought as he squeezed the hand tighter. There was a comfort in that which could last a lifetime. He smiled and watched Derling light up in the sun once again.

THE END